More praise for
THE TALE OF HILL TOP FARM

Don't miss the new Cottage Tale of Beatrix Potter,
THE TALE OF HOLLY HOW

Jan 24, 2008
SMP

continued . . .

Praise for Susan Wittig Albert's
China Bayles Novels

"Albert's characters are as real and as quirky as your next-door neighbor."
—*Raleigh News & Observer*

"[Albert] improves with each successive book . . . artful"
—*Austin American-Statesman*

"Albert's dialogue and characterizations put her in a class with lady sleuths V.I. Warshawski and Stephanie Plum."
—*Publishers Weekly*

"The denizens of Pecan Springs are sympathetic and insightful, grand livers with flinty wit—a combination of the residents of Lake Wobegon and the Texas villages in Larry McMurtry's novels. Albert's writing and outlook suggest Molly Ivins, while China's independence and sunbelt sleuthing will appeal to readers of Earlene Fowler's Benni Harper series and Allana Martin's Texana Jones novels."
—*Booklist*

"A marvelous addition to the ranks of amateur detectives."
—*Linda Grant*

THE TALE OF
HILL TOP FARM

The Cottage Tales of
BEATRIX POTTER

Susan Wittig Albert

BERKLEY PRIME CRIME, NEW YORK

THE BERKLEY PUBLISHING GROUP
Published by the Penguin Group
Penguin Group (USA) Inc.
375 Hudson Street, New York, New York 10014, USA

Penguin Group (Canada), 90 Eglinton Avenue East, Suite 700, Toronto, Ontario M4P 2Y3, Canada
(a division of Pearson Penguin Canada Inc.)
Penguin Books Ltd., 80 Strand, London WC2R 0RL, England
Penguin Group Ireland, 25 St. Stephen's Green, Dublin 2, Ireland (a division of Penguin Books Ltd.)
Penguin Group (Australia), 250 Camberwell Road, Camberwell, Victoria 3124, Australia
(a division of Pearson Australia Group Pty. Ltd.)
Penguin Books India Pvt. Ltd., 11 Community Centre, Panchsheel Park, New Delhi—110 017, India
Penguin Group (NZ), Cnr. Airborne and Rosedale Roads, Albany, Auckland 1310, New Zealand
(a division of Pearson New Zealand Ltd.)
Penguin Books (South Africa) (Pty.) Ltd., 24 Sturdee Avenue, Rosebank, Johannesburg 2196,
South Africa

Penguin Books Ltd., Registered Offices: 80 Strand, London WC2R 0RL, England

THE TALE OF HILL TOP FARM

A Berkley Prime Crime Book / published by arrangement with the author

PRINTING HISTORY
Berkley Prime Crime hardcover edition / October 2004
Berkley Prime Crime mass-market edition / October 2005

ISBN: 0-425-20101-5

BERKLEY ® PRIME CRIME
Berkley Prime Crime Books are published by The Berkley Publishing Group,
a division of Penguin Group (USA) Inc.,
375 Hudson Street, New York, New York 10014.
The name BERKLEY PRIME CRIME and the BERKLEY PRIME CRIME design
are trademarks belonging to Penguin Group (USA) Inc.

PRINTED IN THE UNITED STATES OF AMERICA

10 9 8 7 6 5 4 3 2 1

Acknowledgments

I am especially grateful to the many people whose biographical research into the life of Beatrix Potter has made this fiction possible; their names and the titles of their studies are listed in the Resources section at the end of the book. Special thanks go to Dr. Linda Lear, Senior Research Scholar in History at the University of Maryland, Baltimore County, whose eagerly awaited biography of Beatrix Potter will be published in 2006. Dr. Lear read and commented on this book; she helped to confirm the accuracy of the background research but, even more importantly, to affirm the validity of this fictional approach to Beatrix Potter's life. Thanks also go to Liz Hunter, House and Collections Manager, Hawkshead and Beatrix Potter Properties, National Trust; and to Peter Tasker, the gardener at Hill Top.

I continue to be grateful to my editor, Natalee Rosenstein, whose wit and humor enliven all our interactions, and whose patience I especially appreciate. And of course, to my husband, Bill Albert, for his careful research, his constructive criticism, and his attentive reading.

Susan Wittig Albert

To Judy Taylor,
with grateful appreciation for
her studies of the life and work of Beatrix Potter

Author's Note

This book and others that follow in the Cottage Tales series trace the arc of Beatrix Potter's life from 1905, when she purchased Hill Top Farm in the village of Sawrey, through 1913, when she married William Heelis and went to Sawrey to live. If you have visited the Lake District of England, you may recognize the names of villages, towns, lakes, woods, and even actual houses, for I have chosen many of these lovely and very real places as settings for these books. But with the exception of Beatrix, her family, her friends, and her animal companions, the characters and their stories are entirely imaginary. The "real" people are noted with an asterisk in the Cast of Characters; all others appearing in this book are flights of the author's fancy.

Susan Wittig Albert
Bertram, Texas, 2003

INSERT: CUCKOO BROW WOODS

11

To Cuckoo Brow Woods

6.

5.

4.

3.

2.

N

To Hawkshead

7.

8.

9.

10.

To Willow Cottage

Post Office Meadow

NEAR SAWREY

1.

To the Bridge and Far Sawrey

INSERT: FAR SAWREY

13.

12.

1. Hill Top Farm
2. Rose Cottage
3. The Forge
4. The Joinery
5. The Post Office
6. Castle Cottage
7. Belle Green
8. Anvil Cottage
9. Tower Bank House
10. Lakefield Cottages
11. Owl's House
12. The School
13. The Vicarage

Cast of Characters

(indicates an actual person or creature)*

Beatrix Potter*, children's author and illustrator, has recently purchased Hill Top Farm. She has brought her animals to Sawrey for this visit: *Mrs. Tiggy-Winkle**, *Josey and Mopsy Rabbit**, and *Tom Thumb Mouse**.

Dimity Woodcock and *Captain Miles Woodcock* live in Tower Bank House, a large house overlooking the road to Hawkshead. Dimity, who always has something good to say about everyone, volunteers for parish activities; her brother Miles is Justice of the Peace for Sawrey District. *Elsa Grape* keeps house and cooks for the Woodcocks.

Abigail Tolliver, recently deceased, lived in Anvil Cottage, with *Tabitha Twitchit**, the senior village cat. Miss Tolliver's nephew, *Henry Roberts,* a draper from Kendal, expects to inherit her estate, and employs a house agent, *Mr. Oscar Spry,* to sell Anvil Cottage. *Sarah Barwick,* from Manchester, has a certain mysterious connection to Miss Tolliver.

Mathilda Crook boards guests in her home, Belle Green, at

the top of Market Street. Mathilda's husband, *George Crook,* who has a cranky temperament, owns and operates the village forge. He has a Jack Russell terrier named *Rascal. Charlie Hotchkiss* (George's helper at the forge) and *Edward Horsley* room with the Crooks. Beatrix Potter also stays here during her 1905 visit to Sawrey.

Grace Lythecoe is the widow of the former vicar. She lives in Rose Cottage and plays an important role in village affairs.

Lucy Skead is the village postmistress; her husband *Joseph Skead* is sexton at St. Peter's. Lucy's elderly mother, *Dolly Dorking* (reputed to be a witch) lives with them in Low Green Gate, which is also the village post office.

John Jennings farms Hill Top Farm, his wife *Becky* manages the dairy. They have two children, *Sammy* and *Clara,* and a cat named *Miss Felicia Frummety.*

Myrtle Crabbe, the teacher of the junior class and the head-mistress of Sawrey School, lives in Castle Cottage. Her two younger sisters also live here: *Pansy Crabbe* (who gives piano lessons and leads the Sawrey Choral Society) and *Viola Crabbe* (who gives dramatic readings). Their cat *Max the Manx* lives with them.

Margaret Nash teaches the infants class at Sawrey School, and lives with her sister Annie in Sunnyside Cottage.

Bertha and *Henry Stubbs* live in the left-hand cottage in the row of Lakefield Cottages. Bertha cleans Sawrey School; Henry is a ferryman. Bertha has a gray tabby cat named *Crumpet.*

Jeremy Crosfield and his aunt *Jane Crosfield* live in picturesque Willow Cottage, on Cunsey Beck. Jeremy is in Miss Crabbe's junior class at Sawrey School; Miss Crosfield is a spinner and weaver.

Rose Sutton, wife of *Desmond Sutton,* the veterinarian, lives in Courier Cottage.

Roger Dowling and his nephew *David Dowling* do light carpentry work in the joinery, just up Market Street from Meadowcroft Cottage, where Roger lives with his wife *Lydia.* Meadowcroft is also the village shop, which is operated by Lydia and will later become famous as the Ginger & Pickles Shop in one of Beatrix Potter's books.

Vicar Samuel Sackett is the vicar of St. Peter's Church in Far Sawrey, and lives at the Vicarage. *Mrs. Thompson* keeps house for him.

Dr. Butters, a much-loved physician, lives in Hawkshead and cares for all the people in the vicinity.

Lawrence Ransom owns an art gallery in Ambleside.

Louie and Sophie Armitt*, friends of Beatrix, live in Rydal Cottage, Ambleside. Later in her life, Beatrix donated her botanical drawings, as well as her father's books, to the library established by the Armitt sisters in Ambleside.

William (Willie) Heelis* is a solicitor with an office in Hawkshead.

Galileo Newton Owl, D.Phil., is a tawny owl who lives in Cuckoo Brow Woods. He studies celestial mechanics and the habits of small furry creatures, and makes it his business to know everything that goes on in the neighborhood of Sawrey.

Ridley Rattail is a country-gentleman rat who gets involved with *Roger-Dodger* and *Newgate Jack,* a pair of bad rats from London who want to cheat him out of his money.

1

Miss Tolliver Departs

NEAR SAWREY, OCTOBER, 1905

It was a splendid morning in October when Miss Abigail Tolliver departed this world—one of those brilliant, breezy days that sets the heart singing and stirs the blue English lakes and the blue English sky into a grand and glorious celebration of clouds and color. It was one of those perfect days that seem to promise the beginning of all good things, but because the leaves were whirling from the trees, it promised endings, too.

Dimity Woodcock discovered what had happened at eleven o' clock, when she went to Anvil Cottage to consult Miss Tolliver about the School Roof Fund. There was no answer to her tap at the back-garden door, but since it was always kept off the latch, she called and went in, expecting to find Miss Tolliver in the kitchen. She found her, instead, slumped in her upholstered chair in the sitting room, where the previous afternoon Dimity had presided over tea and cake at a village celebration of Miss Tolliver's sixty-fifth birthday.

"Oh, dear!" Dimity gasped as she touched dear Miss Tolliver's cold hand. Her heart leapt straight up into her throat. "Oh, sweet Miss Tolliver!"

"She died last night," Tabitha Twitchit said. She gave a long, sad sigh. *"I've been keeping watch."*

Dimity looked down at the old calico cat, Miss Tolliver's companion of many years. "What a plaintive meow," she said, bending over to stroke her fur. "But of course you and Miss Tolliver have been together for ages and ages. You'll miss her." She straightened up. "You must be hungry, Tabitha. Come home with me, and I'll give you something to eat."

"Thank you all the same, but I'll just stay here with Miss Tolliver," Tabitha said, tucking her paws neatly under her fur bib. *"I had a mouse last night, but if you would be so kind as to bring me a bowl of milk with a bit of bread in it, that would be quite nice."*

Dimity regarded the cat thoughtfully, reflecting that animals seemed to feel death as keenly as people. "On second thought, perhaps you'd rather stay with your mistress for a while. Tell you what, dear—I'll bring you a bowl of bread and milk when I come back."

And with that, Dimity hurried home to Tower Bank to fetch her brother, Captain Miles Woodcock, Justice of the Peace for Sawrey District, who was always called upon when someone died and knew exactly what must be done.

The news of Miss Tolliver's unexpected death spread swiftly through Near Sawrey. Agnes Llewellyn, who lived at High Green Gate, the farmhouse next up Market Street, met Dimity coming out of Anvil Cottage and heard what had happened. Agnes hurried back home to fetch the black crepe mourning wreath she had hung on her own mother's door some months before. Some might say it was unlucky to use the same crepe, but Agnes, a practical person, could not see the sense in letting a very good bit of crepe go to waste—and now that Miss Tolliver was departed, what worse luck could there be?

Betty Leech, gathering the last striped marrows in the frost-kissed garden of Buckle Yeat, heard the sad news from Mary, Agnes Llewelyn's daughter. She set down her garden basket, told ten-year-old Ruth (who was home from school with a bad cold) to mind the babies, and went to help Agnes hang the crepe. That done, she hurried round to the back of Anvil Cottage, where Miss Tolliver kept two hives of bees, to tell them the news of their mistress's passing. It was always good practice to tell the hive courteously and with respect for their feelings, so that the bees did not decline and die in sympathy with the departed, or take offense and fly off in search of new quarters. The bees properly informed, Betty went knocking on the doors of the cottages on Market Street, and sent her oldest daughter Rachel to tell those who lived on Graythwaite Lane.

Up the hill, at Castle Cottage, Viola Crabbe learnt of Miss Tolliver's death from the baker's boy from Hawkshead, when he delivered the usual weekly order of two loaves, a half-dozen glazed currant buns, and three seed wigs, one for each of the three Misses Crabbe. The boy had stopped at Anvil Cottage on his way up Market Street and heard the news from Dimity Woodcock, who had answered his knock at the door. Viola Crabbe immediately went to tell her sister, Pansy, who—clad in a voluminous purple morning dress that expressed her artistic nature—was playing the piano in the sitting room.

"Oh, dear," Pansy exclaimed, flinging the end of her

fringed purple scarf over her shoulder. "Whoever will I find to take dear Abigail's soprano solo in 'Let Us with a Gladsome Mind'?" Pansy led the Sawrey Choral Society.

"I'm sure I don't know," Viola said, in her shrill, reedy voice. "Mathilda Crook, perhaps, although her high G is liable to be appallingly flat. Abigail reached it so easily and truly. She shall be missed." She took out her handkerchief and touched her eyes. "Oh, yes, she shall be *sorely* missed." Her voice trembled. Viola gave dramatic readings, and had schooled herself in the effective expression of grief.

"It's odd that Myrtle didn't mention an illness," Pansy said, referring to the third Miss Crabbe, their older sister, who was a teacher and headmistress at Sawrey School. "Didn't she stop to have a chat with Abigail yesterday evening?"

"I believe so," Viola replied, and put her handkerchief away. "Now I must go and look out my good black. I shall want it for the funeral."

Within the half-hour, Joseph Skead, the sexton at St. Peter's, was ringing the passing bell in slow and steady strokes, six strokes and a pause, then six more, to let the parish know that it was a woman who had died. (If the departed had been a man, Joseph would have rung nine, or three for a child.) Around the twin hamlets of Near and Far Sawrey and out on the waters of Lake Windermere, the men looked up from their work to tally the peals and wonder who had died. And in all the cottages and gardens within earshot, the women paused as they stirred soup on the stove or picked the last runner beans in their gardens, listening and counting and feeling a little shiver as the ringing went on and on. Six strokes, pause, six strokes, pause.

"What a pity about dear Miss Tolliver," said Margaret Nash, the teacher of the infants class at Sawrey School, to Myrtle Crabbe, headmistress and teacher of the junior class.

The two of them were standing in the school doorway, watching their exuberant charges race around the yard after lunch. "It is the end of an epoch." Margaret shook her head, feeling dazed. "We will all be lost without her."

Miss Crabbe, who had lately begun to seem rather nervous about things, pulled at her long upper lip. "It is sad—and so sudden. I do hope she arranged to have the roof repaired. Water dripped on my desk yesterday, and I had to put a bucket to catch—" She raised her voice. "Harold, stop pushing Jeremy! That is not at all nice!"

Margaret gave her headmistress a startled look. "But the Roof Fund Committee hasn't got properly underway yet, Miss Crabbe. I doubt that there's been any money at all collected."

"It is my understanding that the solicitation has been completed, Miss Nash," Miss Crabbe said in a reproving tone.

Margaret knew there was no point in arguing the matter. Miss Crabbe's memory could not be relied upon at all these days, but the headmistress was far too proud to acknowledge the problem, and any attempt to correct her only led to unpleasantness. The week before, she had misplaced her attendance book, and they'd turned the school upside down before it was finally found, under a stack of song-sheets on a shelf in the map locker. In the interval, Bertha Stubbs, the school's daily woman, had been blamed, and there had been a great deal of rancor and ill will all round.

"I think you mentioned that you intended to see Miss Tolliver yesterday evening after supper," Margaret said, tactfully returning to the subject. "Did she show any signs of illness?"

"I didn't see her," Miss Crabbe said shortly. "It was late and I could not take the time."

"Ah," said Margaret, and sighed. "Well, we shall all miss her dreadfully."

* * *

Margaret Nash's view of the situation was shared by everyone. In the post office at Low Green Gate Cottage, there was distress and dismay.

"I simply can't b'lieve it," mourned Lucy Skead, the plump, cherub-faced postmistress. "Miss Tolliver wasn't that old, and never a day's ill health. Who will take her place in the Mother's Union?"

Mathilda Crook, who had stepped into the post office to buy a stamp for her letter to her sister in Brighton, replied with a dramatic sigh. "And the May Fete? That's been Miss Tolliver's doing for thirty-five years." With a resolute frown, she added, "If anybody should take it in mind to ask me, I want nothing to do with it. That job is more 'n' two people can manage, and I've my hands busy at Belle Green, with a house full of boarders."

"*She's exaggerating, as usual.*" Rascal, a small fawn-colored Jack Russell terrier, spoke in a low voice to Crumpet, a smart-looking gray tabby cat with a red collar. Rascal, who had a great passion for detail, always liked to state things precisely. "*The house isn't nearly full. There's only two boarders, and two empty bedrooms.*"

"*Now is not the time to quibble, Rascal,*" said Crumpet sternly. She shook herself so that the little gold bell on her collar tinkled. Some cats might not like being belled by their owners (in this case, Bertha Stubbs), but Crumpet was not one of them. She thought the bell lent her a certain authority. "*The real question is, what's to become of Tabitha Twitchit, now that Miss Tolliver is gone?*"

In the queue behind Mathilda, Hannah Braithwaite, wife of the village constable, spoke up sadly. "There was never a more generous soul than Miss Tolliver. Why, last Christmas, she gave my Sally a new pair of boots, and Jack a knitted cap." She paused and added, "I s'pose the vicar will telegraph her nephew in Kendal, won't he?"

"That one!" Mathilda snorted. "Never came, never wrote. No other family, though, so I s'pose he'll get the cottage, more's the pity." She frowned at the little dog, who had followed her into the post office. "Tha's mud on thi paws, Rascal. Wait for me outside, and doan't go runnin' off."

"Come on, Rascal," Crumpet said comfortingly, seeing Rascal hang his head. She knew he hated to be scolded in public—it made him feel foolish. *"We'll both go outside. We need to talk, anyway."*

"There's a woman in Manchester," Lucy Skead said. "Sarah Barwick is her name. She's not kin, though. She writes twice a year, and always sends a little something for Miss Tolliver's Christmas and birthday. Home-baked tea cakes, 'twas, just day before yesterday. Almond, I b'lieve." Lucy, an inveterate snoop, could be counted on to know the names of everyone's relations and how often they kept in touch, since all their letters and cards and packages came and went through her hands. Some minded, of course, but it did them no good, for Lucy could no more keep herself from noticing names and relationships than the sun could keep itself from peering into the windows.

By this time, Crumpet and Rascal had gone a little way down the path. *"I think we should go and see Tabitha,"* Crumpet said, pausing for an appreciative sniff at a bit of fragrant, low-growing mint. *"It makes me sad to think of her staying in Anvil Cottage all by herself. And there's no one to feed her, now that Miss Tolliver is gone. We have to help her find somewhere to stay."* Crumpet was an organizer who could be counted on to take charge in a difficult situation. Show her a stray kitten and she'd find a home for him before any of the Big Folk could say, "Somebody ought to get rid of that extra cat."

"Well," Rascal replied judiciously, *"there's room at Belle*

Green, and since the Crooks keep a cow, there's always plenty of milk. And now that old Cranberry's dead and gone, the mice have rather taken over the place. Tabitha certainly wouldn't lack for work."

"Good," Crumpet said. *"I'll let her know."*

Rascal looked over his shoulder to see if Mathilda Crook had come out of the post office yet. She hadn't, so he said, *"I'll catch up to you later, Crumpet. I want to stop in at the joinery. Mr. Dowling usually has a bit of something in his lunch pail for me."*

Down the way, in Roger Dowling's joiner's shop, Roger and his nephew David were already at work on Miss Tolliver's coffin. Both undertaker and coffin-maker, Roger took pride in having the coffin ready when the family came to lay out the deceased, a task which in this case would probably be performed by the women of the village, since the nearest relation was the nephew in Kendal.

"Wonder what's t' become of Anvil Cottage," young David Dowling said to his uncle as they fitted the last plank of seasoned oak. "Fine place, that," he added enviously, "with t' garden 'n' all. Bees, too. Hope somebody thought to tell them the news, so's they don't go flyin' off."

Roger Dowling picked up his joiner's plane and began to true the edge of the coffin, the shavings curling in golden ringlets to the sawdust-covered floor. "Cottage'll be sold up, most like," he grunted. "There's only just that nephew. A draper, he is, in Kendal, with several shops to look after. He woan't want t' bodderment of a cottage here. He'll sell it for what he can get and be done wi' it." He glanced at the little dog who had just come in through the open door. "Hullo, Rascal. Come fer thi bone?" He reached into his lunch pail, took out a small ham bone, and tossed it to the dog.

Rascal caught it deftly in his mouth. *"Kind of you,"* he muttered, around the bone.

"Doan't mention it." Roger Dowling chuckled, as Rascal

turned and trotted back out the door. "Odd thing how old George's dog manages to be so near human. More human than old George hissel, sometimes."

David was still thinking about the cottage. "If tha ask me, it'd be a girt pity if that place was sold to an off-comer," he remarked, a little ungraciously, since he knew he could not afford to buy it himself. But David's feelings were understandable, for Anvil Cottage had been owned by Tollivers since Sawrey's earliest days, and the villagers, rightly or wrongly, thought of it as belonging to them, or nearly so. And none of them welcomed off-comers, especially in the village proper. The cottages were small and close together, as if they all belonged to one family, as in a way they did, and most of the villagers thought of Sawrey village as one large family, which in a way it was. People from outside the village were not exactly welcome.

At George Crook's smithy, next door to the joinery, Rascal's master was expressing similar sentiments to his helper, Charlie Hotchkiss. The two of them were shoeing Big Bonny, one of the great shire horses that belonged to Tobias Llewellyn at High Green Gate farm.

"T'will be sold to another of t' city folk," George predicted gloomily as he pushed a horseshoe into the coals of the forge, where it began to glow, turning from cherry to bright orange. "Like t' spinster writer lady who's bought Hill Top Farm, right out from under Silas Tadcastle's nose. Silas is that put out 'bout it, and I don't blame him a bit."

Charlie nodded. "Nice farm," he said wistfully. "Silas could've made something verra fine of it."

"Lord only knows what t' spinster lady'll do with t' place," George went on, "her bein' from Lonnun and not a brain in her head for animals—so sez Jennings, anyway." John Jennings was the tenant farmer at Hill Top. He lived in the farmhouse with his wife Becky and two children. "Anybody puts dressed-up rabbits and suchlike in books will nivver do well as a farmer."

"Oh aye," Charlie agreed. He lifted Big Bonny's massive left hind hoof, holding it between his knees and beginning to extract horseshoe nails with an iron pincer. "Shame to see cottages and farms sold off to city folk who comes and goes and takes small mind of t' land and t' village." Miss Tolliver, an active member of the Lake District Defense Society, had actively opposed the building of sprawling summer villas along the lake shore and the incursions of the hundreds of day trippers who came to eat their lunches by the side of the road and leave their greasy fish-and-chip wrappings in the ditch.

"Even more of a shame to see good farms bought by rich ladies with no head for farmin'—or fer land-buyin', either," said George, pulling the hot shoe out of the fire and measuring it over Big Bonny's massive hoof. "Did tha hear what she's paid fer it? Nearly three thousand pounds, fer only thirty-four acres. Auld Jepson sold it to her fer double what he paid t' timber merchant, just a few months ago. Took fer a reet fool, she was." With a scornful grin, he tapped the shoe with his hammer on the anvil to size it, then quenched it in a wooden bucket, where it gave a satisfying sizzle, as if it had been the spinster writer lady herself.

"That's t' trouble with rich folk," Charlie said, taking the steaming shoe in one callused hand and filling his mouth with horseshoe nails from the pocket of his leather apron. "They got too much money. Jepson would've sold Hill Top to Silas Tadcastle more reason'ble, if t' rich lady hadn't happened along and bid up t' price. 'Tis a nice auld house, though," he added. "Wouldn't mind livin' in it, mysel." He picked up the hammer and began to tap, whilst Big Bonny placidly munched her extra ration of oats.

"Dairy wants repair," George replied, pumping the leather

bellows with his foot. "And where are t' Jennings to go, I ask. Farms aren't easy to find these days." He paused, frowning. "Come to think, wasn't t' spinster lady to arrive this week, and board with Miss Tolliver?"

"B'lieve ye're right, George," Charlie said. "So now that Miss Tolliver's gone, where's t' lady t' stay?"

That very same question was being voiced in the street outside. Mrs. Grace Lythecoe, widow of the former vicar, had just left Rose Cottage with her basket, on her way to the village shop next door for some cheese and crackers. She encountered Mathilda Crook and pretty little Hannah Braithwaite, accompanied by Crumpet, the gray tabby cat who lived with Bertha Stubbs, and George Crook's dog, Rascal, who was carrying a large ham bone.

"Oh, Mrs. Lythecoe," Hannah Braithwaite exclaimed breathlessly. "A'n't it just dreadful about poor dear Miss Tolliver? Who would've thought, and her always so hale and hearty? We'll all be lost without her."

"It's very, very sad," Grace replied. Then she frowned and remarked on something that had been troubling her since she had heard the news. "If I'm not mistaken, Miss Tolliver was expecting Miss Potter to stay with her for a fortnight. She's due to arrive shortly."

"She's right!" Crumpet exclaimed to Rascal. "I'd forgotten, but Tabitha told me that she and Miss Tolliver were expecting a guest. Miss Potter is an eccentric, apparently. She keeps a pet hedgehog." Crumpet wrinkled her nose distastefully. "Fancy her keeping a foolish hedgehog when she might have a clever, sophisticated, useful cat!"

"Tha's right, Mrs. Lythecoe," said Mathilda. "Miss Tolliver mentioned it to me just yesterday, when I was handing her birthday cake around." She rolled her eyes heavenward. "Death in t' midst of life," she added piously. "We never knows when 't will come to us. Best to be always prepared."

"Who is Miss Potter?" Hannah Braithwaite wanted to know.

Mathilda's reply was tinged with scorn. "The spinster lady writer who's bought Hill Top Farm."

"Bought Hill Top Farm?" Crumpet exclaimed, twitching her tail. *"Tabitha didn't tell me that!"* Since Crumpet made it her special responsibility to learn about everything that was going on in the village, she was nettled that someone else—especially Tabitha Twitchit—hadn't shared this interesting snippet of information with her.

Rascal lay down in the street, dropped his bone between his paws, and began to lick it solicitously. *"Maybe Tabitha wanted to keep it a secret,"* he said. *"Maybe she doesn't feel that she has to tell you everything that goes on."*

Crumpet made a growling noise deep in her throat. *"I just like to stay informed, that's all. Somebody has to mind things."*

"Oh, now I remember," Hannah said. "Miss Potter is t' lady who sent t' books when t' children all come down with scarlet fever and t' school closed. Our Sally got *Benjamin Bunny,* and has read all the words right off t' page. She loved it when Mr. McGregor's cat sat atop t' basket, with t' two rabbits under it."

Hearing this, Crumpet forgot all about her disagreement with Rascal. *"A cat on top of a basket of rabbits?"* She giggled. *"How very clever. Maybe this Potter person has her heart in the right place after all."*

Frowning, Mathilda nudged the cat with her foot. "Go home, Crumpet. We can't hear oursels think over thi yowling."

"But Mr. Braithwaite sez that Miss Potter's nivver e'en even seen t' farm," Hannah went on. "He sez he can't think why she wants it, 'specially at t' price she paid." In an awestruck voice, she added, "Nearly three thousand pounds, he sez."

"Nay, o'course she's seen Hill Top," Mathilda replied with a knowing air. "Miss Potter and her mother and father took their holidays at Lakefield, 'fore tha married Mr. Braithwaite and come to t' village." Lakefield was a large and elegant home near the village, with a wide garden overlooking Esthwaite Water. It was let by its owners, the Beltons, to summer visitors. "Miss Potter was ivver underfoot about t' village, sketchin' all she could lay eyes on. She spent a whole morning drawin' t' door of t' post office, if tha'll believe it, and two more making pictures of Miranda Rollins's two Pomeranians. And I saw her danderin' 'round Moss Eccles Tarn, on t' hunt for toadstools."

"Toadstools!" Hannah exclaimed, her blue eyes widening. "Whatever for?" She lowered her voice. "She a'n't a witch like Auld Dolly, is she?"

A witch? Now, that's interesting, Crumpet remarked, pricking her ears forward. Cats have more than a passing interest in the occult, and have for centuries volunteered as companions to Big Folk who are considered witches. Crumpet had sometimes thought that it might be interesting to be a witch's familiar.

"Don't be silly, Hannah," Grace said sharply. Hannah was impressionable and inclined to gossipy exaggerations. If she wasn't stopped, it would be all over Sawrey that Miss Potter was a witch, and she and Old Dolly would be spoken of in the same anxious breath.

"Why was she lookin' out toadstools, you ask?" Mathilda repeated Hannah's question. "She said she was drawin' pictures, but I never seen a toadstool in her stories. Leastwise, not in *Peter Rabbit,*" she added. "That was t' book I read."

"Miss Potter likes to study fungi," Grace said sternly. "When I met her several years ago, she expressed a great interest in them, and in fossils, too. She's a naturalist, as well as an author."

"A naturalist, eh?" Mathilda snorted disdainfully. "If tha

ask me, that Peter Rabbit of hers ain't any too natural, with that little blue coat and them slippers. Nivver saw a rabbit wearin' a coat and slippers, and that's a fair fact."

Hannah shook her head, still not quite comprehending. "But fancy a lady buying a *farm*. 'Tis a girt puzzler."

"Fancy indeed," harrumphed Mathilda. "Becky Jennings, poor thing, is worrit right out of her mind, frettin' where they'll find another place when they're turned out, and her with a babe on t' way."

"I'm sure Miss Potter won't turn the Jennings out," said Grace, not liking the direction the conversation was taking.

Hannah, open-mouthed, added, "O' course she woan't. She can't possibly mean to farm t' place herself."

"I should hope not," said Mathilda emphatically. "Ladies got no business with farms, Crook sez, and I agree."

"*My feeling, too,*" Rascal remarked, with a sly, side-long glance at Crumpet. "*Women-folk belong in the kitchen, where the good Lord put them.*"

"*That's as much as you know, you daft ha'p'orth,*" Crumpet replied loftily. She licked her paw. "*There's no reason on earth why a woman can't manage a farm just as well as a man.*"

"I'm afraid that the question is more pressing in the short term," Grace went on quickly, to forestall any more discussion of Miss Potter's intentions. "With Miss Tolliver gone, Miss Potter obviously can't stop at Anvil Cottage. She can't put up at the Tower Bank Arms, either, since both of the Barrow children have chicken pox. Do you suppose you could take her at Belle Green, Mathilda? I understand that Ben Drysdale has moved to Ambleside, so his room must be empty."

"I suppose I could take her," Mathilda said with a great show of reluctance, "although Crook woan't like it. He's that put out at her for snatchin' Hill Top away from a serious farmer who would've made something of t' place."

"Perhaps you can speak to George," said Grace soothingly,

who had known the Crooks for many years and had long ago come to terms with George's tempers. "I'm sure he can manage to be civil for a fortnight."

"But if Miss Potter doan't mean to farm," Hannah wondered once again "what's she want with a place like Hill Top? Seems reet daft to me."

Grace avoided the question with a little smile, but Mathilda seized on it. "I've not a glimmer what t' lady wants, Hannah." Her eyes narrowed. "But I nivver could abide a mystery, so I mean to find out."

"Well, good," Hannah said, with satisfaction. "Soon's ye find out, you can tell me."

And when that happened, Grace thought, resigned, everyone else in the village would know, as well.

2

Miss Potter Arrives

Miss Tolliver's funeral—celebrated in Lakeland fashion, with the traditional arval bread, cheese, and ale given to each of the mourners—took place on Friday. On the following Monday, Dimity Woodcock rode the ferry across the lake to Windermere to spend the day with her old nurse, who had retired to a little cottage there. On the return trip, late in the afternoon, her charabanc arrived at the Bowness ferry landing just behind the coach from the railway station. Since the ferry was over on the Sawrey side, there would be a wait. Dimity climbed out of the coach and walked to the shore.

It was a clear, cloudless afternoon, and Lake Windermere, England's largest lake, was a beautiful sight, its blue waters ruffled by a fresh southern breeze, the trees on the western side of the lake dressed in splendid autumn reds and yellows. Dimity was enjoying the bright sun, the cries of the gulls, and the tug of the brisk breeze in her hair when her felt hat suddenly went sailing.

"Oh, blast!" she exclaimed, grasping futilely for the treacherous thing.

"I have it!" a woman called triumphantly, from a little way up the shore. She held up the hat. "A lucky catch."

"Thank you," Dimity said gratefully, going to get it. "I should have tied it on, I'm afraid." She took the hat and smashed it firmly on her head. Then, as she got a proper look at its rescuer, she recognized her. "Why, Miss Potter!" she exclaimed, and held out her hand. "How very nice to see you again!"

With a shy smile, the other woman hesitantly took Dimity's hand and then let it go. In her late thirties, she was of medium height, dressed with an unfashionable plainness in a gray serge skirt, black jacket, and black gloves, with a narrow-brimmed gray hat decorated only by a plain black ribbon and a small posy of black ribbon flowers. She had a certain youthful prettiness, but her brown hair was pulled back artlessly from her round, rosy-cheeked face, giving her the look of a woman who was indifferent to her appearance. Her nose was prominent, her chin and eyebrows firm, and her bright blue eyes sharp, betraying a penetrating intelligence. At the moment, though, her expression seemed weary and her eyes shadowed with sadness, as though something unspeakably dear to her had been lost.

"I understood that you were to arrive today," Dimity said. She hesitated. "I didn't expect to see you, but now that I have, perhaps I had better ask whether you've heard our sad news."

"Sad news?" Miss Potter asked, startled. Her voice was sweet, and rather high-pitched.

"Yes. I'm very sorry to tell you that Miss Tolliver has died."

"Died!" Miss Potter exclaimed, greatly dismayed. "It

must have been terribly sudden. I received a letter from her not a fortnight ago, confirming my visit. There was no mention of an illness."

Dimity shook her head. "There was no illness. Doctor Butters says that her heart simply stopped. She was buried on Friday, at St. Peter's, poor thing."

Miss Potter's eyes filled with tears and she turned away, biting her lip. "Oh, dear," she said, very low.

"Oh, Miss Potter!" Dimity said, instinctively putting out her hand. "Please don't take it so hard. It was a mercifully quick end, Dr. Butters said. She did not linger in pain."

"That's some comfort." Miss Potter took a deep breath and with an effort, straightened her shoulders. "We must be grateful when the end comes swiftly. Thank you for telling me, Miss Woodcock. It seems, though, that I must find another place to board for my visit to Sawrey—a fortnight, I was hoping, perhaps a few days longer. I'm sure Anvil Cottage will not be available."

"I'm afraid that's true," Dimity agreed, adding quickly, "but the Crooks have a room to let at Belle Green. It's very pleasant, overlooking the garden, and spacious and quite private. They are anxious for your coming." That might not be entirely true, Dimity thought ruefully, thinking of the way George Crook was going on about Miss Potter's purchase of Hill Top Farm. But George and Miss Potter would see each other only at meals, and Grace Lythecoe had assured Dimity that George would hold his tongue. They ought to get along well enough—for a fortnight, at any rate.

"Well," Miss Potter said, managing a smile, "it's all taken care of, then. I'm grateful to whoever made the arrangement."

"That would be Grace Lythecoe," Dimity said. "She suggested—" Her sentence was interrupted by the piercing shriek of a steam whistle, as the ferryboat, an open wooden-hulled scow loaded with horses, a carriage, and a half-dozen passengers, approached the landing, belching black coal smoke.

"I'll see you in Sawrey," she mouthed over the noise, and went back to the charabanc.

Miss Potter also went back to her coach, where Mrs. Tiggy-Winkle's wicker hamper, Josey's and Mopsy's box, and Tom Thumb's traveling cage were all safely stowed on the back, along with her trunk and portmanteau and a large box of drawing supplies.

"*I don't fancy ocean passages,*" squeaked Tom Thumb, a small gray mouse. He was a recent widower (his wife, Hunca Munca, had fallen off a chandelier the previous July), and inclined to be a twittery traveler. "*I wish we'd stayed in London.*"

"*It isn't an ocean,*" Mrs. Tiggy-Winkle replied haughtily. "*It's only a lake, and a narrow one, at that.*" Mrs. Tiggy-Winkle, Miss Potter's hedgehog, was a seasoned traveler and inclined to look down on those who had not had her experiences. "*Traveling is educational,*" she was often heard to say. "*I am glad I don't live in a muddy bank, with no one for company but a few ignorant moles and a stupid rat. What kind of pleasure is there in that?*"

"*I certainly hope there's a garden where we're going,*" Josey Rabbit put in, twitching her nose. "*I am thoroughly sick of leftover salad with oil-and-vinegar dressing on it. Fresh greens—that's what I need. A bit of parsley, a few carrots, some fresh cabbage.*" Josey's life had begun in the wild and had nearly ended in a gardener's trap, where she had been rescued by Miss Potter. She still hankered after the old days, when she was free to go anywhere she liked, although she had to admit that it was rather nice to be indoors during the winter—so long, of course, as she had fresh greens.

"*Don't talk about food, please,*" Mopsy Rabbit moaned. She settled back in a corner of the cage she shared with

Josey and closed her eyes. Mopsy, who had a flighty disposition and a nervous stomach, found travel unsettling. If she could choose, she'd never leave Number Two Bolton Gardens in South Kensington, where she lived with Miss Potter.

It may seem strange that a grown woman would travel with a collection of animals, especially since there wasn't a cat or dog—the usual choices in animal companions—among them. But animals had always been an important part of Beatrix Potter's rather lonely life. Left to inattentive nannies and nursery maids in the large London mansion where they were born, Beatrix and her brother Bertram, five years younger, consoled themselves by bringing an immense number of mice, rabbits, bats, snakes, frogs, birds, and insects into the nursery on the top floor of the house, where their parents seldom ventured, not even for tea. Both of the children were keen naturalists, and their animals were not only pleasant companions of hearth and heart, but a scientific challenge, as well. They had been known to boil the flesh from the bones of certain dead specimens they had collected, so they could study the skeletons.

Bertram gave up most of his pets when he went away to school. But for Beatrix, who stayed behind with a series of governesses in the third-floor schoolroom, animal companions—furred, feathered, scaled, and gilled—took the place of her brother and the friends and schoolmates she would never have. She drew them, of course—and when her parents remarked nervously about the latest acquisition, it was easy to say that she needed this or that animal model for her sketches. But the truth was that she loved them. She loved even the unlovely and unlikely ones, like Judy (a lizard) and Punch (a green frog), and loved them deeply, in the way that a desperately lonely person loves a little creature who seems to return that love without condition. Like many other solitary people, Beatrix often felt that the only real love in her life came from her animal friends—a sad truth that had become even sadder and more true in the past few months.

Back inside the coach, Beatrix was glad that the only other passenger—a bald, portly gentleman in a flowered waistcoat—was sound asleep. She gazed with unseeing eyes out of the window as the coach was pulled onto the ferry and the horses unhitched for the short trip across the narrow lake. The bald gentleman stirred and snorted but did not waken.

The steam ferry was a flimsy affair and Beatrix always felt nervous as a passenger, especially when the wind blew from the south and the waves broke over the ferry's low prow. But this time, she didn't notice the choppy water or the gathering twilight. She had not meant to let Miss Woodcock see how sharply she had felt the unexpected news of Miss Tolliver's death—although it was not Miss Tolliver for whom she mourned. Beatrix had been pleased by the generous offer of bed and board during her visits to the village, but she had scarcely known the lady who offered it.

No, it was Norman Warne she mourned. Norman, the news of whose death had reached her by telegram whilst she was visiting her uncle in Wales scarcely two months before. Gentle Norman, whom she had loved with all the fierce, pent-up passion of a heart that had long ago despaired of loving or being loved. Kind, compassionate Norman, who had known her as she was and had loved her in spite of all her defects and shortcomings. They had been engaged for only a month when (to her parents' great distress) he died, suddenly and unexpectedly. Now, all Beatrix's plans and hopes for a bright future lay buried in Highgate Cemetery, in a new grave still covered by raw earth, as raw as her heart.

The steam whistle shrieked again, and Beatrix resolutely closed her mind to thoughts of Norman and all that might have been of their life together. She had not come here to mourn, but to get on with the daily business of living, as he would have wanted and as her own nature—usually optimistic and hopeful—urged. She took out a handkerchief, wiped her eyes, and was blowing her nose when the gentleman opposite awoke with a hiccup and shook himself.

"Whazzit?" he asked. "Whuzzum?"

"The landing," Beatrix said distinctly. "We've arrived on the Sawrey side."

In a moment, the horses were hitched again and the coach bumped off the ferry. Beatrix felt her heart quicken, realizing that she was so near her destination, so near to the place where she hoped to begin a new life—if not now, then someday.

The village of Far Sawrey was just at the top of Ferry Hill, and less than half a mile beyond was Hill Top Farm and the hamlet of Near Sawrey. The names of the twin villages, which seemed so perversely backward, always confused visitors who came across Lake Windermere. Why was one village called *Far* Sawrey, when it was a half-mile nearer the lake, the ferry, and the railway? And why was the other village called *Near* Sawrey, when it was farther away and altogether less important?

All became clear, however, when the visitor realized that "near" and "far" were measured not from the lake but from the ancient market town of Hawkshead, three miles to the west, for centuries the most important settlement in the area. The village of Near Sawrey (*sawrey* was an Anglo-Saxon word for the rushes that grew along the shore of Esthwaite Water) was nearer to Hawkshead by about a half-mile.

To the tune of the coachman's shout, the snapping whip, and the creaking harness, the four horses pulled the lumbering coach up the climbing, twisting road to the top of Ferry Hill and through Far Sawrey. Off to the left, on a green hill some distance away, Beatrix could see St. Peter's and the churchyard where Miss Tolliver lay buried. She did not allow her glance to linger, but she could not quite suppress the sadness that welled up inside her. Norman lay in a fresh grave in Highgate Cemetery, in the shadow of a large fir. She had not been able to talk of her grief to anyone other than Norman's sister Millie, for her parents had been deeply opposed to the match, and no one other than their immediate families knew that they had exchanged rings.

It had all happened so suddenly, too suddenly to comprehend. So much unspeakable joy, so much unbearable pain, all of it sharply compressed into so few days, too few days: Norman's proposal of marriage on the twenty-fifth of July, his death on the twenty-fifth of August. And the news from Hill Top Farm only added to these difficulties, for soon after Norman had proposed to her, Beatrix had discovered that the farm (which had been purchased by a Hawkshead timber merchant earlier in the year) was once again for sale. The price, although still unreasonably high, was now within her reach, for the acreage had been reduced from 151 acres to thirty-four, and she had telegraphed her intention to purchase it.

Her parents, of course, had been initially opposed to her purchase. There was nothing novel in their opposition, for any suggestion that their daughter might want to lead an independent life was met with displeased frowns and gloomy sulks, and often outright antagonism. But Beatrix was glad, now, that she had persisted. Hill Top Farm would give her a place to escape from the buried dreams of might-have-been, from her father's deplorable tempers and her mother's exacting demands.

The driver shouted and the coach jerked to a stop in front of the Tower Bank Arms, Near Sawrey's only pub. Beatrix got out, retrieved Mrs. Tiggy and the others, and saw to it that their boxes and cages were safely stowed on the wooden cart that Spuggy Pritchard had pulled around the corner.

"These go up to Belle Green," she said when Spuggy had added her trunk and bag, and gave the old man sixpence. "Please tell Mrs. Crook that I'll be right along."

"Mind, now!" Mrs. Tiggy-Winkle cried imperiously. *"Don't jostle my basket! And keep that dog away from me!"* A small fawn-colored Jack Russell terrier was dancing around the cart, barking gaily at the strange animals.

"Dog?" Mopsy moaned. *"Did someone say 'dog'?"*

"Dog? Dog? Oh, woe!" twittered Tom Thumb, who had come all the way across the lake with his head buried under a heap of wood shavings in his traveling cage. *"Where in the world have we got to? The ends of the earth? Oh, rural life will never do, never do at all, at all! I'm a town mouse! A town mouse, I tell you!"*

"We've reached Sawrey village, Tom," Josey said briskly. *"And don't fret about the dog. He's just being friendly."*

The charabanc pulled up behind the coach, and Dimity Woodcock climbed down. "Welcome to Sawrey, Miss Potter," she called. "Shall I see you up to Belle Green?"

Beatrix hesitated. It wasn't that she didn't want Miss Woodcock's company; it was rather that she preferred to see the lovely little village alone, without the distractions of polite conversation. On another, earlier day, she would likely have agreed, rather than hurt Miss Woodcock's feelings. But in the few months since she had accepted Norman's proposal and endured all that difficult business with her parents, she had begun to learn how good it felt to say what she wanted, rather than what someone else wanted for her.

"Thank you," she replied, "but I shan't trouble you. It's twilight, and I'm sure you have things to do at home."

Dimity Woodcock seemed to understand. "Of course," she said warmly. "But you must agree to come to Tower Bank House for tea tomorrow. The late roses are glorious just now, and the first sharp frost will put an end to them."

"I should be glad to," Beatrix replied. She was not a very

sociable person by nature, but she thought she would like Miss Woodcock.

"Wonderful," Dimity Woodcock said. She laughed. "Now that I know you're coming, perhaps it will give me an incentive to do something unspeakably rash, such as clearing out the groundsel along the path. And if I'm going to the trouble of pulling the groundsel, I'll invite a few friends, so you can get acquainted. I promise not to overwhelm you, though. Would four o'clock suit?"

"Of course," Beatrix said, admiring Miss Woodcock's easy friendliness and casual manner. Apart from her cousin Caroline Hutton and Norman's sister Millie, she did not have friends in the usual way. It might be comforting to have someone to talk with from time to time—not on this first day, but later. And no doubt Dimity Woodcock knew everything about the village and its inhabitants, for she and her brother had lived here for quite a long time.

Beatrix turned now, and went along the road, past Buckle Yeat Cottage, which had a lovely garden within a fence made of large slabs of slate, standing on end. In the twilight, the village looked just as she remembered it from her earlier visits, and the sight of the little cluster of slate-roofed cottages tucked into the lap of a gentle green hill brought her a quiet calm, a peaceful at-home feeling that was difficult to explain—especially to her parents, who professed to find everything about her decision completely inexplicable. They had enjoyed their visits to the Lakes as much as they liked visiting anywhere, but having exhausted all the local distractions, professed to find Sawrey frightfully dull. And while her father reluctantly acknowledged that a farm might be a prudent way for Beatrix to invest her growing income, her mother was aghast at the thought of her daughter actually spending time away from Bolton Gardens.

To be sure, there was nothing very extraordinary about

the hamlet. As Beatrix turned from the main road into
Market Street, she could look to her right and see Meadowcroft Cottage, which housed the village shop, and through
the open door glimpse Lydia Dowling in her embroidered
apron, having a cup of tea with her niece Gladys, who helped
out twice a week. Across the narrow lane was Miss Tolliver's
Anvil Cottage, where a disconsolate-looking calico cat sat
on the stoop, and High Green Gate Farm was just up the
hill, with Tower Bank House behind it. Next door to the
shop was Rose Cottage, where Grace Lythecoe had lived
since Vicar Lythecoe died some ten years ago, and then
George Crook's smithy and after that Roger Dowling's joinery (Roger was Lydia's husband). Off to the right, up a narrow lane, was Low Green Gate Cottage and the village post
office. The streets were deserted, except for Spuggy Pritchard
toiling away with his cart at the top of the lane. There was no
village green, and St. Peter's Church and Sawrey School were
a ten-minute walk away, in Far Sawrey. Altogether, it had to
be said that Near Sawrey was not a very prepossessing village, although comfortable in its way, with an almost
eighteenth-century air about it.

But as Beatrix turned to look westward, toward the ma-
jestic Coniston fells rising against a sunset sky painted
with lavender and gold, she knew very well what had
brought her here. This was October, the trees of Cuckoo
Brow Woods were as richly colored as a medieval tapestry,
and the meadows along Esthwaite Water, still green, were
dotted with serenely grazing sheep and black-and-white
cows and flocks of white geese. When she first visited the
village with her parents some ten years before, she had
thought it as nearly perfect a little place as one might
imagine, the people hard-working and earthy and old-
fashioned. The whole place had seemed somehow to speak
to a deep and compelling sense of home and hearth, deep
inside her. She felt that same sense again now, and she

pulled in a deep breath, thinking with pleasure that finally, at last, she had come home.

Then, as she walked up Market Street to Belle Green, Beatrix reflected that perhaps a large part of her pleasure in coming here lay in the fact that she was not *known* in the village. Oh, she had visited here several times, and sketched some of the cottages, and made the acquaintance of a few of the villagers, but they knew very little about her, other than the fact that she wrote and illustrated books for children. After everything that had happened—Norman's death, and the increasing difficulties with her parents—the idea of a new beginning had a powerful appeal. A fresh start was what she wanted, and a place to get away from her mother and father, and from the city, and from the wreckage of her lost dreams. And though she couldn't have the love that she had hoped for, she could still have her work, and Hill Top farm, and Sawrey. And that, she thought as she gazed at the enchanted landscape around her, would do. It would do very well.

A little while later, Beatrix was installed at Belle Green. She found her second-floor room to be a clean and agreeable accommodation, even more pleasant for its view of the garden, where she had taken Mrs. Tiggy-Winkle and the rabbits for a brief outing before it grew very dark. Then she unpacked her clothes, set the animals' boxes and basket on a low shelf, and glanced with satisfaction at the fresh white curtains, the quilt-covered bed, the old oak dresser, and the faded landscape prints on the wall. She had looked forward to staying with Miss Tolliver in Anvil Cottage, but Belle Green was an acceptable substitute.

Mr. and Mrs. Crook, however, were another matter. Mathilda Crook, a narrow, middle-aged woman with a ferret-like nose and sharp eyes, was disconcertingly curious about Beatrix's plans. And George Crook, as Beatrix discovered when they all sat down to supper together in the large, comfortable kitchen, seemed to have something against her, although she couldn't think what. He scowled fiercely at her and muttered something into his black mustache. Charles Hotchkiss, Mr. Crook's forge helper, was as surly as his employer, but Edward Horsley, the other boarder, was nicer, and managed a shy smile and a handshake as they were introduced.

For supper, Mrs. Crook had made a tatie pot, a large oven-baked dish made of lamb, black pudding, and potatoes, served with pickled cabbage, mashed turnips, and fresh bread. Despite Beatrix's weariness, she ate with a greater appetite than she did at home, where meals were a trial, especially when her mother was cross and her father preoccupied. Tonight, the supper-table conversation mostly consisted of speculation about poor Miss Tolliver's will (which had not yet been found), the tale of a cow that had strayed from High Green Gate Farm, and the news that the ferry would be out of service tomorrow for a repair to its steam boiler, and that anyone who wanted to go to Windermere should have to go round by Ambleside. The idea that there was a lake between her and London rather comforted Beatrix. If her parents demanded that she return home, she could plead the extra travel occasioned by the repair of the ferry.

Mrs. Crook also managed to put a few questions to Beatrix, sometimes unsubtly concealed, sometimes asked straight out. What had made her think to buy Hill Top Farm? What did she plan to do with the place? Would she be living there? What about the Jennings family? Would they be staying on? Beatrix didn't want to be rude, but she didn't want to answer, either. She was glad when the uncomfortable meal was over and she could escape upstairs.

In her room, Beatrix settled her animals for the night, stroking Mrs. Tiggy-Winkle, tickling the rabbits' ears, and dropping a kiss on the end of Tom's twinkling nose.

"I know that some of you don't enjoy traveling," she whispered to them, "but I'm very glad you're with me. I've wanted this so much—the farm at Hill Top, I mean—but now that I almost have it, I'm afraid I'll lose it, the way I lost . . ." She stopped and stood quietly for a moment, stroking the little mouse. "You understand, don't you, Tom? You lost someone you loved."

"*She's thinking of Norman,*" said Mrs. Tiggy, an incurable romantic who always spoke from her heart. "*She misses him awf'ly.*"

"*You're right, Mrs. T.*" Mopsy licked a paw and smoothed her gray whiskers. "*A terrible tragedy, and so soon after they were engaged.*"

Tom sniffed. "*She'll never love anyone else. Just as there'll never be anyone for me but my dear, sweet Hunca Munca. My precious little mouse-wife.*" He began to sob loudly.

"*Oh, piffle!*" exclaimed Josey with an impatient stamp of her hind foot. "*She'll find someone else to love, someone who'll love her just as much as Norman did.*" She twitched her nose at Tom. "*You will, too, Tom. Just you wait and see.*"

"*Never!*" cried the little mouse dramatically. "*Never, never, never! My heart belongs to Hunca Munca!*"

"What a conversation you're all having," Beatrix said with a smile. "But you've had a long day, and it's time you went to sleep. Tomorrow we'll have lots of adventures."

She gave them each another quick kiss, then sat down and wrote a dutiful letter to her parents—not so much because she wanted to, but because she knew they would telegraph if they didn't hear that she had arrived safely. That chore done, she took out the exercise book in which she kept her journal, turned up the wick in the paraffin lamp, and began to write.

Beatrix had begun her journal when she was fourteen. Because she was a very private person and didn't want her brother or the nursery maids to read what she wrote, she had invented her own secret code inscribed in miniature, a kind of cipher shorthand. The writing was entirely secret and she never expected that it would be read, so she always wrote with complete honesty, about all her feelings. Tonight, she wrote about the tiring journey, and the sad, shocking news of Miss Tolliver's death, and her discomfort at dinner. But she also wrote about her hope for the future, and her plans for an exciting day tomorrow.

After a while, Beatrix put down her pen, put away her journal, and got ready for bed. But she didn't go to sleep right away. Instead, she pulled the curtains open so that the moonlight spilled over the wooden sill and onto the braided rag rug on the floor. Then she lay very still, watching the flickering shadows and thinking.

Tomorrow, she would walk over Hill Top Farm's fields, get a good look at the barns and the animals, and try to formulate some sort of plan for the future of the place. She felt very much at sixes and sevens where the farm was concerned. She had long wanted a little place of her own, and she had no doubt that Hill Top was exactly right. But there were a great many puzzles yet to be sorted out, and they all seemed rather daunting, especially since she was not used to making such important decisions.

For one thing, she had hoped to take possession of the farmhouse as soon as the final papers were signed next month, so she could begin to furnish the house and arrange it against the day when she would no longer have any obligation to her parents and could choose for herself where to live. But it was currently occupied by a tenant farmer named John Jennings, his wife, and their two children, with another on the way. She had considered asking the Jenningses to leave, but she knew nothing about farming and could not hope to be here often or long enough to learn properly, at least while her mother demanded so much of her time and attention. She had also considered keeping the Jenningses on to manage the farm, but asking them to move so that she could have the house. But she knew it would be difficult for them to find a nearby place at a rent they could afford, and she hated the thought of turning them out, especially with a baby on the way.

But if the rapidly multiplying Jennings family filled up every room of the little farmhouse, where could *she* stay? She had thought perhaps she might arrange a more or less permanent lodging with Miss Tolliver, but that was no longer possible. Would she have to lodge here at Belle Green every time she came, with the ferretty Mrs. Crook prying into her business and Mr. Crook scowling at her over every meal, like an irate walrus whose territory she had invaded? She could not ask her father for advice, for he thought the entire idea was ludicrous. Her brother Bertram generally supported her efforts, but he was preoccupied with his own life these days, having just this year bought a farm in Scotland and married a neighboring farmer's daughter—all without saying a word to anyone but Beatrix. Norman would have helped, of course, generously and without question. He had always been able to suggest clever ways out of the dilemmas that had come up with her little books, and over the five years of their collaboration and friendship, she had come to rely on his sound advice, always offered with regard for her feelings.

But Norman was dead, Bertram unavailable, her father unapproachable. She was going to have to face these difficulties, however unpleasant, all by herself. She sighed and pulled the blanket up to her chin. She had hoped that she was opening a fresh new chapter in her life—but it was certainly full of unwelcome complications. And with that ambivalent thought, and a murmured goodnight to her animals, she fell asleep.

3

A Town Mouse Meets a
Country Cat

The moon had shifted so that its beams silvered the shelf where Mrs. Tiggy-Winkle, Josey and Mopsy, and Tom Thumb were napping. Mrs. Tig, who looked very like a stout, bristly little person, stirred, blinked, and sniffled. The sniffling turned to snuffling, and in a moment she was seized by a loud *a-chew!*

"*My pocket handkerchief,*" she muttered, rooting around on the floor of her wicker hamper, which had a convenient window let into it so that she could see out. "*Where is my pocket handkerchief?*"

"*Where are we?*" shrilled Tom Thumb, startled out of a sound sleep. "*Are we back in London? Oh, please tell me that we're back in London!*"

"*No, we're not back in London,*" Josey said in an irritated tone, and rolled over against Mopsy. "*We're in Sawrey Village. Stop that squeaking and go back to sleep!*"

The door opened noiselessly and a small terrier slipped into the room. He studied the shelf for a moment, then got up on his hind legs and sniffed at Tom's cage.

"*Oh, my whiskers, it's a dog!*" Tom cried frantically, running in circles around his cage.

The door opened again, and a shadow slipped into the room.

"*And a CAT!*" Tom shrieked, jumping up and down. "*We're doomed! Doomed, I tell you! Doomed, doomed, doomed!*"

"*For pity's sake, stop that racket,*" said the dog in some disgust. "*I don't eat people's pets. That's as distasteful as eating their shoes, which I've never been fond of. And I certainly wouldn't eat a guest.*" He sat down on his haunches and looked at the cat. "*What about you, Tabitha Twitchit?*"

"*I never eat anything I've been introduced to,*" the cat replied. A handsome calico, she sat down as well, and gave her paw a suggestive lick.

"*My name is Tom Thumb,*" said the mouse, hurriedly recollecting his manners, "*and these are my traveling companions, Mrs. Tiggy-Winkle Hedgehog, and Josey and Mopsy Rabbit. We've come from London with Miss Potter.*" With another uneasy glance at the cat, he pointed to a pillowy mound in the middle of the bed, lowering his voice to a whisper. "*That's Miss Potter, asleep.*"

"*I'm Tabitha Twitchit,*" the cat said, and licked the other paw.

"*I'm Rascal,*" the dog said, surveying them with some curiosity. "*And if you don't mind my asking, why does your mistress travel with you lot? Seems a bit strange to me.*"

Mrs. Tiggy-Winkle came to the window in her basket and looked out. "*There's nothing at all strange about it,*" she said haughtily. "*Miss Potter is a widely respected illustrator, and we are her models. She draws pictures of us and puts them into the books she writes for children. Although,*" she added with a condescending sniff, "*I very much doubt that you've read them, here in the country.*"

"*Well, you're wrong about that,*" Tabitha Twitchit replied, annoyed by the hedgehog's aristocratic manner. "*I used to sit on the back of Miss Tolliver's chair whilst she read Miss Potter's books out loud to the village children. The Tale of Two Bad Mice, I think, was the name of one of them.*"

"Two Bad Mice!" cried Tom Thumb excitedly, "*why, that's my book! My very own little book! My wife Hunca Munca and I are in it!*" A large tear squeezed out of his right eye and trickled down his fat, furry cheek. "*My wife, sadly, fell from a chandelier. She's dead, and I am all alone.*" He began to sob unrestrainedly. "*Woe, oh woe.*"

"*I am truly sorry, Tom.*" Tabitha put out a consoling paw to the mouse. "*My dear Miss Tolliver died quite unexpectedly only last week, and I am left without a family. I know just how you feel.*"

Tom Thumb ducked nervously away from the cat's paw, consoling or not, for it had claws in it, and sharp ones, at that. His mother had admonished him from his earliest days to beware of cats, all cats, but most especially country cats, who had no breeding and could not be trusted. This one seemed well-mannered and good-natured enough, to be sure, and her sympathy appeared genuine, but one never knew what dark intentions might lurk in a cat's heart.

"*How did Miss Tolliver die?*" asked Mopsy curiously.

"*It happened as she was eating some teacakes and reading a letter,*" Tabitha said with a sigh. "*She seemed very sad and cried a bit, and then she clutched at her heart, and then she was dead. I sat with her all that night, until Miss Woodcock came the next morning, and then the Justice of the Peace, and the village constable.*"

Mrs. Tiggy-Winkle gave a loud gasp. "*The constable?*" she whispered in a hollow voice. "*Was it foul play? A poisoned cake?*"

"*Oh, don't be silly, Tig,*" Josey said scornfully. In an explanatory aside, she added, "*Our Tiggy likes to dramatize events. She does it so that people will notice her.*"

"*Rubbish!*" Mrs. Tiggy-Winkle exclaimed inelegantly. "*I am by nature dramatic. My book,*" she added smugly, bringing the conversation back to herself, "*has my name on it.*" Her smile faded. "*Unfortunately, it's about a silly old washerwoman.*" She raised the stiff prickles on her back until she looked like a brown clothes-brush. "*I do so wish Miss Potter had drawn me as I really am. I am nothing at all like a washerwoman.*" She sneezed again, and got down from her window to look for her handkerchief.

Josey chuckled. "*Tiggy would rather have been drawn as a duchess with a diamond tiara than a washerwoman with a basket of clothes to be ironed.*" She came to the front of the rabbit cage and glanced curiously at the dog. "*Since you're a villager, maybe you can tell us about Hill Top Farm. That's where we're going to stay when we come up from London. Miss Potter has purchased the place.*"

"*I don't see how you're going to stay there,*" Rascal said in a musing tone, "*unless the Jenningses move out. There are quite a few of them. The house is full to overflowing already.*"

"*Oh, there you are, you old thing!*" Mrs. Tig crowed triumphantly, having found her handkerchief (made of delicate pink lawn, with the initials *TW* embroidered in one corner) under a lettuce leaf. She blew her nose twice, hard, then got up and looked through her window at Rascal. "*You mean,*" she said, as the dog's words sank in, "*we have nowhere to stay?*"

"*Nowhere to stay?*" echoed Tom Thumb with a squeak, his whiskers twitching. "*Nowhere to stay? Then we shall have to go back to the city. Hurrah! I am definitely not cut out to be a country mouse. I loathe open fields and haystacks. The possibility of owls terrifies me.*"

On the bed, Miss Potter stirred and sat up, rubbing the sleep out of her eyes. When she saw the dog and the cat, she swung her bare feet out of bed and onto the floor. "What are you two doing here?" she asked, pushing the hair out of her eyes. She got out of bed and shooed Rascal and Tabitha Twitchit out the door, closing it behind them. Taking up a gingham cloth, she spread it over the three cages on the shelf.

"And as for you," she said firmly, "it's time to stop chattering and go to sleep." With that, she got into bed and pulled the covers over her head.

And then all was silent, except for Tom Thumb, who whispered to himself over and over, in a small and disconsolate voice, *"Not cut out to be a country mouse, no, never, never, never,"* until he, too, fell asleep.

4

Losses, Mix-Ups, and Confusions

Dimity Woodcock looked up with a smile as her brother, Captain Miles Woodcock, came into the breakfast room at Tower Bank House and sat down at the table across from her with a cheerful "Good morning, my dear." Dimity did not have to ask what he would like; she poured tea, passed toast and Elsa Grape's freshly made orange marmalade, and dished up a plate of eggs and bacon from the warming pan.

Dimity had never for a moment regretted her decision, some ten years before, to come to live with Miles when he retired from the Army and set up housekeeping in the Lakes. Her choice had not seemed entirely wise at the time; she had lived at home in Plymouth the whole of her twenty-four years and had seen very little of the world. When their parents were both killed in a train wreck on the south coast, there had been enough money for her to spend a year or two globe-trotting, as her cousins urged her to do, and then take up residence in London, with the aim of finding a husband, preferably rich.

But globe-trotting did not appeal to Dimity. Furthermore, she had her own income and was not in want of a husband, rich or otherwise; in fact, she had the idea that men (except for her brother, of course) were more bother than they were worth. To placate her cousins, Dimity had taken two sight-seeing trips, one to Italy and the other to Switzerland, and then accepted Miles's invitation to visit him at the house he had just purchased in the village of Sawrey. A few weeks later, he broached the subject of her staying permanently.

"I'm afraid there isn't much excitement," he had said, "but it's a pretty place, and quiet. Rather ideal, actually." He sighed and rubbed the bad leg he'd got in Egypt, along with malaria and the Victoria Cross. "I've no great yearning for society, and quiet and peace have a many charms, at least for me." And Dimity, who had very much enjoyed her walk down to Esthwaite Water, with the view of Coniston Old Man shrugging its mountainous shoulders beyond, had happily agreed.

But although life had been on the whole peaceful, it had not been very quiet, for either of them. Captain Woodcock soon found himself serving as Justice of the Peace for Sawrey district, a post that required him to hear complaints, witness documents, certify deaths, and the like. And his sister, when it became known that she was a sensible woman with abundant goodwill and energy, found herself asked to volunteer for all manner of village and parish activities. She had finally to say no to some things, simply in order to have time to garden and take the long tramps across the fells that she so much loved.

Dimity poured herself another cup of tea. Miles had attended a meeting of the Hawkshead Bell Ringers the night before, and she had not seen him since breakfast the previous day. "Miss Potter arrived yesterday afternoon," she said, adding two lumps of sugar. "I met her as we waited for the ferry."

"Ah, Miss Potter," Miles said dryly. "The worthy London authoress who aspires to become a tiller of the soil. Where's she putting up whilst she's here?"

"With the Crooks, at Belle Green."

Frowning, Miles put down his cup. "Belle Green, eh? I hope George Crook will keep a civil tongue in his head, at least in Miss Potter's presence. He's fairly well put out with her. Says ladies have no business farming. Not to mention that this particular lady outbid Silas Tadcastle for Hill Top." He chuckled without amusement. "Fancy you, Dimity, trying to manage a farm. You'd have it all topsy-turvy in a minute. And so, no doubt, will she."

If this patronizing remark had come from the lips of anyone but her brother, Dimity would have taken offense on her own behalf and that of Miss Potter, who would surely not undertake such an extraordinary project had she not felt qualified. But since it was Miles, she merely smiled.

"It's hardly a farm, is it? Just thirty-four acres."

Miles frowned. "She could have bought twice that amount of land, and more, for what she paid."

"P'rhaps she didn't want twice the land," Dimity persisted. "P'rhaps she's earning enough from her books so that it doesn't matter. They're in all the shops, you know, and selling as fast as ices on a hot afternoon."

"It's not the size of the farm that matters." Miles spread marmalade on his toast. "It's the idea of a 'lady farmer' that galls Crook and the others. That, and her buying it out from under Tadcastle's nose."

"If Mr. Tadcastle had wanted Hill Top badly enough, he should have paid Mr. Jepson's price," Dimity retorted tartly. "I don't understand why anybody should hold that against Miss Potter."

Miles gave his sister a generous smile. "I can see that the lady has one friend, anyway." He went on to something else. "I don't suppose you've heard, Dimity. Miss Tolliver's will turned up a day or two ago. It's to be read out tomorrow."

"But I thought there *wasn't* a will," Dimity said, surprised. "At least, that's what her nephew told me." The nephew, a fat, red-faced draper named Henry Roberts, from Kendal, was the only relative to come to the funeral. Dimity had found the man to be a blustery sort, very different from the modest Miss Tolliver, and not altogether pleasant. He had spoken about selling Anvil Cottage and using the money to open yet another draper's shop, an idea that Dimity found repugnant. She was sure that Miss Tolliver would have thought so, too.

"Well, there was a will," Miles replied definitively. "Is, rather. Willie Heelis—Miss Tolliver's solicitor—was away in Scotland for a fortnight, fishing. When he got back to his office and heard the news, he sent word straightaway that he had the original in his possession, all properly signed and witnessed."

"Well, then," Dimity remarked, "that should please Mr. Roberts. He was unhappy about the idea of having to go through the intestate process to prove his claim."

"I'm not sure it *will* please him," Miles replied off-handedly. "According to Heelis, Miss Tolliver didn't much like the fellow. Maybe she left her estate to somebody else altogether. Of course, Heelis didn't give me any of the details," he added, forking up another rasher of bacon. "Wouldn't've been professional of him."

"I see," Dimity said, and then trailed off, distracted by the thought of the robust Mr. Roberts, who had been so sure of his inheritance and might be inclined to make an unpleasantness should he lose it. She picked up her coffee cup. "There's a young woman friend, Sarah somebody-or-other. Lucy Skead mentioned her. She lives in Manchester and sends little parcels to Miss Tolliver from time to time. The last one came just before she died—homemade teacakes, Lucy said."

"Lucy Skead is a snoop and a gossip," Miles said, and went back to his eggs. "What are your plans for the morning?"

"I'm going down to Sawrey School, to hand in the money the ladies collected for the School Roof Fund. Two whole pounds, which is quite a lot, really. I'm sure Miss Crabbe will be glad to see it. Bertha Stubbs says she's been awf'lly upset over the leaks in the roof. One of them is right over her desk."

"Miss Crabbe," Miles replied, "seems to be having a difficult time of it lately. If she can't find one thing to be upset about, she finds another." Miles was involved with the county school board, and took a personal interest in Sawrey School. "But I'll speak to Joseph about seeing to the roof as promptly as possible. Two quid won't do nearly the whole job, but at least it will be a start."

After breakfast, Dimity consulted with Elsa, their cook and housekeeper, about dinner. Since today was Harry the Fish Man's day, they would be having fish.

"See if you can get some char, Elsa," Dimity said, "and we'll have it with gooseberry sauce." Char, a favorite local fish, came from Lake Windermere, and the gooseberries from the bushes at the foot of the garden. Dimity and Elsa had bottled enough during the summer to last most of the winter. "And for this afternoon's tea," Dimity added, having reminded Elsa that Miss Potter and one or two others would be dropping in, "please make some of those wonderful jam tarts."

"And the sponge that the vicar likes," Elsa said. "We have to have the sponge."

"And the sponge," Dimity agreed.

This done, she put on her jacket, hat, and gloves and walked the half-mile to the school in Far Sawrey, timing her visit to coincide with the morning exercise period. The children were in the yard, playing "Three Tinkers" under the supervision of Miss Nash. Miss Crabbe was at her desk in the junior room. Her gray hair was coming down around her ears and her expression, Dimity thought, was distraught. She seemed to be searching for something. She shut the drawer of her desk with a bang as Dimity approached.

"I've stopped in at a bad time, I'm afraid," Dimity said with some reluctance. She always felt like a slothful scholar in Miss Crabbe's presence, and had the sense that if she held out her hands, the headmistress would take out a ruler and whack her fingers soundly.

"Yes." Miss Crabbe frowned. "No. I mean, of course not. I was only—" She bit her lip. "I seem to have mislaid my spectacles. I had them just a moment ago, but I—"

"I think they might be there, on the windowsill," Dimity said with some diffidence.

Miss Crabbe rose, snatched up the spectacles, and put them on. She turned. "Well?" she asked in a peremptory tone, looking down her very long nose. "What can I do for you, Miss Woodcock?"

Feeling as if she were eight years old again, Dimity reached into her purse and took out an envelope, which contained one gold sovereign, two half-crowns, three florins, and nine shillings. "Actually, I've come about the School Roof Fund," she said apologetically. "After Miss Tolliver's funeral, the Sawrey Ladies' Society collected two pounds. It's not enough to pay for the entire roof, of course, but it ought to manage the repairs." She put the envelope on Miss Crabbe's desk.

Miss Crabbe actually smiled. "Oh, thank you," she said, and snatched up the envelope. "I must say, I am really very glad to see the money. When it rained last, there was a very bad drip directly over my desk, and—"

But Dimity did not get to hear the rest of the tale, for the door burst open, and a boy came in, weeping loudly. He was small and thin, with a delicate, almost pretty, face, and he had a bloody nose. He was accompanied by Miss Nash.

"Jeremy Crosfield!" Miss Crabbe exclaimed, rising. "What on earth is the matter with you? Stop that blubbering this instant! Eleven is much too old for such childish noises."

"Harold pushed him off the coal pile," Miss Nash said sympathetically. "He's scraped his arm rather badly, and his nose is spouting."

"Get a wet cloth and clean him up and make him stop crying, then," Miss Crabbe said tersely. "I'll tend to Harold." She stalked to the door. "Harold!" she shouted. "Harold, come here this instant! I want to see you!"

Dimity left hastily, feeling that she would rather be the unfortunate victim, bloody nose and all, than the culprit who had to face Miss Crabbe's terrifying wrath.

The Reverend Samuel Sackett, vicar of St. Peters, was not a man who paid a great deal of attention to his physical surroundings. On the whole, he was far more interested in the life of his parish and the lives of his parishioners than in the landscape around him. This morning, for instance, the Reverend Sackett was oblivious of the fact that the sky was cloudless, a light southern breeze was shaking a shower of golden leaves from the trees, and the bittersweet berries gleamed like rubies in the hedge. He was deeply occupied with a minor but nonetheless disturbing parish problem.

The vicar had been out for a walk and was on his way back to the vicarage, carrying his favorite rosewood walking stick, which was carved in the shape of a snake. He would have been recognized throughout the parish, even without his collar and black vest, by his habit of carrying carved sticks from his collection, a different one each day. One, elaborately carved from a gemsbok horn and given to him by a missionary friend in Kenya, had provoked an awed Sunday School child into asking if it mightn't be Aaron's rod that parted the Red Sea so the Israelites could cross over. Samuel Sackett could have wished for such a rod today, to part the sea of parish troubles that would open before him if he were not able to find—

"Good morning, Vicar," said a bright voice. "A glorious day, isn't it?"

Startled, the vicar looked up from his musings to find that the sun was shining, the trees were golden, his path had intersected the Hawkshead road, and one of his favorite parishioners was standing before him.

"Good morning, Miss Woodcock," he said, lifting his hat. "Yes, it is indeed a pretty day. And so nice to see you." He especially liked Dimity Woodcock, who always had a good word to say about everyone. She and her brother Miles were willing volunteers for the many necessary little tasks that kept the parish sailing on an even keel through occasional storms of difficulty and disharmony.

And at this moment, Miss Woodcock was reporting on one of those tasks. "You'll be glad to hear," she said with a smile, "that I've been to the school to give Miss Crabbe the money that the Ladies' Society collected for the School Roof Fund. It came to exactly two pounds."

"Two pounds!" the vicar exclaimed, greatly surprised. "Well, now, that is a fine accomplishment, I must say!"

"Yes," Miss Woodcock said. "Lady Longford gave a sovereign, in memory of Miss Tolliver." She paused, her smile widening, and added, "It's one of those funny old Young Victoria sovereigns—1838, if you can believe it, although it looks newly minted. She must have had it for ages."

The vicar could believe it. Her ladyship, who lived in seclusion at Tidmarsh Manor, did not make it a practice to give to charitable causes, as he well knew, having suffered her rebuffs in the past. But he didn't say this, of course. Instead, he said, "Lady Longford was indeed generous. And I'm sure Miss Crabbe was pleased. The leaks in the roof have upset her."

The vicar frowned, for "upset" was too mild a term to describe Miss Crabbe's feelings. She had complained bitterly to him at least twice about having to put a bucket on her desk to catch the drips. In fact, she had spoken of leaving her post if something were not done about the situation straightaway. She had heard, she said, of a position at a school near Bournemouth, on the south coast, where the winters were much warmer and, presumably, the roofs did not leak. She had even said that she intended to ask Miss Tolliver, who was acquainted with a member of the Bournemouth school council, for a letter of reference.

The vicar had replied, and not entirely out of politeness, that he would be very sorry to see her go. It was true. Although Miss Crabbe's manner was often peremptory and impatient and her students feared rather than loved or even admired her, they did their work and there were few discipline problems in her class. And what would Viola and Pansy Crabbe do if their sister should decide to leave the village? Would they go with her, or stay at Castle Cottage, where they had lived for most of their lives? It would be terribly disruptive, all the way round, and Vicar Sackett was not a man who welcomed disruptions. But one way or another, he had to admit that Miss Crabbe was in serious need of a change. If she felt that Bournemouth was the answer, he would ask the Lord to bless her going.

"She did seem very concerned about the leaks," Miss Woodcock said. "I mentioned it to Miles, and he said that he would speak to Joseph about getting the roof mended."

"I'll speak to him, too," the vicar said, and paused, thinking of his own troubles. "I'm reluctant to bring this up, Miss Woodcock, but I wonder if—" He took a deep breath and forged ahead. "You were in charge of decorating the church for the Harvest Festival, I believe."

"I was indeed," Miss Woodcock said brightly. "I thought the volunteers did quite a splendid job, didn't you? Lydia Dowling's pumpkins were extraordinary. I don't think I've ever seen such large ones."

"Oh, my goodness, yes," the vicar said, although he himself had thought Mrs. Dowling's pumpkins, piled in orange heaps around the base of the altar, rather overwhelming. "But I was wondering if you happened to . . . that is, if you might know . . ." He hesitated, finding it difficult to bring himself to give voice to what was occupying his thoughts. "Actually, it's the Parish Register," he said at last. "I discovered it missing when I went to record Miss Tolliver's burial. I was hoping that you might . . . well, that you might have an idea where it has got to."

"Missing?" Miss Woodcock asked blankly. "How can the Parish Register be *missing?*"

The vicar tried to swallow his disappointment. "Then you didn't happen to . . . oh, perhaps, just put it away somewhere? To get it out of the way of the decorations, I mean."

The Parish Register—the record of all the marriages, baptisms, and burials at St. Peter's—was a handsome leather-bound book with a gold-colored clasp. It was not the sort of thing that one put away somewhere and forgot, since everyone who had anything to do with the parish knew of its importance. Still, he had hoped—

"No, of course I didn't put it away somewhere," Miss Woodcock said. "When I saw it last, it was—" She frowned. "Well, I don't know when I saw it last, exactly. But I'm sure it was on the shelf beside the baptismal font. Have you asked Joseph?"

Joseph Skead, the sexton, put things right after services, swept the leaves out of the entry, and mowed the churchyard. He did not do any of these things speedily and without complaint, of course, but he did them, most of the time.

The vicar sighed. He had asked Joseph first thing, of

course. "He has no idea of its whereabouts, I'm afraid," he replied, adding anxiously, "I trust I don't sound accusatory, Miss Woodcock. It's just that I can't think where it might have got to. It's a worry, I must say." He blamed himself, as he usually did when things went wrong. It was easier to shoulder the blame and the responsibility than to hand it off to someone else, even when that might have been appropriate.

"Yes, of course it's a worry," Miss Woodcock said consolingly. "I'm sure it will be found, though. It's not the sort of thing that anyone would . . . well, *take*." She paused. "Actually, I'm glad to have run into you this morning, Vicar. Miss Potter is coming to tea this afternoon, and I thought you might like to come along and meet her."

"Miss Potter? Miss Potter? I don't believe I—" The vicar's mind cleared, and he raised his walking stick in salute. "Oh, Miss *Potter*! Miss *Beatrix* Potter! Why, bless my soul, Miss Woodcock, of course I should like to meet her. I was delighted when I heard that she had purchased Hill Top. I readily confess to being an ardent devotee. In fact, when I was visiting in Ulverston yesterday, I purchased a copy of *The Pie and the Patty-pan* for my brother's daughter—the two-shilling edition, in blue cloth binding with a little medallion printed on the cover, quite handsome and in the shops just this week, I believe. I shall bring it, and if Miss Potter is willing, I should like her to write her name in it, and an inscription to my niece." He paused. "I don't suppose you've seen the book yet, have you? It is set in Sawrey, and there are a great many pictures of familiar things."

"There are?" Miss Woodcock asked. "How nice."

"Oh, indeed, yes," the vicar said, happily punctuating his words with his stick. "I recognized Bertha Stubbs's sitting room, and the path that slopes down to the Lakefield cottages, and Mrs. Kellythorn's wooden pattens, sitting beside the cottage entrance."

Miss Woodcock blinked. "Mrs. Kellythorn's pattens?"

"The wooden shoes are a sweet, homely little detail," the vicar went on enthusiastically, "although perhaps from Mrs. Kellythorn's point of view, a trifle too homely." Mrs. Kellythorn was interested in fashion, and might not be entirely happy that her pattens—old-fashioned clogs used by farm wives to go about the barnyard when there was mud—had been painted for posterity. "And there is the fan light over the post office door," the vicar continued, "except that Miss Potter drew Mrs. Dowling's splendid tiger lilies in the front of the post office, which is bound to disappoint Mrs. Dowling. The two main characters are a cat named Ribby Pipstone, and Duchess."

"Duchess? Miranda Rollins's brown Pomeranian?"

"Yes, that's the one." Mrs. Rollins had two Pomeranians, one black and one brown. The vicar sighed. "It's rather unfortunate that Miss Potter made a mix-up of the names, for she has drawn Darkie, but called her Duchess. There are no people in the book," he added hurriedly, feeling that this might be a good thing. If Miss Potter had drawn Darkie for Duchess and misplaced Mrs. Dowling's favorite tiger lilies, the residents of Sawrey would probably consider it a very good thing that she had not drawn any of *them*.

"I think," Miss Woodcock said, "that I should like to take a look at the book. Would you mind if I borrowed it? I could take it now, and give it back when you come to tea tomorrow."

"Oh, by all means, indeed yes," said the vicar warmly. "I am delighted to share the treasure. Come along, and I'll get it for you." And when he sent Miss Woodcock on her way, she had in her bag a small two-shilling book with a picture of a cat on the blue cover.

5

Miss Potter Surveys Her Domain

Beatrix got up with the sun that morning to take Mrs. Tiggy for a ramble among the dewy, sweet-smelling roses. The little hedgehog had served as a model for the drawings in *The Tale of Mrs. Tiggy-Winkle.* The book, Beatrix's sixth, had been published just last month, and a second printing was already planned, so it seemed clear that it would enjoy the same success as the others—a success that still continued to amaze Beatrix. She somehow could not quite believe that so many people wanted to read stories about rabbits, mice, and squirrels, and every time she received a royalty check she was astonished to see how all those shilling purchases had added up. She was earning quite a respectable sum.

The money was wonderful, in itself, of course, and she was using the income from the first books to purchase Hill Top Farm. But even more wonderful than the money or what she could do with it was what it represented: "It is pleasant to feel I could earn my own living," she had written to Norman, in a triumph of conscious understatement. In fact, she rejoiced at the idea that her writing might allow her to lead an independent life, hugging the glorious thought to herself with a kind of incredulous jubilance several times a day, like a young woman with a letter in her pocket from a secret lover. Her books not only gave her many pleasant tasks with which to fill the empty hours; they were her ticket to independence, to a life of her own, away from Bolton Gardens.

Beatrix always felt very much at loose ends when she had finished a project. She felt this now, perhaps because *Mrs. Tiggy-Winkle* was the last book she would do with Norman. She would have to find a new way of working, and she had come to Sawrey, in part, to sketch. Before Norman died, they had discussed the possibility of a book that would feature a frog named Jeremy Fisher. She already had some drawings, mostly modeled from her pet frog Punch, who had died some years before. But if she could find another frog to draw, particularly a large, self-satisfied green frog, that would be a help.

Having stowed Mrs. Tiggy-Winkle in her basket upstairs, Beatrix went down to the dining room. Mr. Crook and his helper had already gone to the smithy, and Beatrix sat down to a bowl of steaming oat porridge and a boiled egg. Edward Horsley was there, finishing his meal. He smiled at her and offered to build a small hutch for her animals in the back garden.

"I'm sure they'd like that very much," Beatrix said, surprised by his kindness. "It will be a nice change for them. They do so like to be outdoors in fine weather."

Mrs. Crook frowned. "Put it in the corner by the hedge out of the way," she said shortly. "I don't want to be fallin' over it. And mind you make the door fast, Edward. If they get out, they're bound to be lost." She gave Beatrix a dark glance that said, plain as day, that she wouldn't have been so quick to rent her the room if she'd known about the animals.

But Edward only grinned and winked at Beatrix. "Oh, aye," he said easily. "I'll make it so they woan't 'scape." He took his hat and went off to work with a cheerful whistle.

At seven-thirty, Beatrix put on her tweed jacket and wide-brimmed felt hat. With the Crooks' dog Rascal tagging along behind, she walked down Market Street, then through the wicket gate beside the Tower Bank Arms and up the path to Hill Top Farm. She paused as the house came into view, savoring the moment and thinking how absolutely amazing it was that Hill Top was actually *hers*—or would be, when the papers were signed the next month.

It was hard for Beatrix to explain to herself, much less to anyone else, how much she wanted her very own house. She had always loved houses—oh, not grand mansions, like her cousins' Melford Hall in Suffolk; or gloomy, respectable houses like her parents' three-story brick house in South Kensington. What Beatrix loved more than anything else were tiny cottages with crooked roofs, their stone-flagged floors brightened by rag rugs, the ceilings hung with braids of onions and fragrant herbs, the rooms furnished with old-fashioned oak sideboards and grandfather clocks and chairs with woven rush seats. Farm houses with no pretensions to grandeur, with mullioned windows and thick walls and narrow passages turning and twisting every which way. Houses that reminded her of the rooms and hallways in her uncle's house at Gwaynynog in Wales, or the room she slept in at Camfield Place, her grandmother's yellow-brick house. Houses that made her want to reach for her pencil and *draw*.

Yes, perhaps it was her artist's heart that coveted the warm glow of firelight reflected from copper-bottomed pans, or her artist's soul that longed for shafts of dusty sunlight falling through windows bright with blooming flowers. She sketched these whenever she could, and in a way, these sketches of cozy rooms and sunlit windows and comfortable furniture, peopled with cats and mice and little dogs, substituted for a home of her own and a family that didn't sulk and glower at her. But Beatrix knew that she could never be entirely happy until she lived in her own house, a real house, exactly the *right* house. It didn't matter that she would have to put all of the royalties from her little books into it, along with the small legacy Aunt Burton had left her. And it didn't matter that she had paid more for it than anyone else thought it was worth. It was worth the world to her.

Beatrix had admired the farm house at Hill Top since she first saw it some years before. The modest two-story house, over two hundred years old, was simple and almost severe. The exterior was covered with a pebbly mortar, painted with limewash; the roof was made of blue slate; and the chimneys wore peaked slate caps, as did most of the chimneys in the village. A staircase wing and a larder had been built on the rear a hundred years ago, along with a one-story kitchen on the side nearest the barn. And there was a little porch, with two large, flat slates for the sides and two more for the peaked roof. But these few additions could not detract from the house's lovely simplicity. It was all perfect. Perfect in every way—or it would be, if she could sort out the difficulties.

At that moment, two of the major difficulties—Sammy and Clara Jennings—came dancing around the corner of the house and nearly collided with her and Rascal. Clara, the six-year-old, stopped and put her thumb into her mouth, but Master Sammy, eight, came forward and regarded her soberly as she introduced herself.

"Clara and me wuz on our way to school," he said, "but I'll tell m'fadder tha's come."

Clara's large brown eyes filled with tears. "Ye're t' lady who's come t' take our house away?" she whispered fearfully, around her thumb.

Beatrix knelt down, dismayed. "Take your house? Why, whoever says so, Clara?"

"Our mum." The tears brimmed over and spilled in twin rivulets down the child's cheeks. "She sez we've got to find us another house to live in, 'cause Miss Potter is comin' t' live in ours."

Oh, dear! Beatrix thought in alarm. "Your mother and I must have a talk," she said out loud, but her words did not sound comforting, even to her own ears.

A ginger-colored cat sauntered out from behind a large rose bush and joined them, ignoring the terrier at Beatrix's heels. Clara dropped her thumb and scooped up the cat, which was nearly as large as she was.

"And who is this?" Beatrix asked, rubbing the cat's ears.

"She doan't have a name," Clara said.

"All cats have names," Beatrix replied. "Otherwise, how could they answer when we call them? Let's see." She put her head to one side, studying the cat. "What would you think of calling her Miss Felicia Frummety?"

The little girl began to giggle, her fears momentarily forgotten. "But frummety is what I eat," she said. "Barley and milk, cooked up together."

"I daresay Miss Felicia likes frummety, too," Beatrix said. "And she likes her new name. See her twitch her whiskers?"

Rascal pranced forward. *"Frummety, eh?"* he teased. *"What kind of a name is that?"*

"It's a very nice name," Felicia replied with some asperity. *"Nicer than Rascal, and much nicer than having no name at all."* She jumped out of Clara's arms. *"P'rhaps you can tell me what's going on at Anvil Cottage. Crumpet and I were out hunting mice late last night, and we saw—"*

Her story was interrupted when a man came around the corner of the house. He was tall, brown-haired, and brown-bearded, and he had a gruff voice. "T' boy told me you were here, Miss. Come to walk over t' place?"

"If you have the time to go with me this morning, Mr. Jennings," Beatrix said. "I've been looking forward to it very much."

The man glanced down at Beatrix's feet. "T' missus can make t' loan of her pattens," he said curtly. "T' barn yard's a mire, and tha'll spoil thi town shoes."

Beatrix colored. She should have thought to provide herself with something suitable to country walks. "I'd be glad of the loan," she said, and followed him around to the front of the house.

The sturdy leather clogs, Mr. Jennings told her as she took off her town shoes and slipped her feet into them, were made by a cobbler in Hawkshead from an old pattern that was favored by the local country women. They fit perfectly, and as Beatrix walked down the farm lane beside Mr. Jennings, the terrier and the ginger cat trailing behind, she felt very much like a country woman herself. As she looked around, an ecstatic joy welled up inside her, and perhaps she might be forgiven for thinking that Hill Top Farm was the most beautiful farm in the whole world. After all, it was *her* farm, and the grass was like emeralds, the sky an azure blue, the wind off the fells was as fresh and clean as if it had been newly laundered, and smoky London and her mother and father were quite far away.

For the next several hours, as the morning sun lifted the mist from Esthwaite Water and the clouds wandered across the fells and moors beyond, Beatrix and John Jennings made their way around the small acreage, through the stone-built barns and the muddy barnyard, along a narrow cart-track through the grassy meadows, past the stone quarry and stacks of hay and the little autumn-colored coppice. They paused on the lane at the foot of the farm, so that Beatrix could look out over the green meadow toward Esthwaite Water, where a flock of white geese sailed on the placid surface. As they walked, Beatrix inquired about the farm carts and farm tools, the garden soil, the health of the animals, the state of the winter grass, the size of the summer's hay crop, and the availability of quarry stone for walls and walks. Mr. Jennings replied in an increasingly respectful tone that revealed his surprise at the breadth and depth of her questions. Beatrix found pleasure in their conversation; for her, at least, the time passed quickly—and if Mr. Jennings would rather have been doing something else that morning, he didn't reveal it. And Rascal, who was trotting along close behind, was as surprised as Mr. Jennings at the questions Miss Potter asked. Who would have thought that a famous lady author from London could care so much about a little farm in the Lake District?

As they walked down the lane that marked the southern edge of the farm, Beatrix noticed a whitewashed cottage beneath an overhanging willow tree, some little distance away, in the direction of the lake. Looking at it, she suddenly felt the tingling in her fingers that always signaled an irresistible desire to draw a beautiful object—and the tiny cottage *was* beautiful, with its clean white walls and slate roof and chimney cap, and a tumble of roses in the door yard.

"What's that place?" she asked curiously, pointing to the cottage.

"That's Willow Cottage," Mr. Jennings said. "Miss Crosfield and her nephew Jeremy live there. She spins and weaves for folk and keeps a few sheep for t' wool. But since t' steam looms 've come, times is bad for t' likes o' her. Bad for t' sheep, too, now that linoleum's come in to replace carpet."

"Linoleum is bad for the sheep?" Beatrix frowned, thinking of the linoleum on the floor of the Bolton Gardens servants' quarters. "Why is that?"

"T' native sheep are Herdwicks, suited to t' harsh winters in t' fells. Their wool is coarse and springy, and best used to make carpets. But modern folk wants linoleum in their houses, and there's no market for t' fleece, so sheep farmers are turnin' to other breeds." He paused. "Pity, too. Herdwicks are a fine sheep for the fells, strong and hardy. They're heafed to their home places and thrive on even a poor pasture."

"Heafed?" Beatrix asked.

"They know where they belong, and they doan't wander."

"An admirable quality," Beatrix murmured. She thought to herself that it was a gift to know where home was, whether you were a sheep or a person.

"Aye. And when t' winter storms come roarin' down t' fells, they can live in a snowdrift for nigh on a fortnight— on their own wool, if need be."

Still thinking about the Herdwicks whose wool was no longer wanted, Beatrix followed Mr. Jennings through the meadow and up the slope to the garden, or, rather, where she hoped to put the new garden. The existing garden, with its raggedy flay-crow (the Lakelanders' name for a scarecrow), was small and terribly untidy. There were disappointingly few animals, too, although that could be easily remedied. Hill Top seemed to have specialized in pigs that year, for there had been quite a number. Most had already been sold—and a good thing, too, Mr. Jennings remarked with a wry smile, since the pigs had eaten nearly all the potatoes. Any that remained should have to go on short rations.

"What do you think, Mr. Jennings?" Beatrix inquired seriously, as they paused at the barnyard fence. "Shall we have pigs again next year?"

"Oh, aye," Jennings agreed, not looking at her. "Allus good to have pigs. If they does well, tha can get a name, sellin' pigs here and there." Leaning against the fence, he took his pipe out of his pocket and began to fill it with tobacco from a leather pouch. "But afore tha has more pigs, tha'll need to put some money into fixin' t' broken boards on t' pigsty. Can't have pigs runnin' loose and frettin' t' village, now, can we?"

"No, of course not," Beatrix said, although she privately

thought that, as far as the villagers were concerned, a few loose pigs might provide a welcome distraction on a dull day. She reached down to pet Rascal, who had been following them on their walk. "And cows?" she pressed. "I counted only four."

"Aye, cows." Jennings nodded impassively. "O' course, tha'd have to buy t' right stock—Ayrshires, I'd say. And if tha has more cows, tha'll need a new stone floor in t' dairy, and a new roof. T' missus sez t' old dairy isna fit t' keep cheese and butter in, for t' rats. Rats is so big, they could just about carry off t' cats."

"D'you hear that?" Rascal said to the ginger cat. *"Why aren't you out in the barn, taking care of those rats?"*

"That's the barn cats' job," Felicia Frummety explained. *"We all have our territories, you know, and the barn cats don't much like it if I trespass. I'm responsible for the house—and believe you me, no rat dares to show his whiskers whilst I'm on duty. Or her whiskers,"* she added, thinking of Rosabelle Rat, who lived in the attic and had so far proved too wily to catch.

"I see," Beatrix said, mentally adding the cost of a new dairy to the cost of the pigsty and the cost of the Ayrshires. It was clear that the next few books would have to return enough royalties to manage the improvements she wanted to make. "I noticed that there aren't any sheep," she added after a moment. "It would be good to have at least a few Herdwicks, wouldn't you say? It would be a pity to see a fine breed die out."

"Herdwicks?" Rascal said in some surprise. He personally liked the Herdwicks, who seemed to him more intelligent than most other sheep. But the farmers always complained that they couldn't make any money from their wool, and there wasn't any market for the meat. Didn't Miss Potter intend to turn a profit from her farm?

"Herdwicks, then," Jennings said, seeming pleased. He tamped the tobacco in his pipe. " 'Tis a bit late in t' year, but we might find four or five draft ewes for sale at Penrith. No-vember is tuppin' time, and tha'll want to hire a tup."

"Tupping time?" Beatrix asked.

Jennings didn't look at her. "When t' ram—t' tup—is put in with t' ewes. April is lambin' time."

Felicia chuckled. *"Look at her face, gone all red. Well, that's a lady for you. Her nanny probably told her that lambs are brought by the stork."*

Beatrix felt her cheeks flush. This was not the sort of sub-ject she had ever discussed with a person of the opposite gender. But if she wanted to be a farmer, she would have to learn to talk like a farmer. She squared her shoulders.

"Go to Penrith and buy five good ewes for us, then," she said bravely, "and hire the best tup you can find to breed them. And when April comes, we'll have the beginnings of our flock."

Now it was Rascal's turn to chuckle. He leaned over and spoke into Felicia's ginger-colored ear. *"Did you hear that, Felicia? This lady might make a farmer yet."*

"Maybe," Felicia said. *"It's going to take a lot more than words, though. She'll have to get her hands dirty—which might not be easy for a London lady."*

"April." Jennings scratched a match against his boot, put it to his pipe, and pulled. "T' missus and me, we'll have a babe oursels in April. Three, make it." He studied the flay-crow critically. "With pigs and cows and sheep and hay and t' like, there'll be work a' plenty, and you mostly in London. I'm wondering what tha means t' do for a farmer."

"That's it," Felicia said approvingly. *"Ask it straight out, Mr. J., so she knows she has to make up her mind."*

Beatrix had not been sure what she should do about John Jennings, but now it was time to come to a decision. She took a deep breath. "I hope," she said, very seriously now, "that you and Mrs. Jennings will agree to stay on and man-age Hill Top. I'm sure that, working together, we could have quite a good farm. It will be small, but that's for the best, while I'm learning my way." She paused. "Will you do it?"

There was a long silence, long enough for Beatrix to fear that Mr. Jennings was going to say no. In the barn, a hen began to cackle, announcing the arrival of a new egg, and after a moment, a second hen (who always took credit, even when the egg wasn't hers) joined the celebration. Somewhere nearby, a cow made a soft lowing sound, and up at the house, someone was banging on a tin pan.

"I'd do it if she asked me," Rascal said. *"I think it'd be fun. And I like her, in spite of that foolish hedgehog she keeps."*

"Well, maybe," Felicia replied, *"but the problem is Mrs. J., y'see. She's not at all in favor, and she's already told him so."*

"Will I do it?" Jennings repeated. "Well, now, I s'pose it all depends." He looked up at the house. "T' missus was wonderin' what tha had in mind about t' living arrangements. Will tha be wantin' to stay here at Hill Top?"

Beatrix followed his glance. Mrs. Jennings was standing in the porch, holding a large pot and looking in their direction. Even at this distance, she could see that the woman was scowling. She sighed.

"Yes, I should certainly like to stay here when I come. But I must confess that I'm not at all sure how that might be managed. As you yourself say, there will soon be five of you, and we six would be very crowded." Beatrix knew enough about her own need for privacy to be sure that she would not enjoy living in the midst of the noisy family for more than a day or two, and she was very sure that Mrs. Jennings would not be happy about sharing the small house.

"Very crowded," repeated Felicia firmly. *"Somebody would have to sleep on the floor—and it won't be Mrs. J., I can tell you that."*

"Well, then, what's t' be done?" Jennings asked. "T' missus is 'specially worrit about t' house. If we can't conclude an arrangement, I fear tha may need to find another farmer."

"I understand her position entirely," Beatrix said, adding, with more confidence than she felt, "but I'm sure we can work something out. Will you speak to Mrs. Jennings about it, or shall I?"

Jennings puffed on his pipe. "I'd best do't," he said at last. "She's not o'er happy about t' idea of us stayin' on here, I'm sorry to say." He turned, and his serious blue eyes lightened, although he did not quite smile. "I'll be takin' t' pony cart t' Hawkshead on Saturday, to sell butter and eggs. Would tha like t' come wi' me?"

"I would, very much," Beatrix said. She looked down at her feet. "Perhaps I could visit the cobbler and have him make me a pair of clogs just like these."

Rascal turned to Felicia, who wore a surprised look. *"There,"* he said, with satisfaction. *"She talks like a farmer and walks like a farmer. The lady will make a farmer yet."*

On her way back to Belle Green for lunch, Beatrix went to the post office, where she said hello to Lucy Skead, the postmistress, and asked for her mail. It proved to be a substantial bundle: two letters from Millie Warne, Norman's sister; a letter from her mother; a letter and a check from her publisher; and a package labeled as containing six copies of *The Tale of Mrs. Tiggy-Winkle.*

"Welcome to the village, Miss," Lucy Skead said primly. "Ye'll be with us long this visit?"

"Until the end of the month," Beatrix replied. She glanced at her letters and added, "unless I'm needed at home." Her mother had a way of developing an ailment or creating a crisis among the household servants the minute Beatrix was out of the house. She hoped this letter wasn't a summons.

"I couldn't help noticin'," Lucy confided in an innocent tone, "that thi package was full o' books. Mayhap there's a new one? Me mum has read all that tha's written. Her fav'rite is *Benjamin Bunny.* Reads it over and over to my girls, though they can read fer thersels." She trilled a light laugh. "She says thi rabbits put her in mind of folks she knows."

Beatrix opened the paper package of books and took out a copy. "This is the book that came out last month. There's another new one, but they haven't sent it yet." She smiled at Lucy. "Perhaps your mother would like to have it."

Lucy Skead's eyes grew round. "Tha'd *give* it to Mum?" she asked in a whisper.

"I'd be glad to sign it if you like," Beatrix said diffidently. "What's her name?" Lucy told her, and Beatrix took up the pen on the counter, dipped it into the glass inkwell, and wrote, with care, "To Mrs. Dolly Dorking, with kind regards, HBP."

"Oh, thank you!" Lucy exclaimed. "Mum'll be that pleased." She peered at the inscription. "H?" she asked curiously. "What's that stand for?"

Beatrix, feeling that Lucy was a busybody, did not want to tell her that she had been named Helen, for her mother. She was relieved when a shadow darkened the doorway. It was a stooped old lady in a gray dress, a black tippet around her shoulders, leaning on a cane.

"Ooh, look, Mum!" Lucy cried excitedly, holding up *The Tale of Mrs. Tiggy-Winkle.* "It's a new book, and Miss Potter has put her initials in it, and thi name. See? It says 'To Mrs. Dolly Dorking.' She wants tha should have it, with her kind regards!"

The old lady came closer, peering up at Beatrix. She was very short, just above five feet high, with shrewd blue eyes, a face as wrinkled and brown as a scrap of wash-leather, and a strong scent of lavender about her. "Thank'ee," she said, in a cracked, high-pitched voice. "Thank'ee much. Is this 'un about a rabbit? I did admire that Benjamin Bunny, for all his mischief. Put me in mind of my own brother, when he was young."

"Actually, this one is about a hedgehog," said Beatrix, who was always delighted to find an eager reader. "I used my own pet hedgehog—Mrs. Tiggy—as a model."

"Well, I'll read it," the old lady said, "and tell tha how I like it." She sniffed. "But I won't lie, mind. If it's not up to *Benjamin Bunny,* I'll let tha know."

"Mum!" Lucy protested, scandalized. "She *gave* it to you!"

"Well, that's no reason for a body to lie, now, is't?" muttered the old lady, and shuffled off down a dark passage.

Amused, Beatrix gathered up her mail and was about to leave the post office when a woman came in. She was dressed in a neat gray skirt and jacket and white blouse, and her dark, silver-streaked hair was twisted up under a wide-brimmed hat. She was accompanied by a handsome gray tabby cat with a red collar and a little bell.

"Why, Miss Potter," she said pleasantly. "How very nice to see you again. Perhaps you'll remember me—I'm Grace Lythecoe."

"Of course," Beatrix said shyly. She glanced down at the cat. "And this is Crumpet, isn't it? I recall her from my earlier visit."

"Yes," Mrs. Lythecoe replied, smiling. "I'm surprised that you remember her name."

"So am I," Crumpet purred, flattered. She wound herself around Beatrix's ankles. *"But then, I'm a memorable cat."*

"I remember," Beatrix replied, "because I put Crumpet into a book called *The Pie and the Patty-Pan.* I called her by another name—Ribby Pipstone—but it's Crumpet, all the same." She bent down and stroked the cat's sleek fur. "You didn't notice, Crumpet, but I made several sketches of you whilst I was here."

"You put me into a book?" Crumpet sat down and stared up at Beatrix, wide-eyed. *"Just wait until Tabitha Twitchit hears this!"*

"I included one of Mrs. Rollins's little dogs, as well," Beatrix added, straightening, "and several village scenes."

"Oh, what fun!" Mrs. Lythecoe exclaimed. "I know that the children loved the books you sent when they were ill." She stepped up to the counter. "Hello, Lucy," she said. "I'll have a stamp, please."

Beatrix stood by, waiting, as Mrs. Lythecoe paid for the stamp, affixed it to a letter, and handed it to Lucy Skead. As they walked out of the post office, followed by the cat, Beatrix said, shyly, "I wanted to thank you for arranging my stay at Belle Green. Miss Woodcock told me that you suggested the idea to Mrs. Crook."

"You're quite welcome." Mrs. Lythecoe gave her a bright smile. "I do hope George Crook is behaving himself. He's a very nice man, but he's apt to be a bit gruff now and then."

"A bit gruff, is it?" Crumpet laughed. *"Why don't you tell her about the time he chased the gypsy tinker down the street?"*

"So it's not just me, then," Beatrix said in some relief. "Sometimes one feels . . . rather awkward, when it comes to strangers."

"If you don't mind my speaking frankly," Mrs. Lythecoe said, "I'm not sure George likes the idea of a woman buying Hill Top Farm. Some of the men are a bit . . . well, a bit uncertain about the idea of a lady farmer, and especially one from the city." Her gray eyes twinkled. "They predict disaster, of course. Men always do, when a woman plans something out of the ordinary."

Beatrix had to smile, for that was exactly the way her father behaved. "Well, they'll just have to get used to the idea," she said briskly, "for I am determined. I spent the morning with Mr. Jennings, looking around the farm. We talked about repairing the dairy and the pigsty and getting some sheep."

"So the Jenningses are staying on, then?" Mrs. Lythecoe asked, in a serious way. "I really don't mean to pry, but I did wonder how you were going to manage."

"I've asked them to stay," Beatrix answered. "I'm not sure they'll agree, though. Obviously, there's not room at Hill Top for all of us. I—"

"Mrs. Lythecoe!" came a blustery shout. "I say, Mrs. Lythecoe! Hold up there!"

Beatrix turned to see a very stout man in a brown waistcoat, a red tie, and a mustard-yellow tweed suit hurrying across the meadow. Another man, also short and stout but with a fuzzy brown beard, was two paces behind him, almost running to catch up. They looked, Beatrix thought, rather like Tweedledum and Tweedledee.

"Hello, Mrs. Lythecoe," said the first man breathlessly. "So nice to see you again, ma'am."

"Hello, Mr. Roberts," Mrs. Lythecoe said, in a cool, remote voice that gave Beatrix to understand that Mrs. Lythecoe did not consider the man a friend. "I should like you to meet Miss Potter."

Crumpet frowned. *"Roberts, is it? Haven't we met before?"*

"Pleased, I'm sure," Mr. Roberts said, with the slightest nod for Beatrix and none at all for the cat peering out from behind her skirt. He gestured to the shorter man. "Mrs. Lythecoe, Miss Potter, Mr. Spry."

"I am sure we've met," Crumpet said, narrowing her eyes. *"The other night, after dark, outside Anvil Cottage, wasn't it?"* She and the ginger cat from Hill Top had been out and about, mousing. The hunting was always good in the back gardens after dark, when most of the other village cats were content to doze beside the fire.

Mr. Spry bowed twice, muttering his pleasure into his fuzzy beard, and without looking up, reached into his waistcoat pocket and took out two cards, handing one to Mrs. Lythecoe and one to Beatrix. *Houses for Sale and to Let,* Beatrix read.

"Spry's a house agent in Kendal," Mr. Roberts announced. "He'll be selling Anvil Cottage for me."

"One of a cat's most reliable assets," Crumpet remarked, *"is her ability to see in the dark. That was you I saw the other night, sir, trying to climb through the window at the back of the cottage!"*

"Splendid cottage, splendid," Mr. Spry said, in a buttery voice. "Should fetch quite a nice price. Lake District cottages are much in demand these days, you know. The older, the better, of course."

"And Anvil Cottage is as old as they come, if not older." Mr. Roberts pulled down his waistcoat over his bulging stomach. "Been in Tolliver hands since the days of King George."

"Then I am even more surprised that it's not staying in Tolliver hands, Mr. Roberts." Mrs. Lythecoe's voice was now glacial. "It is such a shame to let a nice old family cottage go to strangers."

Mr. Roberts waved a careless hand, rings flashing. "Oh, there isn't any more family. Only me, and I have no use for an old cottage."

"If you have no use for an old cottage, why were you trying to get in through the window?" Crumpet demanded. *"Was there something inside that you wanted?"* She gave a wicked little laugh. *"Too bad that you were too fat to get in, isn't it?"* She and the ginger cat had watched him struggle until he finally gave it up and went off into the dark.

"No use at all," Mr. Roberts repeated emphatically. "I've a fine new house in the newest suburb of Kendal." He puffed out his round cheeks. "All the modern conveniences, water and gas laid on, and a carriage house. Very fine, isn't it, Spry?"

"Oh, very fine," Mr. Spry muttered under his breath. "And modern, yes, indeed. Quite modern. Water and gas, paved street. Carriage house, quite large, with a loft over. Extra-size building lot."

Pressing her lips together, Mrs. Lythecoe inclined her head. "I am glad to hear that you are so admirably accommodated, Mr. Roberts. Miss Potter and I must be going along now. Delighted to meet you, Mr. Spry."

"You don't sound delighted," Crumpet commented dryly. *"And I certainly don't blame you. At the very least, the man is a housebreaker. He was trying to—"*

"One moment, please," Mr. Roberts said, stepping in front of them. "I understand that Aunt Tolliver gave you a spare key for safekeeping, Mrs. Lythecoe, and I should like to have it. Spry was here with me earlier, just after the funeral, so he has already had the ha'penny tour, as it were. But there are a few points we need to clear up before he writes the advert." He made a face. "Unfortunately, I have no key, and the cottage seems to be very tightly locked up. I'd be obliged if you'd let me have yours."

Mrs. Lythecoe straightened her shoulders and pressed her lips together. "I regret to say, Mr. Roberts, that I am not able to give you the key until Miss Tolliver's will has been read out and the matter of the inheritance is settled. I understand that this is to take place at the solicitor's office tomorrow morning. When I am assured that you are the legal heir, I shall be glad to give you the key."

"You can't— But . . . but that's nonsense!" Mr. Roberts rose to his tiptoes, his face becoming as red as a rooster's. "I am the last Tolliver. There's nobody left but me! Anvil Cottage is *my* cottage, and I demand that you give me the key, this instant!"

"Demand all you like, Mr. Roberts," Mrs. Lythecoe said between her teeth, "you shall *not* have the key." She took Beatrix's arm. "Now, if you will excuse us, Miss Potter and I have business elsewhere." And leaving Mr. Roberts staring incredulously after them, and Mr. Spry muttering "Most extraordinary, most extraordinary!" into his beard, they swept away.

"My goodness," Beatrix said, when they had gone a little way. "I certainly admire the way you spoke to that disagreeable little man!" She could not help adding, with a chuckle, "He is very like a rooster, isn't he? Brown waistcoat, red tie, yellow suit. All that's wanted is a red hat."

"A rooster! You have it exactly!" Mrs. Lythecoe laughed, and then sobered. "But I'm afraid that Mr. Roberts can be *very* disagreeable, when he gets it into his head that he wants something. Miss Tolliver had as little as possible to do with him. She was quite attached to Anvil Cottage, and I would be truly surprised if she left it to him—although I can't think who else she might have left it to." They had come to the corner of Market Street, and she paused. "Dimity Woodcock has invited me to tea at Tower Bank House this afternoon. I shall look forward to seeing you there, Miss Potter." She put out her hand, her gray eyes warm.

"Thank you," Beatrix said with genuine feeling, taking her hand. Turning toward Belle Green and reflecting on Grace Lythecoe's firmness in the face of that dreadful man, Beatrix thought that she should not like to have her for an enemy.

And Grace Lythecoe, for her part, walking in the direction of Rose Cottage, smiled once again at Miss Potter's remark that Mr. Roberts was very like a rooster. The lady might be shy when it came to meeting strangers, but there was nothing wrong with her powers of observation.

6

Dimity Woodcock Serves Tea

Dimity Woodcock had spent the early part of the afternoon, as she had promised herself, pulling groundsel along the front path and raking the leaves that had fallen on the grass. At four, she changed her dress, combed her hair, and went downstairs to the small sitting room, with windows overlooking the garden. A fire burned on the hearth, its glow reflected in the oaken furniture that had belonged to the Woodcock side of the family. Vases of fall asters and bowls of late roses brightened the room, and tea was laid on a white damask cloth. Elsa Grape, a plain, sturdy woman with the proprietary air of one who has served the family for a long time (as indeed she had, having been hired by Dimity's brother the day after he settled himself at Tower Bank House) came in with a tray of cakes.

"Ring if ye want more hot water, ma'am," she said. "Mrs. Lythecoe sent to say that she might be a bit late, and I meant t' tell thi that Harry the Fish Man only had trout, so that's what'll be for dinner tonight, with t' gooseberries, instead of t' char. And oh, yes, Jane Crosfield brought t' woolen skirt with t' tear that she darned for the, and a reet good job of it she made, I must say. Tha can't hardly see the t'mend at all." She surveyed the tea tray critically. "Should we have more sponge?"

"Don't we have enough already?" Dimity looked at the laden table, where seven china cups and saucers were set out. "We're only four, you know. Just the vicar, Mrs. Lythecoe, Miss Potter, and myself. Mr. Woodcock has business in Hawkshead and will not be back until dinner."

"Oh?" Elsa asked. "Must be important, to keep t' cap'n from tea with t' vicar." She paused, and raised her eyebrows. "T' bisness wouldn't be about poor Miss Tolliver, would it?"

"I'm sure I don't know," Dimity said, and began counting the spoons. Elsa's greatest flaw was her indomitable curiosity. She was determined to find out what was going on in the household, even when nothing was going on; Dimity, consequently, was determined to keep Elsa from discovering anything, even when there was nothing to discover. The game had amused the two of them for the past ten years, and neither wanted to give it up.

"Humph," Elsa remarked in a slightly acid tone, and departed for the kitchen.

Not long after, the bell rang, and Elsa was back. "T' vicar is here, ma'am, with Miss Crabbe and Miss Nash. He met them on their way home from school, and says if it's no trouble, might they come to tea and meet Miss Potter."

"Oh, by all means," Dimity said, flustered. She would be very glad to see Margaret Nash, but she hoped that Miss Crabbe would not take it into her head to lecture them in her headmistressy way, as she sometimes did, and which was most unpleasant. And it was rather awkward to have Myrtle Crabbe to tea, without having invited her sisters, Pansy and

Viola. She sighed. To make amends, she should have to have all three of the Misses Crabbe to lunch. And it would have to be on a Saturday or Sunday, since Myrtle was at school the other five days. Village life might seem simple on the surface of things, but underneath, it was very complicated.

But Dimity hid these distracted reflections behind a bright smile and held out her hand as the trio came into the room. "Vicar," she said cordially, "and Miss Crabbe and Miss Nash. How *very* kind of you to come and meet Miss Potter."

Miss Crabbe was looking tidier and less distraught this afternoon, and more fully in command of herself, which also meant that they were more likely to be lectured. "Where is Miss Potter staying?" she asked, as Dimity poured tea. "Milk and sugar, if you please."

Margaret Nash smiled at Dimity. "Lemon for me, please, Dimity."

"Just sugar," said the vicar. Today's walking stick was dark oak, carved with heavy clumps of leaves and acorns. He leaned it against the wall and rubbed his hands together. "Miss Potter is staying with the Crooks at Belle Green, I believe. Isn't that right, Miss Woodcock?"

"Yes," Dimity said, pouring. "We can only hope for the best, of course," she added obliquely.

"I suppose I might have a word with George," the vicar said doubtfully as he took the cup Dimity handed him, "although I'm not sure it will do any good. He is not entirely happy with the idea of women farmers. And there was that unfortunate business with Silas Tadcastle."

"I've forgotten," Miss Crabbe said, "just who Miss Beatrix Potter is, although I'm sure I've heard the name any number of times." She stirred her tea vigorously. "Political, is she?"

"Some sponge, vicar?" Dimity asked. "Mrs. Grape wanted you to know that she made it especially for you."

"Why, how nice," said the vicar, taking two pieces.

"Please thank Mrs. Grape. Her sponge is always most delicious."

"I believe you're thinking of Beatrice Potter, Miss Crabbe," Margaret Nash said tactfully. "She is a Socialist, and spells her name with a *c*."

"*Our* Miss Beatrix Potter writes and illustrates children's books," Dimity said, "and spells her name with an *x*. A bit of sponge cake, Miss Crabbe? Or perhaps a jam tart?" To the vicar, she added, "Miss Potter's new book is there on the table. Thank you so much for lending it to me. I found it quite delightful."

"You're most welcome," the vicar said, picking up the book. "Here it is, Miss Nash, the book I was telling you about. *The Pie and the Patty-Pan.*"

"Jam tart, I think, Miss Woodcock." Miss Crabbe's eyebrows rose. "I didn't know you enjoyed children's literature, Vicar," she went on archly. "We shall have to ask you to read it to our classes—if it is not too political, that is. I always say that we should not bother the children's heads with political matters." She leaned forward. "What was the unfortunate business with Silas Tadcastle that you mentioned?"

The vicar was saved from answering the question when the bell pealed and Elsa reappeared at the sitting-room door. "It's Mrs. Lythecoe, ma'am," she said. "She says to say that Mrs. Rose Sutton dropped in to return a tray she borrowed, and she thought it'ud be lovely if Mrs. Sutton was invited to welcome Miss Potter, 'specially since Mrs. Sutton is t' veterinarian's wife and if Miss Potter aims to have cows and sheep and pigs and such at Hill Top they'll cert'nly become acquainted, so t' sooner t' better."

"Of course," Dimity said, counting the cups. "Do ask them in, Elsa." Really, it was of no use to try to give a *small* tea party in a village. One might as well put out all the china and resign oneself to a crowd.

"So Miss Potter's bought Hill Top, has she?" Miss Crabbe's

thin eyebrows went higher. "What's to become of the Jenningses? I suppose she's going to turn them out."

"Dear Dimity," Grace Lythecoe said from the doorway. With her was a disheveled, youngish woman with bright hazel eyes, chapped lips, and reddened hands that looked as if they spent a great deal of time in hot water. Dimity was well acquainted with Rose Sutton, who might be a trifle harum-scarum at times but was one of the hardest working women in the parish. Not only did she keep the accounts for her husband Desmond's practice, but she helped to make up his medicines and manage his supplies, as well as deftly managing a houseful of small Suttons—five, at last inventory, although from the look of Rose, the count would be going up soon.

"What does Miss Potter think she will do with a farm?" Miss Crabbe was asking the vicar in a skeptical tone. "Really, I can't understand these political women, always wanting to make people *notice* them by doing one outrageous thing or another."

"I don't believe our Miss Potter is especially political," the vicar said uncomfortably.

"I'm afraid I can't stay very long," Rose Sutton said, taking the cup and saucer Dimity handed her, "as I must see to the children's tea. But I did so want to thank Miss Potter for her thoughtfulness. My Lizzy received one of the books she sent when scarlet fever closed Sawrey School. It kept all the little ones quiet for days." She stirred in sugar, then glanced around brightly. "I wonder, if I may be so bold as to ask, what anyone's heard about Miss Tolliver's will. My husband heard that Mr. Heelis has it in his office, but no one seems to know if the draper from Kendal is to inherit, or someone else altogether."

Everyone looked expectantly at Dimity, for Captain Woodcock, as Justice of the Peace, always knew what was going on. Dimity cleared her throat. "My brother told me just that much at breakfast this morning," she said apologetically. "The will is to be read out tomorrow. I'm afraid I don't know anything more about it than that."

"Miss Potter and I were coming back from the post office this morning," Grace Lythecoe said, choosing a jam tart, "when we met Mr. Roberts. He demanded the key to the cottage."

"Demanded?" the vicar asked, raising his sparse gray eyebrows. "Oh, dear."

"Oh, yes," Grace said in a dry tone. "I must say, he became quite unpleasant. There was a house agent with him, a Mr. Spry, from Kendal. Mr. Roberts has apparently engaged him to sell Anvil Cottage. He said he expects to dispose of it quickly."

"You didn't give him the key, I hope," Dimity said anxiously, thinking that this was something Miles ought to hear. He might want to tell Miss Tolliver's solicitor.

"Of course not," Grace replied. She smiled. "I don't know whether I should repeat this, but Miss Potter remarked that Mr. Roberts looked like a rooster. Very apt, I thought." Rose Sutton giggled, Margaret Nash laughed out loud, and the vicar chuckled.

Miss Crabbe, as might be expected, was not amused. "That's the trouble with political women," she said, with a disapproving *harrumph*. "They are much too quick with their criticism. And the Socialists are quite the worst of the lot. Nothing seems to suit them."

"Miss Crabbe," said the vicar diplomatically, "Miss Potter is not a political person, but an artist, and quite well known. She writes and illustrates children's stories." He held up a copy of *The Pie and the Patty-Pan*. "This is her latest. It appeared just last week."

"Well, I do hope she keeps Socialism out of her books." Miss Crabbe lowered her chin and peered at the vicar over the tops of her gold spectacles as if he were one of her juniors. "Especially if she's going to suggest that people are like *animals*. What sort of example does that set for the children?"

"I'm afraid I shouldn't have mentioned it," Grace said, with an apologetic glance at Dimity.

The doorbell rang again, and a moment later, Elsa opened the door with a flourish and announced, "Miss Potter *and* Mrs. Crook." To Dimity, who was mentally tallying up the numbers, she confided, "I'll bring more china straightaway, ma'am, and another kettle of hot water."

Dimity hurried to greet the guest of honor, but Mathilda Crook put herself forward. "I told Miss Potter that tha'd likely be having several to tea," she said energetically, "and tha wudn't mind if I popped in for just a minute. T' more t' merrier, as my old mother used to say. In Sawrey, we nivver stand on sermons." She glanced around the crowded little room. "Just look, Miss Potter, at t' girt gang o' folk! How nice of ivverboddy to come!" Having cast herself in the role of the gracious hostess, Mrs. Crook went to the tea table and took the last cup.

The next few moments were filled with the sort of confused hubbub that attends the arrival of a celebrated guest. In this case, however, the guest was shy and hung back by the door, looking as if she wanted to make her escape as soon as possible. But finally she was lured to a chair beside the fire, introductions were managed, Elsa produced another cup and saucer and the kettle, and Dimity handed the last of the cakes around. Rose Sutton thanked Miss Potter for the book her little Lizzy had received, Margaret Nash reported that Clara Jennings had told her schoolmates that Miss Potter had given her cat the enchanting name of Miss Felicia Frummety, and the vicar asked Miss Potter to sign his niece's copy of *The Pie and the Patty-Pan,* which apparently its author had not yet seen.

"The amount of detail in your pictures is nothing short

of miraculous," the vicar said admiringly, when Miss Potter had written an inscription on the flyleaf. He opened the book to the third page. "This drawing of the post office door, for instance. It's exactly like, down to the very detail in the fanlight."

"But tha's put Lydia Dowling's tiger lilies along t' post office path!" Mathilda Crook exclaimed in a horrified tone, peering over Miss Potter's right shoulder. "And tha's drawn them much too tall. Why, they're as tall as t' post office door!"

Miss Potter seemed abashed by the criticism. "But I meant the door to seem small, you see," she explained, "the same size as the little dog. The tiger-lilies suggest the scale."

"Confusing, is what it is," Mathilda Crook said, with a frown. "Things ought to be t' same as they *are*."

"It's artistic license, Mathilda," Margaret Nash commented. "In pictures, things are never exactly as they are in real life."

"And here is Bertha Stubbs's parlor," the vicar went on hurriedly, turning the page, "with Miranda Rollins's little dog Duchess climbing up to look into the cupboard for the mouse pie. Why, it is exact in every detail, down to the red cushion on Mrs. Stubbs's loveseat." He turned another page. "And here is Duchess and Bertha Stubb's tabby cat Crumpet—whom you will recognize even though she is called Ribby Pipstone—sitting down to a fine mouse pie."

Miss Crabbe frowned over Miss Potter's left shoulder. "But this is not Duchess," she said, planting a disapproving finger on the drawing of the dog. "This is *Darkie,* for she has a black coat, whilst Duchess is brown. And why has the cat's name been changed, I wonder. If one is drawing from life, one should render one's subjects exactly."

Dimity saw that Miss Potter's cheeks were by now quite red. "I think," she said, coming quickly to the rescue, "that

Duchess is a prettier name for a story-book character than Darkie. And Ribby Pipstone is a very clever name." Then, with a hasty change of subject, she added, "You had a lovely morning for a walk around Hill Top Farm, Miss Potter. Did you find everything as you expected it?"

"Yes," Miss Potter replied. "It's a beautiful place. Mr. Jennings and I discussed some repairs to the dairy and the pigsty. I should like to enlarge the garden, too, although perhaps not right away."

Miss Crabbe sat down on the sofa beside Margaret Nash. "I suppose the Jenningses will be leaving." She pursed her lips disapprovingly. "Where are they to go? There are no cottages to let nearby."

Miss Potter gave her a direct look. "I've asked them to stay on," she said, "although we shall have to work out the details of living arrangements."

"Perhaps," Rose Sutton ventured, "they could take Miss Tolliver's cottage. She died, as I suppose you know, very suddenly and mysteriously, only last week."

Miss Potter cleared her throat. "Yes, I know," she said in a low voice. "It was quite a shock to hear of her death."

"What did she die of?" Rose asked Dimity. "I don't think I heard."

"That's what we'd all like t' know," Mathilda remarked in a meaningful tone. "Nivver sick a day in her life."

"It was her heart, Dr. Butters said," Dimity replied, picking up the plate of sponge cakes that Elsa had just put down. "More cake, Vicar?"

"It wasn't poison, then," Rose said, and gave a nervous little laugh. "One always wonders, doesn't one? When it's unexpected, I mean." She laughed again, looking from one to the other. "It's the sort of question Sherlock Holmes would ask."

Dimity looked up to see that Elsa was standing with the kettle in her hand, listening intently to the conversation.

"Thank you, Elsa," Dimity said, taking the kettle. "That will be all for the moment." When Elsa had reluctantly left the room, Dimity returned to the conversation.

"I should have thought, Rose," Miss Crabbe was saying, "that your children would keep you so busy that you wouldn't have time for those silly detective stories."

"Oh, but they're such *fun,* Miss Crabbe," Rose protested. "Everyone likes a mystery. And surely there's no harm in a little entertainment."

"The harm is in wasting one's time," Miss Crabbe replied sternly. "One should read to improve one's mind, not just to entertain oneself. For instance, I am reading a wonderful book about genealogy, called——" She frowned. "Bother. I can't remember the title, exactly, and the author's name escapes me, which is odd, since I never forget an author's name. But it was an enormously enriching book, and well worth anyone's time to read. I have recommended it to both of my sisters. It——"

"I'm afraid there's no chance of getting Anvil Cottage for the Jenningses," Dimity interrupted hurriedly, for Miss Crabbe showed every sign of launching into one of her lectures. "Mr. Roberts will ask a pretty penny for it."

The conversation turned to other village matters. Mathilda Crook told Dimity that her hens were laying unusually well for the time of year, and if she were in need of some large brown eggs, to send Elsa Grape with a basket. Margaret Nash, in a low voice, offered to lend Rose Sutton *The Return of Sherlock Holmes,* which had only been published the month before. And the vicar, in a very confidential whisper, asked Grace Lythecoe whether she had noticed that the Parish Register was missing from its accustomed place and wondered if she might possibly have a clue as to its whereabouts.

"The Register?" Grace asked, startled. "Oh, dear! No, I don't have the foggiest, I'm afraid. You don't suppose someone *took* it, do you?"

"That's the only explanation I can think of." The vicar sighed heavily. "But I can't imagine who would want it, or why. Now, if it were the chalice cup gone missing, I could understand it, for the cup is fine silver and very old. But it's not the cup, it's the Register, and I really can't think what to do about it."

"I understand that you don't want to raise a general alarm," Grace said. "But it might be well to spread the word. Quietly, of course."

The vicar glanced at Miss Crabbe, who was popping the last sponge into her mouth. "Perhaps I should ask Miss Crabbe. Her sisters are often in the church, since both of them are involved with the Choral Society. And she has had occasion to—"

"Another cup of tea, Vicar?" Dimity asked, going round once more with the pot.

These changes of subject were much to Beatrix's relief, for she had not expected to be the center of attention at so large a gathering. She had felt quite out of place and awkward, especially when Miss Crabbe and Mrs. Crook began to criticize her drawings for such silly reasons. But now everyone was talking to someone else about other things, and she could simply watch and listen and rather enjoy herself. She decided that she liked Rose Sutton (Beatrix herself had devoured every single one of the Sherlock Holmes stories), and Margaret Nash, who had a practical, down-to-earth air. She was already acquainted with Grace Lythecoe and Dimity Woodcock, both of whom she wanted to know better, and with Mathilda Crook, whom she did not, as least, not especially. The vicar was a fuss-budget but kindly. And Miss Crabbe—

Beatrix suppressed a smile. With her gray hair, very long nose, and reproachful glance, Miss Crabbe reminded her of a cross old stork who couldn't quite remember where she had delivered the most recent arrival, and hated to admit it.

* * *

Given her interest in Sherlock Holmes, Beatrix might also have been interested in the conversation that was taking place in the kitchen, among the three friends who had gathered at the scrubbed-pine table. Elsa Grape was pouring tea for her sister-in-law, Bertha Stubbs, the Sawrey School caretaker, and Hannah Braithwaite, the wife of the local police constable. Like Elsa, both Hannah and Bertha had healthy curiosities. Because little of importance ever happened in the village, anything out of the ordinary—a wandering cow, a new hat or a new baby, or a death—was a matter for vigorous discussion.

"Poison!" Bertha Stubbs exclaimed, with just the right mixture of frozen horror and wide-eyed enjoyment, when Elsa had told them what Mrs. Sutton had said upstairs.

"Poison?" Hannah Braithwaite repeated doubtfully. "Really, now, Elsa. Mr. Braithwaite didn't mention anything 'bout poison, and tha'd think he'd know, him bein' t' constable an' all. If that's what she died of, I mean."

"I didn't say Miss Tolliver died of poison." Elsa sat down at the table and picked up her teacup. "I only said that Rose Sutton said she wondered. Doctor Butters didn't seem to think so, though. He told Cap'n Woodcock that Miss Tolliver's heart just stopped." She paused. "It's awful'y queer, though. What would make a person's heart just stop? There's got to be a reason."

"Mappen Dr. Butters doan't *know* what made it stop," Bertha Stubbs replied significantly, helping herself to the last jam tart. She pinched off a piece and gave it to her cat Crumpet, who had followed her into the kitchen and taken up a place just under the edge of the tablecloth.

"*Thank you,*" Crumpet said politely. She liked Elsa Grape's jam tarts and found her way into Elsa's kitchen as often as possible.

"Doan't know?" Hannah asked, pulling her brows together. "But he's a doctor, and doctors are s'posed t' understand about things like that."

"But there's secret poisons," Bertha replied in a mysterious voice. "And there's accidental poisons, and poisons of all sorts. Remember when auld Mr. Davies died at Stone Well Cottage a few years ago? That was accidental poison, or so 'twas said. His daughter-in-law gave him a tea that had foxglove leaves in it. Stopped his heart, quick as tha please." She frowned. "O' course, there were others who said that t' daughter-in-law brewed it a-purpose, 'cause t' old man was sick and sufferin'. They had her up 'fore t' magistrate in Hawkshead, and Dr. Butters had to testify. But t' jury couldn't decide whether she meant to kill him or not, so they had to let her go. 'Twas a real percadillo."

"A predicament?" Elsa asked doubtfully.

"Whatever," Bertha replied, with a wave of her hand.

Crumpet was more interested in something else Bertha had said. *"Foxglove?"* she exclaimed. *"My goodness gracious! Why, there's a patch of foxglove growing in Miss Tolliver's garden, right beside the path!"*

Elsa frowned. "Now that tha mentions it, Miss Tolliver did tell me once that she used foxglove regular, to strengthen her heart. But she said she was always careful with it, 'cause it was dangerous. I doan't think she'd've done it accidental-like. If she was poisoned, like Bertha says, it had to be somebody else done it."

"I didn't say she was def'nitely poisoned," Bertha said stiffly. "I was just spectacularizing, is all."

"Speculating," Crumpet amended.

Hannah shook her head, frowning. "But who would do such a thing? And why? Miss Tolliver was t' very soul of kindness."

"Who?" Elsa gave them both a knowing look. "Doan't tha read t' newspaper? People kill other people because they think they're going to get something out of it."

Bertha leaned forward. "That fat nephew from Kendal, for instance, who's getting t' cottage, and any money Miss Tolliver had. A draper, he is, name of Henry Roberts. If anybody did it, he did."

Crumpet was so excited that she jumped into Bertha's lap and stared her right in the face. *"Roberts is the man I saw the other night, when I was out hunting. He was trying to climb through the casement window at the back of Anvil Cottage."*

"Ay, that one," Elsa remarked, rolling her eyes. "Miss Tolliver told me once that her sisters's side of t' family was always after her about money, but they weren't going to get a penny out of her, alive or dead." She folded her arms and sat back, satisfied. "Alive or *dead*. Her words 'xactly."

"Get down, Crumpet," Bertha said in a scolding tone, pushing the cat out of her lap. "Tha knows better than to make yersel a nuisance in somebody else's kitchen." She turned to Hannah. "Ye're sure Constable Braithwaite hasn't said anything 'bout how she died, Hannah?"

Crumpet gave a low, disgruntled meow. *"I wish, just for once,"* she said crossly, *"that you would try to understand me, Bertha Stubbs. I tell you, that man Roberts was trying to break into Anvil Cottage!"*

"I'm sure," Hannah said. "But I'll ask him, I will, when he comes home t' supper." She cast a look at Elsa, changing the subject. "What does tha think o' Miss Potter, Elsa? I saw Becky Jennings at t' village shop this morning, and she says Miss Potter has asked 'em to stay on at Hill Top Farm."

"Humans!" Crumpet exclaimed in disgust. *"There's no point in telling you anything."* And she stalked out the door, her tail held straight up, twitching the tip to show her displeasure. She only went as far as the porch, though, where she sat down and curled her tail around her front paws, watching a beetle move ponderously across the flagstone and half-listening to the conversation.

"Miss Potter seems a nice sort," Elsa replied, in an appraising tone. "Pretty enough, but plain, if tha takes my meaning. Seems not to care o'er-much for t' way she looks."

Crumpet put out a paw and flicked the beetle over on its back. It was always so much fun to watch the little legs waving frantically in the air.

"Aye, I recall that about her," Bertha said. "She was in my sitting room, y' know, drawing my cupboard. Made some pictures of my cat, too." She shook her head. "Seemed reet queer t' me, it did. Tha'd think a rich London lady would care more for curls and pretty frocks than cupboards and tabby cats."

Crumpet flipped the beetle right-side-up again and watched it run in mad circles. Beetles were barmy. Always good for a laugh.

"She put that cat of yours into her latest book," Elsa replied. "Big as life and twice as nat'ral. I didn't see it mesel, but they was sayin' so, upstairs. G've it a diff'rent name, though. Pippy Ribstone, or something like that."

"*My* cat?" Bertha asked, breaking into a pleased smile. "My gray Crumpet, ye mean?"

Crumpet abandoned the beetle and trotted back into the kitchen. *"Yes, that's right,"* she said proudly. *"Miss Potter told me herself."*

"That's t' one," Elsa said. She looked down at Crumpet, who was rubbing herself against the leg of a chair. "Cats are funny, aren't they? She knows we're talking about her."

"Fancy Crumpet, in a book." Bertha was shaking her head in amazement. "I reckon I'll have to buy it and send it to my cousin Ruth. She's allus braggin' 'bout how pretty that Persian cat of hers is, though she's a poor mouser, not near as good our Sawrey cats." She looked down at Crumpet and laughed uproariously. "What d'ye think, Crumpet? You're famous! And Ruth'll be that jealous, she'll turn green as gooseberries. She woan't be doin' any more braggin' on that silly auld Persian of hers."

"*Well, it is rather nice to have one's better qualities recognized,*" Crumpet purred happily. "*I won't let it go to my head, though, the way some would do.*"

"Are t' Jennings goin' t' stay at t' farm?" Elsa asked curiously. "If they're not, I have a bachelor cousin who'd be interested."

"A bachelor woan't do at all, Elsa," Bertha said disapprovingly. "Miss Potter couldn't stay in t' same house with a man. Wouldn't be at all proper, now, would it? Even if she is an auld maid. Wonder why she never married. Tha'd think somebody as rich as her would've had lots of chances."

Hannah frowned. "Mr. Jennings wants to stay and farm, Becky says. T' trouble is t' house. Miss Potter wants it for hersel, which she's not to be blamed for, o' course, since it's her money what's payin' for it. But if she takes t' house, where are t' Jennings to go?"

Elsa sighed with pleasure and poured another cup of tea all around. It was very agreeable to have so many interesting things to discuss, and all at the same time, too.

7

Tabitha Twitchit Has a Bright Idea

Crumpet also had something interesting and important to discuss, and she hunted and called until she located Tabitha Twitchit and Rascal in the garden at Belle Green, lounging lazily on the grass and watching Edward Horsley, who was building a pen for Miss Potter's animals. It took only a moment to summarize what she and the ginger cat had seen in the back garden at Anvil Cottage, what people were saying about poisons, and what she knew about the foxglove in Miss Tolliver's garden. And of course, she thought it necessary to say that Miss Potter had put her into the latest book, although she didn't mention that Miss Potter had changed her name.

Tabitha Twitchit sat up straight, narrowing her eyes and laying her ears flat against her head. *"You're in a book? Why?"*

"Because I'm clever, I suppose." Crumpet lifted her paw, admiring her sharp claws. *"I'm also a superb mouser, of course."*

"*No better a mouser than I am,*" Tabitha snapped. "*Last night, I caught two in Mrs. Crook's larder.*"

"*That's nothing!*" Crumpet retorted tartly. "*The other night, the ginger cat and I—*"

"*Girls, girls!*" Rascal barked. "*Stop the babblement this instant! Crumpet, are you sure it was Henry Roberts who was trying to break into Anvil Cottage? I know cats can see in the dark, but it's been pitch black the last several nights.*"

Crumpet paused, wanting to answer as honestly as she could. "*It's true that it was awf'lly dark,*" she admitted. "*What I saw was a very short, very stout man trying to push himself through the window at the back of the cottage. Who else could it have been but that Roberts fellow?*"

"*Well, did he get in or didn't he?*" Rascal asked.

"*I don't know,*" Crumpet said, beginning to feel defensive. "*A vole scurried past just about that time, and I was distracted for a few minutes.*" The vole had been very fat and very tasty—a distraction worth the effort. "*When I looked back, he was gone.*"

"*You mentioned poison,*" Tabitha said, frowning. "*What's that about?*"

"*All I know,*" Crumpet said with a dark look at Tabitha, "*is what I've already told you. People are wondering whether Miss Tolliver might have been poisoned with foxglove, accidentally or . . .*" She did not finish her sentence.

Tabitha flicked her tail, giving Crumpet an irritated glance. "*I am quite sure that Miss Tolliver did not poison herself accidentally. Yes, she used foxglove, but she knew it was dangerous and she was always especially careful with it.*" She sighed. "*As I said, she was eating a teacake someone sent her and reading a letter when she died. And she hadn't taken any medicine at all that evening. She seemed to be feeling quite well. It was her birthday, and she had enjoyed the party.*"

"*Did the letter come with the cakes?*" Crumpet asked.

Tabitha frowned. "*No, I don't think so. If I remember rightly,*" *the teacakes arrived on the day before the birthday party, and the letter in the afternoon post."*

"*I wonder . . .*" Rascal said, and stopped, cocking his head to one side, his bright eyes intent.

"*Wonder what?*" Crumpet asked. When Rascal looked like that, he was usually thinking something important.

"*Whether somebody put something in those cakes.*" Rascal frowned. "*Remember Old Ebenezer the shepherd, up on Raven Crag? He put poison into a sheep's carcass and murdered the vixen and three of her little fox kits.*" He spoke fiercely, for Jack Russell terriers were bred to chase foxes, and Rascal often went out with the Hunt. He had developed a very great fondness for the foxes on the fells, who allowed the dogs to chase them and give the hunters an exciting day's pursuit. The thought of anyone poisoning a fox turned his stomach.

Crumpet turned to Tabitha, beginning to feel that this was a matter that needed looking into. "*Who sent those cakes, Tabitha? It wasn't that Roberts fellow, was it?*"

"*I have no idea,*" Tabitha replied. "*I was so shocked and upset about poor Miss Tolliver that I didn't even think to take a look at the packet and see who might have sent it.*"

"*You couldn't have read the address, anyway,*" Crumpet said. She batted at a moth that had landed on a blade of grass at her feet. It annoyed her when Tabitha put on airs.

Tabitha twitched her whiskers disdainfully. "*That's all you know, Crumpet. I have spent a great many afternoons perched on the back of Miss Tolliver's chair whilst she read out loud to the village children. I might not know every single word, but I could make an educated guess.*" She stood up to stretch, showing off her calico markings. "*I have an idea. Do you two want to hear it?*"

"*Of course,*" Rascal said eagerly. He was always ready for any new adventure. "*What do you have in mind?*"

Crumpet didn't say anything. She was wishing she had taken the trouble to look over Mrs. Stubbs' shoulder when she read the *Westmoreland Gazette* out loud to Mr. Stubbs in the evening. If Tabitha Twitchit could learn to read, she certainly could, too. And then she'd be able to read what Miss Potter had written about her.

"*I'll wager Anvil Cottage is just as it was left after Miss Tolliver died,*" Tabitha said in a conspiratorial tone. "*I think we should take a look at that package and see who sent it. Want to go with me?*"

"*But the cottage is locked,*" Crumpet objected. "*And Mrs. Lythecoe has the only key. I heard her tell Mr. Roberts so.*"

"*Of course it's locked,*" Tabitha replied. "*But I know a secret way in, don't I?*"

Rascal gave three excited yips. "*I say, Tabitha, old girl, that's a topping idea!*"

"*We should wait until dark,*" Crumpet said cautiously. She always hated it when somebody else's ideas were better than hers—Tabitha's, especially. "*We don't want anybody to see us going in.*"

"*Don't be such a scaredy-cat, Crumpet,*" Tabitha scoffed. "*Nobody pays any attention to a pair of cats and a dog. As long as we stay out of the Big Folks' way, we can go anywhere we like.*"

"*Right-o!*" Rascal exclaimed. "*Tally-ho, girls!*" And he was off.

Crumpet had to admit that Tabitha might be onto something. And since she didn't want to be left behind, she joined the others as they scrambled under the fence and dashed off down the hill.

Seeing them go, Edward Horsley put down his hammer and straightened up. "Wonder what got into that lot all of a sudden," he remarked out loud. He shook his head. "Funny things, them little creatures. Sometimes you'd think they was ivver bit as smart as people."

Tabitha Twitchit found the expedition to Anvil Cottage interesting, in more ways than even she might have anticipated.

Feeling quite proud of herself, she showed Crumpet and Rascal the hidden opening in the stonework at the back of Miss Tolliver's kitchen, which she had always used as her own private come-and-go-as-you-please door. She went through first, with Crumpet following after. And although Rascal found it a bit of a squeeze, he managed almost as easily, for Jack Russells can never resist the opportunity to squirm through narrow openings.

Feeling rather melancholy at the sight of her old home, Tabitha led them through the cozy kitchen—cold now, since there had been no fire in the range for several days—and down the hall to the sitting room. The cottage held all the pleasant smells of home: lavender, Earl Grey tea, washing-up soap, lemon-oil furniture polish. Tabitha felt a sudden pang, remembering how many happy evenings she and Miss Tolliver had spent together in front of the fire.

"*It doesn't look as if anything's been changed,*" she said, as they went into the sitting room. She frowned. "*Although . . .*" Her voice trailed off.

"*Although what?*" Crumpet demanded.

"*Something isn't quite right,*" Tabitha said uneasily. "*I'm not sure what, but—*"

"*Never mind,*" Rascal said, impatient. "*Where are the cakes?*"

"*Up here,*" Tabitha said, and a surprisingly easy grace for a cat of her advanced age, she jumped up on the table and sniffed at a cardboard box, empty now except for a trace of crumbs. There was a trail of crumbs on the table, as well.

"*I'm afraid the mice have been here.*" She shook her head, disapproving. "*I've always done my best to keep them in their place, but the minute I'm off somewhere, or busy about other things, they will take advantage.*"

The look Crumpet gave Tabitha was clearly disdainful. Tabitha sighed. She knew that Crumpet, who was younger and a great deal more competitive, would never tolerate even one mouse in the house. She herself found them occasionally useful, though, and felt that it was good to cultivate a working relationship with them.

Rascal, not so graceful as Tabitha, scrambled up on a chair, put his paws on the table, his nose twitching as it always did when he was on a scent. He took a deep breath, then frowned. *"If there's something poisonous here,"* he said, *"I don't smell it."* He sneezed, having inhaled one crumb too many.

Crumpet leapt up beside Rascal. *"Just a minute,"* she said, the tip of her tail flicking back and forth. *"If the cakes were poisoned, any mice that nibbled on them ought to be dead. Right?"*

"Right!" Tabitha cried, and jumped off the table. Trotting to the corner behind the chair, she tapped the floor with her paw and meowed several times, authoritatively. Then she put her ear to the wall, listened for a moment, and meowed again.

Rascal hurried over to join her. *"What are they saying?"* he asked. Tabitha knew he didn't have much respect for mice and had never bothered to learn their language.

"Nothing of any real consequence," Tabitha reported with a toss of her head. *"Mice are such silly creatures, chattering endlessly about the weather, the food, the neighbors. But apparently they all ate the cakes, and nobody's been reported sick. Which means—"*

"Which means that the cakes weren't poisoned," Crumpet replied, from the vantage point of the table. *"So there's no point in trying to figure out who sent them. But you mentioned a letter, Tabitha, and there's one right here."* She put her paw on it. *"Maybe it will give us a clue."*

But it turned out that although Tabitha Twitchit could read words printed in a book, handwritten words in a letter were an entirely different matter.

"Oh, dear," she murmured, after studying the page top-to-bottom for several moments, then turning herself to

study it bottom-to-top. *"I'm afraid I can't make head nor tail of this. These little marks and squiggles—they're all Greek to me."*

Crumpet looked down her nose as if she wanted to say "I told you so" out loud. But she only flicked her gray tail. *"I suppose we'll need to think of a way to get a human to read this for us. Perhaps we could—"*

"What's that noise?" interrupted Rascal urgently.

"It must be that dreadful man," Crumpet hissed, the gray fur rising along her back. *"The one I saw last night. He's trying to climb in the window again!"*

"It's not the window," Tabitha said. She might be older, but her hearing was just as acute as Crumpet's. *"It's someone at the front door, someone with a key."*

Impetuously, Rascal launched himself off the chair. *"I'll take care of whoever-it-is! I'll show him my teeth! I'll have a nip of—"*

"No, Rascal!" Tabitha exclaimed. *"Let's hide and see what he's up to!"* And she darted behind the green sofa, with Crumpet and Rascal close behind. The animals crouched down, making themselves very small.

But it wasn't that dreadful man, after all. A moment later, the sitting room door opened and Mrs. Lythecoe came in, accompanied by Miss Potter. They were talking about a book that Mrs. Lythecoe had loaned to Miss Tolliver—a new book called *A Rambler's Notebook at the English Lakes,* by Canon Rawnsley—which she had come to retrieve.

Mrs. Lythecoe shivered, feeling saddened by the empty chill of the cottage and the even emptier feeling of Miss Tolliver's absence. She went to the shelf beside the window and found the book.

"Here it is, Miss Potter," she said, picking it up. "There are some lovely descriptions of the lakes in it, and some amusing stories about Lake District traditions. I'm sure you'll find it interesting, especially as you know the author."

"Canon Rawnsley is a family friend," Miss Potter said, taking the book. "We first knew him when my parents took their holiday at Wray, where he was vicar, and he calls at Bolton Gardens whenever he is in London. I'm sure I'll enjoy the book immensely."

At that moment, a calico cat leapt out from behind the sofa, startling both ladies. "My gracious, Tabitha!" Grace said breathlessly, when she saw that it was her old friend's cat. "You're not supposed to be here! How did you get in?"

"Let's not talk about that now," Tabitha replied urgently. With an agility that would have done justice to a much younger cat, she jumped to the table and planted both front paws on the letter. *"Read this,"* she commanded.

Grace reached for the cat. "I'm afraid it's out the door with you, poor old thing," she said sympathetically. "I know you miss your dear mistress, as we all do. But Anvil Cottage belongs to somebody else now—and he's not the sort of fellow who is likely to want a cat." To Miss Potter, she added, "Mathilda Crook is taking Tabitha. She said she needs a good mouser at Belle Green. Tabitha was a sterling mouser in her day, although she's getting a bit slow in her old age."

"I am not!" Tabitha exclaimed indignantly. *"There's nothing at all slow about me."*

Miss Potter was looking at the letter. "I wonder," she said in a low voice, "whether Miss Tolliver's correspondent has been notified of her death. I lost a . . . a friend recently. I know how important it is that people learn about it as soon as possible."

"You're right, of course," Grace said, hearing the sadness in Miss Potter's voice and wondering what it meant. She put Tabitha on the chair and reached for the letter, which was written in a slanting feminine hand on beige linen letter-paper. "I suppose I had better contact the writer. I'm sure that Miss Tolliver's nephew won't think to do it." She scanned the first page quickly, noting the address at the top. "It's from a Sarah Barwick, in Cumberland Lane, Manchester. I'll drop her a note." She put the letter back on the table.

"But what does it say?" Tabitha insisted, stretching out her paw.

Grace glanced down at the table, seeing the box and the crumbs. "My goodness, Tabitha," she said, "what a dreadful mess the mice have made since you've left the cottage." She swept the cake crumbs off the table and into the empty box. "I'll carry this home and put it in the dustbin." To Miss Potter, she added, "We have such a problem with mice in this village. Without a cat in the house, they simply take over."

"Read the letter!" Standing on her hind legs, Tabitha put both forepaws on the table and switched her tail from side to side in an imperative gesture. *"It might contain a clue to Miss Tolliver's death!"*

Miss Potter fixed her blue eyes on Grace. "Perhaps you will think this silly," she said in a half-apologetic tone, "but you might consider keeping the package safe, rather than disposing of it. One does not wish to leap to conclusions, of course, but I believe someone mentioned poison whilst we were at tea, just a little while ago. I'm quite sure there's nothing to it, but as long as someone in the village is thinking of poison, the possibility does remain, if only in the mind."

"There!" Crumpet exclaimed into Rascal's ear. *"You see? I told you so! Poison!"*

"But the mice said—" Rascal began.

"Oh, what do mice know?" Crumpet growled impatiently. *"Stupid creatures! Almost as stupid as snails. Half of them could have died and never been missed."*

Grace chuckled, albeit a little uneasily. "Why, Miss Potter," she said in the lightest tone she could manage, "I do believe you've been reading your Sherlock. And you do know a thing or two about villages, don't you? The way people gossip—" She gave her head a disapproving shake. "Rose Sutton is likely to have poor Miss Tolliver murdered twice over—in her imagination, of course. But you're right. I'll take the box and keep it safe, in case it's ever wanted."

"The letter!" Tabitha cried, and reached up to catch at Miss Potter's sleeve with her extended claws. *"There's nothing wrong with the cakes, but do read the letter. Aloud, please!"*

Miss Potter smiled down at the cat, her blue eyes twinkling. "Such an expressive creature. My own little animals often seem to have an understanding that is almost human. One quite imagines that Tabitha is trying to tell us something important." Her eyes went back to the letter. "I wonder if Miss Tolliver was reading this when she suffered her attack. Do you happen to know if this Sarah Barwick was a friend?"

"I'm afraid I can't say," Grace replied regretfully. "Miss Tolliver and I were rather close, certainly, but she was never one to share confidences." She paused, thinking about how kind and understanding Miss Tolliver had been when her husband the vicar had died, and how much she had come to depend upon her unquestioning friendship.

Miss Potter nodded thoughtfully. "I suppose it is easy to have acquaintances in a village. Indeed, one must find it hard not to be acquainted with everybody. But I daresay it is exceedingly difficult to find a friend one can trust with one's interior secrets."

Exactly! Grace thought, looking at Miss Potter with respect. She had received that kind of friendship from Miss Tolliver, and had freely shared her hopes and fears. But it had not worked the other way round, and Grace had to admit that the older woman's interior life had remained a mystery to the end.

"I think Miss Tolliver never found that kind of friend," Grace replied. "She was born in this cottage, and lived here her entire life. She never left the village, you see, and never married. She was devoted to her elderly father, who was rather a difficult person. She took care of him until he died, ten years or so ago, without question or complaint." She paused and added, "I understand that he did not want her to marry."

"Parents can be unreasonably demanding," murmured Miss Potter, averting her glance.

"They can indeed," Grace replied. Frowning, she glanced around at the furniture, the windows, the walls. "It's curious," she said, "but I have the feeling that something's not quite right in this room. That something is missing."

"Missing?" Tabitha repeated. She raised her head and followed Mrs. Lythecoe's glance from one wall to another. *"Yes, I had thought about that earlier. Something is definitely—"*

"I rather think," Miss Potter said quietly, "that the Constable miniature is gone."

"The . . . Constable?" Grace asked, nonplussed.

Miss Potter pointed to a spot on the wall, above a mahogany writing table on which stood several photographs. "It was there, in a gilt frame, the last time I was in this room."

"Of course," Grace exclaimed, going across the room to the table. "Why, how very perceptive you are, Miss Potter! It was a framed miniature landscape of the English countryside, no more than a few inches wide and high. You can even see where it hung, since the print wallpaper around it has faded." Frowning, she turned back to Miss Potter. "But—a Constable? Surely you're not referring to John Constable, the great English landscape master?"

"Oh, but I am," Miss Potter said, her face growing animated and almost pretty. "I recognized the painting the moment I first saw it, when I visited her several years ago. Both my brother Bertram and I are admirers of Constable's work, you see. Bertram likes to paint large landscapes, although rather gloomier than Constable's." She paused and added diffidently, "I daresay this little landscape needed cleaning. But of course it was quite a valuable piece, especially since Constable painted so few miniatures—only nine or ten, as I recall. Perhaps Miss Tolliver did not like to entrust it to anyone for cleaning."

Even more surprised and perplexed by this deepening mystery, Grace looked back at the wall. "A Constable," she mused. "I certainly had no idea, and I'm sure that no one else in the village suspected that the painting had any particular value." She paused, now very much disturbed. "But what on earth could have happened to it? It must have been there when we celebrated Miss Tolliver's birthday on the day before she died, or I should have noticed its absence, especially owing to the way the wallpaper has faded around it."

"Has anyone been in the cottage since Miss Tolliver died? Other than those who removed her body, I mean."

"Not to my knowledge," Grace answered, "and as I told Mr. Roberts, I have the only key." She stared at Miss Potter. "Mr. Roberts was certainly anxious to get in, wasn't he? But I hardly think that he would have—"

"*Listen!*" Crumpet exclaimed, jumping out from behind the sofa. "*I saw that Roberts fellow last night, trying to break into this very cottage! It was dark, of course, but I'm sure it was him. I don't believe he got in whilst the ginger cat and I were watching, but he might have come back after we left.*"

"Crumpet!" Grace exclaimed. "What are you doing here?" She went to the sofa and looked over the back. "And Rascal! My goodness! Are there any more of you? Get out of here, right this minute! You know better than to come into a house uninvited!"

"*But we were invited,*" Crumpet protested. "*Tabitha Twitchit asked us in.*"

"Out with you," Grace repeated. And with a squirming

cat under each arm and Rascal creeping guiltily at her heels, she marched to the front door and thrust all three outside.

Returning to the sitting room, she continued with her thought. "I hardly think, though, that Mr. Roberts could have gotten into this cottage during the daylight hours—and especially after making all that fuss about the key."

"But perhaps Mr. Roberts had already entered the cottage and taken the painting," Miss Potter remarked. "He may have raised the commotion over the key to mislead us, feeling that—when the painting was discovered to be missing—he would not be suspected."

Grace smiled. "Why, my dear Miss Potter, you astonish me. You are a skeptic at heart!"

"I'm afraid so," Miss Potter said ruefully. "I come from a long line of Dissenters—obstinate, hard-headed, matter-of-fact Lancashire folk, and skeptics to the very bone. For better or worse, I have inherited their spirit."

"My husband, the former vicar, always used to say that he cherished the skeptics in his parish," Grace said, "because they were the only ones from whom he was likely to hear the truth—especially when it wasn't a truth he wanted to hear." She paused. "Speaking of the vicar, I'm reminded that something else has gone missing in the village. The Parish Register."

"The Register?" Miss Potter looked surprised. "That's an odd thing for someone to take. I'm sure it's quite valuable, of course, but only for the information it contains."

"Indeed," Grace said. She folded the letter and put it into the pocket of her brown skirt. "Shall we go?" she asked briskly, thinking of the supper waiting for her on the back of the kitchen range.

Miss Potter hesitated. "Don't you think that someone should be notified? About the missing Constable, I mean."

"Yes, of course," Grace said. "Well, perhaps our village policeman." John Braithwaite kept the peace and dealt deftly with troublesome daytrippers, but she did not have a great deal of confidence in his ability to trace the whereabouts of a stolen painting.

Miss Potter cleared her throat. "I was thinking of Miss Tolliver's solicitor, rather than the police," she replied hesitantly. "You said this morning, if I remember correctly, that there is a will."

"Why, of course," Grace exclaimed. "Why didn't I think of that? Mr. Heelis, in Hawkshead, was Miss Tolliver's solicitor. I'll send a message to him straightaway, and leave the entire matter to him." Satisfied that they were making the very best of a bad thing, she picked up the empty cake box from the table. "We should be going now, don't you think?"

"I do," Miss Potter said, and cast one last look at the spot on the wall where the Constable had hung. "I'm afraid there isn't much more to be learnt here."

8

Charlie Hotchkiss Has News

October in the Lake District brings variable weather, with early snows almost as likely as late summer sunshine, and there is always a great rush to get the last vegetables in from the garden before winter begins in earnest in November. But there had not yet been a frost this autumn, and although the air was crisp, the rising sun and clear sky offered the promise of a warm day.

Beatrix got up and took her rabbits and hedgehog into the garden at the first light of dawn. The sky was serene and cloudless, the fells across Esthwaite Water were turning from smoky gray to lilac, and the hill behind Belle Green was brushed with a dewy sheen. The robins practiced their sunrise chorale in the sycamore tree, the rooks cawed lustily, and the farmyard roosters crowed in a raucous chorus. It was a lovely morning, Beatrix thought, turning to glance toward the woods, where the beeches and larches paraded in their gold-and-bronze autumn finery. A splendid morning to go down to the lake and draw.

Beatrix settled Josey, Mopsy, Tom, and Mrs. Tiggy in the new pen that Edward Horsley had built for them behind the chicken coop, gave them each a bowl of their favorite food, and went in to breakfast. She was in such good spirits that she even managed to ignore George Crook's brusque greeting as she sat down to a bowl of hot oat porridge, with milk and a sprinkling of sugar. Charlie Hotchkiss was more cheerful than usual, too, for he had picked up a bit of intrigue at the pub the night before.

"What dust tha think, George?" he asked, sitting down at the table across from Beatrix. "Seems like Miss Tolliver might've been poisoned. Foxglove, 'tis said."

Beatrix stared at him. The question of poison had not been far from her mind since Rose Sutton had mentioned it during Dimity Woodcock's tea party. Poisonings weren't terribly unusual, of course, and one read about such dreadful accidents in the newspaper every now and then. Foxglove, she knew, contained something called digitalis, which acted on the heart in ways that weren't very well understood. Beatrix somehow didn't think it was likely that Miss Tolliver would have been careless with foxglove, which was well known to be dangerous. But when the inhabitants of a village began gossiping, what counted was what people *thought* to be true, rather than the truth itself.

"Poisoned!" Startled, George Crook looked up from his eggs and rasher of bacon. "Why, I nivver in t' world would've thought it!"

Mathilda came to the table with a basket of warm bread in one hand, a pot of tea in the other, and a look of disapproval across her narrow face. "Tha ought not t' say something like that, Charlie Hotchkiss, unless tha knows it for a pure fact. There's enough talk about poor Miss Tolliver as 'tis, without addin' to it. Bread, Miss Potter? There's honey in that jar."

"Thank you," Beatrix said. Mathilda Crook might have her failings—her caution to Charlie was definitely hypocritical, given her penchant for passing along any little tidbit that came her way—but her breads were without fault and her honey was deliciously reminiscent of elder flowers in the spring.

"But it's true!" Charlie said, defending himself. "Constable Braithwaite told me. Seems Miss Tolliver took foxglove for her heart." He picked up his spoon and attacked his bowl of steaming porridge. "He said not to tell nobody, though," he added importantly, with a warning glance at Beatrix. "T' matter is still under" (he dropped his voice) "investy-gation."

"Miss Potter and me was at Tower Bank House yesterday, to tea," Mathilda said importantly, with a nod to Beatrix. She wiped her hands on her apron and sat down at the table. "There was talk of poison then. Rose Sutton mentioned it, as I recollect."

"I nivver," George said again, leaning back. He blew out an incredulous breath. "Well, if tha heard it at Tower Bank House, there must be something in it, Tildy. Cap'n Woodcock bein' Justice of t' Peace, and all, I mean. There's not a thing in this village goes on what he doan't know."

"T' cap'n weren't there," Mathilda said. "It was Rose who brought it up."

"But bein' t' wife of t' veterinary," Charlie said judiciously, "Rose Sutton 'ud be one to know all 'bout poisons, I reckon."

"And Desmond Sutton is a friend of Constable Braithwaite, which is likely where t' news come from. Out of t' horse's mouth, so to say." George, now satisfied that he had traced the information to its source and found it to be true, went back to his eggs.

"'Tis a bad business," Mathilda said, shaking her head sadly. "But if Miss Tolliver died from poison, it had to've been a mistake. Mappen she weren't wearing her spectacles when she mixed it up."

Charlie leaned forward. "Constable says it could've been *foul play*," he reported in a very low voice, with the confidential air of a man who has had access to official secrets and has been warned against passing them on.

Beatrix gave him a surprised glance. George *well-I-nivver*ed for the third time, Charlie added that the nephew from Kendal had been very ugly to Mrs. Lythecoe about the key to Anvil Cottage, and Mathilda said she hoped that Constable Braithwaite and Captain Woodcock would talk to the magistrate in Hawkshead about their suspicions, " 'cause it was appalling to have such unfortunate goin's on in t' village, with new folk comin' in and all."

And with a meaningful glance at Beatrix, she began to talk about the School Roof Fund, to which Lady Longford had with amazing generosity contributed a gold Young Victoria sovereign, and which Dimity Woodcock had handed over to Miss Crabbe the day before, so that the roof could be mended before the next rain.

" 'Cause if it isn't," she concluded, dolloping honey on her bread, "Miss Crabbe is likely to have a breakdown over it. At least, that's what Bertha Stubbs says."

And having cited the ultimate authority on events at Sawrey School, she settled down to her breakfast.

9

Myrtle Crabbe Makes a Dreadful Discovery

Miss Crabbe herself was already on her way to school, hurrying a bit more than usual. She had just remembered that she had forgotten to put the envelope containing the School Roof Fund collection into her purse the night before and was anxious to retrieve it from the desk drawer where she had left it. She was walking quickly across the bridge over Wilfen Beck when she saw Bertha Stubbs just ahead.

Bertha had been the school's caretaker for nearly as long as Miss Crabbe had been headmistress, which would soon be a full quarter-century, and, at sixty, she was getting a bit too old to be doing the hard work around the school. Miss Crabbe had pointed this out on occasion, and had recently spoken to the vicar about giving Bertha notice and hiring someone younger and less cantankerous. But the vicar had replied that Bertha still seemed capable of doing the work, which involved stoking the stoves several times daily during stove season, cleaning out the cinders every morning, hauling buckets of water twice a day, scrubbing the floors weekly, and washing the windows monthly. He had added, deferentially, that he hoped that Miss Crabbe would allow Bertha to keep the job as long as her performance was up to scratch.

Hearing footsteps on the gravel, Bertha turned and waited for Miss Crabbe to catch up to her. "Well, then!" she said in an amiable tone, "What dust tha think of our Miss Potter?"

Miss Crabbe frowned crossly. "I shall keep what I think to myself, and I advise you, Bertha, to do the same. It is not a good idea to gossip about one's neighbors, especially if they are political."

"Ain't a neighbor yet," Bertha remarked with an enigmatic lift of her eyebrows. "May not be, if Becky Jennings has her way." She glanced up at the sky, sniffing. "Shouldn't be surprised if we don't get some rain. Could come down smartish by afternoon. Pity that roof ain't got fixed yet." She gave Miss Crabbe a toothy smile. "Guess we'll need to put that rain-bucket on thi desk. Pity it makes such a racket. Plink-plinkety-*plink,* all afternoon. Enough to addle thi wits, I'd warrant."

Miss Crabbe, who had the feeling that Bertha was baiting her, picked up her pace. It was true that the roof could not be repaired by the afternoon and that she should have to endure the maddening plinking, but she could certainly see to it that the work got underway immediately. She would send one of the older boys with a note to Joseph Skead, the sexton at St. Peter's, who handled the major repairs to the school. Barring misfortune, the roof should be mended by next week, and that horrible rain-bucket would be a thing of the past.

Miss Crabbe set her mouth in a thin, hard line, thinking that if she had been successful in securing the Bournemouth position, she would not have had to deal with any of these difficulties. Bournemouth, where the sun shone brightly even in the winter, and where the warm southern breezes meant that there was a great deal less rain and hardly any snow. And where she could have had a small cottage to herself, without the clattering nuisance of her sisters, well-intentioned, both of them, but nuisances just the same. She and Pansy and Viola had lived together all their lives, but recently it had become more and more difficult to tolerate their silly meddling, always giving her this advice and that, as if she were a child instead of their older sister and due a proper deference and respect. If only she had got the Bournemouth position, she could have put all this behind her.

But Bournemouth was not to be. Despite her pleadings—really, she had lowered herself quite appallingly, to the point of shameless begging—Abigail Tolliver had refused to sign the letter of reference she had helpfully typed out for her signature. And why, Miss Crabbe simply hadn't a clue. It had all been infuriating, really, to abase herself in such a way, when Abigail refused to tell her why she would not sign the letter, and even threatened to write and tell the school council that she was not suitable for the position! And as she had stood beside the flower-heaped coffin, listening to the vicar drone on and on about Abigail's contributions to village life and how much she would be missed, Miss Crabbe had had to suppress a small, mean smile. She might not be going to Bournemouth, but Abigail Tolliver wasn't going *anywhere*.

Miss Crabbe squared her narrow shoulders. She would have to put all that behind her, the small regret about Abigail Tolliver, the larger and more persistent bitterness about Bournemouth and the new beginnings that might have been. She would see to it that the roof repairs were completed as soon as possible, which would put that annoyance out of the way. Her sisters . . . well, they were another matter. She would have to think about how to deal with them.

But Miss Crabbe's plan for the repair of the school roof was destined to be thwarted. For when she reached Sawrey School, went to her room, and opened the drawer of her desk, she saw to her horror that the envelope that Dimity Woodcock had given her—the envelope that contained one bright gold sovereign, two half-crowns, three florins, and nine shillings—was gone.

She was still standing at her desk, staring uncomprehendingly into the empty drawer, when Margaret Nash came into the room carrying a stack of song-sheets and a large box of drawing pencils.

"Why, Miss Crabbe!" Margaret exclaimed, seeing the look of consternation on her headmistress's face. She set down the things she was carrying and went to the desk. "Whatever is the matter?"

"The School Roof Fund is gone," Miss Crabbe whispered faintly, and dropped into her chair, as if her legs could no longer hold her. "It's been stolen." She buried her face in her hands.

"Stolen!" Margaret exclaimed, bewildered. "But how? All three of us—Bertha, you, and I—left at the same time yesterday afternoon. We locked the building behind us, and it was still locked this morning when I arrived." She cast a quick look at the room's windows. "None of the windows have been broken, and there's no sign of a forced entry."

"Of course there's no sign of an entry." Miss Crabbe's voice was flinty, her face very white, her lips pressed into a thin, hard line. "There's no sign because there was no break-in. That *boy* took it."

"That boy?" Margaret asked blankly.

Miss Crabbe's mouth twisted. "The child who was left alone here."

"You can't mean little Jeremy Crosfield!"

"What other boy was alone in this room yesterday?" Miss Crabbe demanded furiously. "I went out to the schoolyard to tend to his tormenter, you went to get some water and soap to wash his face, and he was here alone—with the money lying right there, in an envelope." She pointed to a spot on the desk. "I can see it all now, as clear as a picture. I didn't put the money into the drawer, after all. I left it on the desk, and he took it!"

"But Jeremy was still sitting in his seat when I—"

Miss Crabbe's voice rose. "Are you prepared to swear that he didn't have time to jump up and pocket that money? The Crosfields are poor as church mice. It would be a fortune to him."

Margaret swallowed. "Well, no, of course I couldn't swear. But how he could have known there was money in the envelope?" She took a deep breath. "Miss Crabbe, this is a very serious accusation. We don't have any proof that Jeremy is a thief. We—"

"We have all the proof we need." Miss Crabbe rose from the chair and stood, rigid with rage, rapping her knuckles in an irregular tattoo on the desk. "Go out to the gate and wait. I want the boy brought to me the instant he puts in an appearance. And don't you defend him, Miss Nash! You are far too soft on these dirty little urchins. This child needs to be taught a lesson, and I am going to administer it!" Her voice became a half-hysterical quaver. "And when I am through, I intend to turn him over to Constable Braithwaite. He'll see to it that we get the school's money back."

"But Miss Crabbe—"

"I will not tolerate impertinence!" Miss Crabbe cried, now completely beyond remonstrance. "Do what I tell you, you wretched creature, or I shall demand that the board terminate your contract."

Gulping back sobs, Margaret almost ran from the room. As she closed the door behind her, she found herself face-to-face with Bertha Stubbs. Finding Bertha outside a door was not unusual, of course, since it was her habit to listen to as many conversations as she could. Usually, she was embarrassed by being caught; now, though, her face was red as a beet. She was plainly angry.

"I believes in speakin' my mind, Miss Nash," she said gruffly. " 'Speak t' truth and shame t' devil,' is what I allus say. And that auld she-devil in there ought to be ashamed—"

"Hush, Mrs. Stubbs," Margaret said, trying to pull herself together. She straightened her shoulders and managed to calm her voice. "Miss Crabbe is under a great deal of strain just now, and—"

"A girt deal o' strain is purely reet," Bertha Stubbs said grimly. "She's strainin' t' rest of us to death, she is, with her unperdictamus tantrums. Week afore, it was t' attendance book in t' map locker—and her accusin' me of takin' it! Now it's t' Roof Fund, and she's blamin' that poor little boy." She narrowed her eyes. "What're tha aimin' to do?"

"Do?" Margaret asked, with a helpless shrug. "I'm going to wait at the gate for Jeremy, that's what I'm going to do. Miss Crabbe may be wrong but she is, after all, my superior."

"Well, she may be thi superior but she ain't mine, not no more," Bertha said with a dark significance. She jerked off her coverall apron and threw it on the floor. "I'm givin' in my notice, is what I'm goin' to do, and reet this verra minute, too. It's a matter o' principality!"

This was not a new threat, of course. Bertha threatened to give in her notice every few weeks, and usually with a loud declaration of principle. But this time, her words had the ring of conviction. Margaret shook her head wordlessly, feeling the weighty burden of daily buckets of coal and clinkers added to the burden of Miss Crabbe's capricious wrath. Trying hastily to compose her face so that the children in the schoolyard would not glimpse her apprehension, she hurried out to the schoolyard gate to wait for Jeremy.

Miss Crabbe, however, was to be thwarted yet again. The yard filled with children from Far Sawrey and Near Sawrey and the surrounding cottages and farms. But although Margaret lingered until the last assembly bell had pealed across the yard, Jeremy Crosfield did not appear. Her feet dragging, she went inside, picked up Bertha Stubbs's cover-all apron from the floor where she had flung it, and told Miss Crabbe that their thief was now a truant, and that they would have to find someone else to look after the stoves and scrub the floors.

Then she pasted a falsely cheerful smile on her face and went to greet her children.

10

※※※

Miss Potter Faces Facts

As all this commotion was going on at Sawrey School, Beatrix was walking to Hill Top Farm with her sketch pad and a tape measure, intending to survey the area in front of the house, where she planned to put the new garden. She had never had much of a chance to garden, since her mother preferred that the care of the formal flower beds at Bolton Gardens be left to the once-weekly gardener. But she loved to sketch the gardens of the various country houses where her family spent their holidays. What she admired most were the little kitchen gardens, with flag-stone paths and glass-topped vegetable frames and wooden trellises and hives for the bees, and rows of cabbage and rhubarb and old-fashioned herbs— thyme and rosemary and lavender and mint—all growing in a tangle of blossoms and leaves against a wall or under a hedge.

Now, as Beatrix stood in front of Hill Top, she saw a

space occupied by a weedy garden, enclosed on all four sides by low stone walls. She began to sketch a plan, deciding that she would keep two of the walls and put in a new iron gate. She would replace the third with a tall hedge and the fourth with a brick wall, against which she would plant fruit trees. The walks would be laid with the local blue-green slate, and a new gravel lane would redirect the carts and farm wagons through the farmyard, rather than past the house. These projects would take some time, of course—they would give her something interesting to look forward to when she came next.

"Would tha care to step in for a cup o' tea, Miss Potter?"

Startled, Beatrix turned to see Mrs. Jennings standing in the porch, the ginger cat at her feet. "Oh, yes, thank you," she said with real pleasure, for she had wanted badly to see the inside of the house, but had been timid about asking Mr. Jennings for a tour. She closed her sketchbook and tucked her pencil behind her ear. "I was just drawing out a plan for the garden," she explained, coming up to the porch. "I would like to make it larger, and plant a hedge, and—"

"I doan't have time t' garden," Mrs. Jennings said in a vexed tone, and turned to go inside. "Jennings does t' milkin' and I do all t' dairy. Separatin' t' cream and churnin' t' butter takes more time than tha'd think. What with washin' and cookin' and cleanin' t' house, there's not a minute left."

Beatrix followed Mrs. Jennings into the house—*her* house now, she thought with a barely suppressed delight. She had not been in it for several years, since her parents had spent the holiday at Lakefield and boarded their coachman and his wife at Hill Top, and as her vision adjusted to the shadowed interior, she looked around with great curiosity.

They had entered a dark, narrow entrance hall, at the end of which was a staircase leading to a windowed landing and then up to the left, to the second story. On the right side of the entrance hall, a door opened into the Jennings' bedroom, and on the left, another led into the main downstairs room of the house, which the family used for cooking and eating, for indoor work and relaxing.

This room, the largest in the house, had a slate floor, partly covered by a rag rug. It was somewhat brightened by a window and warmed by the iron range that had been installed in the fireplace alcove, which had panel-door cupboards on either side. As Beatrix glanced around, she decided that, as soon as she could, she would tear out the partition that created the narrow entrance hallway, so that the front door would open directly into the main room and bring in light and fresh air. The place could certainly do with an airing-out, for it was smoky and smelled of boiled cabbage and onions.

Mrs. Jennings, a thin, angular woman whose plain features were set in a unfriendly expression, did not invite her guest to tour the house. Instead, she poured tea from a china pot nestled in a crocheted wool cozy, and motioned Beatrix to a chair. The ginger cat leapt lightly onto the wide stone windowsill, where she raised one paw and delicately licked it, regarding Beatrix with bright, curious eyes.

Beatrix, glad to see a friendly creature, smiled at the cat. "Hello, Miss Frummety. I trust you are keeping well."

"*I am, thank you very much for asking,*" Felicia Frummety replied decorously. "*And yourself, Miss Potter?*"

"Frummety." Mrs. Jennings snorted. "Foolish name for an animal. If a cat has to have a name, it ought to be simple, like Puss."

Miss Frummety sniffed distastefully. "*I'd rather have no name at all than be 'Puss.'*"

Beatrix felt rebuked, and her delight evaporated like a puff of smoke. "I'm sorry, Mrs. Jennings. I was only trying to make friends with your little girl and—"

Mrs. Jennings didn't let her finish. "Jennings sez tha're

wantin' us to stay on here and farm," she said brusquely, and took a chair on the opposite side of the table.

"That's my hope," Beatrix replied, "if we can work out the living arrangements." She stirred sugar into her tea. "I don't think—"

"Tha has to face facts, Miss Potter," Mrs. Jennings interrupted. "There's nay room for all o' us here at Hill Top. There'll be five Jenningses come April. There's nay room for visitin' off-comers, even if they own t' place."

Miss Frummety scowled. *"Really, Mrs. J.!"* she exclaimed. *"I call that rude!"*

Beatrix flushed. "I know it wouldn't be convenient," she said, "but I—"

"If we can't live here," Mrs. Jennings went on with a kind of grim satisfaction, "I doan't see as how we can stay and work t' farm. Which is just what I said to Jennings last night, when he told me what tha wanted. 'We got to face facts,' sez I to him. 'Fact is, Miss Potter means to live here when she visits from Lonnun, and who's to blame her,' I sez, 'since it's her house now, which she bought 'n' paid good money for, more'n she should, mappen, though there's no help for that now. But there's nay place for us to live in t' village, so I doan't see how we're to stay.' That's what I sez to Jennings, and that's a fact."

"What about Anvil Cottage?" Beatrix heard herself asking. When Mrs. Jennings stared at her, uncomprehending, she added, in a desperate tone she hardly recognized as her own: "Miss Tolliver's cottage, I mean. It's only a few steps away, and it's every bit as large as this place. You could live there, couldn't you?"

"Anvil Cottage?" Mrs. Jennings frowned. "Well, I s'pose we cud. But I doan't see as how we could afford it."

"Anvil Cottage?" Felicia Frummety brightened. *"Plenty of mice there."*

"If I paid part of the rent?" Beatrix hazarded. "If it were

available, I mean. If you thought it large enough." *What was she saying?* She didn't have the money, either in hand or in prospect, to buy the cottage. And the place wasn't likely to be let, since Mr. Roberts intended to sell it as soon as his aunt's will was read out.

There was a long silence, broken only by the hiss of the fire in the iron range. "I doan't know about Anvil Cottage," Mrs. Jennings said finally. "But we got to face facts some-how. I'll talk to Jennings."

"Please do," Beatrix said. She hurriedly swallowed the last of her tea and rose, feeling that she had confronted quite as many facts as she could manage for the moment. "Thank you for the tea, Mrs. Jennings. I must go now."

And with that, she escaped from the house and almost fled past the barn and down the long slope to the green bank of Esthwaite Water. Miss Felicia Frummety sat on the flag-stone porch, watching her until she disappeared from sight.

If you should visit Esthwaite Water, you will find it to be a clear, stream-fed lake, some eighty acres in size, cupped in a green glacial valley just to the west of Lake Windermere. The word *thwaite*, which means "a clearing in a woodland," reflects the Norse influence in this part of England, and many of the local customs, like the arval bread made of the best wheat flour that was given at Miss Tolliver's funeral, were brought from Norway by the Vikings in the early Middle Ages. The old Norse market town of Hawkshead— a little gem of a town, with higgledy-piggledy streets, un-expected squares and gardens, and whitewashed dwellings— lies at the upper end of the lake, while the two Sawreys lie near the lower end. On the west side of the lake, you can still see the remains of the pits where wood was burned down to charcoal for the iron foundries and forges in the Furness Fells. On the Sawrey side, along the eastern bank, reeds and rushes flourish in the clear, shallow water, fished by kingfishers, herons, and great crested grebes. Esthwaite is much frequented by human fishers, as well, who pull brown and rainbow trout from its sparkling waters, and great numbers of pike and perch.

During her earlier holiday visits to the area, Beatrix had spent a great many hours foraging in the woods and along the lakeside, and not far from here she had found and painted some lovely mushrooms and toadstools, in which she was greatly interested. She was younger then, and firmly believed in fairies, and would have not been at all surprised to see one of the Wee Folk pop out from under a toadstool or behind an oak tree, with a clover blossom cap on his head and a bundle of wild thyme sprigs tucked under one arm. In those days, everything she discovered in the Westmoreland woods and meadows and ponds and ditches seemed wonderfully, imaginatively enchanted, a stark contrast to the formal, frozen life of Bolton Gardens.

Today, though, the fairies, real or not, were quite far from her mind. She had come to the lake to draw, and drawing would help to quiet the litany of Mrs. Jennings' unpleasant facts echoing uncomfortably in her thoughts. So she walked along the bank, looking for possible subjects. Water hens, small black birds with bright red bills, were swimming close to the shore, almost within arm's reach, their heads bobbing as they poked under the lily-pads for water snails. A half-dozen lapwings stood on one leg in the shallow water, napping, with their heads tucked under their wings, and a pair of great crested grebes, sorely threatened by the demand for their feathers for ladies' muffs and hats, swam leisurely through the reeds. But although Beatrix walked for some distance, looking closely, she could find not a single frog—and a frog was what she needed, a cooperative frog who might be persuaded to sit for the drawings of Mr. Jeremy Fisher she planned to use in what she and Norman had laughingly called her "frog book." Finally, she found a dry, sheltered spot, warmed by the sun, and sat down to sketch whatever she could see.

Beatrix's early books had begun as picture letters, written to the children of her favorite governess, Annie Moore. A dozen years before, when she was on holiday with her parents at Dunkeld, on the banks of the Tay, she had written an illustrated letter about the adventures of a mischievous rabbit named Peter to Noel Moore, Annie's oldest son. The very next day, she wrote to Noel's brother Eric: "My dear Eric, Once upon a time there was a frog called Mr. Jeremy Fisher, and he lived in a little house on the bank of a river. . . ."

Beatrix's new book—the one she was supposed to be working on just now—would tell more about Jeremy Fisher, a gentleman frog who gets more than he bargains for when he puts on a mackintosh and galoshes and goes fishing. Jeremy is snapped up by a hungry trout, and saved only by the fact that the fish doesn't like the taste of his mackintosh and spits him out. Norman had chuckled out loud at her preliminary sketches, and seeing the project through his eyes, she had looked forward to completing the twenty-five or so detailed watercolors that would make up the book.

But the memory of Norman settled over Beatrix like a sad, gray fog, and the sunshiny morning, already darkened by the gloomy Mrs. Jennings and her melancholy facts, grew even darker. Over the four years she and Norman had worked together, she had come to associate the happiness she felt in her drawings with his childlike delight in them, and she had always been inspired by his playful encouragement and gentle suggestions. In fact, as their relationship grew closer, she had begun to draw as much for *him* as for the children. And now that her most appreciative audience was gone, so was all her joy in her work. How could she draw without Norman's smile and light-hearted chuckle of approval to confirm her sense of what was right about her drawings? How could she imagine a story without Norman's exuberant imagination to inspire her?

Despairingly, Beatrix looked down at the sketches of reeds and lily pads and water hens and lapwings that she had made in the last hour. They had no spirit, no energy, not a spark of life. They looked exactly the way she felt, flat and gray and gloomy. She ripped the pages out of the sketch book and crumpled them into a ball. There wasn't any point in going on with the book—with any of the other books she'd planned, for that matter—if all of her drawings were going to look so lifeless. But if she didn't go on with the books, she couldn't earn any money, and if there was no more money, she couldn't do anything with the farm. There would be no repairs, no new walls around the garden, no cows, no sheep.

Beatrix wrapped her arms around her legs, propped her chin on her knees, and stared out across the water, her worries draped like a heavy shawl around her shoulders. Perhaps her parents were right. Perhaps she didn't have any business trying to manage a farm, after all. What *was* she going to do about the Jenningses? If they stayed in the house, where was she to stay when she came from London? If she took the house, where were they to live? Mrs. Jennings may have been rude, but she was right. She had to face the facts, no matter how unpleasant.

Beatrix had endured some very dark days in her life. There had been times when she was dangerously ill with rheumatic fever and confined to bed for months and months, and times when she felt totally paralyzed by the confining limits imposed by her parents. And since Norman's death, there had been many times when she despaired of escaping from the prison of Bolton Gardens to find freedom and happiness of her own in the world. But she could not remember a time when she had been confronted with more difficult questions, or when she had less confidence in her ability to find answers, or felt more in need of help.

She gave up trying to fight the hot, bitter tears and simply lowered her forehead onto her knees and gave way to wrenching sobs. She cried for what seemed like a long time, and then, exhausted with the effort of dealing with so many problems and facing so many facts, lay down on the grass, pillowed her head on her arm, and fell asleep.

11

✖⟨❦⟩✖

Freedom!

As their mistress was sleeping the sleep of discouragement and despair, Mrs. Tiggy-Winkle, Josey, Mopsy, and Tom Thumb were in quite a different frame of mind. The four of them were exploring their comfortable new hutch, which Edward Horsley had built of freshly sawn boards and wire netting and placed between the chicken coop (occupied by a dozen self-satisfied red hens and a cocky red rooster) and the lilac hedge, in the farthest corner of the back garden at Belle Green.

"This is quite a lovely cage, I must say," Mopsy remarked with pleasure. She nipped a dainty sprig of clover and nibbled it contentedly. Mr. Horsley had not built a floor for the hutch, but had merely set it down on the ground, so that the animals could enjoy a bit of fresh grazing.

"Oh, yes, indeed," Mrs. Tiggy-Winkle said happily, above the sound of a chicken cackling. She spoke with her mouth

full, for she had pushed aside a clod of fresh earth and discovered a plump, wriggling worm nearly three inches long, a perfect mid-morning snack. *"It's pleasant here under the hedge. I do enjoy the cool shade."*

"I would prefer more sun," Tom Thumb said in a complaining tone. *"My dear wife Hunca Munca felt that if we were going to the trouble of exercising out of doors, we should get a bit of warm sunshine whilst we were at it."* His eyes brimmed with tears. *"Dear, darling Hunca Munca. She may be dead and gone, but she will live on in my heart."* He began to sob, so loudly that the words were almost swallowed by his weeping. *"I shall always be true to her."*

A large blue-black magpie wearing a tidy waistcoat of white feathers landed on the top of the hutch. *"What's this noise?"* he cried, with a saucy show-off flutter of his iridescent wings. *"What's all this squeaking? Who are you?"*

"We're visitors from London," Mrs. Tiggy-Winkle said haughtily. *"We're here with Miss Potter."*

"Tourists," said the magpie, with a disgusted squawk.

Josey, in her usual lively search for adventure, had been poking her nose into various corners of their new outdoor quarters. *"Look at this,"* she called excitedly, over her shoulder. *"Mr. Horsley forgot to fasten the wire netting!"* She pushed at the netting with her nose, and by the time the others had come over to see what was happening, she had shoved her head and shoulders through the flap of loose netting.

"Josey," Mopsy said, quite alarmed, *"stop that this minute! What do you think you're doing?"*

"I'm escaping from this cage, that's what I'm doing," Josey said, pushing with her back feet and wriggling her hindquarters energetically.

"Oh, no!" Mopsy exclaimed, horrified. *"You mustn't!"*

"Oh, but I must," Josey said, caught up in the sheer delight of her own happy mischief. And with a gleeful shake of her fat white tail, she slipped under the wire. *"I'm free!"*

she cried, hopping back and forth in great delight. *"I'm free!"*

"So you are," said the magpie. *"Free to make trouble—for yourself and everybody else."*

Mrs. Tiggy-Winkle stood up on her hind legs and regarded the rabbit with displeasure. *"Josephine,"* she said sternly, *"you must come back into the hutch. You know you're not allowed out unless Miss Potter is with you."*

Tom covered his eyes with his hands. *"Oh, do come back, Josey! It's dangerous out there in the wilderness! You'll be snapped up by a dog or a fox."* And then, overcome by his own fearful prediction, he began running about in mad circles, squeaking tremulously, *"A dog, a dog, a fox, a fox, a dog!"*

"Come back," Mopsy cried, in an imploring tone, pressing her pink nose against the wire netting. *"Oh, Josey, do come back where it's safe, please, please do! You'll get tangled in a gooseberry net, like Peter. Or Mrs. McGregor will put you in a pie!"*

"Mrs. McGregor?" Josey gave a derisive laugh. *"Don't be silly, Mopsy. That's Miss Potter's make-believe."* And with that, she hopped through the hedge and was gone.

"She'll be eaten," cried Tom in despair. *"We'll never see her again, never more, never more!"*

With a shake of his feathers, the magpie flew into the air, cackling crazily. *"Of course not, you silly mouse. She's free, free as a bird! And once free, only a fool would go back to a cage."*

"I'm afraid the magpie is right," Mrs. Tiggy-Winkle said sadly. *"Josey is no fool. She's a clever and resourceful rabbit. She has abandoned us."*

But Josey was back again in a minute or two. *"I didn't see anything that looks even remotely like a gooseberry net,"* she reported, *"or a dog or a fox or Mrs. McGregor."* She rolled her eyes ecstatically and wiggled her ears. *"But I did see a lovely patch of wild salad burnet. And there's a glorious golden haystack, and an orchard full of the most beautiful red fallen apples."*

Mrs. Tiggy-Winkle's brown eyes became suddenly bright,

and she rubbed her little clawed forepaws together. *"Fallen apples?"* she whispered reverently. *"Fallen apples, you say? And where there are fallen apples, one might just find a worm or two, mightn't one?"*

"Oh, I should think so." Josey gave her ears a careless toss. *"Worms and beetles and grubs and snails."*

"Snails," said Mrs. Tiggy-Winkle. *"Worms! Beetles!"*

"But we can't leave the hutch," Mopsy said desperately. *"We can't leave Miss Potter! She's our friend!"*

"We're not leaving forever, silly." Josey lifted up the corner of the wire netting, squeezed under it, and was back inside the hutch in a flash. *"You see? We're just going on holiday. We can slip out with no trouble and duck right back in whenever we feel like it."* She grinned at Mrs. Tiggy-Winkle. *"You can come back here after you've eaten all the worms and beetles and grubs your little hedgehog heart desires. Well, Mrs. T? What do you say?"*

"Just say no!" Mopsy implored wildly. *"It's the voice of temptation, dear Mrs. Tiggy-Winkle! You must not yield!"*

"It's the voice of freedom," cried the magpie with a raucous laugh, and flew to the top of the hedge.

Josie pushed back out through the loose wire netting. *"Come on, Tig,"* she beckoned. *"Consider the worms!"*

Mrs. Tiggy-Winkle, her eyes dancing, considered them for all of five seconds. Then she cried joyously, *"I shall have worms! Indeed I shall! And beetles and snails!"* And with that, she pushed her way through the flap. In an instant, the little brown hedgehog had scampered through the hedge and was running through the green grass and into the orchard, just as fast as her small feet could carry her.

"Well away!" shrilled the magpie from the top-most twig of the hedge. *"Hoop-hoop, tally-ho! Never say die!"*

Josey turned to look at Mopsy and Tom, who were still sitting inside the hutch. *"Well?"* she asked cheerfully. *"Who's next?"*

"Certainly not I," Tom said. He picked up the tip of his

tail and began to nibble it in a forlorn sort of way. *"I am a town mouse, and have no use for the country. I'll just stay here in this cage and be true to Miss Potter and to my dear Hunca Munca."* He sighed deeply. *"True, true, always true."*

Mopsy sat up on her haunches and folded her forepaws, her teeth chattering, her whiskers twitching fearfully. *"I'm not coming either, Josey. It's simply too dangerous. There are too many risks. Bears and panthers and wolves—"*

"Don't be silly," Josey said. *"There have never been any wild bears in England, or panthers. And the wolves have been gone for centuries."*

"How do you know?" Mopsy persisted. She shivered. *"Just because you've never seen one—"*

"Personally, I don't much care whether you come or not," said Josey, with a shrug of her shoulders. *"You're such a nervous Nellie that you're likely to spoil the fun, anyway. But you'll be lonely all by yourself."*

"I have Tom," Mopsy said, moving closer to the mouse.

Josey smiled. *"Tom,"* she said, lowering her voice to a whisper. *"Come here, Tom. I want to tell you something. Something important."*

Mopsy put out a paw to restrain him, but Tom, who was always more curious than was good for him, crept close to the wire. Josey whispered in his ear. Tom's eyes widened as he listened, and he took a step back.

"You're making it up," he cried. *"It can't be true."*

"Cross my heart and hope to die," said the rabbit. *"The spitting image of Hunca Munca. Could be her twin. She's sitting right beside the haystack. I saw her with my very own eyes."*

"Hunca Munca's twin sister!" cried Tom, now so giddy with joy that he turned two flying cartwheels. *"Can it be true? Can it be true, true, true?"*

"Come and see for yourself," Josey said, and lifted up the flap of netting.

And with that, Tom Thumb was gone, streaking through

the hedge in the direction of the haystack, his white tail straight out behind him.

Josey smiled mischievously. *"Any time you're ready, Mop, old girl,"* she said over her shoulder. *"You'll find me in the salad burnet patch."* And with that, she hopped through the hedge.

It took Mopsy quite a time to work up her courage, but at last, driven by loneliness and an overwhelming desire to be with Josey, she wriggled through the netting flap. For a moment, she crouched just outside the hutch, gazing back at its comfort and safety with longing. Then, her ears flat against her head, her eyes wide with fear, she crept through the hedge.

From the topmost twig of the hedge, the magpie surveyed his wide domain. In the orchard, seized by a joyful ecstasy, the hedgehog was rooting gaily among the fallen apples, crying *"Worms, grubs, and beetles, beware! Worms, grubs, and beetles, beware!"*

Beside the haystack, the mouse was murmuring romantic poetry into the ear of another mouse, who appeared to be impressed by his courtship.

And in the salad burnet patch, the two rabbits, shoulder to shoulder, were munching in oblivious pleasure.

"Well, they won't last long in the wild," the magpie said to himself, and gave a raucous, mocking laugh. *"Tourists, every silly one of them."*

12

Miss Tolliver's Will Is Read

As Miss Potter's fugitive animals were enjoying their newly won freedom, Dimity Woodcock was setting out with her brother for Hawkshead. Dimity planned to do some shopping, and Miles had business with the solicitors' firm of Heelis and Heelis. Dimity had arranged to meet him at noon and drive back to Sawrey together in time for lunch.

"You'll be in the solicitors' office during the reading of Miss Tolliver's will, won't you?" Dimity asked, as she climbed into the waiting gig.

"Probably," Miles replied, lifting the reins. Topaz, his young filly, pricked her ears and stepped out smartly.

"Please do see what you can find out about it," Dimity said, and smashed her felt hat more firmly on her head. "It's such a mystery, you know. I am absolutely *mad* to know whether that awful man is to have Anvil Cottage after all."

Miles laughed. "You and the entire village. Elsa gave me

a special commission this morning—seems as anxious as you to know about the cottage. And Grace Lythecoe button-holed me as I was waiting for you. She wants me to find out about a miniature Constable that used to hang in Miss Tolliver's sitting room."

"A *Constable?*" Dimity asked, surprised, as they turned onto the Hawkshead Road. It was a lovely morning, the sky was so brilliant that it almost hurt one's eyes to look at it, and the trees made a graceful golden arch over the narrow road. "Miss Tolliver had a genuine Constable painting? I don't remember seeing anything like that. Where was she hiding it?"

"I'm sure I don't know, Dim," Miles said, raising a hand to Spuggy Pritchard, who was leading Biscuit, his billy goat, down the road. "I never noticed it, although I do seem to recall some muddy little painting in a gilt frame that hung in a corner. It seems, however, that our observant Miss Potter saw it when she was visiting Miss Tolliver several years ago. She's the one who pointed out to Grace that it was gone."

"I suppose Miss Potter would notice such things," Dimity said thoughtfully, "being an artist, I mean. But when did it go away? And *how?* Surely not since Miss Tolliver died, for the house has been locked."

Miles pulled Topaz and the gig onto the grassy verge, to make way for a draft horse hitched to a heavily loaded hay wagon, coming from the other direction. "Good morning, Mr. Everett," he called, to the craggy, gray-bearded farmer driving the wagon. To Dimity, he said, "As to how and when, Grace hadn't a clue. She seemed to think the painting was there when Miss Tolliver had her birthday party. Anyway, she sent a boy with a note to Heelis yesterday evening, letting him know it's gone missing. She thought Miss Tolliver might have given him an inventory of her possessions."

Dimity folded her white-gloved hands in her lap. "Well,

then," she said decidedly, "you can find out about *that,* too."

"Yes, ma'am," Miles said dryly. "I shall add it to my list." His tone become sterner. "You didn't mention that there was talk at tea yesterday of Miss Tolliver's having died of poison."

"Poison!" For a moment, Dimity was startled. Then she recalled. "Oh, yes. It was Rose Sutton who mentioned it. She'd been reading Sherlock Holmes, I think. She said something to the effect that when somebody died unexpectedly, one ought to consider all angles." She paused. "It seemed an innocent enough remark. No one took it up, at least not in my hearing." She frowned. "Why do you ask?"

"Because Constable Braithwaite came to see me this morning, very early. He was at the pub last night, and heard several of the men talking about it. It seems that there is a general consensus of village opinion that she died of an excess of foxglove, self-administered or . . ." He lifted the reins and Topaz stepped faster. "Otherwise."

"Oh, dear," Dimity said. Soberly, she added, "There's no truth to it, is there?"

"To be perfectly honest," Miles replied, "I don't suppose there's any way of knowing. Dr. Butters saw no reason to perform any toxicological tests." He gave his sister a sideways glance. "You knew Miss Tolliver rather better than most, Dim. Did she dose herself regularly with foxglove?"

"Foxglove?" Dimity asked, feeling suddenly apprehensive. "She did talk to me about it once. She grew it in her garden, and made up her own 'heart tonic,' as she called it. But knowing Miss Tolliver, I'm sure she was very careful." She drew in her breath sharply. "Oh, Miles, this is dreadful! If there's no way of knowing for certain how she died, people will simply go on talking forever!" Then something else occurred to her, and she felt even more apprehensive. "They aren't mentioning the names of . . . suspects, are they?"

"The constable said that the men at the pub were inclined to believe that the nephew had something to do with it. Of course, he's the one who's expected to benefit from his aunt's death." He chuckled wryly. "Unfortunately, he appears to fit people's idea of a proper villain. He is said to have accosted Grace Lythecoe and Miss Potter yesterday, rather aggressively."

"That must have been the business about the key," Dimity said. She sighed. "What are you going to do?"

"There's not much I can do," Miles said. "I'm seeing the magistrate this morning, and I'll mention the matter to him. And to Heelis, as well." He raised his voice. "Get along a little faster, there, Topaz."

Dimity had always thought that Hawkshead—named after the tenth-century Norseman "Haukr" who established it— was a perfectly wonderful little town, so clean and neat and friendly. She loved to stroll through the narrow streets, which bore names like Leather, Rag, Putty, and Wool, reflecting the medieval crafts and trades that had flourished in earlier times. Wool was especially important, of course, for it was the fleece that had been marketed and processed here for shipping to the weavers at Kendal that brought prosperity to the town and surrounding countryside.

The buildings were quaintly medieval, too, none of that solemnly pretentious red-brick Victorian stuffiness here! The pebbly walls were whitewashed, and buckets and pots of chrysanthemums, Michaelmas daisies, and lobelia sat on every sill. The south end of town was dominated by St. Michael's Church, sitting "like a throned lady" on a hill, as the poet William Wordsworth had described it. And on her way to Miss Stanley's millinery shop, Dimity walked past the little grammar school, still open to the local children, where Wordsworth himself had studied in the late 1700s, and where he had carved his name on his wooden desktop.

Miss Annabelle Stanley kept her tiny shop between the cobbler and the chandler, under a wooden sign that bore the faded painting of a ruffled bonnet, first displayed by her mother, Mrs. Ada Stanley. That worthy woman, now some ten years departed, had opened the shop in the same year that Victoria ascended the throne. A few of her serviceable straw bonnets were still on the shelf at the rear of the shop, while Miss Stanley's modish hats, lavished with lace and silk flowers and swathed with yards of tulle, were prominently displayed in the window.

The fashionably dressed Miss Stanley, who had two gold teeth and wore black false hair and daintily rouged cheeks, brought out a tray of satin ribbons, averting her eyes from Dimity's unfashionable felt hat. When Dimity had chosen two yards of a narrow yellow ribbon and a yard of green, Miss Stanley wrapped the purchase in a bit of tissue paper. As she handed it to Dimity, she remarked, with a delicately affected lisp, "You've heard, I suppose, about Miss Tolliver's will."

"Heard what?" Dimity asked, startled. It was no surprise that Miss Stanley had been acquainted with Miss Tolliver, of course. She and her mother, between them, had constructed hats and bonnets for three generations of Hawkshead women. But Dimity hadn't known that the business about the will was common knowledge so far away from Sawrey. Of course, three miles was not far by London standards, where one might flit here and there by Underground and drive here and there by motor car. But in the countryside, where the roads toiled up and down and around the stony hills, three miles was still a substantial journey.

Miss Stanley leaned closer, nearly submerging Dimity in a wave of lilac perfume. "My sister keeps Ivy House, you know," she said, in a voice meant to convey an important secret. "Miss Sarah Barwick arrived late yesterday, from Manchester. She said she came for the reading of Miss Tolliver's will, which is to be this morning." She added, with a meaningful look, "I doubt if she'd have come all that way if she hadn't been a beneficiary, do you?"

Dimity stepped back and took a breath of clearer air. "From Manchester?" She hadn't known that Miss Tolliver had any relations there—or anywhere other than Kendal, for that matter.

"Just so," said Miss Stanley. "And when she was asked if she was related to Miss Tolliver, Miss Barwick said no, although she might have been, if things had been different." She frowned. "Now, what do you make of that?"

"I'm sure I don't know," Dimity replied. "Is she an . . . older lady?" Given Miles's stature in the community, Dimity usually felt that it was inappropriate for her to gossip. In this case, however, she felt rather justified, since so little information was available that really, one owed it to oneself to latch onto whatever odd bit one could.

"A younger lady, my sister says, scarcely out of her twenties. Quite pretty, in a hoydenish sort of way, but modern." (The last word was spoken with marked disapproval.)

Dimity tucked her purchase into her handbag and stepped back, wondering what "hoydenish" and "modern" might mean, in this context. "I'm sure she must be very nice," she said primly, recollecting her role as the sister of a Justice of the Peace.

"But who *is* this Miss Barwick?" Miss Stanley asked, stepping forward and speaking urgently. "I've always understood that Miss Tolliver had no relations, other than that draper fellow from—"

"I'm sure I shall find the ribbon quite delightful, Miss Stanley," Dimity said, making her exit. "Thank you so much." Once on the street, she took a deep breath to clear her lungs of lilac perfume, concluding that perhaps she should be grateful that Miss Stanley had not mentioned anything at all about poison.

A cup of tea, several errands, and a half-dozen variously sized parcels later, Dimity arrived in the street outside the office of Heelis and Heelis. Miles emerged, swinging his stick jauntily and whistling between his teeth.

"Well, that's all settled," he said as they went off round the corner to Holtby's Stable, where Topaz had been left to enjoy a ration of oats.

"What?" Dimity demanded. She plucked at Miles's sleeve. "What's settled? Were you there when the will was read?"

"I was," Miles said, and gave the stableman a half-shilling to hitch the gig and bring it around to the lane. "Just inside the door, on a very hard chair. Willie Heelis wanted me as a witness. Can't think why, though. There were only two bequests, both very straightforward."

"Did the draper get the cottage?" Dimity asked breathlessly. "Who is Sarah Barwick? And what about the Constable?"

Miles's eyebrows went up. "How did you find out about Sarah Barwick?"

"She's staying at Ivy House," Dimity replied, not very informatively. *"Did he?"*

"Roberts, from Kendal?" Miles chuckled. "No, he didn't, as a matter of fact."

"Oh, my," Dimity said faintly.

"Oh, yes." He chuckled again. "You never saw a man so heated, Dim. Heelis hadn't even finished with the reading when Roberts jumped out of his chair and began to rant and rave. I thought he was going to explode, just like a volcano— as indeed he might, if Heelis hadn't stopped and calmed him down." He paused as the stableman brought out horse and gig. "Ah, here's Topaz, combed and curried and bright as a new penny. Climb in, my dear, and let's be off. I'm ready for lunch."

"I'm going to explode just like a volcano," said Dimity

fiercely, as she got into the gig, "if you don't tell me who got the cottage. *This minute!*"

When Miles wanted to tell a story, he could tell it swiftly and without embellishment, and since Dimity really wanted to hear it, she did not interrupt him. Miss Tolliver's will had been short, simple, and quite specific about the disposition of her property. She had bequeathed Anvil Cottage and all its contents to Miss Sarah Barwick of Manchester. To Mr. Henry Roberts of Kendal, she had left the sum of one farthing—the smallest coin in the realm—as well as a box of letters that had been written to Miss Tolliver by Mr. Roberts' mother and a funeral locket containing his mother's hair. There was indeed an inventory, made the year before, which listed a gilt-framed miniature painting, with no artist mentioned and no value assessed. Willie Heelis had told Miss Barwick that he had been advised by a neighbor that the painting might have some value, and that it seemed to be missing. He suggested that Miss Barwick undertake an immediate search for it and offered to drive her over to Sawrey that afternoon, so this could be done straightaway.

"But *who* is this Miss Barwick?" asked Dimity, helplessly, feeling that whilst one mystery had been solved, another now rose before them.

"A friend of Miss Tolliver," Miles said. "That's all I know, Dim. Every bit of it."

"But if she was Miss Tolliver's friend," Dimity persisted, "why didn't she—"

"You'll have to ask her," Miles said shortly. "And with regard to that gossip about poison, I mentioned it to the magistrate and to Heelis. Neither of them think poison at all likely, since Dr. Butters seems not to have considered it. And both agree, there's nothing to be done unless some specific evidence comes to light."

"Which means," Dimity said regretfully, "that there's no way to stop people from talking."

"Too true, I'm afraid." Miles gave a little shrug. "They'll talk about it until something else comes along they'd rather talk about."

Dimity shivered. She hated to think what *that* might be.

13

Miss Potter Sees Herself in a New Light

Beatrix was awakened by the kiss-kiss-kissy sound made by the water hens, who were discussing the important business of snails for lunch, the best nesting sites, and the education of young water hens. The sun, higher in the sky now, had burned the mists from Esthwaite Water and a light breeze ruffled its blue-gray surface. She sat up and rubbed her eyes. Very close by, along the shore to her right, a half-dozen brown and white cows stood knee-deep in the water, velvety-brown eyes regarding her thoughtfully beneath a luxuriant fringe of eyelashes. Away to her left, smoke rose in a delicate spiral from the chimney of Willow Cottage, and she could see someone sitting in the door yard.

With a sigh, Beatrix stood, brushed bits of grass off her woolen skirt, and tucked her sketchbook under her arm. If she could not draw, she could spend her time more productively than by sleeping—she could drop in on a neighbor and introduce herself. Besides, she was curious about Miss Crosfield's occupation as a spinner and weaver. Beatrix herself was descended from a long line of industrious cotton spinners, calico printers, and cloth merchants, and she had often thought she would like to have a spinning wheel. Perhaps Miss Crosfield would teach her how to spin. She set off along the edge of the lake, and when she got to the dry-stone wall, hiked up her skirt and climbed over.

But the person sitting on the step in front of the little low cottage was not Miss Crosfield. It was a slightly built boy of ten or eleven, red-haired and barefoot, wearing a faded blue shirt and ragged trousers, held up with red hand-made braces. On one side was a pile of bright, clean spelks—thinly shaved strips of oak—and a half-finished swill basket, of the sort that Lakeland people used to carry animal feed, harvest vegetables, or fetch coal.

But the boy seemed, for the moment, to have abandoned his basket-making. With a piece of half-burnt coal, he was sketching a black-and-white cat, asleep on the sun-warmed flagstones of the path. He looked up from the bit of rough paper on his lap as Beatrix came up the path, and she saw that his eyes were wide-spaced and gray, his pale face liberally dusted with sandy freckles.

"Hello," Beatrix said. "I'm Miss Potter, your new neighbor at Hill Top Farm."

"If you've come to see my aunt," the boy said, going back to his sketching, "you've missed her. She's gone to Hawkshead to sell a piece of cloth. I'm Jeremy," he added, rubbing out a line with one finger.

"Jeremy!" Beatrix exclaimed. "Now, there's an interesting coincidence."

"A coincidence?" The boy lifted his eyes and regarded her curiously. "Why?"

"Because," she said, gathering her skirt and sitting down on the stone step beside him. "I'm making a book about a frog named Jeremy. Mr. Jeremy Fisher." She leaned over to look at his sketch. "That's a first-rate cat," she said. "I especially like the way you've drawn his ears."

"*Her* ears," Jeremy amended. "Her name is Baffles." At the sound of her name, Baffles stirred, opened one green eye, and closed it again. The boy nudged her with his toe. "Roll over, Baffles," he commanded, and Baffles, her eyes still closed, obligingly flopped from one side to the other.

"How clever of her," Beatrix said admiringly. "I have never been able to persuade cats to do tricks. They don't seem to like obeying orders. Rabbits," she added, "are quite another matter."

"You have rabbits?" the boy asked.

"Oh, I've had all kinds of animals," Beatrix replied. "Mice and hedgehogs and squirrels and owls and frogs and lizards. I use them as models for my drawings, you see. But it's the rabbits who do the very best tricks." She smiled reminiscently. "I once had a dear fellow named Peter, an absolutely splendid Belgian rabbit. He would hop over my hand for bits of biscuit, and jump through a hoop, and do all manner of amusing things."

Baffles sat up and yawned widely, and Beatrix laughed. "But I see we are boring Baffles. Cats don't think very highly of rabbits."

The boy was eyeing the sketch book under her arm. "I don't suppose you've got any drawings of rabbits with you?"

"I'm afraid not," Beatrix said. "I've been working on Jeremy." She opened her book to the page of frog sketches she had shown Norman.

Jeremy studied them silently. "These are good," he said at last, in a tone of honest appraisal. "I didn't suppose a lady would know what a frog really looks like."

"I once had a green frog named Punch," Beatrix said reflectively. "Most of these are sketches of him. He lived with me for five or six years, and went everywhere with me in a bamboo cage. He liked to eat live grasshoppers." She smiled. "There'll be a grasshopper in the story. Roast grasshopper, I think. Mr. Fisher has invited a few dinner guests, you see, quite like a country gentleman. He plans to have fish, but he has to settle for grasshopper."

"If I were a frog," Jeremy said decidedly, "I should like somebody to catch grasshoppers, to save me the trouble. But I should *not* like to live in a bamboo cage, or have my grasshoppers roasted."

Beatrix closed her sketchbook. "You'd rather be a frog along Esthwaite Water, I'm sure. But that would mean you'd have to find your own grasshoppers, and worry about being snapped up by a heron or a pike. There are advantages either way." She paused and looked at him speculatively. "This is rather an impertinent question, Jeremy, but I wonder if you know where I might find a frog to sketch. I always do much better when I have a real creature in front of me."

"Of course I know where there are frogs," Jeremy said, as if it really *were* an impertinent question. "There's a whacking great colony of them above the stone bridge over Cunsey Beck. The frogs live in the reeds, and swim and catch bugs. There's one fine, fat fellow who likes to sit on the bank in the afternoon sun." He gave Beatrix a sidelong glance. "It's rather a hidden place, though, and you're not likely to find it by yourself. Would you like me to take you there?"

"I would indeed, very much!" Beatrix exclaimed, delighted. "I am truly in need of a frog." She stopped suddenly, with a glance at the half-finished swill. "But shouldn't you finish your basket? And why aren't you in school, if you don't mind my asking?"

"I can work on the basket later," the boy said shortly. "And I'm not going back to school." He pushed his red hair out of his eyes, leaving a smear of charcoal on his forehead. "Not *ever*."

"I see," Beatrix said. "I would have given anything if my

parents had allowed me to go to school. My brother did, of course, and had all sorts of interesting adventures. But I was taught at home by governesses." Baffles began to curl herself around Beatrix's ankles. "Now, though," she went on absently, reaching down to stroke the cat's soft fur, "I often think that if I'd gone to school, some of my originality might have got rubbed off. Teachers do rather seem to want pupils to do everything their way, and I'm quite sure I wouldn't have liked that. I am rather independent I'm afraid."

There was a silence, as Jeremy considered this. "Well?" he asked at last. "Don't you want to know why *I'm* not going back to school?"

"Why?" Beatrix asked.

"Because," Jeremy said sadly, "there's a beastly big bully named Harold. He pushed me off the coal-pile and hurt my arm." He extended his pale arm and Beatrix saw a long, reddened scratch.

"I see," Beatrix said, shaking her head at the sight. "*How* odious. I quite agree with you, Jeremy. If I were you, I would never *ever* go back to school again—at least until I felt brave enough to face down that horrid bully."

Jeremy frowned at that. "I'm brave, of course, but—"

"No matter." Beatrix stood up. "We can't be brave all the time. I know I'm not, at any rate. Mostly, I'm a coward." She sighed, thinking that if she had been brave enough to stand up to her parents, she and Norman might have had a longer time of happiness together, before the end.

"Really?" Jeremy looked interested. "I didn't think grown-ups could be cowards."

"Of course they can. It happens all the time." Beatrix summoned a smile. "Well, since you don't seem to have anything else to do just now, let's go along and find the frogs. You can have a page or two of my sketchbook for your own pictures, if you like," she added. "I've also an extra drawing pencil. Charcoal does very well for cats, but a pencil is better for drawing frogs."

"Hurrah!" Jeremy cried exultantly. "Hold on, and I'll leave a note for Aunt Jane; She'll worry if she comes home and finds me gone."

He went inside, and Beatrix followed him into the pleasant, low-beamed kitchen. In one corner stood a tall grandfather clock with a border of flowers around its face and the moon's phases turning inside a gold circle at the top. Over the fire, a black chimney-shelf held pewter mugs, a copper kettle, and two china candlesticks stuck with half-burned candles. A woven rag rug covered the floor. A large wooden spinning wheel sat beside the fireplace, its bobbin filled with fine gray yarn, and a heavy wooden jack loom, on which a length of gray tweed was being woven, took up an entire wall. It was a poor place, yes, but there was something brave about it, Beatrix thought, something brave and hopeful.

In a few minutes, Beatrix and Jeremy were on their way to the stone bridge over Cunsey Beck. The frogs lived upstream, near the lake, in their own private marshy cove. The banks were rimmed with bracken and shrubby willows and the shallow water was thick with reeds and fragrant water mint. It was an enchanted spot, Beatrix thought, and perfect for frogs. There really were quite a number of them—swimming, snapping at dragon flies, hopping along the bank. One was, as Jeremy had said, an especially handsome fellow, who sat by himself a little apart, blinking with lazy contentment in the October sunshine. He seemed entirely oblivious to the barefoot boy and the lady who made a place to sit in the bracken and draw pictures.

They talked as they worked, and Beatrix discovered that Jeremy had been to school in Oxford; that he had lived with his aunt since his mother died of influenza the year before (his father having died before he was born); that he was often sick but didn't like to talk about it; and that he meant to be an artist when he grew up, an ambition that had attracted a certain amount of unfortunate attention at Sawrey School, where the village boys (who aimed to be ferrymen, black-smiths, or farmers, like their fathers) found it amusing.

Jeremy's aunt, he said, felt it would be quite wonderful if he could be an artist, although she did sometimes remind him that it might be difficult to sell enough work to buy food and lodging, and that he might have to do other things just to keep body and soul together. This was a challenge that she herself understood, since being a spinner and a weaver was something like being an artist, only in wool. But these days, people did not like to pay the price for hand-woven wool, when the machine-made stuff was much cheaper. It was a very good thing, Jeremy added prudently, that he could make swill baskets, and that their hens laid so many eggs, the cow gave so much milk, and the bees made so much honey that they could sell what they didn't use and bring in a few extra shillings a week. It was obvious, Beatrix thought, that money was hard to come by in the Crosfield family. But that didn't seem to have daunted their creative energies or their willingness to work.

"Well, what do you think?" Beatrix asked, after a time, and showed her drawings to Jeremy.

"Oh, topping!" Jeremy exclaimed, leaning over to look. "Those are ever so good, Miss Potter! I rather like that one," he added, pointing. "The fat, funny one with the cravat and spats. He looks terribly smug and pleased with himself. He seems to fancy himself an important country gentleman, with foxes in his fields and trout in his stream, when he's re-ally only an insignificant green frog on a muddy bank." He giggled happily.

"I like that sketch, too," Beatrix said, looking down at her work and then at the complacent frog on the bank, feel-ing that she had at last met the real Mr. Jeremy Fisher—pompous, self-important, just a little conceited—and that meeting him in the company of Master Jeremy Crosfield, who obviously knew his frogs, made Mr. Fisher seem an even more interesting character than she had at first imagined.

"To tell the truth," she went on, "I was feeling rather dumpy this morning, before I met you. I was afraid I might never be able to draw another frog—but now I'm sure I shall. At least, as long as I can come here and draw Mr. Fisher." She smiled. "Now, show me what you've drawn."

"My frogs aren't as good as yours," the boy said without rancor, "but I like them. I haven't drawn frogs before, but now I think I shall draw lots of them."

"Oh, yes," Beatrix said earnestly, as she looked at Jeremy's work, thinking that it showed a great deal of promise. "You *must*!"

Jeremy regarded her. "Your frog—he's really named Jeremy? And he's really going to be in a book?"

"Yes, to both," Beatrix said, more confidently now. This morning, she had wondered whether she could begin again, and now she knew she would. It had felt very good to draw the frogs, and it felt even better to have an appreciative child look at her work. She was glad she had come.

But Jeremy's thoughts were taking another, more practical direction. "And will people give you money for the pictures?"

A pragmatic question deserved a pragmatic answer. "The book will be sold for a shilling," Beatrix replied, "if it's paper-bound. If it's cloth-bound, one and six. Of that, the publisher will pay a certain royalty to me."

Jeremy thought about this for a minute. "It must feel very good to be able to sell your pictures."

"It does, of course," Beatrix said, thinking that she ought to give Jeremy several of her books. "Having my own money makes me sure that I can take care of myself. But I think I should draw even if the work didn't sell. There are things, sometimes, that make my fingers itch to make pictures of them."

"Oh, yes!" Jeremy said, and smiled broadly. "I feel that way about cats." He jumped up. "Come back to the cottage with me and I'll show you my cat pictures. And I'll put on the kettle and we can have a cup of tea."

Beatrix closed her sketchbook and stood. "I should like to see your pictures, but we'll have to save the tea for another time. I'm sure it is already past lunchtime. I'm staying with Mrs. Crook, at Belle Green, and she will wonder what's become of me."

Back at the cottage, Jeremy spread several pictures on the kitchen table and Beatrix admired them for a few moments, then reminded him that she had to go. She was saying goodbye when they heard an angry rapping at the door.

"Jeremy Crosfield!" a woman's irate voice shouted. "This is Miss Crabbe. I know you're in there, you horrid boy! Open the door and let me in!"

Jeremy's eyes grew large and the sandy freckles stood out on his pale face. "It's the headmistress," he whispered, frightened. "She's come to make me go back to school. Oh, please, Miss Potter. Tell her I'm not here!"

"I can't do that," Beatrix said and added, putting a comforting hand on Jeremy's shoulder, "But I'm sure she'll understand when we explain why you didn't go to school today." She went to the door and opened it. "Hello, Miss Crabbe," she said politely. "Miss Crosfield is not here just now, but perhaps I can help."

Miss Crabbe's eyes narrowed. She seemed to have put her hat on back-to-front, with the feathers hanging down over her nose, and her jacket was buttoned crookedly. "I want to speak to Jeremy Crosfield. Where is he?"

"Right here," Beatrix said pleasantly. "We've been having a drawing lesson—drawing frogs, actually. After his unpleasant encounter with Harold yesterday, he felt he would not be able to—"

Miss Crabbe came into the room, shutting the door

behind her. "I know all about what happened after yesterday's encounter with Harold," she said ominously. "All right,
young man, hand it over."

Jeremy's gulp was audible. "Hand . . . hand what over,
please, Miss Crabbe?"

"The money you stole from my desk when you were alone
in the classroom, that's what!" Miss Crabbe blazed. "One
sovereign, two half-crowns, three florins, and nine shillings.
The money that was collected to repair the school roof."

Beatrix gasped, scarcely believing her ears.

"But I didn't steal any money!" Jeremy cried desperately.
He turned to Beatrix, imploring. "Please believe me, Miss
Potter. I didn't!"

Beatrix put her hand on Jeremy's shoulder. She was quak-
ing inside, but she tried not to show it. "Miss Crabbe," she
began, "I am sure that Jeremy—"

"Miss Potter," Miss Crabbe said, in a biting, bitter voice
that was remarkably like Beatrix's mother's, "this affair is
none of your business. You political females are all alike.
You defend the ones you call the 'down-trodden,' whilst
they steal and cheat and cause trouble for honest, upstand-
ing folk. I don't want to hear another word out of you. If
this child won't hand over the money he stole, I shall drag
him off to Constable Braithwaite. And the constable, young
man, will see that you're put in jail!"

Helplessly, Jeremy began to cry.

Afterward, Beatrix would wonder what in the world
came over her. She didn't know whether it was the fact that
Miss Crabbe sounded so infuriatingly like her mother, or
whether she felt a natural sympathy for Jeremy and a strong
inclination to take his word over Miss Crabbe's. She only
knew that she did not for a single instant doubt the boy's
complete innocence, or imagine that, no matter how much
in need he and his grandmother might be, he would stoop
to theft. And while she had been brought up to be respectful

to her elders and never to answer back, regardless of the circumstances, she could not stand silently by and allow Miss Crabbe to wrongfully accuse him.

She put a protective arm around Jeremy's shaking shoulders, drew herself up to her full height, lifted her chin, and spoke quite loudly and firmly. "Miss Crabbe, I will not allow you to bully this child. If you cannot keep a civil tongue in your head, I must ask you to leave."

"But he stole the money!" Miss Crabbe cried angrily, reaching out as if to seize Jeremy. "He's a thief! I demand that you hand him over."

"Demand all you like," Beatrix said distinctly, putting the boy behind her, "you are *not* taking Jeremy. If you have proof of your claim, you should lay it before the constable. He will see that the matter is handled correctly. All you've done is shout accusations without offering a shred of proof. As a teacher, you should be ashamed."

"Ashamed!" Miss Crabbe cried shrilly. Her face had grown quite red and she was panting. "You dare to tell me that I should be *ashamed*!"

"I do indeed," Beatrix said. "As a teacher, you know better than to make unsubstantiated accusations against a helpless child. You should be truly ashamed of yourself." Marveling at her calm, she stepped forward and opened the door. "And now you must leave."

Miss Crabbe raised her hand as if she meant to slap Beatrix. Her heart thudding in her chest, Beatrix stood quite still, fixing her eyes steadily on Miss Crabbe's face, until the other woman's eyes wavered and her hand dropped. Miss Crabbe, still furious but clearly defeated, took a step backward, and then another, and then she was gone.

And in the next moment, Beatrix was on her knees and holding the sobbing Jeremy in her arms, his tears wet against her face. "It's all right," she whispered. "It's all right, Jeremy. She's not going to hurt you."

"You're so brave," Jeremy said, between sobs, "and I'm such a coward. I wish I could be brave like you."

As Beatrix held him closer, she could feel herself shaking. She had resisted her parents when it came to Norman's proposal and to her purchase of Hill Top, but her resistance had been quietly passive. She had never before spoken out so vehemently in the face of opposition, and with such a strong conviction of being in the right.

It gave her an entirely new view of herself.

14

The Mystery of Miss Barwick

Grace Lythecoe, accompanied by Crumpet, was just returning from the post office when she looked up to see Miss
Potter hurrying up Market Street. Her sketch book was
tucked under her arm and her round, cheerful face wore a
troubled look.

When Miss Potter saw Grace, she lifted her hand in
greeting. "I'm so glad to have caught you," she said breathlessly. "If you have a moment, I should very much like to
have your advice."

"By all means," Grace said, and opened the front door of
her cottage. Crumpet, feeling that it must be time for
lunch, stepped daintily over the threshold. Strictly speaking, Crumpet belonged to Bertha Stubbs and was supposed
to take all her meals at home, but the village cats—of whom
there were many, since there were a great many mice—were
welcome in most of the village households. Mrs. Lythecoe

had a canary called Caruso, after a famous opera singer who had recently performed in London, and out of respect for Caruso's feelings, did not keep her own cat. Crumpet could be trusted to stay away from the cage, however, so Mrs. Lythecoe often invited her in for a bowl of milk or piece of fish in the kitchen.

Grace followed the cat into the house, hung her wide-brimmed straw hat on the wooden peg next to the door, and dropped her mail on the hallway table to be looked over later. "The kettle is hot," she said to Miss Potter, "and I was about to have a cup of tea and a sandwich. You've had lunch, I suppose?"

"*I haven't,*" said Crumpet pleasantly, "*and to tell the truth, I'm quite hungry.*"

Miss Potter looked uncomfortable. "Actually, no," she said, "but I—"

"Then you'll have a something with me," Grace said decidedly. "It's well past lunchtime, and there's a nice bit of joint left over from yesterday and fresh bread from this morning's baking." She looked down. "I daresay Crumpet would like a little something, as well. Wouldn't you, Crumpet?"

"*Thank you,*" Crumpet said with a smile and a flick of her tail. "*You are very kind.*"

And with that, the three of them went along the passageway to the small kitchen at the back of the cottage, where Grace took her guest's hat and jacket, hung them up, and pulled out a chair beside the oak table. She flaked a bit of cooked fish onto a saucer for Crumpet, then took out her blue china teapot and measured tea into it.

"We'll have tea," she said, pouring hot water from the kettle into the teapot, "and while you can tell me what's on your mind, Miss Potter. I must say, you look as if you're disturbed about something."

"I certainly am," Miss Potter said decidedly, sitting back

in her chair. "I have just had a most unfortunate encounter." And without further prompting she related the tale of Miss Crabbe's visit to the Crosfield cottage.

Crumpet, having finished the fish, was washing her paw. She stopped and looked up, startled. *"Jeremy Crosfield, a thief?"* she exclaimed. *"Why, he's the only boy in the village who doesn't pull the animals' tails or throw rocks. He's no thief."*

"Jeremy Crosfield?" Grace asked incredulously. "That's rubbish! He's a very well-behaved child." She picked up the teapot and poured two cups of tea. "Of course," she added, putting the sugar bowl and a small pitcher of milk on the table, "children can surprise us with their mischief, but I shouldn't have expected him to be a *thief.*"

"But his being well-behaved isn't really the point," Miss Potter said. "The point is that Miss Crabbe offered no evidence for her accusation, beyond the fact that the boy had the opportunity to take the money." She dropped two lumps into her tea and stirred it so violently that the tea slopped over into the saucer. "I'm sure she must have been dreadfully upset when she discovered the loss, but that was no excuse for bullying the boy. Jeremy is intelligent and sensitive. He's likely to bear the scar of this for a very long time." She put down her spoon. "We must do whatever is necessary to clear him of suspicion!"

"Bravo!" Crumpet exclaimed. Crumpet's mistress Bertha Stubbs had plenty to say about the erratic behavior of Miss Crabb, whom she considered a "proper dictation, and every inch as revoltin' as the Jar of Russia." And Crumpet had heard a few interesting tales from Max the Manx, who lived with the three Crabbe sisters. Viola and Pansy were eccentric, he said, but reasonable, when you got right down to it. Myrtle, on the other hand—

"Of course we must think of the child," Grace said soothingly. "And you're right, there can be no excuse for that kind of behavior." She sighed. "However, Margaret Nash—she's the other schoolteacher—tells me that Miss Crabbe has been rather more nervous than usual lately, and forgetful. She misplaced her attendance book, and it was only found by accident. In the meantime, there was quite a commotion over it at the school."

"Quite a commotion? That's not the half of it." Crumpet gave a knowing laugh. *"Bertha threatened to hand in her notice if Miss Crabbe didn't apologize for accusing her."*

"You're suggesting that Miss Crabbe herself might have mislaid the money?" Miss Potter asked dubiously.

"It's possible. Perhaps she put it somewhere for safekeeping and simply forgot." Grace got up, put out the roast beef and some cheese and mustard, and began to slice the bread.

"Then what's to be done?" Miss Potter asked, frowning. "My row with her didn't do anything more than stave things off. She says she's going to talk to Constable Braithwaite." She picked up her tea cup. "And you can guess how Jeremy feels. I stayed until his aunt came home and tried to explain the situation to her. She was upset, as well. To them, two pounds is an enormous amount of money."

Grace spread the bread with butter and put the slices on two plates. "I'll speak to Margaret Nash and see what she knows about the situation," she said, thinking out loud. She put the bread and sliced roast beef on the table. "And I'll go up to Castle Cottage after lunch and enlist the aid of Miss Crabbe's sisters. Perhaps you could come with me," she added. "You were there when she accused Jeremy." Grace didn't like to subject Miss Potter to such a trial, but the two Misses Crabbe would prefer to hear Beatrix's story directly from her.

"Castle Cottage—now, there's an idea," Crumpet said approvingly, thinking that she would go along and chat up Max the Manx. Max was a gloomy cat who kept to himself, but he might be willing, if approached nicely, to talk about what was going on at Castle Cottage.

"Her sisters?" Miss Potter asked doubtfully.

"Myrtle Crabbe is the eldest of three. Pansy leads the Sawrey Choral Society, and Viola gives dramatic readings. Both of them are younger than Myrtle, and perhaps a little . . . well, more amiable. They have both been good friends to me, and are very nice, once you get to know them."

"Nice, if a bit bizarre," Crumpet added. The younger Crabbe sisters had a reputation around the village for being rather daft.

"I see," Miss Potter said. "Well, if you think I'd be helpful, I should be glad to go with you." Her smile was less than enthusiastic, and Grace guessed that she did not relish confrontations. "I only hope that the money can be found and Jeremy's name cleared."

"Amen," Crumpet said fervently.

"So do I," Grace said, and added ruefully, "You must find this affair a disagreeable introduction to our little community. I'm sorry you were dragged into it."

"It does rather overturn one's idea of an idyllic, harmonious village," Miss Potter commented wryly.

"That's an idea that needs to be upset," Crumpet remarked, *"and the sooner, the better. A more inharmonious village never existed than Sawrey. There are always rows and discontents and tittle-tattling and—"*

"Crumpet," Grace said sternly, "there is no more fish, so be quiet, please." She poured two more cups of tea. "Now, Miss Potter, tell me about your morning. You said that you did some drawing?"

Miss Potter smiled. "I did indeed. In fact, Jeremy took me to see what he calls a 'whacking great colony' of frogs, above the bridge over Cunsey Beck. I've some very nice sketches to take back to London to work on, and I hope to get more whilst I'm here." She gave a self-deprecating laugh. "Now, if I could only think of a way to take possession of my house! I found myself suggesting to Mrs. Jennings that I might try to obtain Anvil Cottage for them, although I know only too well that I can't afford to rent it for them, much less buy it."

Some time later, their lunch finished, Grace and Miss Potter were preparing to walk up the hill to see the Misses Crabbe, when a horse and a red-wheeled gig drew up in front of Anvil Cottage, across the way, and a man and lady got out. The man was tall and thin, clean-shaven and quite good-looking, with brown hair brushed back and a pleasant smile. The lady was young, scarcely out of her twenties, with an intense expression and an obvious physical vitality. She was dressed in a costume that suggested that she was one of the New Women: a severely tailored plum jacket over a white shirtwaist and a plum-colored skirt, cut quite short and showing an inch of ankle clad in sensible black boots. Her dark hair was coming loose under a small plum-colored hat decorated with two stiff black feathers.

"Why, Mr. Heelis," Grace said with pleasure, as the two came across the lane toward Rose Cottage. "How nice to see you!" Willie Heelis, who was in his middle thirties, was the younger partner in the Hawkshead solicitors' firm of Heelis and Heelis and a frequent visitor to Sawrey. He was a likable man, although painfully shy.

"Good afternoon, Mrs. Lythecoe," Mr. Heelis said, lifting his bowler hat. "I should like to introduce Miss Sarah Barwick, from Manchester." He added, with a little hesitation, "Miss Barwick is the beneficiary of Miss Tolliver's will, and has inherited Anvil Cottage."

Grace caught Miss Potter's quick glance, and knew that she too was remembering the letter from Sarah Barwick they had found the day before, on the table beside Miss Tolliver's chair. She was taken aback by the unexpected announcement of the inheritance, but she smiled nonetheless, and held out her hand.

"Welcome to Sawrey, Miss Barwick," she said. "And congratulations on your inheritance."

"I am glad to meet you, Mrs. Lythecoe," said the young woman, shaking Grace's hand energetically and speaking in a clipped, mannish voice. Her face was too long and narrow for conventional prettiness, her mouth too wide, her expression strained. But her sharp glance was undeniably intelligent. "I understand that you were Miss Tolliver's friend."

"Indeed I was," Grace said, and introduced Miss Potter.

"Miss *Helen* Potter?" Mr. Heelis asked, in some surprise. "The purchaser of Hill Top?"

Miss Potter nodded. "Yes. I was planning to come to your office in the next day or two and introduce myself properly." To Grace, she added, "Mr. Heelis's firm is handling the deed and survey and the purchase documents—all those sorts of legal details. We've exchanged numerous letters, but never met."

"Well, you two will want to get acquainted, then," Grace said, and smiled hospitably. "Shall we all go in and have a cup of tea?"

Miss Barwick was brusque and to the point. "Thank you, but we were wondering if you might open Anvil Cottage for us. Mr. Heelis says that you have the key. And there's something about a painting?"

"Miss Barwick is referring to the Constable miniature, Mrs. Lythecoe," Mr. Heelis added with a shyly apologetic glance, as if feeling the need to explain. "Miss Barwick wondered whether Miss Tolliver might have simply taken it down and put it somewhere, and we hoped you might help us search the cottage. Neither of us have the slightest idea what we're looking for."

"We need to eliminate that possibility, you see," Miss Barwick said, in a businesslike way, "before we bring the police into the matter."

"It was that Roberts fellow," Crumpet put in. *"I—"*

Grace frowned down at the cat. "Crumpet, you're making a nuisance of yourself with all that meowing." She smiled at Miss Barwick. "Of course I'll help look for the painting."

"Perhaps I'd better go on to Belle Green," Miss Potter said, and made as if to leave.

"Oh, no, please," Grace said, putting her hand on Miss Potter's arm. "You're the one who's familiar with the painting. We need you to help us look. And anyway," she added, thinking of their proposed visit to the Crabbe sisters, "we still have our errand at Castle Cottage." She smiled at Miss Barwick. "If you'll excuse me for just a moment, I'll get the key."

She hurried back into the house, took the cottage key off its peg, and picked up Miss Barwick's letter from the hallway table. The four of them went across the way, with Crumpet at their heels. When they went into the cottage, the first thing they saw was Tabitha Twitchit, in her accustomed place in Miss Tolliver's chair.

"I suppose this is Miss Tolliver's cat," Miss Barwick said, in a tone that implied strong disapproval. She sneezed.

"I lived with Miss Tolliver for years," said Tabitha, offended. She switched the tip of her tail. *"Who, pray tell, are you?"*

"You're not going to like it when you hear," Crumpet growled, jumping onto the chair beside Tabitha. *"She's inherited Anvil Cottage. And she is obviously not a lover of cats."*

Tabitha lifted her chin. *"Then she can learn to live with the mice. Let's see how she fancies that."*

"Mathilda Crook has volunteered to take Tabitha," Grace said to Miss Barwick, "unless you'd like to keep her, of course."

"She's a lovely creature," Miss Barwick said in a determined tone, "but I simply cannot tolerate cats. They make me sneeze. Please, Mr. Heelis, be so kind as to put both of them out." She took off her gloves, her hat, and her jacket, as if she were making herself at home.

"You don't have to put me out," Tabitha announced grimly, jumping off the chair and stalking to the door. She was followed by Crumpet, who added, *"I wouldn't stay in this house if you begged me."*

Miss Barwick took a handkerchief out of her purse and blew her nose. "Now, then," she said in a practical tone, tucking her handkerchief into the sleeve of her tailored blouse, "where shall we start? The bedrooms? Mrs. Lythecoe, please lead the way."

It didn't take long to look through the tidy drawers, neat kitchen cupboards, and well-equipped pantry, but after a while, they had to admit defeat. The painting had not been taken down and put somewhere.

"You mentioned in your note," Mr. Heelis remarked to Grace, as they assembled once more in the small sitting room, "that you remember the painting being in its accustomed spot on the wall when you helped Miss Tolliver celebrate her birthday."

"Not exactly," Grace amended. "I said that I would have noticed if it had been gone that day. I think it must have disappeared at some point after that."

"You don't suppose Miss Tolliver might have given it away?" Mr. Heelis asked uncertainly.

"I shouldn't think so," Grace replied. "Anyway, she was discovered dead the morning after her birthday, so there wouldn't have been time. And to whom would she have given it? Certainly none of the villagers."

Miss Barwick, who had been sneezing occasionally during the search, now sneezed again. "Really," she said, in a resigned tone, "one would think from the way my nose is behaving that those cats were still in the room."

"Observant, isn't she?" Tabitha whispered sarcastically to Crumpet, in their hiding place behind the sofa. *"A regular female Sherlock Holmes."*

"Her nose knows," Crumpet said, and giggled.

"I'm afraid, then," Mr. Heelis went on regretfully, "that we must assume that the painting has been stolen."

"Someone from the village, I suppose," Miss Barwick said, and blew her nose. "Is there a policeman?"

"*I keep telling them,*" Crumpet whispered to Tabitha, "*about that fellow Roberts. But of course they don't listen.*"

"*They can't,*" Tabitha said. "*Their ears don't work right.*" She frowned. "*Or maybe it's their brains.*"

"Our policeman is Constable Braithwaite," Grace said slowly. She had suddenly remembered that this was the *third* thing to go missing in the village in the past week or so— the painting, the Parish Register, and the School Roof Fund. "It's hard to think who would have taken it," she added, feeling slightly bewildered. "Everyone loved Miss Tolliver and wouldn't do anything to trouble her. And anyway, none of us had any idea that the painting had any sort of significance or value. I'm sure we all saw it hundreds of times, but no one ever gave it a second look."

During this conversation, Miss Potter had been sitting quietly on the sofa, listening. She coughed deferentially. "Perhaps it would be worthwhile to inquire of the art dealers in the surrounding area. If it has been stolen, someone may try to sell it."

"Then we should have to have a description," Miss Barwick said. She looked at Grace. "Perhaps you could you tell us what the painting looked like, Mrs. Lythecoe."

"I certainly couldn't," Grace replied, "but Miss Potter may be able to. And since she is an artist, perhaps she'd be willing to draw a sketch of it."

"What a good idea!" Mr. Heelis exclaimed heartily. "Do, Miss Potter. It would be such a help."

The three of them turned to Miss Potter. "I suppose I could try," she said with a small smile, "although one feels a bit . . . presumptuous, sketching a Constable." She got up, took her sketchbook from the table where she had left it, and opened it to a blank page, considering for a moment. "There was a hay wain in the right-hand corner," she said, sketching swiftly, "and a large tree—a copper beech. And a small, grassy stream in the foreground, with three or four white sheep on the bank. And white clouds piled against a blue sky, so."

"And the size of the painting?" Miss Barwick asked.

"The canvas was no larger than three inches by four," Miss Potter replied. "It was matted with—I think—green paper, and not a very nice shade of green at that. And of course, there was the usual gilt frame, rather ornate. Although if it's been stolen, the thief may very well have taken it out of the frame." She took the page out of the sketchbook and handed it to Mr. Heelis. "I hope this may be of some help."

Mr. Heelis looked down admiringly at the drawing. "I must say, Miss Potter, you have a first-rate eye."

"And an excellent memory for detail," Grace added.

"Thank you, Miss Potter," Miss Barwick said, in a friend-lier tone than Grace had heard her use so far.

"You're very welcome," Miss Potter said, closing her sketchbook. She looked curiously at Mr. Heelis. "What will you do with the sketch?"

"I like your idea of taking it to art dealers. I am going to Ambleside tomorrow, and I shall drop in on a man I know there. He has a small shop—mostly local artists, of course, but I'm sure he's familiar with Constable. Perhaps he can make a suggestion or two, and help us put out the word to other dealers."

Miss Potter cocked her head to one side. "If you're going to Ambleside," she said, "I wonder if I might go along. Three acquaintances of mine, the Armitt sisters, live at Rydal, and I promised to spend a day with them. I'm sure I can find my own way back."

"I'd be glad of the company," Mr. Heelis replied. "I was

planning to leave at nine, if that's not too early, and I shall drive over and pick you up. You're staying at Hill Top?"

"At Belle Green, with the Crooks," Miss Potter said. Her shy smile lightened her blue eyes and made her almost pretty, Grace thought. "I am very grateful."

Mr. Heelis turned to Miss Barwick. "Before we go back to Hawkshead, it might be a good idea to speak to Constable Braithwaite about the missing painting." He gave her a lop-sided smile. "This is not a very pleasant introduction to your new cottage, I'm afraid."

"It's something that has to be settled, one way or another," Miss Barwick said pragmatically. She glanced around. "It is quite a homey place, isn't it? I think Miss Tolliver must have been very happy here—at least, she seemed so, in her letters."

"You didn't visit her here, then?" Miss Potter asked.

"No, I didn't," Miss Barwick replied, with a little shrug of her shoulders. "In fact, I didn't know her at all until we began corresponding a year or so ago."

Grace tried not to show her surprise at that bit of news. "Do you plan to live here?" she asked. "I daresay the question sounds inquisitive," she added hastily. "But this is a small village, and all the neighbors are anxious to know what's to become of the cottage."

"I'm sure they are," Miss Barwick said crisply. "To answer your question, Mrs. Lythecoe, yes, I do intend to live here. I had my doubts when I first learnt of the bequest, since I've lived most of my life in Manchester. But now that I've seen the cottage and have had a glimpse of the village, I must say it looks an ideal place for the business I have in mind. My father died not long ago, you see, and it seems a good time to start over." She picked up her jacket. "If we're going to speak to the constable about the painting, Mr. Heelis, p'rhaps we had better go."

Grace was burning to know what sort of business this young woman was referring to. The cottage had no land and only a small garden. There was a pub across the road—the Tower Bank Arms—and the village shop was only a step away, so she couldn't be thinking of opening a pub or a shop. What else did she imagine would be profitable in a village as small as Sawrey?

But Grace had learnt a long time ago, as the vicar's wife, to curb her curiosity. She handed Miss Barwick the key. "Here," she said. "This is yours."

Miss Barwick took it. "Thank you," she said. "I'll be back in the morning. I'm expecting to spend a few days here, getting acquainted with the cottage and the village—and with my benefactress, as well." Her voice seemed to soften. "There is a great deal I don't know about Miss Tolliver. I'm hoping you will be able to tell me."

Grace regarded her thoughtfully. She still could not imagine who Miss Barwick was, or why Miss Tolliver had given her cottage to this stranger, whom she had never met. But these were mysteries to be unraveled later.

"I'll do my best," she said, "although Abigail Tolliver was a very private person. All of us in the village loved and respected her, and some of the older ones knew her for the entire course of her lifetime. But I'm not sure that anyone knew her very well." She took something out of her pocket and held it out.

"This letter is yours," she went on. "Miss Potter and I found it lying on the table next to the chair in which Miss Tolliver died. In fact, she may have been reading it when she died. I took it home with me, intending to write, in case you hadn't heard. I didn't read it," she added reassuringly. "I only intended to copy the address."

"It wouldn't have mattered if you had," Miss Barwick said, taking the letter. "It's nothing very secret—just about my dad dying." She sneezed again. "I'm afraid that my first order of business," she added, blowing her nose, "is a good housecleaning. The place must be full of cat fur."

"I wonder," Tabitha said to Crumpet, very quietly, *"how this person feels about mice. I'm thinking of arranging a small present or two, strategically placed."* She smiled, showing her teeth. *"In her tea cup, for instance. Or in the milk jug, or on her pillow."*

Crumpet chuckled, imagining the effect such interesting gifts might have on Miss Barwick's composure. She leaned closer and said, into Tabitha's ear, *"I'm going up to Castle Cottage to have a bit of a chat with Max the Manx. Want to come along?"*

"No, thanks," Tabitha said, folding her paws. *"As soon as that woman is out of here, I'm going to run upstairs and shed fur all over the bed."*

15

✧❦✦

True Love

Despite the magpie's dire prediction, Miss Potter's animals—tourists though they certainly were—encountered no serious dangers in the field beyond Belle Green's back garden. They spent a delightful morning foraging in the drowsy meadow and orchard. The warm October sunlight lay like a golden mantle over the grass, its gentle rays lighting the brown and orange wings of the Wood Tiger moths that clung to the fuzzy blossoms of hemp agrimony. The orchard buzzed and hummed and droned as if it were alive—as it was, alive with drunken insects feasting in giddy pleasure on the wine-sweet apples that lay fermenting in the grass.

Mrs. Tiggy-Winkle was the first to make her way back to the hutch. After several hours of blissful snacking, she waddled back across the meadow, through the hedge, and under the loose netting flap. Her large meal had made her quite sleepy, so she rolled herself into a snug little ball, covered her head with her pocket handkerchief to keep out the light, and fell fast asleep. Since hedgehogs are known to nap for weeks at a time, and since Mrs. Tig had not enjoyed a good, sound sleep for quite a while, it was not likely that the others would wake her as they returned.

Mopsy and Josey were the next to come back to the hutch. Mopsy seemed to have lost a little of her fear, although she still cast nervous glances over her shoulder, as if expecting to be attacked by a panther or a bear. She kept close to Josey, too, relying on the larger rabbit's greater strength and confidence.

Josey, for her part, was somewhat more vigilant than she had been when she started out, for she had caught a glimpse of an immense crow flying overhead, his shadow like an ominous finger moving across the land. She knew herself to be brave, but she was not foolhardy, and she had a proper respect for crows, who might dive down and peck out rabbits' eyes. When she saw the shadow, she had pulled Mopsy under the shelter of a stone fence, where the two huddled until the danger was past.

But that had been a momentary alarm, and both rabbits were in fine spirits when they returned to the hutch, having feasted on wild clover, sainfoin, and dandelion blossoms, with a bit of thyme and self-heal for dessert. They found Mrs. Tiggy-Winkle fast asleep and knew better than to try to rouse her.

"*I feel drowsy myself,*" Mopsy said, her ears drooping. "*I'm full of clover. And anyway, it is very tiring for the nerves, being constantly on the alert for things that might snap at one's ears or tail. I think I'll have a little nap.*" And suiting the action to the word, she curled up beside the hedgehog and fell fast asleep.

Josey looked around. Three of them had safely returned, but where was Tom? She glanced up at the sun, thinking that it must be after two o'clock. Miss Potter would be back before long, and she would come straightaway to check the hutch. She was fond of Tom, and would be upset if she returned to find him gone. What was more, she would likely discover and repair the loose netting, and then they'd never have another lovely holiday like this one.

So Josey ducked out of the hutch and set off for the haystack, where she had last glimpsed Tom, sharing a bit of grain with a field mouse with velvety gray ears, pretty white whiskers, and a very long tail. She should have to fetch him back home.

But Tom was not in a mood to return. *"What?"* he exclaimed, when Josey found him at last, sitting just outside the opening of a cozy-looking mouse house on the sunny side of the haystack. *"Go back to the hutch? Never!"* He put a proprietary paw on his companion's shoulder. *"This is Teasel. She's the most beautiful mouse I've ever seen. She and I are engaged."*

Josey was nonplussed. She had thought it would be good for Tom to get out into the open and get some exercise, and she had used the little female mouse as bait to lure him out of the hutch. But she had never imagined that he might fancy himself in love and refuse to go back home!

"But what about Hunca Munca?" she asked finally. *"I thought you had vowed to be true to her forever and ever."*

Teasel turned to Tom, her eyes narrowing. *"Who is Hunca Munca?"*

"Tom's wife," Josey replied.

"Your wife!" Teasel squeaked, jumping up. *"But you told me you weren't married!"*

"I'm a widower," Tom said. *"My dear Hunca Munca died last July. She was quite acrobatic, you see. She fell off a chandelier and broke her neck."* His eyes brimmed and a big fat tear ran down his cheek. *"I've been terribly lonely ever since I lost her. And then I met you, Teasel. You've filled the empty place in my heart. It's true love, that's what it is. True love."*

Teasel, although appeased, looked warily at Josey. *"Is it*

true that his wife is dead? My mother told me never to have any-thing to do with a married mouse."

"It's true," Josey conceded, feeling bound to tell the truth.

"*Well, I suppose that's all right, then.*" Teasel smiled pertly and rubbed her two white paws together, glancing at Tom under her long lashes. "*I must say, it will be ever so nice to have a town mouse for a husband. Before I met Tom, I was engaged to a common field mouse named Acorn. Tom seems more sophisticated—a mouse of the world.*"

Josey was a clever rabbit. Seeing a possible opening, she said, "*I'm sure you do see a difference, Teasel. Compared to country mice, Tom is quite well traveled, and cultured, too. He has accompanied Miss Potter to Scotland and Wales, and to any number of resorts in the south of England. And when we are at home in London, there are musical entertainments, and readings-aloud, and games.*"

Teasel looked worried. "*I hope you won't be dull here in the village, Tom. There's not much opportunity for travel, unless you hop into the baker's basket and ride over to Hawkshead. And the only musical entertainments are the fairy dances in the oak woods on Midsummer's Eve, and the Big Folks' country-dancing at the Tower Bank Arms. But we have animal shows,*" she added with greater enthusiasm, "*and there's always an egg-rolling on Easter Monday, and a jolly great bonfire on Guy Fawkes Night.*"

"*Animal shows, egg-rollings, and bonfires,*" said Josey, with a sidelong glance at Tom. "*A world of fun, I'm sure.*"

"*Oh, I'll be all right,*" Tom said with a careless smile, "*as long as there's plenty to eat. I'm especially fond of calves' foot jelly, Teasel. And a meal isn't complete without a thimbleful of wine. And of course, I do enjoy dressing for dinner. White tie and tail,*" he said, looking proudly at his own, which was very long and white.

"*Oh, dear,*" said Teasel apprehensively, "*I think the calves in the barn would be terribly upset if someone suggested making jelly out of their feet. But there's plenty of corn to eat, and we have oats for breakfast every day, and sometimes a bit of cheese, if the dairy is left unattended. And there are turnips and dried peas and—"*

"*I don't like turnips,*" said Tom, frowning, "*and I prefer green peas to dried. And what about wine? I am quite fond of fine French champagne.*"

Teasel looked doubtful. "*We have elderberry wine, of course, and dandelion wine, and cider, but—*"

"*And dressing for dinner?*" Tom persisted. "*I am really quite accustomed to that, my dear Teasel. Hunca Munca had a delightful blue silk dress with a white lace ruffle and ribbons, which once belonged to a doll named Lucinda.*" His eyes took on a far-away look. "*I loved to see her wear it. So stylish, she was.*"

Teasel looked down, her pretty ears suffused by a pink blush. "*I'm afraid I don't have a dress, Tom. Clothing does rather get in the way out here in the country. When you're running from owls, you see, it's much better to be unencumbered.*"

"*Owls?*" Tom cried, scanning the skies anxiously.

Teasel held up one paw. "*Don't speak so loudly, please! They don't often come during the day, but one never knows.*"

"*No one said anything to me about owls,*" Tom snapped. "*You might have mentioned it before we got engaged.*"

Teasel stared at him. "*I just didn't think. Acorn never seemed to be afraid of—*" The rest of her sentence was drowned out by a loud mooing from a barn not far away.

"*What's that?*" Tom cried, his whiskers twitching in fright. "*What's that noise?*"

"*It's just the cow,*" Teasel said in a comforting tone. "*You don't need to be afraid of Honeysuckle, Tom. She's harmless, unless she happens to step on you.*"

Tom was by now quite pale, and his voice was high and thin. "*Are there any other dangers I should be aware of?*"

"*Well,*" Teasel replied reluctantly, "*there's the stoat, of course. We always have to be on the lookout for him. And the hay harvester's sharp scythe, which cut off my father's tail, and—*"

"*I wonder,*" Josey said thoughtfully, "*whether you have considered asking Teasel to come and live with you, Tom. That would be rather nice, don't you think? And I'm sure Miss Potter wouldn't mind."*

Tom brightened. *"Why didn't I think of that? Come on, Teasel!"*

"Where?" Teasel asked, bewildered.

"To a wonderful place where you'll have the very best food, and wine with dinner, and a dry place to sleep," Tom replied. *"And best of all, there are no owls, or scythes, or stoats. Come on!"* And with that, he scampered off across the meadow in the direction of Belle Green.

Teasel stood still, looking after him. *"What do you think?"* she asked Josey, in a hesitant tone. *"Should I go with him?"*

"Do you love him?" Josey asked. She herself had never loved anyone, other than Miss Potter, that is, and did not feel quite equal to giving advice.

"I . . . I think so," Teasel said, looking a bit unsure. *"It was all very sudden, though. Tom rather swept me off my feet, and I didn't have time to tell Acorn that I was breaking our engagement."*

"Well, if it's true love, I suppose you should go with him," Josey said. *"And if you're going, now's the time. We must get back in the hutch before Miss Potter returns."* And she started off after Tom.

"Who is Miss Potter?" asked Teasel, running to catch up.

"You'll see," Josey said. *"You'll like her, I'm sure. She's kind, and she takes very good care of us."*

The rabbit felt quite proud of herself for having the presence of mind to fetch Tom, so that their exit would not be discovered. It wasn't until they got back to the hutch that she realized that when Miss Potter saw *two* mice instead of just one, she would look for the way Teasel had got in. She would quickly discover the way they had gotten out.

But Josey was quite clever indeed, and in a few minutes, she had taken care of the situation—or at least, so she hoped.

16

Behind the Walls of Castle Cottage

Beatrix and Mrs. Lythecoe left Anvil Cottage and walked up the lane in the direction of Castle Cottage, which sat on the hill above the post office. They went along in silence for a moment, until Mrs. Lythecoe said, "Well, Miss Potter, what do you think of Miss Barwick?"

Unaccustomed to being asked to frankly express an opinion about another person, Beatrix hesitated. "I rather like her," she said finally. "Some might think her a bit brusque, but I admire a woman who is firm in her judgements. And she is certainly direct—no beating about the bush." Directness was something that Beatrix valued a great deal. She had never seen any purpose in saying things just because another person wanted to hear them—which accounted for her habitual silence in Bolton Gardens, where she could not say the things that her mother and father expected to hear, and where anything she did say was more likely than not to be taken as impertinent.

"I liked her, too," Mrs. Lythecoe said, and chuckled. "A no-nonsense sort of person, isn't she? I wonder how George Crook will take that short skirt. She'll be a bit modern for his taste, I suspect." Her chuckle became a laugh. "First a lady farmer, and now a woman who displays her ankles. What's the world coming to?"

Beatrix, imagining the expression on George Crook's face when he saw Sarah Barwick's short skirt, had to join the laughter. After a moment, she said, "I wonder what sort of business she means to operate. Do you suppose she's a seamstress, or perhaps a milliner?"

"Oh, I *hope* not," Mrs. Lythecoe replied, raising her eyebrows. "Most of the Sawrey ladies sew for themselves and their children, and they certainly don't go in for high fashion. As for hats, there's a perfectly good shop in Hawkshead. If that's the sort of thing Miss Barwick has in mind, she'll be greatly disappointed, I fear." She paused, and added, almost to herself, "And I do wonder about her connection to Miss Tolliver. She's obviously not a relative, and only a recent correspondent, apparently. And it seems they've never met. So how in the world did she come to inherit Anvil Cottage?"

Beatrix, having no answer to that, looked up to see where they were going. They had left Market Street and were walking up a narrow private lane, approaching a foursquare eighteenth-century house that was rather in need of repair and repainting. It was built in the same style as the farm house at Hill Top, with a slate roof, gray walls, and peaked porch. It sat against the green hillside, overlooking a tangle of overgrown garden and the Post Office meadow. Beyond, Beatrix could see the Tower Bank Arms and the roof of Hill Top Farm.

"It's a pretty house," she said, "or it would be, if it were better taken care of. Have the Crabbe sisters lived here long?" Beatrix, who usually went out of her way to avoid an argument, was more than a little apprehensive about the meeting. If Viola and Pansy proved to be anything like their sister, the encounter might be unpleasant.

"They came here when they were young women," Mrs. Lythecoe said. "The farm belonged in their father's family, I believe. The pastures are let to the neighboring farmers now, and the barns, too. It's quite a lovely place, although the garden has gone rather wild, as you can see. None of the sisters care to garden." She smiled. "You'll like Pansy and Viola, I think, although both are a bit . . . well, eccentric. I enjoy them, though, and count them among my friends."

They had reached the house, and Beatrix stood aside as Mrs. Lythecoe raised the brass knocker and dropped it. After a moment, the door was opened by a young girl in a dark cotton dress and white ruffled apron. She bobbed a curtsey, with a mumbled "G' afternoon, mum."

"Good afternoon, Laura," Mrs. Lythecoe said cheerfully. "Please tell your mistresses that Mrs. Lythecoe has come calling, with their new neighbor from Hill Top Farm." She stepped in. "We'll show ourselves into the sitting room, thank you."

The small sitting room was crowded with a piano, a dark green settee, three overstuffed chairs filled with bright-colored cushions, several tables cluttered with photographs and bric-a-brac, and two large potted palms. In a few moments, an apparition darkened the door, a short, round woman of perhaps fifty, her yellow hair curled in massive ringlets in what had to be (Beatrix thought in some amazement) a blonde wig. Her substantial bulk was loosely swathed in a chiffon tea gown of an astonishing chartreuse color, and beneath its flowing sleeves, her plump arms were covered, wrist to elbow, with jingling bangles. She wore a gold pince-nez on a ribbon around her neck.

"Why, Grace!" she cried. "So delighted!" She raised her

voice and shouted over her shoulder. "Viola! Guests!" She came forward, lifting her pince-nez to peer at Beatrix. "And who, may one ask, is this?"

"This is Miss Beatrix Potter," Mrs. Lythecoe said. "She is the author and illustrator of a number of very fine children's books. She has just purchased Hill Top Farm. Miss Potter, allow me to present Miss Pansy Crabbe."

Beatrix found herself seated on the slippery horsehair settee, very like the one in her mother's drawing room. She allowed her attention to wander as Mrs. Lythecoe and Miss Crabbe chatted amiably about village matters. In a few moments, out in the hall, there was a clatter and rattle, and the maid wheeled a tea tray into the room, followed by the second Crabbe sister.

Where Miss Pansy was short and round and soft as a suet dumpling, Miss Viola was thin and willowy, with very white hands and long, polished nails, and she moved with an exaggeratedly graceful motion. She wore a heavy oriental kimono of black china silk covered with gold-colored figures of peacocks and tied with a gold silk sash. Her hair was dead black, parted in the center, and drawn dramatically back from her face and secured in a chignon at the back of her neck. Her lips had been rouged and her dark eyes, very large, sparkled brilliantly in her pale face. Beatrix remembered that she was accustomed to give dramatic readings, and thought that she certainly looked the part.

"We are *so* very glad to meet the new owner of Hill Top Farm," Miss Viola said in a shrill soprano voice. She poured tea into porcelain cups and handed them round. "Our windows look down to your orchard, you know, Miss Potter. We can see the village children raiding your apple trees."

Taking the proffered cup, Beatrix glanced toward the partly raised sash window, curious to see what her orchard might look like from this height, and wondering which trees the children raided. She could see little, however, except for an untidy tangle of vines and the shadow of a black cat sitting placidly on the outer sill.

"It's a pity our sister Myrtle isn't here," Miss Pansy said, settling her large, round self comfortably into her chair. "She will want very much to meet you, Miss Potter—especially since you write for children. She is a teacher, and the head-mistress of Sawrey School."

"Yes," Beatrix said. "In fact, I have met her, briefly." She looked to Mrs. Lythecoe for a cue as to how to go on.

"That, I am afraid," Mrs. Lythecoe said, "is the real reason we have come." She put down her teacup and sat forward. "This is all rather awkward, and I am very sorry for it. However, both Miss Potter and I feel that you need to know what has happened, and give us your advice." She glanced at Beatrix. "Miss Potter, could you tell them about your meeting with Miss Crabbe, please?"

Feeling wretchedly uncomfortable, Beatrix put down her cup and related what had happened at the Crosfield cottage that morning. When she finished, there was a long silence.

Outside, Crumpet, sitting under the window, looked up at Max the Manx, on the windowsill. "You see?" she said in a low voice. "What did I tell you?"

"Not good," Max growled, deep in his throat. He was a solid, stocky all-black cat, with a noticeable absence of tail, a trait that was shared by most Manx, caused (as Max himself was fond of explaining) by Noah himself, who shut the ancestral tail in the door of the ark. Max was also rather a pessimist. "Not good at all," he repeated morosely. "But there's nothing to be done. Miss Myrtle is quarrelsome, you know. She does just what she wants, and Lord help everyone else."

"There's many a slip twixt does and will do," Crumpet said enigmatically. "We have to find a way to stop her from going to the constable."

Inside the room, there was shock and consternation. "Oh, dear!" Miss Pansy exclaimed in distress, raising a plump hand to her round mouth. "Oh, dear, dear, *dear*!" The yellow curls trembled all over her head.

Miss Viola's eyes grew larger and darker. "I am appalled, Miss Potter," she said, her reedy voice quavering. "I scarcely know what to say, except that I'm sure that our Myrtle wouldn't have behaved in such a disgraceful fashion if she hadn't been under a terrible strain. Please accept our apologies." With a dramatic flourish, she put her hand in the region of her heart and pressed. "Our most *heartfelt* apologies."

Beatrix relaxed a little. "There is no need for apology," she said. At least they weren't going to blame her for what had occurred.

"We were sure," Mrs. Lythecoe said, "that you would want to know. And to tell the truth, we hoped that perhaps you might agree to . . . well, help us keep Myrtle from carrying out her plan."

"Her plan to go to the constable, you mean?" Miss Viola asked. Her rouged lips were tight and puckered, as if she were tasting something tart.

Beatrix nodded. "If there were only some proof, even a little scrap, no one could object. But there seems to be none, other than your sister's feeling that the boy is guilty."

Miss Viola sat up straighter. "And Myrtle's feelings," she said, "can no longer be relied upon." She turned to her sister, and her voice became tinged with bitterness. "We must acknowledge that, Pansy. Sadly, we must acknowledge *that*."

"Oh, but, Viola," Miss Pansy cried, anxiously fluttering a chartreuse sleeve, "don't you think you are stating the matter too harshly? Myrtle has always been such a forceful person, so firm of spirit."

"But it is her *forcefulness* that makes these episodes so very difficult!" Miss Viola said. "Both of us love her, Pansy, but this is getting entirely out of hand." She turned back to Beatrix, a pained expression on her pale face. "These are private family matters, and you may feel that we should not discuss them with a stranger such as yourself, Miss Potter. But our sister has already involved you in her affairs—most unfortunately, of course, but there it is. I feel you are owed the whole truth." *Whether you like it,* her tone implied, *or not.* "And of course, Grace is the widow of our own beloved vicar, and is a trusted friend. We know that both of you will respect our confidences."

Beatrix, taken aback and not at all sure that she wanted to hear any more of this unpleasant truth, whatever it was, gave a murmur that might be taken as assent. Mrs. Lythecoe said quietly, "Of course, Viola."

Outside, Crumpet leapt up to join Max on the windowsill, so she could hear a bit more clearly. *"The whole truth?"* she said to Max. *"There's more to this situation than meets the eye, I suppose."*

"You don't want to know, Crumpet," Max replied in a gloomy voice. *"Things have gone on in this house that would curl your whiskers."*

"But Viola," Pansy protested, "I don't really think—"

Miss Viola turned back to her sister. "Please recall if you will, Pansy, the scandalous scene last month over the money she thought she had left out to pay the baker's boy. And then there was the unnerving disagreement over what happened to the gold locket that dear Aunt Adrienne gave you, which is yet to be found." She dropped her voice to a throaty whisper. "And Myrtle's diary, of course. What a dreadful debacle!"

"Ah, the diary," Max said, with a heavy sigh. *"Accusations and recriminations and denouncements. You'd have thought that it was as valuable as the crown jewels, the way she went on."*

Intrigued, Beatrix looked from one of these oddly paired sisters to the other, feeling that there must be a fascinating story behind the oblique references to money and lockets and diaries. Obviously, something unsettling was happening behind the walls of Castle Cottage, and the sisters were deeply troubled by it.

Miss Pansy sighed heavily, her round face a mass of misery. "Yes, the diary. Most unfortunate. And all too reminiscent of Dear Mama's irrational behavior. Oh, Viola, I do hope we are not going to have to go through *that* again! That would be too dreadfully appalling!"

"We won't go into that just now, Pansy," Miss Viola said in a warning tone, and Beatrix understood that there were still more secrets, and darker ones. She had the feeling that Viola, at least, was afraid. But of what? Not of their sister, surely.

"*Irrational behavior?*" Crumpet asked. "*They're talking about their mother? What was wrong with her?*"

"*In the last year of her life,*" Max replied, "*old Mrs. Crabbe was as mad as a March hare. She actually tried to kill Myrtle. Of course, they made out that it was an accident—although how you can accidentally hit someone over the head with an iron skillet is beyond my powers of comprehension. Anyway, Myrtle took Mrs. Crabbe up to Carlisle and put her into a hospital—a lunatic asylum. She died the next year, stark, raving mad.*" Max glanced darkly at Crumpet. "*There. I told you it would curl your whiskers.*"

"*For pity's sake,*" Crumpet marveled, astonished by these sensational revelations. She flicked her tail. "*All this was going on, and the sisters managed to keep it a secret—in this village?*"

"*They brought a girl up from London to see to the house,*" Max said, "*and when Mrs. Crabbe got worse, they sent her back to the city and took on the work themselves. When the old lady was safely in the asylum, they told everyone she had gone to visit her sister, and continued with their lives just as if nothing had happened. It was Myrtle who made them keep it a secret. She was determined that the truth wouldn't get out.*"

"*And now it sounds as if the other two fear for her state of mind,*" Crumpet commented.

"*As well they might,*" Max said ominously. "*As well they*

might. You have no idea what it's like around here, Crumpet."

Inside, the conversation was continuing. "The worst of it is," Miss Viola said with a dramatic gesture, "that these episodes are no longer confined within the family. Myrtle accused Bertha Stubbs of taking her attendance book, and involved Margaret Nash in the disagreement as well. And there was her unfortunate quarrel with Abigail Tolliver over the letter. And now this business about the Roof Fund." She shook her head despairingly. "Two pounds! I suppose there will have to be an investigation of some sort."

Beatrix frowned. Beside her, Grace Lythecoe stiffened. "A quarrel with Abigail?"

Miss Pansy's ample bosom rose and fell in a heavy sigh. "Myrtle decided to have a change of scene for herself, Grace. A warmer climate, where there are not so many annoyances, including her sisters." She pushed back a lock of yellow hair that had fallen across her cheek. "I rather think she would be glad to be rid of us, actually. She planned to make application to a school near Bournemouth, and went so far as to inquire of the school council there. But—"

"But Miss Tolliver apparently refused to sign the reference letter after Myrtle had prepared it for her," Miss Viola said, cutting the story short. She put her cup down and straightened, her expression dark. "Miss Tolliver said that she did not feel that Myrtle's health was up to it. Myrtle has been . . . quite upset about the matter."

"What you're telling us," Mrs. Lythecoe said quietly, "is that what happened with Miss Potter this morning is not an isolated affair."

"Yes," Miss Viola replied, with theatrical huskiness. "That's exactly what we're saying, Grace. Things are progressing from bad to worse, and very quickly, too."

"We're at our wits' end," Miss Pansy said desperately. "We've tried reasoning with her—"

"—appealing to her better nature—"

"—reminding her of her position at the school and in the village—"

"But none of it seems to help," Miss Viola concluded, with a dramatic sigh. Her hands fluttered into her black silk lap. "We have tried to be gentle and considerate, but when we raise even the smallest question, she complains that we are undermining her authority. As Pansy has said, we're at our wits' end. She pays no attention to us at all."

"That's because she knows they're afraid of her," Max said sourly. *"She's the eldest, and she's always had the upper hand. Can you imagine three spinster sisters living together in one house their whole lives, their mother gone mad, and now their sister, mad herself and driving them mad?"* He gave a bitter, sardonic laugh. *"Driving me mad, too, come to that. I tell you, Crumpet, it's all going to the very devil."*

"This is getting serious," Crumpet said. *"Somebody needs to do something before everything goes to wrack and ruin. But what should we do?"*

"What indeed?" Max raised his voice querulously. *"You're welcome to make all the suggestions you like, but personally, I think we'd be wasting our time. It has not been my experience that—"*

"Max!" Miss Viola said sharply, getting up to shut the window. "Our dear old Manx is a delightful companion," she said, returning to her chair, "but it's always distracting when he decides to join the conversation." She went back to the subject. "Pansy and I will speak to Myrtle as soon as she comes home from school this evening. But we cannot promise that we will be able to keep her from going to Constable Braithwaite, if that's what she intends to do."

"Perhaps," Beatrix suggested, "Mrs. Lythecoe and I should speak with the constable first. Then he would at least be . . . well, prepared."

"That is an exceedingly sensible idea, Miss Potter," Miss Viola said, inclining her head. "By all means, do speak to the constable. And we'll do what we can here, of course."

Mrs. Lythecoe rose. "I think, Miss Potter, it is time for us to be going."

"Thank you for the tea," Beatrix said, standing. She held out her hand. "I enjoyed meeting you both, very much."

"And we enjoyed meeting you," Miss Pansy cried, fluttering her sleeves so that she looked for all the world, Beatrix thought, like an oversize green moth. "Perhaps next time, you'll bring one or two of your books."

"Oh, do, please do!" trilled Miss Viola. "I could give a reading from them for the children!"

Beatrix smiled and nodded, but she was thinking that Miss Viola's black kimono and snugged-back hair were scarcely appropriate to a reading of *Peter Rabbit*.

As they walked down the lane to Market Street, Mrs. Lythecoe said to Beatrix, "My dear Miss Potter, I must compliment you. You handled that situation splendidly."

"Thank you," Beatrix said. "I found it . . . difficult." She shook her head, remembering her earlier idea that the village was quiet and peaceful, which now struck her as naive. The three Misses Crabbe, hidden behind the gray walls of their Castle Cottage, certainly appeared to lead dramatic lives. There was also a mystery about Miss Tolliver and her connection to Miss Barwick. And the missing painting, and the lost Parish Register, not to mention the Roof Fund. Mysteries upon mysteries. "I suppose," she added, "we should go and find the constable now, before Miss Crabbe finishes with school for the day."

Mrs. Lythecoe took her arm. "We won't have far to look," she said. "Here he comes, with Captain Woodcock. The captain is our Justice of the Peace, you know—Dimity Woodcock's brother, and entirely dependable. We can talk about this matter in front of him."

The captain, Beatrix noticed with some curiosity, was a slender, brown-haired man in his forties, dressed in gray tweeds of an admirable cut and wearing a jaunty gray fedora with a cockade of red feathers. His hazel eyes were sharp and penetrating and Beatrix imagined that they might be cold, under the right circumstances. But his voice was soft and his pleasant smile warmly reminiscent of his sister's. She felt immediately comfortable with him.

Constable Braithwaite was short and stocky, with a florid complexion and hair and eyebrows so blond they were nearly white. He wore a blue serge uniform with polished brass buttons and a tall constable's hat fastened with a chinstrap. There was no one else about, so the four of them stood in the lane as Mrs. Lythecoe introduced Beatrix and outlined their problem. Beatrix then explained, in as economical and nonjudgmental fashion as possible, what had happened at Willow Cottage that morning.

Captain Woodcock was the first to speak. "You say she offered no evidence that the boy was involved in the theft, Miss Potter?"

"If Miss Crabbe's accusation was based on anything other than opportunity," Beatrix replied carefully, "she did not say what it was."

"I see," said the captain, his appraising glance resting on Beatrix in a way that made her color.

"This comes on the heels," Mrs. Lythecoe said, "of several other . . . difficulties. One would prefer not to go into the details, of course, but Miss Crabbe seems not to be quite . . . well, quite herself lately."

The captain nodded sympathetically and, Beatrix thought, as if he were already aware of the situation. "I think, Constable," he said, "that you should take these things into consideration. If Miss Crabbe comes to speak to you about it, that is. Otherwise, p'rhaps it's just as well to leave it alone. She may think better of the accusation."

"I take thi meanin', sir," said the constable.

"And I think," the captain added, "that I shall drop in at the school and have a bit of a chat with Miss Nash. Some sort of effort must be made toward recovering the money, of course."

"Exactly, sir," said the constable. He glanced at Beatrix, and a smile crinkled at the corners of his eyes. "And doan't fash thasel, Miss. If I speak to t' boy, I'll deal gently with him." He paused, looking from one to the other. "Tha'rt t' ladies who discovered t' painting missin'?"

"So Mr. Heelis and Miss Barwick found you," Mrs. Lythecoe said.

"Aye, and reported that a val'able painting is gone out of Anvil Cottage." The constable shook his head. "Doan't know what t' world's comin' to," he muttered darkly. "Two quid nipped from the school, a painting gone from Anvil Cottage, and talk of poison."

"And there's also the missing Parish Register," Beatrix remarked thoughtfully.

Captain Woodcock gave her a sharp look. "The Register? Missing from the church?"

Mrs. Lythecoe explained. "It's a minor puzzle, of course," she added, "compared to the others. And I doubt it's connected."

"I don't think we can be sure of that," Beatrix heard herself say, rather to her own surprise. She was not accustomed to disagreeing. At the captain's "Yes?" and Mrs. Lythecoe's inquiring glance, she added, apologetically, "I only mean that the idea of a connection should perhaps not be quickly discarded. The village is so small, and everything and everyone in it all seem related. Perhaps it's best not to leave out a piece of the puzzle, however insignificant."

"I daresay you're right, Miss Potter," the captain said thoughtfully. "I'll speak to the vicar about it."

Mrs. Lythecoe turned back to the constable. "You mentioned poison. That *is* only idle talk, isn't it? There's nothing at all to it, I hope."

The constable glanced at the captain, who nodded

shortly, almost as if, Beatrix thought, he were giving permission.

"O' course it's only talk," the constable said in a comforting tone. "Dr. Butters says she died of nobbut her heart. His word is good enough for me, and for most folk. But tha's lived in this village long enough to know that for some, when a thing is said, it's as good as *did*."

"And the worst thing about talk," Captain Woodcock said quietly, "is that there's no way to lay it to rest. Every fresh breeze brings a new speculation."

"Yes, that's the pity," Mrs. Lythecoe said, and sighed. "So we'll just have to wait it out."

"So it seems," said the captain, and lifted his hat courteously. "Good afternoon, ladies."

A moment later, Beatrix and Mrs. Lythecoe had reached Belle Green. "I'll leave you here," Beatrix said. "Mrs. Crook must be wondering what's become of me. I left early this morning, with a promise to be back for lunch, and now it's nearly time for tea."

"Thank you for all your help, my dear." Mrs. Lythecoe leaned forward and gave Beatrix an unexpected kiss on the cheek. "You have a very sound head on your shoulders, as my dear husband would have said. I have the suspicion that you're going to make an important contribution to life here in Sawrey."

"Thank you," Beatrix said, surprised and deeply touched. "It's very kind of you to say so. I hope I shall be able to—"

"Miss Potter!" a woman called. Beatrix looked up to see Lucy Skead, the postmistress, hurrying toward them. "Oh, Miss Potter," she cried again, "I'm so glad I've caught you." She held up a yellow envelope. "It's a telegram. From London!"

With a sinking heart, Beatrix thanked Lucy and took the telegram. She didn't have to open it to guess what was in it.

17

Miss Nash Shares a Problem

Margaret Nash had been a teacher at Sawrey School for nearly ten years, and in all that long time, she could not remember a more trying day. With Bertha Stubbs gone, she'd had to add sweeping and carrying water and coal to her morning duties, but those were minor difficulties in comparison to her dealings with Miss Crabbe.

After the anguished discovery of the missing money and the noisy departure of Bertha Stubbs, the two teachers had taken their morning classes as usual. It had not been "as usual," of course, where Margaret was concerned, for she had carried out her tasks with an ear to what was going on in Miss Crabbe's room—not at all hard to do, since the wall between the two classrooms was thinner than one would like, and it took an effort *not* to listen. To judge from the impatience of Miss Crabbe's commands and the tentative, half-frightened responses of the children, it was not a usual day for the junior class, either.

At the beginning of the lunch period, Miss Crabbe had disappeared without explanation, and when she returned almost an hour later, she was in such a state—certainly in no condition to face the children—that Margaret had taken pity on her. She had led her into the tiny teachers' pantry, fetched a wet cloth for her face and a comb for her hair, and heated the kettle on the gas ring. With a mug of hot tea in her hand, Miss Crabbe began to regain her composure, and the story came out in bits and pieces. Not a pleasant story, either, Margaret thought, as she listened in growing dismay.

Miss Crabbe had gone to Willow Cottage to confront Jeremy Crosfield and demand that he return the money. But the boy had denied taking it and Miss Potter had unexpectedly taken his part.

"Miss Potter?" Margaret asked in surprise. "What was she doing there?"

"What indeed?" Miss Crabbe asked, her outraged tone implying that Miss Potter was part of a dangerous conspiracy. "There was some sort of nonsense about a drawing lesson, and frogs. *Frogs,* mind you! She spoke quite disrespectfully to me, and when I tried to compel the boy to confess, she pushed me out of the cottage."

"Pushed?" Margaret stared incredulously, trying to reconcile this version of Miss Potter with the shy, mild person she had met the afternoon before, who had seemed rather easily intimidated. There must be something very sturdy hidden deep inside the lady, to enable her to stand up to the formidable Miss Crabbe.

"Yes, *pushed,*" Miss Crabbe said, and banged her mug on the table. "I told the both of them that I should have to go straight to the constable and report the boy's theft. And I would have done, too, had Constable Braithwaite not been out on his rounds. I shall have to see him this evening."

Margaret summoned her courage. "I wonder," she suggested bravely, "if perhaps we shouldn't wait. Before we speak to the constable, that is. We could give both classrooms a good turning-out. The money may have been merely mislaid or—"

"Fiddle-faddle!" Miss Crabbe exclaimed. "That boy took it, and that's the long and short of it. And I don't need you, Miss Nash, to go to see the constable with me. You would just confuse the issue by making excuses for the child. You are entirely too soft-hearted, as I have told you time and again." She stood up, straightened her blouse, and consulted the watch pinned to her lapel. "Let's get on with our work, shall we? We are already five minutes late to class."

The long day over at last, Margaret pinned the children's art work to the wall, tidied her desk, swept the floors, and damped the coal fires with peat. She would have liked to take the time to search for the missing money, but her errand, she felt, had a higher priority. So she put on her green felt hat and kid gloves and, with determination and more than a little anxiety, walked to the Vicarage. She could no longer bear the burden of Miss Crabbe's eccentric behavior entirely alone. It was time to confer with a higher authority.

Sawrey School had long been a church school, although with the recent educational reforms, control of the Westmoreland schools had been handed over to an elected board. Regardless, Margaret knew that Vicar Samuel Sackett's long connection with the school, as well as his position as spiritual adviser to his flock, made him the right person with whom to share her worries. He had been vicar at Sawrey since Vicar Lythecoe died ten years before, and although Margaret might wish that he would exercise his authority with a little less dithering, he was a kindly man with a good heart who knew his parishioners well. She would lay the matter out before him and he would tell her what to do.

But when Mrs. Thompson (who kept house for the vicar) showed her into the vicar's study, Margaret found that Reverend Sackett was not alone. Captain Woodcock was there, seated in an overstuffed chair, his legs crossed, his pipe in one hand and a cup of tea in the other. He put down his cup and stood when he saw her.

The vicar straightened up from the fire holding the poker, his face reddened by his attention to the coals. He was wearing a gray woolen sweater with the elbows worn through; Mrs. Thompson's duties did not, apparently, extend to darning.

"Ah, Miss Nash!" he exclaimed, putting the poker aside. "Captain Woodcock and I were just talking about you."

Margaret glanced at the captain. He was handsome enough to make her wish that she was not so very plain, and she could feel the color come suddenly, vividly, to her face. "Talking about me?" she asked, with a light, self-deprecating laugh. I know I haven't done anything very immoral. I certainly hope I've done nothing illegal."

"Actually, we were talking about the School Roof Fund," Captain Woodcock said, in a half-apologetic tone. "You'll have a cup of tea, won't you?" Without waiting for an answer, he went to the tea table, picked up the china pot and poured a cup, and brought it to her as she sat down.

"Yes, yes, the School Fund." The vicar rubbed his hands together, wearing a worried frown. "We understand that it's gone missing."

Margaret took the cup. "Actually, that's what I came to discuss," she said. "Miss Crabbe spoke to you about it, then?" Another thought struck her, and she added, "Or perhaps Bertha Stubbs?" She had cautioned Bertha strictly against telling others what had happened, but she didn't really believe that her warning would have any effect. Bertha's tongue was a law unto itself. Half the village probably had the news, or some variant of it, by now. The other half would have it by sundown.

"No," Captain Woodcock said, "we didn't hear it from Miss Crabbe. Miss Potter told me, and I told the vicar. He and I were just remarking that we should like to talk to you, when you appeared." He grinned, and one eyebrow went up. "Fortuitous, I should say."

"Miss Potter told you!" Margaret exclaimed, her breathing more affected by that raised eyebrow than she cared to admit.

"She and Miss Crabbe apparently had some sort of altercation regarding the money," the captain said, "in the presence of the boy. Miss Potter feared that Miss Crabbe's accusation—which seemed to her unfounded—might harm the child. She discussed her concern with Mrs. Lythecoe, and the two of them spoke to me and the constable."

"Oh, well, that's all right, then," Margaret said, feeling immensely relieved that she did not have to rehearse the whole unseemly affair. "Miss Crabbe did tell me that she and Miss Potter talked. Of course, I have only Miss Crabbe's version of the episode." With a small smile, she added, "It sounded . . . well, rather unpleasant."

"To say the least," remarked the captain dryly. "I shouldn't have thought that meek little Miss Potter had it in her to stand up to a wrathful Miss Crabbe, who is enough to strike terror into the staunchest soul." He smiled. "But there seems to be an obstinate side to Miss Potter's personality— or perhaps I should say, a side that refuses to yield to bullies." He shot a glance at the vicar. "Forgive me if I seem unchristian, Reverend, but that's how it strikes me. Miss Crabbe may be a pillar of our little community, but she has it in her to behave like a bully."

The vicar sighed. "I'm sorry to say so, but I'm afraid you're right." He turned to Margaret. "We were hoping, Miss Nash, that you might be able to give us some additional insight."

He poured himself another cup of tea and sat down. "How likely do you think it that the boy took the money?"

"I don't think it at all likely," Margaret said, almost fiercely. "Jeremy is a very good boy, the best in that class. And even if he weren't, I doubt that he was alone with the money long enough to take it. Or that he even knew it was there."

"What actually happened?" the captain asked. "My sister Dimity took the money to the school, as I understand it."

"That's right. She brought it in an envelope yesterday morning, whilst the children were out playing. Miss Crabbe told me that she recalled putting it into the drawer of her desk, but when she went to look for it this morning, it wasn't there. She decided then that she must have left it on the desk and that Jeremy had taken it when we were both out of the room."

"Oh, dear, oh, dear," the vicar murmured, in a dithering sort of way. "Has the school been searched?"

Margaret shook her head. "I suggested it, but Miss Crabbe didn't feel it necessary." She was placing herself in a terribly awkward position, of course, tittle-tattling (or so Miss Crabbe would certainly call it) on her superior. But if she took no action, the situation would almost certainly worsen. And of everyone in the village, these were the men in whom she should confide. The vicar was not only connected with the school, he was also Miss Crabbe's spiritual adviser, while Captain Woodcock was Justice of the Peace and served on the Council School Board. Everything of importance that went on at the school eventually came before him.

The captain drew on his pipe and blew out a stream of aromatic blue smoke. "I see," he said. "Well, then, perhaps you and I should conduct a search, Miss Nash."

"Yes, of course, we can do that." Margaret took a deep breath and forged ahead. "But while the missing money is bad enough, I'm afraid it's not the only problem. One doesn't like to criticize or carry tales, and one is certainly grateful to Miss Crabbe for all she's done. But—"

She bit her lip, feeling almost overwhelmed by her disloyalty. Whatever Miss Crabbe's faults, the two of them had taught together for nearly ten years. The vicar was so kind that he wouldn't attribute any ulterior motives to her, but mightn't the captain (who was much more a man of the world) think that she was deliberately undermining Miss Crabbe's authority, or, far worse, angling for Miss Crabbe's position?

"But what?" prompted the captain gently. "Come, come, Miss Nash. If you have anxieties, this is the time and place to be frank about them. Whatever you say will go no further. Both Reverend Sackett and I have a stake in our little school, you know, and a responsibility to make sure that things work as they should. And if you're worrying about being disloyal, don't. Your duty is to the school, not to any individual."

Thus reassured, Margaret felt herself relax. "The thing is, you see, that Miss Crabbe has become . . . well, rather forgetful. Small things, mostly, such as losing her glasses and forgetting that she was supposed to be somewhere or do something. And when she feels she's not entirely in control, she tends to blame others. She misplaced her attendance book a few weeks ago, and accused Mrs. Stubbs, who gave notice straight off, of course. It took a bit of talking to get her to agree to stay on." She sighed. "Mrs. Stubbs gave notice again this morning, I'm afraid, when she overheard Miss Crabbe talking about Jeremy. And this time, I think she means it. Of course, she'll let everyone in the village have her opinion on the matter, which will make it difficult to find a replacement. No one will want to work at the school."

"Because of Miss Crabbe, you mean?"

Margaret nodded wordlessly.

The eyebrow went up again. "Any thoughts, Vicar?" the captain inquired.

The vicar stood, clasped his hands behind his back, and took a turn in front of the fireplace, looking troubled. "I don't like to break a confidence," he said at last, "but there is something I suppose I should mention. Miss Crabbe herself has acknowledged to me that she's not entirely happy here in Sawrey. She is seeking another position."

Margaret stared at him, startled. Miss Crabbe was thinking of going somewhere else? "But what of her sisters?" she blurted. "Would they go, too?" It seemed unthinkable, really. The three Misses Crabbe had lived at Castle Cottage for decades. And Miss Crabbe must be close to sixty—too old to easily find a teaching position somewhere else.

"I don't know about her sisters," the vicar said. "I must confess that it struck me as . . . well, rather odd." He glanced at Margaret. "I, too, have been concerned about her frame of mind."

"Well," the captain said. "Is it likely that anything will come of her idea to relocate?"

"I don't believe so," the vicar said slowly. "She thought she had found a place in a school near Bournemouth. But she told me yesterday afternoon—after tea at your house, Captain, where we all gathered to welcome Miss Potter— that she had abandoned the plan. She was not able to get the letter of recommendation she needed from Miss Tolliver."

"From Miss Tolliver," the captain said thoughtfully. "I should like to know the details of that."

"I believe that Miss Tolliver knew someone at Bournemouth—someone who might be expected to intervene on Miss Crabbe's behalf," the vicar replied. "She is rather older and more senior than most teachers who change schools," he added, as if in explanation. "I suppose that Miss Tolliver died before Miss Crabbe could ask for the letter, and without it, she did not feel confident in applying for the position. She did not ask me to write, and I did not offer. I . . . well, I shouldn't have known what to say, I'm afraid."

"I really think, Vicar," Captain Woodcock said pushing himself out of his chair, "that things have come to the point where you and I should have a word with Miss Crabbe. Tonight, if possible. Shall we drop in at Castle Cottage, say, around seven or so?"

"I suppose we must," said the vicar unhappily. "Yes, seven will be fine. I'll come to Tower Bank House, and we can walk up together."

The captain turned to Margaret. "Miss Nash, if you don't mind playing Sherlock to my Watson, I should like to drive over to the school and have a look for that envelope. My gig is around at the back. Will you join me?"

"Of course," Margaret said, feeling her ears go pink and thinking that there was nothing she would like better.

At the door, Captain Woodcock paused, holding his fedora. "I understand that something else has gone missing," he said to the vicar. "Has the Register been located yet?"

"The Parish Register?" Margaret asked blankly.

"I'm sorry to say that it has not," the vicar said, with a guilty look. He pushed his hands into his trouser pockets. "I've ransacked the church, of course, and inquired discreetly around the village. One doesn't want to raise an alarm."

"That makes three," the captain said.

"Three?" Margaret inquired, pulling on her gloves.

"The School Roof Fund, the Parish Register, and Miss Tolliver's Constable."

"Miss Tolliver's *Constable?*" Margaret and the vicar exclaimed in unison.

"So it seems, I'm afraid," the captain replied, and gave them the details.

"Oh, my," said the vicar helplessly. "Oh, my word! I've seen that painting any number of times, but I had no idea it was a *Constable!*"

"None of us did," the captain said. "It was Miss Potter who identified it."

"A Constable," Margaret murmured, wondering who could have taken such a thing, and how. "Why, it must be worth hundreds of pounds."

"Thousands, I should say. It is one of his miniatures, which are said to be very rare." The captain put on his hat. "After you, Miss Nash. Vicar, we'll let you know straight off if we find anything. And I'll see you this evening, at seven, at Tower Bank House."

Still puzzling over Miss Tolliver's missing Constable, Margaret accompanied the captain to the school. But even though they searched the shelves, the cupboards, the children's desks, and the lockers in the tiny teachers' room, the money was not to be found. At last they had to admit defeat—although, Margaret thought, as the captain let her off at her door, smiling and touching the brim of his jaunty hat, she had had a perfectly splendid time *not* finding it.

And she felt distinctly better, now that she had put the problem of Miss Crabbe into such capable and understanding hands as his.

18

Miss Potter Says No

The last time Beatrix had received a telegram, it had brought the awful news of Norman's death, and this one made her heart pound and her knees wobble. No other blow could be as brutal or bitter as that, however. Now that Norman was gone, there was nothing left to lose and no reason to feel afraid. She opened the envelope as she walked up the path to Belle Green.

It was, of course, from her father, composed in his usual stern, dispassionate style, the telegraphic contractions rendering it even sterner and more dispassionate. Beatrix was wanted at home, without delay. The parlor maid had left without giving notice, and Mrs. Potter was suffering from a cold and could not be expected to interview applicants for the position. He himself had had another bilious attack. Beatrix was to catch the earliest possible train tomorrow morning so that she could be home in time for tea.

Beatrix crumpled up the telegram and thrust it into the pocket of her skirt. It was really too bad that she had to go back to London, she thought sadly, so soon after arriving, and with none of her business settled. She had managed to get a few good drawings done this morning, thanks to Jeremy and his frogs, but she still had no idea of what to do about the Jenningses. She had intended to go to Rydal tomorrow, to call on the Armitt sisters, whom she had not seen for some time. And she had meant to order a pair of clogs from the cobbler in Hawkshead, so that the next time she came, she'd have the proper footwear. There was also the terribly unfortunate matter of Jeremy and Miss Crabbe, which she wanted to see through to the end, and that puzzling business about the missing Constable painting. And she really was curious about the three Misses Crabbe, and what was going on at Castle Cottage. If only she—

At that moment, completely unbidden, Beatrix heard Jeremy's voice echoing inside her head. "You are so brave," he had said, after she had shown Miss Crabbe the door. "I wish I could be brave like you."

Brave? Beatrix laughed, feeling a bitter sense of irony. Well, perhaps she could stand up bravely to the Miss Crabbes of the world, to whom she owed nothing, but not to her irascible father or her vexatious mother, to whom she owed deference and respect and a daughter's duty. No matter how much she wanted to stay here in Sawrey, she should have to swallow her dismay and disappointment and go back to London.

"Brave like you." The words came again, stopping her in her tracks. Why should she go home? What could she do that could not be done equally well by others? Parlor maids came and went, and hiring a new one could be left with confidence to Mr. Cox, the family butler. Her mother's head colds came and went as well, and there was nothing Beatrix could do but fetch cold remedies and hot tea and water bottles. She could do nothing to help her father, either. He was increasingly impatient with physical discomforts, and the least little twinge provoked paroxysms of complaint. He had sent for her out of habit—and most likely also out of pique. If either he or her mother were vexed or uncomfortable, they seemed to feel that it was unfair for Beatrix to be away somewhere, enjoying herself. She should come home and suffer with them.

Suddenly Beatrix felt a strange, hot defiance pushing up from somewhere deep inside, like a lava stream boiling out of a long-quiet volcano. It was wrong of her parents to treat her as if she were a hired nurse or a housekeeper, rather than their grown-up daughter, and entitled to a life of her own! Yes, she could go home and hire a parlor maid and make their tea and hand round their medicines, and return again to Sawrey when things had quieted down. But it would only happen again, and again, and again. If she did not begin to take a stand—any sort of stand, however modest—against their constant demands on her time and attention, she would never escape from Bolton Gardens.

Her hands thrust deep into her pockets, her head down, Beatrix turned and began to walk down the lane, mentally composing a telegram as she went.

URGENT MATTERS REQUIRE ATTENTION HERE STOP
WILL RETURN AS CIRCUMSTANCES ALLOW STOP
MOST SORRY YOU ARE UNWELL STOP YOUR LOVING
DAUGHTER BEATRIX STOP.

She shivered as she imagined the scolding that would greet her when she got back to Bolton Gardens, the angry accusations that she had put herself and her own desires first, once again, ungrateful girl that she was. But she had always known that she was a terrible disappointment to her parents, not at all the daughter they wanted her to be. And wasn't it better to endure their anger for a little while than to suffer her own bitter resentment for a great deal longer?

She squared her shoulders, lifted her head, and walked faster, suddenly noticing that she was going in the direction of the post office. Her feet were taking her where her heart knew she needed to go.

Ten minutes later, having written out her telegram and handed it over to Lydia Skead, she went back in the direction of Belle Green, walking now with a lighter, more buoyant step. All of her life she had said *yes,* even to the point of compromising her pledge to Norman by agreeing not to share the news with anyone else but their families. Now, at last, she had said *no.* She was surprised at how good it felt.

There was another surprise waiting for Beatrix at Belle Green. She stepped into the house to let Mrs. Crook know that she had returned and would be glad to have a cup of tea. Then she went out immediately to the garden to retrieve her animals, who had spent the entire day in the hutch Mr. Horsley had built for them under the hedge. She found Mrs. Tiggy-Winkle and Mopsy Rabbit fast asleep, Josey contemplatively nibbling on a stem of green clover, and two mice—*two!*—sitting quietly together in a corner, affectionately grooming one another's fur.

"Why, Tom Thumb!" Beatrix exclaimed. "Who is this?"

"Her name is Teasel," Tom said, looking up brightly. His whiskers twitched. *"She's a country mouse, and we're engaged. Teasel, this is Miss Potter. She takes care of us."*

"Pleased t'meet ye, I'm sure, Miss," said Teasel shyly, bobbing her head.

"It's polite for a lady mouse to curtsy," Tom hissed.

"I don't know how," Teasel said.

"Well, you must learn," Tom replied sternly. *"In the city, curtsys are taken quite seriously. Hunca Munca had a very pretty little curtsy."*

Beatrix bent to look closely at the hutch. "I wonder how

that mouse managed to get in?" she said to herself, searching around the bottom. In a minute, she found it: a small but conspicuous tunnel dug under one end of the hutch, exactly the right size to admit a mouse.

"Well, that's easy enough to remedy," she said aloud, filling in the dirt and tamping it down with the heel of her boot. "It's lucky that the rabbits or Mrs. Tig didn't decide to make the tunnel a little bit bigger. They might have escaped, and I'd never have found them again." She opened the door and picked up Josey, who opened one sleepy eye and twitched a whisker in greeting. "But I suppose you're all too lazy to do any digging," she said, stroking the rabbit's soft ears. "And you're probably far too comfortable in this nice hutch Mr. Horsley built to think of wanting to get out."

"Oh, of course," Josey said, and pushed her nose into the crook of Beatrix's arm.

Beatrix reached into the hutch and picked up Mopsy as well, meaning to take the rabbits back to her room. Then she closed the hutch and smiled down at the pair of mice, who looked quite contented together. However it had happened, she was delighted that Tom had found a companion, for she knew he'd been terribly lonely since Hunca Munca's death. She hoped they'd be very happy together.

19

Bertha Stubbs Tells All

Bertha Stubbs lived in the third cottage in a row of three side-by-side stone houses called Lakefield Cottages, just outside the village. Having given in her notice that morning at Sawrey School, she walked straight home at a furious pace and did what she always did when she was angry or perturbed. She put on her apron and began to cook and clean and wash and polish.

Bertha was known throughout Sawrey as having a light hand with pastry, and she immediately turned to making a rhubarb pie for her husband Henry's supper, using a jar of the rhubarb she had bottled in the spring and some strawberry jam that Mrs. Lythecoe had given her, made from the strawberries in Betty Leach's garden at Buckle Yeat. Whilst the pie was baking, she stirred up a batch of gingersnaps and put a pot of oxtail stew on the back of the range. She swept the kitchen floor and washed it, then attacked the ceiling-high oak dresser, built by her grandfather and embellished with his hand carvings, which held her best blue Staffordshire platter and dishes, and the Toby jugs that her aunt had sent her from Dover. Beginning at the very top and working her way to the bottom, she washed each plate and cup and saucer in hot soapy water heated on the range. And all the while she worked, she was muttering angrily to herself. "What a way to treat an innercent child . . . Always one to stand on my principalities! . . . Spilt milk won't never go back in the jug."

Bertha was rinsing the last plate and thinking that she had just about worn herself out with cleaning and was ready to have a bit of a sit-down when she heard a knock at the kitchen door. It opened, and Elsa Grape put her head in.

"Hello, Bertha." Elsa never stood on ceremony, and came in without waiting for an invitation. She was accompanied by Tabitha Twitchit, poor Miss Tolliver's calico cat, who was known to enjoy a saucer of milk in a cozy kitchen. "I was leaving a basket of beans for Mrs. Pritchard, and thought I'd pop in for a bit of a chat." Elsa glanced up at the oak-cased clock in the corner, which announced that the time was a quarter past three. "Tha'rt home from school early today."

"I ain't goin' back to that school," Bertha said grimly, polishing the plate with a fierce vigor that betrayed the vehemence of her feelings. "Not nivver again. Leastwise, not so long as Miss Crabbe is there." She nodded toward the copper kettle steaming on the back of the range. "Kettle's hot. Tha'll have a cup of tea, Elsa? And there's gingersnaps, fresh-baked." She glanced down at the cat. " 'Spose tha came for milk, eh, Miss Twitchit?"

"So nice of you to offer," Tabitha said politely, and curled up in Crumpet's favorite spot on the hearth rug, her paws tucked under her orange-and-white bib. She knew that Crumpet had gone up to Castle Cottage to talk to Max the Manx, and wasn't likely to arrive and dispute her possession.

"I wouldn't say nay to a cup," Elsa agreed cheerfully, and settled herself in a chair while Bertha poured hot water over three spoonfuls of tea in her second-best teapot. As far as news was concerned, Elsa felt, today had already proved to be quite remarkable, and she was eager to share what she knew with Bertha. At lunch at Tower Bank House, she had overheard Captain Woodcock and his sister discussing the fact that Miss Tolliver's will had been read out that morning at the Heelis office in Hawkshead, and that a certain female person from Manchester—a Miss Sarah Barwick, whose mysterious connection to Miss Tolliver could only be guessed at—had inherited Anvil Cottage, whilst the draper from Kendal had got nothing but a box of old letters his mother had written to her sister. And then Miss Barwick herself had arrived with Mr. Heelis (Elsa had seen this with her very own eyes when she went to the village shop to buy a reel of cotton and a half-pound of castor sugar), and had chatted for a short while in the lane with Grace Lythecoe and Miss Potter, and then all four of them had gone together into Anvil Cottage. Elsa had come prepared to relate this interesting tale, and to remark on the scandalous shortness of Miss Barwick's skirts and the agreeable way that the handsome Mr. Heelis had handed her up into the gig when they left.

But Elsa was already in possession of these entertaining bits of gossip and Bertha looked fair bursting to tell her something else entirely. So she sat back in her chair, took a still-warm gingersnap from the plate on the table, and asked, in an interested tone, "What's Miss Crabbe gone and done now?"

"What's she done?" Bertha cried, putting down a saucer of milk in front of Tabitha. "What's she done? I'll tell thi what she's done." And she did, in detail, with only one or two slight embellishments.

"*Jeremy Crosfield?*" Tabitha said in amazement, licking milk from her whiskers. "*I can't believe it!*"

"Jeremy Crosfield?" Elsa exclaimed indignantly. "Fancy her accusin' that lit'le boy, and him not able to defend himself. And where's t' School Roof Fund got to, I wants to know? Two pounds is a girt lot of money."

"A great lot of money indeed!" Tabitha exclaimed, performing a quick calculation. Most of the men in the village brought home only ten shillings a week, so two pounds represented the income of four whole weeks, or two months' cottage rent, or the purchase of three or four sheep.

"I've no notion where t' money's got to," Bertha said angrily, pouring the tea. "I've considered goin' to t' vicar, or talkin' to Constable Braithwaite mesel, or—" She paused, frowning. "O' course, Miss Nash did tell me to keep it quiet, so I doan't 'spose I should. And I'll thank ye to keep it to thasel, too, Elsa Grape. There's no good causin' a lot of talk, which'll hurt nobbut the boy. Tha knows how folk in this village are. They see a mouse, pretty soon it's a hittopopomus."

"Ye're right, of course, Bertha," Elsa said, and stirred sugar into her tea. "Not but what there'll be a girt deal o' talk anyway, once it gets out that tha's give notice. People'll be wonderin' why, and what am I t' say?"

"Just say it's all along o' principality," Bertha said in a righteous tone. "Say that Bertha Stubbs won't stand to work for somebody as mean and unjustified as Miss Crabbe."

And that's what Tabitha Twitchit told Crumpet and Rascal when they joined one another after dark that evening, in the bushes beside the pub.

It's also what Elsa Grape told her cousin, Florrie Stokes, when Florrie dropped into the Tower Bank House kitchen to borrow a cup of sugar while Elsa was cooking dinner for Captain and Miss Woodcock. Florrie took the story home, along with the sugar and the tale of Miss Barwick and her inheritance, to share with her mother and father and her cousin Ruth Birkett, who happened to be visiting the Stokes house that evening. Florrie repeated the tale of Miss

Barwick's mysterious inheritance with a reasonable degree of accuracy and only the usual speculations. But she had theatrical aspirations, and her rendering of the encounter between Miss Crabbe and Mrs. Stubbs (which had particularly caught her fancy) was performed with a great many dramatic flourishes. The plot and dialogue were improved upon, as well.

"Oh, it was a row, all right!" Florrie reported with great enjoyment, "a row to end all rows! Bertha Stubbs, she was outside t' classroom door, sweepin' t' floor, when she heard Miss Crabbe start accusin' that pore lit'le boy of stealin' t' three pounds t' ladies collected. She stormed straight in and let her have it, then and there. 'Leave this school and nivver darken its door again!' Miss Crabbe screams, and Bertha Stubbs says, very dignified-like, "I am a-leavin', this verra instant, and I'm nivver a-comin' back, no matter if tha falls down on them bony knees and begs me!"

Florrie widened her eyes dramatically, and placed her hand on her heart. "If it'ud been me, o'course, I'd a been so frightened I'd've swooned dead away, on the spot. But our Bertha's not one to be bullied, oh, no! She stands up to Miss Crabbe and shakes her fist in her face and gives her a fair piece of her mind!"

When Florrie had finished her performance, Mr. and Mrs. Stokes and Ruth Birkett were loud in their praise of the intrepid Bertha, and Florrie herself could not help feeling gratified by the family's appreciation. They adjourned to the supper table, where they continued the discussion over plates of Mrs. Stokes's Cumberland sausage, boiled cabbage, and fried potatoes, carrying it on through dishes of treacle pudding and cups of hot tea, until Ruth Birkett declared that it was getting late and she should be starting for home.

The number of people to whom Ruth Birkett repeated the tale of Bertha's heroism is unfortunately not recorded. But since Ruth lived with her three unmarried sisters halfway between Near Sawrey and Hawkshead, and since all four Birketts went out for daily work in that market town, it is highly likely that the story found its way into at least four Hawkshead households the very next morning. And it would not be surprising if the School Roof Fund—which had grown to three pounds in Florrie's version of its disappearance—was enlarged to four, five, six pounds, and even more, in subsequent retellings of the tale, enough to put an entirely new roof on the school and perhaps even a new room, if one had been wanted.

Miss Tolliver would have been amazed to learn how much money the Sawrey ladies had collected after she was gone.

20

Miss Crabbe Meets with an
Unfortunate Accident

Max the Manx was not by nature a hopeful creature, and it
had been his experience throughout his life that things
never worked out exactly as they were planned. He did not,
therefore, think highly of Crumpet's scheme to keep Miss
Myrtle from going to see Constable Braithwaite and telling
him to arrest the boy. Oh, the plan was certainly clever
enough, but it required him to climb up to the top of the
steep stairs to Castle Cottage's second floor, something Max
had never before done, because high places made him
queasy. Still, he agreed with Crumpet that Miss Myrtle had
to be stopped, and since he had no confidence that Viola or
Pansy could get the job done, he promised to think about it.

Viola Crabbe, for her part, had been deeply distressed by
what Grace Lythecoe and Miss Potter had told her earlier
that afternoon. Of course, it was very bad that the boy
should have been accused, and that Myrtle should have

spoken so appallingly to Miss Potter, who seemed a very shy, quiet person who wouldn't say boo to a goose.

But what was far more distressing, to Viola's mind, was the pattern of Myrtle's behavior over the past several months. Viola acknowledged that she had a dramatic temperament and often exaggerated things. But she was not exaggerating when she said that her older sister—always so strong, so capable, so very firm of intention—was undergoing a mental breakdown, as had their mother only five or six years before. Dear Mama, however, had been in her seventies when the terrible affliction struck, and the fragility of her physical health had meant that she did not have to suffer for many months in the asylum where Myrtle had insisted on placing her. Viola and Pansy had argued against the asylum, wanting to keep Dear Mama at home where they could take care of her, for they had loved her in spite of her mental frailties. But Myrtle had absolutely insisted, and although they had resisted as long as they could, Viola and Pansy had finally given in, for fear of causing further grief to all concerned.

Now, looking back, Viola had the chilling thought that her sister's violent insistence might have been a clue, a signal, perhaps, that Myrtle herself was beginning to fear some sort of psychological breakdown, and had reacted by wanting to put Dear Mama out of the way. She could not know this for certain, however, and there was no point in speculating about the past, especially when the present was rapidly becoming intolerable.

And it wasn't just the two or three events that Viola and Pansy had mentioned to Grace Lythecoe that afternoon. It was the little things that occurred almost every day now— the abrupt anger over trivial upsets, the groundless accusations of persecution, the inexplicable fits of crying, the subtle changes in physical appearance—that hinted at Myrtle's deteriorating personality. It was clear that their sister was

going to pieces and that Viola—for Pansy was not of much
help when it came to a crisis—should have to take charge.
But first things first. This evening, Viola had to deal with
the most immediate problem, which was to somehow pre-
vent Myrtle from going to the constable with her indict-
ment of little Jeremy Crosfield, who must be innocent, if
dear Grace Lythecoe thought so.

The tea things were put out as usual, and at tea time the
three sisters gathered in the sitting room in front of the
comfortable fire. Viola still wore her kimono, but Pansy had
changed into a mauve velvet tea gown with lace-trimmed
ruffles at the neck and sleeves. Myrtle was, as always, carefully dressed, in a white shirtwaist and black skirt. But the
skirt seemed to hang loosely on her and her face looked thin
and gaunt. Her gray hair had lost its spring and its silvery
luster had faded. She had never been pretty, but the sharp
intelligence that had once brightened her expression seemed
to have faded as well.

Viola waited until Myrtle had finished her biscuit and
cup of tea, then took a deep breath, squared her shoulders,
and told her (with as little drama as possible) about the visitors who had called earlier that afternoon.

"Pansy and I think, Myrtle," she concluded quietly, "that
it is inadvisable for you to bother Constable Braithwaite
about this affair. There doesn't seem to be any proof that the
boy stole the money—in fact, there seems no proof that it
was stolen at all. Pansy and I would like to go with you to
the school and search for it. We can go now, if you like, or
first thing in the morning, if you'd rather."

"That is totally unnecessary, Viola," Myrtle said. "The
money is *not* at the school."

Viola had expected a tirade, not this extraordinary calm-
ness, and it rather unnerved her. "Then where is it?" she
asked uncertainly.

"Why, it's at Willow Cottage—or wherever the boy has

hidden it," Myrtle said airily. "You're not to worry about this, Viola. The child is clever, I'll give him that—clever enough to get people on his side. But I'm sure the constable will ferret out the truth, and the money."

Pansy, always the sympathetic one, put out her hand. "Dearest Myrtle, do consider the possibility that the money was simply mislaid, like the money for the baker's boy, or Aunt Adrienne's locket—"

"Don't talk nonsense, Pansy," Myrtle said, with a gentle air of reproving authority. "That wretched child simply took the opportunity to pocket the money when he was left alone in the room, and that's all there is of that."

"But, Myrtle," Pansy protested, "we really think—"

"Don't," Myrtle said sharply. "Thinking is not your strong suit, Pansy. Nor Viola's. Neither of you have any experience of the world on which to base any opinion at all. If you will keep your thoughts to yourself, they will not be exposed as foolishness."

Pansy looked as if she had been slapped. Her large soft eyes filled with tears that spilled over onto her cheeks.

"There is no need to be rude, Myrtle," Viola said. "We are just trying to help avoid a scandal that might damage the child—and you."

"I am quite aware of what you are trying to do," Myrtle said significantly. She pulled her thin gray eyebrows together in a disapproving line and directed a stern frown, first to one sister and then to the other. "I'd like to know what business this is of Grace Lythecoe's. Just because she was married to the vicar, she thinks she's an emissary of the Lord, I suppose. And that dumpy, disagreeable Miss Potter, sticking her political nose into matters that she has nothing to do with."

"But, Myrtle—" Viola began.

"It is getting on to six," Myrtle said, glancing up at the ormolu clock on the mantle and putting down her teacup in a businesslike way, "and if I mean to have a word with Constable Braithwaite tonight, I had better be on my way." Obviously feeling in command of the situation, she gave her sisters an indulgent smile. "Now, my dears, for the really important question. What are we having for dinner tonight?"

Viola and Pansy exchanged glances. "Mutton cutlets," said Pansy in a small voice, "and a Damson pudding."

"Excellent," Myrtle said, standing. "I shall return shortly, and expect dinner at the regular hour." She set her mouth, looked down her nose, and spoke in a reproving tone. "We will have no more words about this unpleasant business. Do you hear?" When neither of them answered, she repeated it, louder and with a sharp emphasis, as she would in the schoolroom. *"Do you hear?"*

"Yes, Myrtle," Pansy said obediently, and Viola made a silent, sulky nod.

"Very good," Myrtle said, and gave them each a vastly forgiving smile. "Stay and finish your tea, dears. I shan't be gone very long."

Feeling that she had kept her temper admirably under quite a trying circumstance, Myrtle swept out of the parlor and upstairs to her bedroom, where she combed her hair, changed into a clean white shirtwaist, and put on her third-best jacket. She pulled on her gloves, pinned on her hat, hung her purse over her arm, and started down the stairs in the direction of the front door.

But she got no further than the second stair, for that was the point at which she stepped on Max (who, crouched on the shadowy stair, was virtually invisible), and pitched forward, head over heels, giving a wild, piercing shriek. She bumped in a somersaulting tumble down the steep, uncarpeted stairs to the very bottom, where she lay in a heap, unmoving.

In the sitting room, Viola and Pansy had been conducting

an anxious, low-voiced discussion of what was to be done, now that they had failed in their efforts to keep Myrtle from going to the constable. Viola had just said that she was beginning to fear for their sister's mental balance when she was interrupted by Myrtle's alarming shriek and a series of thumps. She and Pansy ran out into the hallway and were greeted by the sight of Myrtle, dazed and moaning, at the bottom of the stairs. Her eyes were closed and her face was ashen.

"Myrtle! What's happened?" Pansy cried in a horrified voice, kneeling beside her. "Are you all right?"

Myrtle's eyelids fluttered. "My right leg," she moaned. "It hurts. It hurts terribly." She tried to raise herself but fell back with a little whimper.

Viola lifted Myrtle's black woolen skirt, exposing the thin, black-stockinged leg. It was bent above the knee at an odd angle. She dropped the skirt. "I daresay it's broken," she said dispassionately. "Above the knee, which makes it much worse."

"Broken!" Myrtle shrilled, attempting once again to raise herself. "You and your histrionics! You're exaggerating the situation, as usual, Viola, for your own purposes. My leg is not broken! I have things to do! I must go and see—"

"Don't be a fool, Myrtle." Viola spoke sharply, feeling a mean sense of triumph. "You're not going anywhere. Pansy, bring the brandy and a glass, and a blanket." As Pansy scurried off, Viola straightened and looked down at her prostrate sister, whose face and figure she had never once viewed from this superior angle. "How in the world did you manage to fall?"

Myrtle turned her head from side to side. "It was Max. He was sitting on the next-to-top stair."

"I doubt it," Viola said, thinking that it was just like Myrtle to blame someone else—in this case, an innocent cat—for something she had done herself. "In all the years we have had that cat, he has never once ventured up those stairs. You know he's afraid of heights. He's never even climbed a tree."

"But I'm sure it was—"

"Don't talk," Viola instructed. She wouldn't have admitted this to a soul, not even to Pansy, but she felt this unfortunate accident had occurred at a most opportune time. Myrtle would doubtless be confined to the house for as long as it took the break to mend—six weeks or more, likely. Perhaps, in that time, her mental balance would be restored, and they could go on as they had before. She stopped herself with a little shake. No—not as before. This time, *she* would be in charge, and some serious changes were going to be made.

Feeling considerably cheered, Viola reached for her shawl, hanging from the peg beside the door. "I'll go over to Belle Green and ask Edward Horsley to fetch Dr. Butters," she said. "George Crook and Charlie Hotchkiss can bring a plank to get you up to bed."

"But I want to see Constable Braithwaite," Myrtle cried weakly, her voice thin and tremulous. Her face was contorted, whether with pain or with anger Viola could not guess. "If I can't go there, you must fetch him, Viola. Bring him to me. I am *ordering* you!"

"No, Myrtle," Viola said in a low, level tone that was all the more dramatic because it lacked drama. "I will not fetch the constable, not now, and not later." As Pansy appeared with a blanket and the brandy, she added, "Give her quite a large one, Pansy." To Myrtle, she said, "Lie still and obey instructions, or you'll cause yourself more pain and us more trouble. I'll be back as soon as I can." And with that, she wrapped her shawl around her shoulders and went out the door, closing it firmly behind her.

Crouched in the shadows on the second stair from the top, Max the Manx had watched silently as this fascinating scene unfolded in the hallway below. Miss Myrtle had made life difficult for everyone in Castle Cottage, and he was not sorry (although of course he should have been) to see her have a taste of it for herself.

Indeed, Max was feeling more than a little pleased with himself. He had not expected Crumpet's plan to work, especially since he feared that he was too much of a coward to attempt the stairs. But he had taken it slowly, one step at a time, and to his great surprise, he had not minded the height—not very much, at any rate. He had not even minded being trodden upon by Miss Myrtle, and he was already thinking how pleased Crumpet would be when she heard what he had accomplished.

However, it was now necessary to give some thought to his exit. He would have liked to creep down the stairs, but the way was blocked by the prostrate Miss Myrtle and the ministering Miss Pansy and he could not escape without being seen. He was much closer to the top than the bottom, anyway—and since he had gotten this far, he told himself, he might as well take full advantage of the situation. What was more, whilst he kept a tight rein on the mouse population downstairs and in the garden, there might be mice up here. He climbed to the top of the stairs, slipped into the shadows, and began to explore the hitherto undiscovered upper regions of Castle Cottage.

Just before seven that evening, Miles Woodcock answered the vicar's knock at the front door of Tower Bank House. He put on his coat and hat, called out to his sister that he was leaving, and went out into the chilly dark. Together, he and the vicar walked up Market Street in the direction of Castle Cottage. The breeze was rich with the smoke of evening fires in cottage kitchens, the smell of sausages hung on the air, and from somewhere in the distance came the low, throaty hoot of an owl. Miles told the vicar about the unsuccessful search of the school that he and Miss Nash had made that afternoon, but other than that, they exchanged few words. He was not looking forward to their discussion with Miss Crabbe, and he suspected that the vicar—who was not of a confrontational turn of mind—was dreading it even more. Both of them knew the lady too well to expect that their interview would be a comfortable one, but it was a duty they could not shirk.

As they reached the top of Castle Cottage lane, however, Miles was surprised to see Dr. Butters's gig parked in front, his horse enjoying a nosebag of oats. Lounging on the front step, a pipe in his mouth, was George Crook. With him was Rascal, his Jack Russell terrier.

"Hullo, George," Miles said. With a frown, he glanced up at the lighted second-story windows. "Has something happened? Why is the doctor here?"

George got to his feet. "G'evenin', Captain," he said, and grinned. "G'evenin', Vicar. Aye, something's happened, a-reet." He lowered his voice. "It's t' elder Miss Crabbe. She's bad, verra bad."

"Dear me, George!" cried the vicar anxiously. "What's happened to her?"

"Broke her leg, she did, poor thing," George Crook said. "Lucky it weren't her neck. Them auld stairs is verra steep."

"My goodness," said the captain, bending over to scratch Rascal's ears. He could not escape the thought that, if Myrtle Crabbe had to go and break her leg, this was not a bad time to do it.

"Aye, broke it verra bad, she did," George went on, adding, with an ominous emphasis, "above t' knee."

The captain straightened, flinching.

"Above t' knee," George repeated with grim relish. "I've been waitin' here in case t' doctor needs a hand settin' it. Sometimes it takes two, y'know." He shook his head mournfully. " 'Specially when it's broke above t' knee."

"Dreadful!" the vicar muttered. "Oh, this is dreadful! I shall go right up and see if I'm needed." And without any dithering at all, he opened the door and went straight in.

The captain took out his pipe, filled, and lit it. "Broke her leg, did she?" he murmured, around the pipe stem. "How under the sun did she manage to do that?"

George Crook shrugged. "Stepped on t' black cat on t' dark stair, she sez. Put a foot wrong, sez t' other two ladies. Either way, she went in a tumble head-first, all t' way down to t' bottom. Me an' Charlie Hotchkiss put her on a plank and lugged her back up," he added. "Wasn't half hard, neither. The lady may not look heavy, but she's solid as a ton o' pumpkins. Charlie, he hurt his back, he did."

The door opened and light fell out onto the little porch. "Captain Woodcock?" Miss Viola asked. "The vicar said you were out here. Won't you come in?" She opened the door wider. "And George, Dr. Butters says to tell you that he's finished setting the break. You're free to go along home now, with our thanks. We're very grateful for your help, and Charlie's, too, of course. We'd never have gotten her into her bed without you."

"Thank'ee," George said. "I hope she mends well. Come on, Rascal. Mrs. Crook'll have our supper ready." He tipped his hat and went into the dark, trailed by his dog.

Miles followed Miss Viola into the sitting room. "How is she?" he asked.

"About as one would expect," Miss Viola said, sitting down in front of the small fire. "She is in a great deal of pain, and very upset. My sister is a woman who likes to be in charge of things. This accident was not in her plan." She paused. "Will you have a cup of tea, Captain? Or I can offer you a glass of port."

"I'd welcome some port," Miles said, still standing. He glanced down at his pipe. "Do you mind if I smoke?"

"Not at all," Miss Viola said, getting up and going to the

sideboard, where she took up a bottle and a glass. "Myrtle doesn't permit it," she added, pouring, "but I do rather enjoy a man's pipe. It reminds me of Dear Father."

Miles took the glass she offered and sat down. "This is rather an awkward question, under the circumstances, but I wonder if you know whether your sister managed to speak to Constable Braithwaite this evening. You see, she—"

"She did not," Miss Viola said firmly. "She was on her way to see him when she met with the unfortunate accident." She looked at him, her head tilted to one side. "I take it by your question, Captain, that you know about the missing money—and perhaps about my sister's encounter with Miss Potter and the boy."

"I do," Miles replied, feeling a great relief that he did not have to explain the situation. "Miss Potter and Mrs. Lythecoe spoke both to me and to the constable about the matter, and I discussed it with the vicar."

Miss Viola visibly relaxed. "So the constable isn't likely to confront the boy?"

"Not without more evidence," Miles said. "The vicar and I have discussed the situation with Miss Nash, as well, who was present when the theft is said to have occurred. She is persuaded that the child did not have the opportunity to take the money—and that he would not, if he had. She knows of no evidence that might incriminate him."

"It appears, then, that the money may have been merely . . . mislaid, rather than stolen," Miss Viola said. She gave a discreet cough. "My sister has not been quite herself lately, you see, Captain, and it's possible that she's put it somewhere and forgotten about it. Pansy and I were wondering whether, once Myrtle is settled comfortably, one of us should go to the school and search."

Miles shook his head. "I don't think that would help. Miss Nash and I made a thorough search of the school this afternoon, and found nothing. I think, however—" He paused uncomfortably, sipped his port, and tried again. "I feel like a cad for asking you this, but I would very much appreciate it if you would have a look around your sister's room. Perhaps she brought the money home for . . . well, for safekeeping."

"You're not a cad, Captain." Miss Viola sighed heavily. "I'm afraid that the scenario you suggest is entirely possible. The doctor will likely give her a sleeping draught before he leaves. When she's safely asleep, I'll have a look."

As if on cue, Dr. Butters entered the sitting room. A much-loved figure in the neighborhood of Sawrey, he was a tall, thin man with a bony, intelligent face, gingery hair going gray at the temples, and a gingery moustache. "Viola," he said, with a nod. "Good evening, Woodcock. Didn't expect to see you here."

Miss Viola rose, clasping her hands. "Will she be all right, Doctor?"

"In time," the doctor said. "It's a nasty break, though. It will be some months before she's ambulatory, and I doubt that she can return to the classroom this year. Knowing how your sister feels about the school, I'd say that this by itself might become a problem." He looked intently at Miss Viola. "She seemed a great deal agitated. Kept muttering about the constable, and stolen money, and a thieving boy." He cocked an inquiring eyebrow. "Anything that needs tending to?"

"We're in the process of setting it right," Miles said. "It's not something she should worry about."

Doctor Butters nodded. "I've given her something to make her sleep, so she won't be worrying about anything for a while. I've sent Pansy to lie down with a draught, as well. She's more anxious and flustered than is good for her." He turned. "Would you mind looking in on her, Viola? The vicar is with Myrtle at the moment, so you're not needed there."

"Of course," Miss Viola said. She went first to the sideboard and poured another glass of port. "Sit for a few minutes before you drive back to Hawkshead, Doctor."

The doctor took the glass from her. "Don't mind if I do," he said. When Miss Viola had left the room, he dropped into a chair and put his feet on the fender. "Well, Woodcock? How are things?"

"Muddled," Miles said ruefully. "The School Roof Fund is missing, the Parish Register hasn't been seen for a fortnight, and someone appears to have taken a valuable painting from Anvil Cottage. Not to mention that there's a good deal of gossip about the manner of Miss Tolliver's death."

"My goodness me," said the doctor. "Where is Holmes when we need him?" He sipped his port. "And what are people saying about Miss Tolliver's death? The usual gossip, I suppose."

"It seems to be a bit more focused than that," Miles replied cautiously. "It's said that she died of poison, specifically foxglove. Perhaps self-inflicted, perhaps administered by some third party."

"Well, I don't know about your other mysteries, but I can certainly solve this one for you," the doctor said. "Miss Tolliver showed no signs of digitalis poisoning—and the symptoms are unmistakable, believe me. Nausea, vomiting, diarrhea. It is not a pretty death, nor an easy one. Miss Tolliver died quickly and, I should think, rather easily, from a heart attack. It was not unexpected, you know."

"Not unexpected?"

The doctor hesitated, as if he were wondering how much to reveal. Finally, he said, "I don't suppose it matters now that she's dead. There were previous attacks, although she did not want anyone to know. A very private person, that lady, who kept herself to herself—not an easy thing to do in a small village. So I wasn't in the least surprised when you summoned me. I had always expected that some sort of sudden shock would do her in."

"Sudden shock?" Miles asked, thinking in a rather disconnected way of the missing painting. Had Miss Tolliver surprised a thief who had broken into the cottage and was in the process of stealing it? Or—

"Oh, bad news, something of the sort." The doctor gave him a slanted look. "Now, tell me this, if you can. What do you know of Myrtle Crabbe's behavior in the past few months?"

Miles sighed. "Not as much as I probably should," he said. "There was a problem today about some money—that business with Constable Braithwaite that she was going on about. I understand from Miss Nash, the other teacher, that there have been additional difficulties." He frowned. "Why are you asking?"

"Just an idea. She was rather incoherent, you see, and she said a few things that rather surprised me." A smile twitched at the corners of his mouth. "Not the kind of things one might expect to hear from a lady of Miss Crabbe's sheltered background and social standing." He tossed back the rest of his port and stood. "Time I was getting back to Hawkshead. I'm expecting Mrs. Forsythe to deliver tonight, and it won't be easy. Are you on foot? Shall I give you a lift to Tower Bank House?"

"I'd like that," Miles said. "I daresay the vicar won't want me to wait for him."

"I shouldn't think so," Dr. Butters said. "Let's be off, then."

Upstairs, the vicar, deeply troubled, was sitting beside Myrtle Crabbe's bed, watching as she fell asleep. Her thin, bony fingers lay stilled on the eiderdown coverlet, and her pale face was peaceful in the light of the oil lamp on the table. Samuel Sackett reflected, as he often did, on the enigma of human nature. A few moments before, Miss Crabbe had been wildly fretful, tossing her head, muttering incoherently about the constable, the money, and Jeremy Crosfield, her fingers plucking restlessly at the covers. Now, her anxiety was gone, the stern lines of her face had relaxed, and she lay in restful, blessed sleep. Restful and healing, not just to the body, but also to the mind.

For this, Reverend Sackett was enormously grateful. In the past half hour, he had become very much afraid that the balance of Miss Crabbe's mind was in serious jeopardy. Of course, the pain of her fracture was probably responsible, but the appalling torrent of profane words that had spilled out of the lady's mouth had been wholly, entirely unexpected, a great shock to him and (he thought) surprising even to Dr. Butters, who had no doubt heard just about everything in his many years of practice.

And then, when the doctor had left, the vicar had heard even more. Miss Crabbe seemed to be glad that Abigail Tolliver was dead because she had refused to sign the letter, and without it, Myrtle couldn't go to Bournemouth and get away from her meddling sisters and her horrible school and this wretched little village. Of course, this was all very incoherent and jumbled and the vicar wouldn't have been able to make any sense of it if he hadn't already known about the letter beforehand. But he was still shocked and horrified by Miss Crabbe's vitriolic anger, and glad that neither of her two sisters had been present. Of course, it was not a question of blame or censure, for Myrtle was obviously not herself. Rather, it was a matter for compassion, and for the hope of healing and self-forgiveness. The vicar put his hands over hers, bowed his head, and translated his hope into a fervent, heartfelt prayer for Miss Crabbe's early and entire recovery, both mental and physical.

A little later, hearing the wheels of the doctor's gig crunching on the gravel outside, the vicar stood and took out his watch. It was not quite nine. No doubt Captain

Woodcock had departed with the doctor, and he must be on his way, too, back to the vicarage. He would stop to say a few words to Miss Viola and Miss Pansy, and then take his leave.

He turned down the oil lamp until it was barely glowing, and moved it so that the light did not fall directly on the bed. He bent over the sleeping woman, touched her quiet hands, and said one last prayer. Then, as he straightened and turned toward the door of the darkened room, he was startled to see a pair of demonic green eyes staring at him from a dark shelf over the dresser that sat beside the door.

Dear God, the vicar thought with a frightened gasp, *what in the—*

Then the eyes blinked, there was a soft *meow,* and he realized with an instant flood of relief that he was looking at the Crabbe sisters' Manx cat, so black that he was invisible in the darkness, only the gleam of his eyes betraying his presence. The vicar had met Max on his earlier visits to Castle Cottage, and had admired him greatly. He reached out his hand to stroke the cat's wiry fur.

"Max," he murmured. "Max, you devil."

"Hello," said Max pleasantly, getting to his feet and arching his back under the vicar's hand. *"So nice to see you."* He had not planned to call attention to himself; after all, no one knew that he was prowling about upstairs. But the vicar was one of the few men who made their way into the women's domain of Castle Cottage, and Max had always rather enjoyed him. He put out his paw with a playful gesture and caught the vicar's cuff.

"Max, you're a funny creature," the vicar said with a chuckle, releasing his cuff and rubbing the cat's ears. And then he frowned, his attention attracted by the book on which Max was sitting. It had a clasp, was bound in leather, and was about the size and shape of—

"Max," said the vicar urgently, "get down." And without ceremony, he lifted him up and put him on the floor. Then he reached for the book.

It was the Parish Register.

21

Rats!

When Tabitha Twitchit met Crumpet and Rascal the Jack Russell terrier in the bushes beside the pub that night, it was getting on to nine o'clock, and Dr. Butters had just dropped Captain Woodcock off at Tower Bank House. The clatter of the doctor's gig died into the dark, and all was quiet, except for the churring call of a nightjar and an occasional burst of raucous laughter from inside the pub, where a half-dozen village men were enjoying a noisy game of darts along with their evening pint.

There was plenty for the animals to discuss. Tabitha (who as senior village cat presided over the meeting) told Crumpet and Rascal what she had heard in Bertha Stubbs' kitchen that afternoon: that Bertha had given notice at Sawrey School because Miss Crabbe had unfairly accused little Jeremy Crosfield (whom the animals all knew and liked) of stealing the School Roof Fund. Crumpet and Tabitha told Rascal what they had learnt about Miss Barwick when they were hiding behind the sofa in Miss Tolliver's sitting room—Miss Barwick's sitting room, now. And Rascal, still rather breathless from his run down Market Street, told Crumpet and Tabitha what had just happened at Castle Cottage.

"Miss Crabbe broke her leg!" Crumpet exclaimed in astonishment, and then related the scheme she had suggested to Max the Morose, as a means of preventing Miss Crabbe from going to Constable Braithwaite. *"Of course,"* she added, *"I had no way of knowing that Max would actually be able to bring himself to do such a thing. He's afraid of heights, you know."*

Rascal patted Crumpet's shoulder with an approving paw. *"I say, Crumpet, that was a topping idea! It stopped her dead in her tracks."* He paused. *"Well, not dead, exactly. You know what I mean."*

"I didn't know she'd break her leg," Crumpet said, frowning. She was a cat who liked to see things done in an expeditious manner, but that didn't include hurting people. *"I'm sorry to have caused her pain."*

"Look at it this way, Crumpet," Tabitha said. *"There was no way to stop that woman, short of flinging her down the stairs. And if she hadn't been injured, she would certainly have done a great injury to Jeremy Crosfield and his aunt. Either way, somebody was bound to suffer."*

Crumpet had to admit that Tabitha was right. What boy could defend himself against a teacher, and the headmistress, at that! In Sawrey village, Miss Crabbe had almost as much authority and prestige as the vicar and the justice of the peace.

Rascal sat down on his haunches and cocked his head to one side. *"I have an idea,"* he said. *"If the money wasn't stolen, it's lost, right? I think we should go to the school and search. If it's there, we'll find it. And that will clear Jeremy completely."*

"But won't that have been done already?" Crumpet asked with a frown.

"*Probably,*" Rascal said, with a careless toss of his head. "*But I'll wager the place wasn't searched by anybody with my expert nose. Don't you remember the time I found George Crook's leather coin-purse after he'd dropped it in the field behind Belle Green? I know what money smells like. And if it's there, by Jove, I'll sniff it out!*"

Tabitha leaned close to Crumpet and spoke into her ear. "*Rascal's right about his nose. He certainly has a better chance of finding that money than any of the humans. All they have to go on is their sight—and even that isn't too good. I think we should let him try.*"

"*Of course we should,*" Rascal barked. "*Come on, girls! We're going on a treasure hunt!*"

And with that, the two cats and a dog set off down the narrow lane that led from Near Sawrey to Far Sawrey. The moon was full, a large, low-hanging globe that floated over the larch trees, and their lane was an intriguing patchwork of bright and dark, noisy with the skitterings and scratchings of small nocturnal creatures. Wilfin Beck, which came leaping down from the tarns of Claife Heights past Cuckoo Brow Wood, was in spate, running bank full, a silver skein shimmering through the shadowy meadows, and the night air was rich and heavy with the autumn scents that all animals love: damp earth, peat and decaying mosses, fallen leaves.

And if there were a few fairies loitering among the roots of the large oaks in Penny Wood that evening—well, would that be any great surprise? Not to the animals, who had the wisdom to acknowledge that there might be things in the world that they did not fully understand. And not to most Lake Country dwellers, either, who still believed in elves, witches, wizards, fairies, and the supernatural in general. Vicar Sackett had once been told, as if it were the gospel truth, of a parishioner who, returning late one night from Hawkshead, was dragged off his horse by fairies. He would have been pushed through a door in a fairy hill, the man claimed, if he hadn't a page of the Bible in his pocket, carried as a charm against just such abductions.

But animals know that fairies and elves do not like to cross running water, so they hurried toward the stone bridge over Wilfin Beck. As they reached it, they heard a scurrying rustle and a sharp hissing. It was the ferret who lived there—not a wilding, but an escaped ferret named Fritz whose master had trained him to catch rabbits—and who often made it unpleasant for the small animals who wanted to go across. Fritz made his living by raiding the large rabbit warren in Sawrey Fold, sometimes with Rascal's help, since Rascal enjoyed going after the bolters that his companion flushed out of the burrows, and was always very keen on a day's rabbit hunting with a skilled and highly motivated ferret. So when Fritz saw that his friend Rascal was leading the trio of animals, he sat up on his haunches and cheerfully waved them on, as they crossed the bridge and ducked through the opening in the hedgerow to take the footpath across the open expanse of Sawrey Fold.

Here, the night air was scented with meadowsweet and wild thyme, and the field seemed very still under the silent moon, which flickered as cloud shapes passed over it. But the animals had not gone far when they heard a soft whispering sigh, and then the sigh was louder, and then it resolved itself with a flutter of heavy wings and a rasp of claws into the dark shape of an owl settling onto the limb of a willow beside the beck. The flat round disk of his large face was ghostly in the moonlight, his staring eyes wild and fiercely luminous. He was annoyed.

The animals ducked under a hazelnut bush. The owl was Professor Galileo Newton Owl, D.Phil., a tawny owl who was much larger and very much older than the common tawny owls of the region. The Professor lived in an enormous hollow beech in Cuckoo Brow Wood and spent the hours between midnight and dawn searching the heavens with his telescope from the observatory he had built at the very top of his tree.

In addition to his scholarship in celestial mechanics, the Professor had a wide reputation for applied studies in natural history, particularly in the nocturnal habits, preferences, and tastes of small furry creatures. His evening hunting forays had made him an expert in all matters having to do with the meadows and woods around Sawrey, and not much went on that escaped his scrutiny. The Professor was an enormously dignified bird who refused to suffer impertinence—and one never quite knew what might strike him as impertinent.

"*Who?*" the Professor called in a cross, quavery interrogative. He turned his head from side to side, repeating his question. "*Who-who-whooo?*"

"*It's Rascal, sir,*" Rascal barked, with the greatest politeness. "*And Tabitha Twitchit and Crumpet. From Near Sawrey.*"

"*Sooo I see,*" said the Professor, sounding even more cross. "*But you are on the wrong side of Wilfin Beck. Your side is the other side.*"

"*That is true, Professor Owl,*" Rascal agreed, aware that it would not do to offend. Galileo Newton Owl was really quite large, his beak razor-sharp, his claws powerful. Every rabbit and mouse in the district fled when the shadow of his wide wings crossed their paths, and even Fritz the Ferret was afraid of him, although he laughed carelessly and pretended not to mind. "*But we're on an important mission, you see, sir,*" Rascal went on. "*We're on our way to Sawrey School to see if we can find the lost money.*"

"*Lost money?*" asked the Professor with an irritated glance down his beak. He found it disagreeable to be told that there was something going on that he did not know about. "*Whooose money was it? Whooo lost it?*"

"*Tabitha,*" Rascal said, with a certain sense of nervous inadequacy, "*p'rhaps you'd better explain.*"

Tabitha Twitchit was a good storyteller and related the tale with such skill that the Professor was intrigued. More than intrigued, though, he was nettled, for he often had occasion to observe Jeremy Crosfield when the boy was putting up his aunt's sheep at dusk, and had found him quite a sensible and respectful young man.

"I'll go with you," he said. *"If there's anything I detest—worse than impertinence, that is—it is the want of integrity. I dooo not hold with people making accusations for which there is nooo foundation. And Jeremy Crosfield is a fine lad."* He flapped his large wings and rose with a hissing whisper into the dark sky, where his black shape hung like an ominous thought between earth and moon.

The two cats and the little dog raced across the meadow, across a lane, and up a steep hill to Sawrey School. The building had a melancholy look, standing alone on the hill in the flickering moonlight, the boundaries of its yard marked by a low drystone wall. It looked as if it missed the children's gay games and laughter.

"How will we get in?" Tabitha asked, as they paused under the trees, surveying the shadowy scene. *"The doors must be locked tight."*

"There's bound to be a way," said Rascal, conscious that the Professor had just settled onto the branch of a nearby elm and was watching them. *"Let's just follow our noses."*

And follow their noses they did, all the way around the stone building to the place where a small frame addition had been constructed to serve as the teachers' pantry, where Miss Crabbe and Miss Nash could hang their coats and hats and brew a pot of tea on the gas ring. And there, just at ground level, in the corner where the little room had been built against the stone wall, was a round hole and a narrow passage, barely large enough for Tabitha and Crumpet and Rascal to squeeze through, one at a time. Rascal wrinkled his nose as he went, for he was smelling a very strong, very disagreeable scent. It was the pervasive, repulsive, disgusting scent of rat.

The animals pushed out through the end of the passage and found themselves in the far corner of a very dark cloakroom. Dogs are not especially known for their nighttime vision, but cats are quite adept at seeing in the dark. Crumpet and Tabitha encountered no difficulty as they led the way past stacks of newspapers and magazines and boxes and broken umbrellas and unmatched wellingtons. They went out into the main lobby, and saw that there were two rooms, one smaller, one quite large.

"Let's take the small room first," Tabitha said. As they could tell from the scrawled pictures pinned to the wall, it was Miss Nash's infants' room, where children aged five, six, and seven learnt their first lessons in reading, writing, and sitting still. There was a window in one wall, and in the gloom, Rascal could make out the rows of empty wooden desks, their seats neatly folded up. He was pleased to see that there were several colorful pictures of dogs, and only one of a cat.

"*Well, Rascal?*" Tabitha demanded. "*Can you smell any money?*"

"*Give me a minute, will you?*" Rascal growled. "*I'm not a magician, you know. This sort of thing takes skill and concentration.*"

As the cats made their own search (not nearly so thorough as Rascal's, of course), the dog applied his nose to the floor and began to sniff, methodically quartering Miss Nash's room, just as he would quarter for the scent of a fugitive fox. He spent ten minutes prowling around the four walls of the room, around the teacher's desk, under the children's desks, and in front of the bookshelves and lockers. He found some polished stones under a desk, several bits of chalk, and some beech leaves that had been tracked in and not swept up, probably because Bertha Stubbs had given notice. He also found a yellow bead, a bright blue marble, and a broken red-painted handle from a skip-rope. But there was no money.

"*Nothing of interest here,*" he reported. "*Let's try the other room.*"

"*What does money smell like?*" Tabitha Twitchit wanted to know, as they went into the larger room—Miss Crabbe's junior room.

"*It smells like gold and silver, brass and copper,*" Rascal said. "*It also smells like sweat and human hands. It smells,*" he added, half under his breath, "*like greed.*"

The junior room had a window that caught the moonlight and spilled it onto the floor, brightening the gloom. Miss Crabbe's wooden desk was at the front, before a long black chalkboard that hung on the wall, beneath a row of pictures showing the letters of the alphabet as they were meant to be written. Bookcases ran the length of one wall, and a piano stood in the corner, with yellowed ivory keys, a decorative bracket for an oil lamp, and a fretwork front cut in an intricate design, its curlicue openings filled with green silk. The students' desks were larger than those in Miss Nash's room—the children who sat in them were eight, nine, ten, and eleven years old—and each one had an inkwell and a slot for pencils and a top that folded down over a wooden box beneath, where books and papers were put. The children were forbidden to keep food in their desks, of course, but Rascal could smell it: the tantalizing odor of crusts of buttered bread and cheese, ginger biscuit, and soft, ripe apples and pears.

He also smelled rat, stronger and more pervasive now. And he heard an odd metallic clinking.

"*What's that sound?*" Tabitha whispered anxiously, pressing very close to Crumpet. Tabitha had a good head on her shoulders, but she was inclined to be uneasy when she got very far away from her village.

"It sounds like somebody rolling something," Rascal remarked, puzzled. He cocked his head, listening, and heard it again.

"It's coming from behind Miss Crabbe's desk," Crumpet said, taking charge. *"Rascal, you go round to the left, and I'll go round to the right. Tabitha, you go underneath."*

Crumpet lowered herself close to the floor and crept slowly forward, whiskers twitching. Her sense of smell might not be as keen as Rascal's, but no cat in the world would be worth her salt if she did not recognize this scent. The odious smell of rat was so strong that it washed over her like a nauseating flood. Cats may be superior mousers, but they are not at all fond of rats, who taste much worse than they smell. To tell the truth, most cats (except for the largest and most combative) are afraid of rats, for their teeth and claws are like steel needles, and they never fight fair.

And then, as she peered fearfully around Miss Crabbe's desk, Crumpet saw them: three brown rats. One was larger and sleeker than any rat she had ever seen, and seemed to think a good deal of himself. He was a country-gentleman sort of rat, in a blue jacket, red waistcoat, fawn breeches, and smart boots. He must, however, have fallen on rather hard times, for his jacket was shabby, his waistcoat was dirty, there was a rip in the right leg of his breeches, and his boots were muddy and down at the heel. In fact, his whole appearance was that of genteel poverty, although he was sitting on a stack of coins: a gold sovereign, three half-crowns, and several florins. Several shillings were scattered on the floor.

The other two rats were smaller and thinner, with pointed noses and half-closed eyes that gave them a sly, shifty look, and shabby fur that looked as if the moths had been at it—or perhaps they had been in a brawl, for they struck Crumpet as the fighting kind. One wore a red-and-white striped jersey, like a sailor; the other sported a green jockey's cap, perched at a rakish angle, and a dirty green silk scarf. Hand-rolled cigarettes dangled from the corners of their mouths, and their protruding front teeth were stained an ugly tobacco-yellow. From the look of the pair, Crumpet thought, they were tough, disreputable rats, and had probably ridden a railroad train up from the London wharves.

The three rats had set up four pieces of chalk in a diamond pattern, standing them on end like pins, and they were playing at bowls, rolling silver shillings in the direction of the chalk pins. They were so intent on this game, and they were having such a great deal of noisy fun at it, that they failed to notice the two cats and the dog, crouched silently in the shadow of the desk, watching.

"*Pop-pop, and they're gone!*" whooped Striped-Jersey, as his shilling knocked down two of the four pins. One of his ears had been chewed and his tail was short and stumpy, as if a cart had recently rolled over it, cutting off an inch or two. He smacked his dirty paws together and danced a celebratory jig. "*Add two to me tally, Newgate Jack! That florin is as good as mine.*"

"*Two on, Roger-Dodger,*" said Newgate Jack calmly, pushing his green cap back between his ears and marking with a bit of pencil on the back of a white envelope which lay on the floor. That is, it had once been white, although now it bore the dusty marks of innumerable rat paw prints, and one corner looked as if it had been gnawed. "*That brings you to twenty-nine.*"

"*Twenty-nine?*" the gentleman rat cried angrily. "*But Roger-Dodger's last bowl but one brought him only to twenty-five, so he's at twenty-seven, not twenty-nine!*"

"*Sorry, old chap,*" Newgate Jack said nonchalantly. "*Twenty-nine, no more, no less. If you don't believe me, you can count 'em yourself.*" He pushed the dirty envelope under the nose of the gentleman rat, who stared at it with consternation. It was obvious that he hadn't a clue as to how to read the tally.

Crumpet guessed that the other two rats knew this, and were busily cheating him out of the money on which he had been sitting.

"*So I'm two up on you, Ridley Rattail!*" Roger-Dodger gloated, going to set up the pins again.

"*Not for long, ye're not,*" growled Mr. Rattail, picking up a shilling and turning it over in his paws. "*I'll take ye in one hurl, I will, ye dirty little rat.*" And with that, he stepped up to the mark and bowled the shilling smartly down the lane. His aim was not true, however, and his shilling wobbled off to the side and under the teacher's desk, very near Tabitha's paw.

"*Too bad for you, Ridley Rattail, old chump—old chum, I mean,*" Newgate Jack said, as the gentleman rat, muttering under his breath, went back to squat on top of the coins. "*Roger-Dodger, your hurl.*"

"*And my florin,*" Roger-Dodger said arrogantly, sauntering up to the mark. "*And after that one, I'll have another.*" He spit first on one paw and then on the other, his whiskers twitching back and forth. And then he lifted the shilling, took two short, scurrying steps up to the line, and hurled hard and true. The shilling struck the nearest piece of chalk with a resounding *chink!* and all four pins went flying.

"*Thirty-one and game!*" Newgate Jack said, making more marks on the envelope. "*The florin is yours, Roger-Dodger old lad!*"

"*It's mine, all right,*" said Roger-Dodger, approaching Ridley Rattail with his paw out. "*I'll have it now, if you please, Rattail old fellow. But I'll be glad to give you a chance to get it back.*"

Grudgingly, Ridley Rattail got off his stack of coins and handed over the florin to Roger-Dodger, who tucked it into the pocket of his striped jersey.

But the winner had no time to celebrate, for the next

thing they knew, the three rats were prisoners. Ridley Rattail was clasped firmly between Crumpet's teeth, while Tabitha held Newgate Jack by the tail, and Rascal smashed his paw flat on Roger-Dodger. There were scratchings and wrigglings and a chorus of shrill shrieks and the sound of wharf rat curses.

"What'll we do with these filthy fellows?" Tabitha asked distastefully, around a mouthful of squalling rat. *"They're not fit to eat."*

Rascal would not have had any difficulty eating the rats, for his sense of taste was not as easily offended as that of the cats, but he had another plan. *"I'll show you what we'll do with 'em,"* he said, and led the way out of the room, through the teachers' pantry, and back to the little hole through which they had entered. He spit Roger-Dodger out on the floor.

"Get out of here and don't even think about coming back," he snapped, baring his teeth and swatting at the rat with his paw. They all stood watching while Roger-Dodger scrambled hastily through the tunnel to the out-of-doors.

"We're letting them go?" asked Crumpet incredulously. Like Tabitha, she had no taste for rat, but it went against her nature to release them. It seemed very clear that Ridley Rattail, down on his gentleman's luck, had stolen the School Roof Fund, and the other two were cheating him out of it. However you looked at it, they were an unsavory lot.

"Oh, they won't go far," Rascal replied with confidence, as the other two rats made their ignominious exits.

Rascal was right. For the instant Roger-Dodger darted out of the hole and into the schoolyard, he was fair game for the Professor, who had been impatiently waiting to learn what had become of the money and who (since owls have very little sense of smell), was not at all offended by Roger-Dodger's disgracefully ratty odor.

"Put me down, Round-Head!" shrilled Roger-Dodger, as the Professor seized the rat in his claw. The rat's striped

jersey was bunched up around his ears. *"Put me down, you pirate!"*

"Don't be impertinent," the Professor admonished sternly, giving the rat a good shake as he flapped his huge wings and lifted into the air. *"Impertinence does not become a rat whooo is invited to dinner."*

"Invited to dinner?" Roger-Dodger cried, turning pale with fear as he looked down to see the ground, now very far below. Unable to bear the sight, he covered his eyes with his paws. *"Oh, I'm done for, I'm dead! I'll never again see the wharves, or dance with the ladies in the Whitechapel pubs. I'll never again see me mates, or Newgate Jack, Gor'bless his bones!"*

Which proved not quite true. For at that moment, the Professor looked down over his shoulder and saw Newgate Jack scrambling out of the hole and staggering off dazedly across the schoolyard. Not being an owl who wasted his opportunities, the Professor made a graceful turn, swooped, and snatched. Then, bearing one rat in each large claw and feeling mightily pleased with his night's work, he flew off to his home in the hollow beech in Cuckoo Brow Wood, where he took out a large iron pot and the recipe for fricasseed rat that had been given to him by his cousin, Old Brown, who lived on an island in a lake not far away. It called for a carrot, a parsnip, a stick of celery, an onion, and two rats (or one squirrel), skinned. These ingredients were to be stewed all together over a slow fire until quite tender, then seasoned with plenty of fresh parsley and a pinch of cayenne and served over dumplings.

As dinner was cooking, the Professor went up to his observatory, which was located at the very top of the beech. There was a ladder, so that he could invite his friends up to have a look at the heavens, but being an owl, the Professor disregarded it and flew, instead of climbing. Over the low observatory door was a hand-painted notice board, reading:

G. N. OWL, D. PHIL.
OBSREVER AT LARJE
MIND YR HED!

The Professor spent the next pleasant hour having a look at the moon through his telescope, which was mounted on a swivel that allowed him to see the entire sky, and making notes in his *Obsrever's Notbook*. Then he flew back down to enjoy his gourmet dinner, taking it, as usual, with a small glass of mead, which he brewed himself from honey and strawberries, with a sprig of rosemary, a few cloves, and some orange peel. He found his plate of fricasseed rat quite satisfactory, and when he had finished, he retired with a cup of dandelion coffee to his favorite chair, where he fell sound asleep over a copy (in translation) of Sir Isaac Newton's *Principia Mathematica*.

It was too bad, of course, that when the Professor made off with the rats, he had only two claws and was not wearing a waistcoat with pockets. For when Ridley Rattail dragged himself out of the hole, he found that he was able to get clean away, which he did as fast as his four paws could carry him. Since it was a moonlit night and he was strongly apprehensive about owls, he kept to the cover of the bushes and brambles, where his breeches were ripped and torn. When he reached Wilfin Beck, he had to swim for it, stripping off his jacket, waistcoat, and breeches and carrying them, rolled, in his teeth. Once on the other side, he was busy wringing out his tail when he was accosted by Fritz Ferret, who actually liked the taste of rat. He had to run very fast—faster than he had ever run in his life—in order to escape with most of his fur and his tail intact. He managed to gather up all of his clothes except for his jacket, and Fritz took it home to use for a duster.

Which is why, when Ridley Rattail arrived at last at Hill Top Farm, where his dear friend Rosabelle Rat lived in seclusion in the attic, he was without a jacket, his breeches were torn, he had lost one of his smart boots, and he was cold and wet right through his fur to his skin. Not only that, but he was overwhelmed with misery at the thought of being forced to abandon his treasure. (Ridley Rattail was not quite clever enough to realize that, had their game gone on much longer, Roger-Dodger and Newgate Jack would have taken every last farthing away from him.)

Rascal, Tabitha, and Crumpet, on the other hand, were rejoicing. They gathered up the coins and counted them to be sure that they were all there: one sovereign, two half-crowns, three florins, and nine shillings (including the florin that had fallen out of Roger-Dodger's jersey when Crumpet held him upside down and shook him). The envelope into which Dimity Woodcock had put the money was rather the worse for wear, of course. The upper right-hand corner had been chewed, there were dusty rat-prints all over it, and a crooked column of tallies where Newgate Jack had scored the game of bowls. But Tabitha held it open with her paw while Crumpet counted the coins into it, one at a time, doing sums in her head to make sure that the whole two pounds was accounted for. Then Rascal took the envelope carefully in his teeth and carried it to Miss Nash's desk. He put it into the top drawer, where she would be sure to see it first thing in the morning.

But not before Tabitha had taken up the stub of pencil and written, in her very best copperplate hand (paw, rather):

NO MORE RATS.

22

Acorn to the Rescue

Sawrey lay sound asleep under the silent, silvery moon, the little village wrapped in a curling mist that rose from the marshes and fields like wisps of fairy web. In his home in the hollow oak, G. N. Owl napped fitfully over *Principia Mathematica,* while Ridley Rattail slept the sleep of utter exhaustion in the attic at Hill Top Farm. Rascal, Crumpet, and Tabitha, satisfied that they had done a good night's work, had also gone home to their beds.

Miss Potter's animals were asleep as well, snug in their traveling boxes in Miss Potter's bedroom. Josey Rabbit dreamed expansively of the fields and meadows and woods that stretched to the horizon and beyond. Beside her, Mopsy dreamed that she was lying on her back in fragrant mounds of wild thyme and clover, kicking her heels and batting at butterflies. Mrs. Tig's nose twitched with delight as she dreamed of beetles and worms and snails and fallen apples.

And in his little wooden cage, his head pillowed on excelsior, Tom Thumb dreamed of a grand wedding at Westminster Cathedral: himself in white tie and tail, with a lavender boutonniere; Teasel in a pink-and-white dress and tulle veil, with a bouquet of primroses and forget-me-nots; and champagne and wedding cake and dancing after.

Teasel, however, was not dreaming, for she was not asleep. Instead, she lay uneasily awake, wondering what she had got herself into. She could understand that her fiancé, because he was a city mouse, had different ideas about what he wanted in a wife—different, that is, from Acorn, who was perfectly content with her just the way she was, and did not demand that she learn to curtsy, or wear a blue silk dress trimmed in lace, or drink French champagne. And now that she thought about it, she wondered whether she could actually love a mouse who was so skittish about owls, and bragged of actually eating calves' foot jelly, and kept comparing her to his first wife.

Teasel sat up and looked at Tom's sleeping form. Yes, he was certainly a handsome mouse, plump and sleek, with elegant paws and polished whiskers and a delightfully long, astonishingly white tail. He had delicate sensibilities, and charming manners, too, and an alluring mouse-of-the-world sophistication. He was nothing at all like Acorn, whose paws were worn with work, whose brown tail and ears had got all tattered in various brave adventures, and whose fur and whiskers were usually dusty and full of cobwebs. But Acorn didn't mind the owls (although he was careful not to tempt them), and he wasn't afraid to go straight up to Honeysuckle and ask her politely for a little bucket of milk. And he actually enjoyed sitting down to a dinner of turnips and corn, or a breakfast of oats, with a bit of cheese now and then for a tea-time treat. No fancy dishes or fine wine for Acorn. He was a country mouse, through and through.

And at the thought of Acorn's cobwebby whiskers and

tattered tail and comfortable, homely ways, Teasel began to cry. She had made a dreadful mistake, leaving her home in the haystack and eloping with a city mouse—without even a note of explanation for her parents or for Acorn. Dear, sweet Acorn, with whom she had shared so many happy times, dancing, and playing hide-and-seek in the meadow, and chasing one another through the sweet, clean hay. What must he think of her, abandoning him as she had? She would never see him again, never hear his cheerful voice calling—

"*Teasel!*"

Teasel sat up straight, her large ears perked forward, her whiskers twitching, her heart pounding hard in her chest. Was someone calling her name? Was it possible that—

"*Teasel, it's me! Acorn! I'm here to rescue you!*"

"*Rescue me?*" she cried, scrambling up and running over to clutch the bars with her paws. "*Oh, Acorn, do you think you could?*"

"*Of course I can,*" Acorn said, with a vigorous determination. "*I've been searching for you ever since I heard you'd been kidnapped by some scoundrel. I won't rest until you're safe.*"

And without a word, he jumped up on the shelf beside Tom Thumb's cage and began gnawing at one of the wooden bars. Acorn's teeth were sturdy and strong, and he had completely gnawed through one bar and started on another almost before Teasel realized what he was doing.

"*Oh, Acorn!*" she said, sighing in breathless admiration as she watched those teeth, those determined country-mouse teeth, so hard at work—at work for her, setting her free.

One more minute, and the second bar was gnawed through, and Acorn was holding out a paw. "*Can you squeeze through?*" he asked anxiously.

"*Of course I can,*" Teasel replied. She pushed herself through the opening and into Acorn's waiting arms. She did not bother to leave a note for Tom.

* * *

The sun rose to the east over Lake Windermere, the cheerful light rousing the village to its daily tasks and waking Tom Thumb from his nightlong sleep. With a dreamy smile, his eyes still closed, he rolled over and put out a paw.

"Teasel," he said. "Oh, Teasel, my love. Come here and give your sweetheart a big kiss."

But Teasel did not reply. Tom opened his eyes and saw, to his horror, that the bars of the cage had been gnawed through and his fiancée was gone. He gave a frantic squeal and began to run in circles. "Oh, woe!" he cried. "Oh, woe, woe, woe!"

Mrs. Tiggy, who slept very hard, slumbered on, but Josey and Mopsy woke up with a start. "What's happened?" Josey cried. "Is somebody dead?"

"Teasel's been kidnapped!" Tom sobbed. "Teasel, my lovely, the love of my heart, the light of my life—she's gone, gone, gone!"

In the bed in the middle of the room, Beatrix sat up straight, threw off the covers, and pulled a shawl around her shoulders. "What's all this squeaking?" she asked, getting out of bed and padding over to the cages. "What's wrong?"

But one glance answered her question. "Oh, I see," she said, and added reasonably, "I suppose your friend got homesick, Tom, and gnawed through the wooden bars to let herself out."

"No, no!" Tom shrieked, growing more frantic by the minute. "She was kidnapped, I tell you! Teasel would never leave me!"

Beatrix picked up Tom, squealing and kicking, and put him into the rabbits' box. "You can stay here until your cage is repaired," she said in a comforting tone. She stroked the quivering mouse with the tip of her finger. "Don't be so sad, Tom. You'll find another companion, I'm sure."

"Never, never," cried Tom. "*I'll never love another mouse the way I loved Teasel!*"

Beatrix sighed, thinking of her own loss. "But if you don't, you know, you'll just have to learn to live alone. Not all stories have a happy ending."

And with that, she threw off her shawl and began to get dressed. Today was a busy day.

23

Miss Nash Is Surprised

It was eight o'clock in the morning, and Miss Nash was walking from Sunnyside Cottage, where she lived, to Sawrey School. It was a pretty October morning, cool and crisp, with the fragrance of autumn. The golden trees seemed to shimmer against the blue sky and the blackberry briars along the lane were covered with red and yellow leaves, making brave patches of color in the sunshine.

But these sights brought Margaret little pleasure, for she was terribly anxious about what the morning would bring. If Miss Crabbe had made her accusations to Constable Braithwaite, it was entirely possible that Jeremy Crosfield had been arrested and taken to Hawkshead for arraignment before the magistrate. If Miss Crabbe had not yet gone to the constable, for whatever reason, there would no doubt be a great deal of turmoil and anxiety and mutterings about the money. And to add to the difficulties, there was no Bertha to clean and light the stove, carry coal and cinders and water, and sweep the floors. All those duties would fall upon Margaret's shoulders. It was no wonder that her heart was heavy, her feet dragged, and the day ahead seemed filled with ominous storm clouds.

But Miss Nash was in for a surprise—several of them, in fact. She had just inserted the key in the lock and was preparing to open the school door, when she heard someone calling her name.

"Miss Nash, oh, Miss Nash!"

She turned to see Vicar Sackett hurrying across the school yard. His scarf was flying, and he thrust his walking stick into the air with a great energy.

"Good morning, Vicar," Margaret said without enthusiasm, and turned the key. This was no time for a chat. She would barely be able to get Bertha's work done before the children arrived.

"Oh, Miss Nash, I have news," the vicar said breathlessly. He lifted his hat and put it back on. "Terrible news, I'm sorry to say. Miss Crabbe has broken her leg."

Margaret turned, appalled. For a moment, she couldn't catch her breath or speak. "Broken . . . her leg?" she managed at last.

"Yes, yes, her leg." The vicar took out his handkerchief and blew his nose. "Dreadful. A very bad break. Very bad. Doctor Butters came, of course. She is confined to bed." He eyed her and added, with deliberate emphasis. "Miss Crabbe is going nowhere."

Margaret still could not quite comprehend. Miss Crabbe was such a *determined* person, so firm of purpose, so resolute. It was inconceivable that anything might arrest her forward motion. "But . . . but how? How could such a thing happen?"

"She fell on the stairs at Castle Cottage," the vicar replied. "She says she stepped on the cat." He cleared his throat, sketched a gesture with his walking stick, and cleared his throat again. "I believe that she was on her way to see Constable Braithwaite when it happened."

Margaret found that she had been holding her breath. "Oh," she said, with enormous relief. "Then she didn't—"

"No," said the vicar. "She didn't."

Margaret straightened her shoulders. "Well, then," she said, and was surprised by the cheeriness in her voice. "Let's make a cup of tea and talk about how we can handle her classroom. I have a suggestion or two to make."

"Wonderful," said the vicar, with obvious relief. He beamed. "I knew we could count on you, Miss Nash."

In the little teachers' pantry, while their tea brewed, Margaret told the vicar what she had in mind. First, the vicar might write a note to Bertha Stubbs, explaining what had happened and asking her to return to her work. Surely, Bertha would not reject the vicar's plea—and in Miss Crabbe's absence, there would be no reason for her to refuse. Second, the vicar might call upon Mrs. Holland, who had come in to take the infants' class when Margaret's mother had fallen ill two years before. If Mrs. Holland, who was very capable, could take the younger children, Margaret herself would take the older ones. The arrangement might be extended for the length of Miss Crabbe's absence, if Mrs. Holland were available.

The vicar sipped his tea and put down his cup. "I might as well tell you the whole truth," he said. "I very much doubt that Miss Crabbe will return to her post. She is . . . not well." He hesitated, started to elaborate, then thought better of it. He settled for: "However, that is a bridge perhaps more easily crossed in future months. In the meantime, I am glad that you are willing to take Miss Crabbe's place. I will contact Mrs. Holland and see when it is possible for her to come in."

"And Bertha Stubbs," Margaret said, thinking of those buckets of coal.

"And Bertha Stubbs," the vicar agreed. "I shall get on it at once." He finished his tea, took his hat, and went to the door, where he paused, his hand on the knob. "Oh, yes, one more thing I thought I would mention. I am glad to tell you that the Parish Register has been found and returned to its rightful place."

"How wonderful!" Margaret exclaimed. "You must be very relieved that it has been returned. Where was it? Who found it?"

The vicar put on his hat. "I must be on my way," he said vaguely, and was gone.

It was indeed a pity that the vicar left when he did, for he was not there when Margaret sat down at her desk in the infants' room and opened the top drawer to take out her attendance book. But she paused with her hand raised, staring down at the drawer in surprise and bewilderment. On top of the book lay an envelope, chewed in one corner, with dirty smudges all over it and an odd, wavering column of tallies down one side, as though someone had used it to keep score. And even more puzzling were the three words penciled in a faintly written script:

NO MORE RATS.

But when she picked the envelope up and spilled the coins onto the desk, Margaret knew what she had found. Before her lay one sovereign, two half-crowns, three florins, and nine shillings.

The School Roof Fund had been returned.

24

Miss Potter Pays a Visit

As Margaret Nash was making her troubled way to Sawrey School that morning, Beatrix was seated in Mr. Heelis' red-wheeled gig, behind a fine brown horse that pulled them swiftly along the seven-mile stretch of twisting road between Hawkshead and Ambleside. She was on her way to visit the Armitt sisters, who lived at Rydal Cottage, a short distance beyond Ambleside.

If she had been in London, Beatrix would have felt terribly uneasy and very shy about riding for miles with a strange man whom she had met just the day before—and a very good-looking man he was, too. Of course, her mother would have absolutely forbidden the journey, as she had so often forbidden Beatrix to be alone with Norman—a demand that, at the time, Beatrix had accepted without complaint and now wished with all her heart that she had disregarded.

Anyway, they were not in London, her mother had no idea what Beatrix was doing, and Mr. Heelis was no strange man, but the respected solicitor who was managing her purchase of Hill Top Farm. What was more, he seemed even more shy than she, and his tongue-tied shyness had the odd effect of making Beatrix more comfortable with him, rather than less. Most people, Beatrix had found, expected a person to make chit-chat and carry on a lengthy conversation about nothing at all, with no other purpose than to make appropriate social noises at the appropriate points: *"Is that right?"* and *"How very amusing!"* and *"Oh, you don't say!"*

But Mr. Heelis seemed to enjoy idle conversation no more than she, so the two of them maintained a companionable silence as they drove along the quiet road. A gauzy autumnal fog lay across the lake, but the sun was already drinking it up, and the blue sky promised another bright morning. It was still very early when they reached Hawkshead, and few were about, and once past the market town they were on the open road, with blue speedwell and white mayweed and pink campion hiding in the grass along the verge, and the cherry-red pips of the dog rose and the even brighter berries of the holly sparking like scarlet flames in the hedgerow, which was busy with finches feeding on the fruit. Mr. Heelis's horse was fast, and before Beatrix knew it they had flown past Outgate and Clappersgate and over the River Rothay into Ambleside and out again. When they arrived at Rydal Cottage shortly after nine, Mr. Heelis remarked politely that he would return after lunch to pick her up. Then he smiled and touched his hat, lifted the reins, and was gone.

Beatrix had been looking forward with pleasure to her planned visit to the Armitt sisters. Louie and Sophia—Annie was away in London—shared many of Beatrix's interests: she and Sophia enjoyed drawing and talking about the Lakeland fungi, and she and Louie held similar views about the importance of preserving the Lakeland customs and old ways. Both of the sisters knew and corresponded with many important people, entertained distinguished visitors, and were ardent supporters of women's right to graduate from Oxford and Cambridge. Sophia was confident and sometimes imperious, while Louie was imaginative, and when Beatrix was with them, she often felt quite overwhelmed, since both sisters were far better educated than she.

But Beatrix should not have worried, for she was widely read in the literary classics and she had an extraordinary memory—she had once memorized six of Shakespeare's plays for her own pleasure. She also read popular novels, her father's political journals, and the newspapers, and when she was asked an opinion on politics or international affairs, she had one to offer. This happened rarely at Bolton Gardens, of course, for her father did not invite her thoughts on any subjects, and her mother talked of nothing but household business or social affairs. But the Armitt sisters treated Beatrix as an equal with opinions worth hearing and considering, and when the three women were together, they got on famously. There were dozens of subjects to discuss and they were never silent for an instant.

And so it was on this visit. The weather was fair and warm, and they walked through the garden, gay with chrysanthemums, dahlias, and Michaelmas daisies. Afterward, they ate a simple lunch of soup and bread and cheese, admired Sophia's drawings, listened to Louie read a paper she had written about the woolen mills that used to operate up and down the river, and talked of the sisters' dream of creating a library at Ambleside.

The Lake Country was known for its unspoiled natural beauty and the slow, sweet, seasonally defined pace of its rural life. But a great many artists, poets, and writers had called it home in the last hundred years, and it had a strong cultural tradition. Ambleside seemed to Louie and Sophia exactly the right place to establish a library for students and scholars, where papers and books that had literary, scientific, or antiquarian value could be housed. Beatrix enthusiastically agreed, and promised to subscribe when the Armitt sisters' library became a reality.

The hours passed all too swiftly, and when in the early afternoon the red-wheeled gig pulled into the cottage drive and stopped, Beatrix felt a sharp pang of regret, for it seemed as if the visit had hardly begun. She bade Louie and Sophia goodbye, promised to write to them often, and hurried out to the gig to join Mr. Heelis, anxious not to keep him waiting.

"You had a good visit, I hope," Mr. Heelis said, when she had settled herself.

"I did, indeed, thank you," Beatrix replied with a smile, and that was all that was said for quite a few moments, as they drove back toward Ambleside.

The earlier part of the day had been sunny and pleasant, but in the last hour, the sky to the north and east had darkened, the thunderheads were piling up like mounds of blue and gray cotton, and gusts of chilly wind swirled the fallen leaves. She was surprised, then, when Mr. Heelis broke the silence to say that that there was something he wanted to show her.

"I hope you won't mind," he said with some diffidence, "if we take a short detour. It shouldn't require more than a half hour."

"Of course not," she said, but she spoke uncertainly, with an eye to the threatening clouds. Another half hour might mean the difference between staying comfortably dry and getting soaked. "Where are we going?"

"It's a bit hard to explain," he said with some awkwardness. "I should rather wait until we get there, and let you see for yourself."

And with that, Beatrix had to be content.

25

Sarah Barwick Shocks
the Neighbors

Dimity had spent the morning tramping through the glorious woods and meadows of Claife Heights and up to the summit of Latterbarrow. There, she sat down and ate the sandwich and apple she had brought, enjoying the magnificent views. To the east, she could see the head of Lake Windermere; to the north, the cloudy slopes of Loughrigg, the Fairfield Horseshoe, Red Screes and Caudale Moor, and the town of Ambleside, with Wansfell Pike and the Ill Bell Ridge beyond; to the northwest, the near-vertical flanks of the Langdale Pikes. The view took her out and away from herself, and from the goings-on at Sawrey: the disconcerting business at Anvil Cottage, Miss Crabbe's accident, the missing money—small matters to city people who were accustomed to murder and mayhem on a large scale, perhaps, but anxiety-provoking enough for those whose lives centered on a quiet village.

Having eaten and rested and filled herself with the sights of the distant fells, Dimity started home, taking the path past Moss Eccles Tarn, a quiet little lake bordered with woodland and brightened by late-blooming wild flowers. It was a good place to fish for trout, and watch red squirrels gathering acorns against the coming cold of winter, and glimpse the bright red flash of a fox, hurrying through the undergrowth.

Eons ago, the mountains of this part of England had been covered with ice, and the large lakes—Windermere and Coniston and Esthwaite—were the work of the glaciers, gouging and grinding the rock. The smaller tarn lakes, such as Moss Eccles and Lily Tarn and the others, lay in the hollows scraped out by the advancing and retreating ice. It somehow pleased Dim to think of those silent, massive, enduring glaciers, as high as the sky and more powerful than the resisting rock, carving and sculpting and shaping the landscape she saw now around her. It was all a great mystery, and she became somehow a tiny part of its vastness as she stood on the windswept height. Altogether, it had been a good morning's walk, she thought happily, as she headed downhill and home.

Dimity was coming down Market Street when she saw the green bicycle leaning against the front of Anvil Cottage. The front door of the cottage stood open, as did all the windows, and several rugs were spread over the side fence for airing. Miss Barwick, whom Dimity had not yet met, must have ridden over from Hawkshead for the day.

Dimity paused, regarding the bicycle with a raised eyebrow. Bicycles were not a novelty in the village, of course. Two or three men rode them, and so did the boy who brought the newspaper from Hawkshead, and occasionally an intrepid woman could be found among the sports cyclists who rode through Sawrey on their way up to the fells and moors.

But although cycling might be all the rage for the New Woman in London, cycling women were still looked on with open suspicion in the rural areas. They were not quite respectable, somehow. They were thought to have loose morals or lack a sense of propriety, or were anxious to call attention to themselves. Dimity suspected, however, that what lay behind most of the criticism was the recognition that a cycling woman was a mobile woman, and the fear that a mobile woman would have a great deal more independence, and the absolute belief that independence in women was not a good thing. In any event, Miss Barwick's bicycle was certain to shock a villager or two.

Dimity stepped up to the open door and knocked. She was not dressed for calling. In fact, she was wearing her stout old boots, a disreputable felt hat, and a tweed jacket and skirt rather the worse for having been worn on many muddy tramps. But it would only be neighborly to stop in and introduce herself—and besides, she was dying of curiosity. Who *was* this mysterious Miss Barwick, this bicycling Miss Barwick? And how in the world had she come to inherit Anvil Cottage?

But there was no answer to her knock. Instead, Dimity heard several fierce sneezes, each one louder than the other, followed by a shriek and a resounding crash. And then silence.

Alarmed, Dimity called, "Miss Barwick? Miss Barwick, are you there? All you all right?"

There were two more sneezes. A muffled voice said, quite crossly, "No, I'm not all right, blast it. I'm dead."

Dead? Dimity pushed the door open wide and ventured into the sitting room. "Miss Barwick?" she asked tentatively, looking around. "Miss Barwick, where are you?"

"In here," said the voice, somewhat strangled. There was another loud sneeze.

Dimity went into the room that Miss Tolliver had used

as a dining room and stopped, shocked. Miss Barwick had apparently been standing on a heavy wooden chair in front of the window when she had fallen, for the chair was on the floor, Miss Barwick was flat on her face half under the chair, and the fringed chintz curtains were draped over her and wound around her legs—which were unmistakably clad, Dimity saw with a stifled gasp, in gray serge trousers.

Swallowing her shock, Dimity hurried forward. "Please, may I . . . may I help?"

"You might begin by taking the chair off me," Miss Barwick said with some asperity. "I seem to be wound round in this horrid chintz." She sneezed again, emphatically. "And the fringe is thick with cat fur. It's sending me into fits. Hurry before I sneeze my head off." And she sneezed again.

Dimity hurriedly tilted the heavy chair upright and pushed it against the wall. She helped Miss Barwick untangle her legs from the curtains, and then extended a hand to help her get up.

Disregarding the hand, Miss Barwick rolled over and scrambled nimbly to her feet. She had a horsey sort of face, long and narrow, her mouth was very wide, and her nose was definitely freckled. No one would ever call her pretty, but her eyes, dark and alert, held humor and a sharp intelligence. Her dark hair had come loose and tumbled in a disheveled way around her shoulders, and her white blouse, which had a blue-edged sailor collar, was smudged with cobwebs and dust. The gray trousers were cut full so that the outline of her legs was scarcely visible—but they were most definitely trousers. They looked, Dimity thought, as her surprise gave way to something like envy, rather comfortable. To tell the honest truth, they also looked quite practical, if one were riding a bicycle, or tramping across the fells, or climbing over a stone wall.

"Sarah Barwick," the woman said, and held out her hand. "I say, thanks for unwinding me. If you hadn't come along, I might have lain there wrapped in my chintz shroud till the last trumpet." Her speech was clipped, with a brusque, downright quality that no doubt startled some, but which Dimity rather liked.

"I'm Dimity Woodcock," Dimity said, finding that Miss Barwick had a firm, emphatic grip. "My brother and I live on the other side of the wall at the foot of your garden, in Tower Bank House."

"Oh, yes, Captain Woodcock. I met him yesterday morning. Justice of the Peace, or something or other, isn't he?" She straightened her hair and looked down at the cobwebs on her blouse. "Pardon my appearance. I've been cleaning house, and I look a dreadful fright."

"Oh, please, no need for apology," Dimity said hastily. She glanced around the room. The slate floor was bare—the carpet and rugs had been rolled up—and the pictures had all been taken down. "Miss Tolliver liked to do her own housekeeping," she added. "I doubt that the cottage has had a good turning out in several years. There must be quite a lot of dust."

"It's not the dust," Miss Barwick said, rubbing her nose. "I'm an indifferent housekeeper myself, and I've learnt to live with dust. It's the wretched cat fur—sends me into sneezing fits. I'll have to clean it up before I can stay here." She looked down at the tangle of chintz curtains. "I say, Miss Woodcock, would you mind giving me a hand? These need to go outside for a good whip in the wind. Easier than beating them."

Five minutes later, the curtains were hung over the clothesline in the back garden, in the company of a two motley coverlets, some rather shabby bed curtains, the up-stairs brocade drapery, faded and patched, and several rugs. Since the wind was beginning to gust, the cat fur would soon be a thing of the past.

"It looks as if you've been hard at work," Dimity said as

they went back into the cottage. "Would you like to come over to Tower Bank House for a cup of tea and a scone?"

"Gosh, I don't know," Miss Barwick replied doubtfully, eyeing the sky, which was darkening to the east. "I think I had better stay here, where I can haul the lot in if it starts to rain. Tell you what, though. I've a fire in the range and the kettle's just on. I haven't yet looked around for tea, but I daresay we can find some. Or coffee, if you'd rather."

"The tea is in the tin canister above Miss Tolliver's sink," Dimity said. "Your sink, I mean. But do let me run home and fetch a few of Elsa's scones to have with our tea."

Miss Barwick thanked her warmly, and Dimity went home to get the scones. Ten minutes later, they were settled comfortably in the kitchen, a plate of Elsa Grape's delectable scones on the table in front of them and a china teapot keeping warm under a crocheted cozy.

"The first order of business," Miss Barwick said firmly, taking out a cigarette and lighting it with a match, "is to shed all this stuffy old Miss-this, Miss-that business. My name is Sarah. Please use it. If you don't mind," she added hastily, as if to soften what might sound like a command. She got up and took a saucer from the shelf to serve as an ashtray. "It does seem rather ridiculous to insist on ceremony after you unwound me from that chintz wrapper."

Dimity was pleased by this straightforwardness, which somehow seemed to go with the trousers and the bicycle—and the cigarette. Dimity had seen women smoke before, when she lived with her parents in the south of England, and many a rural farm wife enjoyed her fireside pipe of tobacco when her chores were done for the day. But cigarettes were generally thought "fast," something that might be used by London's Marlborough House set or women who fancied themselves artistic or emancipated. Sawrey would have yet another reason to be shocked.

"Well, then, you must call me Dimity," Dimity said, eyeing Sarah's cigarette with interest, admiring the casual way she held it between her fingers, so that the smoke curled in front of her face. It looked very attractive and . . . well, modern. "My brother sometimes calls me Dim, although I don't think he means anything by it." She paused. "You're from Manchester, I think he said?"

Sarah nodded and began to talk about herself. Dimity soon found that the mystery of Miss Barwick was unraveling quickly and without a great deal of prompting.

Sarah, who was a few years younger than Dim, had grown up in Manchester, where she worked in the family bakery and confectioner's shop and kept house for her father after her mother's death, some four years before. Her father had recently died, her uncle (with whom she didn't get along) had bought his brother's share of the bakery, and she had decided to strike out on her own. She had floundered around, though, not knowing what direction to take and having only the little bit of money her father had left and what she'd got from her uncle for her father's share of the shop. And then she had learnt, quite unexpectedly, that Miss Tolliver had died and left Anvil Cottage to her.

"I wasn't sure, at first, what I ought to do," she said, pouring Dim and herself a second cup of tea and lighting another cigarette. "My father grew up in this area—Hawkshead. But he left when he was twenty and never came back, and I've never had any cause to visit the Lake District. I'd no idea it was so beautiful, and of course I've never lived in a village. To tell the truth, I was planning to sell this place and use the money to set up a bakery in a city."

"But you've changed your mind?" Dimity asked.

Nodding, Sarah settled back in her chair. "It came to me in a flash when I was here yesterday with Mr. Heelis. I'll open a small bakery and confectioner's shop right here.

Nothing big, of course, not dozens and dozens of loaves every day. Just a bit of fresh bread and cakes, tea cakes, scones"—she glanced approvingly at Elsa's—"and perhaps a few hot pies. And there's a hive of bees in the garden, and I might put in another, to have a little fresh honey to sell. I don't need a great income, you see, just something to supplement what my dad left." She paused and asked, with an anxious look, "Will it do well here, do you think? A bakery business, I mean?"

Another surprise for the village, Dimity thought, with a private smile. A woman baker and confectioner, in Miss Tolliver's cottage? But why not? The kitchen was large enough to accommodate two ranges, if that were necessary. And Sarah would not be the only woman working in her home. Lydia Dowling ran the village shop in the front of Meadowcroft Cottage, just across Market Street. Jane Crosfield was a spinner and weaver, Mrs. Jamison raised chickens, Betty Leach sold vegetables out of her garden at Buckle Yeat, and Agnes Llewellyn, next door at High Green Gate, sold milk and butter from her husband's cows. So why not a bakery?

"I think you might do very well, actually," Dimity replied thoughtfully. "The baker's boy comes over from Hawkshead once a week, but I'm sure we'd rather buy closer to home. Quite a few families still make their own bread, of course, but some would prefer to buy cakes and pies and such. And there are the day-trippers coming through, and the cyclists, all of whom are good for a bun or two. Yes, indeed, I think you might do very well."

"Hurrah, then," Sarah said, with evident satisfaction, and added, as an afterthought, "I'm sure Miss Tolliver wouldn't mind. In fact, I mentioned it to her once in a letter—the idea of going into the baking business for myself—and she encouraged me. She said that every woman ought to be able to make her own way in the world." She tapped her cigarette ash smartly into the saucer. "Of course, I hadn't an idea in the world that she intended to leave me her house. That came as a great surprise, let me tell you. Practically knocked me off my pins."

"You and Miss Tolliver were friends, then," Dimity remarked, in a tone designed to elicit a response without betraying her curiosity.

"I wish I could say that we were," Sarah replied. Her dark eyes grew sad. "We were never able to actually meet, face-to-face, I mean. But I feel that I knew her through our letters. We'd been writing for a year or so, and I used to send her little packages of baked goods. You know, biscuits and sweets and the like. She said she enjoyed them, and sent me back all manner of crocheted and knitted things—doilies and pot holders and gloves. Things she'd made."

"But how did the two of you come to *start* writing?" Dimity persisted. Under other circumstances, the question would have been impertinent and perhaps even rude, but Sarah seemed to want to talk, and Dimity certainly wanted to know.

"Oh, haven't I said? Miss Tolliver and my dad were old friends, from the time before he married my mum. As I mentioned, he grew up in Hawkshead. They kept in touch through the years, in a friendly way. And then, after Mum died, Miss Tolliver wrote a very sweet and proper letter, and asked me to tell her about myself, what I liked to read, whether I was a needlewoman, or kept dogs, how I felt about this and that. I wrote back, and after that, she'd write every few months." She smiled ruefully. "My dad used to say that p'rhaps she was looking for a daughter, since she had none of her own. Never married, he told me, although she wanted to, once. Her father wouldn't allow it. Thought she ought to stay home and care for him, which she did, I understand, till he died."

"I heard something about a sweetheart," Dimity said, "although I don't know the full story. I doubt that anybody does, here in the village, I mean. Miss Tolliver was a dear and so very kind. She was involved with everything that went on and we saw her every day. But for all that, we didn't *know* her, if you take my meaning. She kept herself to herself."

"Sorry to hear that," Sarah said frankly. "To tell the truth, I was hoping that somebody here might tell me more about her." She got up and went to the sideboard, where she picked up a letter. "I wrote to her, you know, to tell her that my dad was dead. And yesterday, Mrs. Lythecoe, from across the way, said she thought that Miss Tolliver was reading my letter when she had her heart attack and died. I'm afraid that maybe the news about my dad came as a great shock to her."

Dimity gave her a wondering look. "You mean, you think that reading about your father's death actually triggered her own? But *why*?"

"Why?" Sarah repeated, frowning. "Yes, that's what I've been asking myself. I mean, I know they were friends, a long time ago. I once asked Dad if they were sweethearts, but he didn't answer me. And now, I suppose, it will be a mystery forever. I—"

Sarah was interrupted by a loud rapping at the kitchen door. "Miss Barwick! Miss Barwick!" a man's voice called urgently. George Crook opened the door and put his head in. "Thi clothesline just fell down. Everything's in a heap all o'er t' ground."

"Oh, gosh!" Sarah cried, smacking her forehead with her hand. She jumped up. "Oh, stupid me! I should have known better than put all that weight on it, in this wind."

"If tha wants, I'll tie it back up," George said helpfully. "I—"

He stopped, staring at Sarah's trousers, shock and consternation written all over his face. He swallowed. And then he saw her cigarette. His eyes got bigger and bigger until (as Dimity said later to Mrs. Lythecoe) they were as big as partridge eggs, and about to pop out of his head.

"Oh, could you?" Sarah said eagerly, stubbing out her cigarette in the ashtray, appearing not to notice the look on his face. "I say, I'd like that awf'lly. I'm such a fumble-fingers—if I did it, the line would be down again in a shake."

And then they were all outside in the back garden, the two women gathering up the drapes and curtains and rugs, George Crook fastening up the clothesline and trying not to look at Sarah Barwick's trousers.

26

Miss Potter Puts a Thief
out of Business

As Beatrix kept an apprehensive eye on the sky, Mr. Heelis drove south, toward Lake Windermere. It did not take long to get where they were going, and even though the sky was growing darker and more threatening, still there was no rain. In ten minutes or so, they were stopping in front of a small stone building near the remains of the old Roman fort.

"This gallery belongs to a gentleman who collects and sells paintings and sculptures," Mr. Heelis replied, at Beatrix's questioning glance. "He has a number of interesting pieces on display—one in particular that I should like you to have a look at." He secured the reins and got out to come around and give her a hand.

"Did you speak to him about Miss Tolliver's Constable?" Beatrix asked as she climbed down.

"I did," Mr. Heelis said. "Come in, please."

Inside, Beatrix saw that the white walls of the little shop

were hung with quite a lot of lovely pieces of art—landscapes of the Lake District's remarkable scenery, watercolors of plants and flowers, photographs of the fells and the moors— and on the shelves were any number of fossils and Roman artifacts that she would have liked to study more closely. But Mr. Heelis was pressing her forward and introducing her to a short, stout, sallow-faced man with a large head of shaggy brown hair, immense mutton-chop whiskers, and the mournful, baggy eyes of a basset hound—eyes that did not quite meet her own.

"Miss Potter, this is Mr. Lawrence Ransom, who owns this gallery," Mr. Heelis said.

"Pleased to make your acquaintance, I'm sure, Miss," Mr. Ransom said, making a small bow, but still not quite meeting her eyes. His voice was as doleful, Beatrix thought, as his expression.

"We shall want to get right to it, Mr. Ransom," Mr. Heelis said, with a quiet authority. "We have some distance to go, and it is beginning to look like rain." Outside, as if to applaud Mr. Heelis's astuteness, there was an emphatic clap of thunder.

Mr. Ransom sighed—a gusty sigh that seemed to be propelled from his toes upward through his rotund torso and finally out of his mouth—and reluctantly took his cue.

"If you'll come this way, Miss," he said, and led them toward a door, which opened onto a small room in the back of the gallery. The room had one narrow window and was piled from floor to ceiling with an untidy jumble of canvases, frames, broken sculptures, odd bric-a-brac, and pieces of pottery. Mr. Ransom went behind a corner screen and came out with a small painting in a gilt frame. He seemed, Beatrix thought, quite reluctant to show it to her.

"If you wouldn't mind holding it up, please, Mr. Ransom," Mr. Heelis said firmly. Prompted, Mr. Ransom held it up, still averting his eyes.

"Why, it's Miss Tolliver's Constable!" Beatrix exclaimed in delight, immediately recognizing the painting. She clapped her hands. "Oh, Mr. Heelis, you've found it!"

"It was your sketch that made finding it possible," Mr. Heelis replied. "All I had to do was show your drawing to Mr. Ransom, and he recognized it straightaway." The sardonic glint in his eye suggested that there was rather more to the story than that, but it would have to wait.

"It's a great comfort to see that it has suffered no damage," Beatrix said, with genuine relief. She looked again at the painting, then at the man who held it, and asked the question that was at the front of her mind. "How did you come by it, Mr. Ransom?"

The little man sighed again, shot a glance in the direction of Mr. Heelis, and licked his lips. "I am holding it for a . . . certain person with whom I have occasionally done business," he said in a mournful voice, so low that Beatrix had to strain to hear him. "Several of my clients in the area are interested in Constable's work, you see, and this person approached me with the idea that I might be able to sell it for him." He coughed delicately and added, "However, now that Mr. Heelis has made me aware that the painting was taken without the permission of the owner—"

"Stolen, you mean," Beatrix said tartly. It was annoying when people beat about the bush and did not come straight out with what they had to say.

"As you wish." The man coughed again. "As I said, the painting was left with the understanding that I would contact my clients and let them know that it is available. *Was* available," he amended hurriedly. "Of course, now that I understand the situation and Miss Potter has positively identified the work, I am quite anxious that it be returned to its rightful owner as soon as possible. Quite, quite anxious, I assure you."

"Then perhaps you would like us to return it," Mr. Heelis suggested.

"Ah, yes, of course, did I not say so?" Mr. Ransom affected great surprise. "'Pon my word, I am sure I said so. You may take it now, if you wish. In fact, that is a very good idea. I beg you to take it now, so that there is no untoward delay. I will wrap it carefully against the weather."

Beatrix frowned. "Theft is a serious business, Mr. Ransom, and you surely don't want to take our word that the painting was stolen. This is a business for the police. I'm sure that Constable Braithwaite would be glad to speak with you about it, or Captain Woodcock, our Justice of the Peace."

"Oh, dear, no!" Mr. Ransom exclaimed, his basset eyes widening in alarm. "Oh, no, dear Miss Potter, that will not be necessary, not necessary at all. Now, if you will give me a moment, I'll wrap the painting for you."

Beatrix stared at the man, beginning to understand. There could be only one reason why an art dealer who was holding stolen property would not be willing to discuss the affair with the authorities. It was because he was afraid of being suspected of being a fence, a receiver of stolen goods— or because he actually *was* a fence. She had read about such people in the newspapers, although she had never thought to meet one. She was immediately glad of Mr. Heelis' company, for she had the idea that this stout, sad little man might, under other circumstances, be dangerous, not a man to be pressed. Still, there was something she needed to know.

"Wait," she said urgently. "Before you wrap the painting, Mr. Ransom, we must know the name of the person who brought it to you."

Mr. Ransom's eyes narrowed and his lips tightened almost imperceptibly. A hard expression crossed his soft face.

"I am afraid," he said in a mournful tone, "that I am not at liberty to—"

Mr. Heelis leaned forward and put his hand on the little man's arm. "Mr. Ransom," he said, tightening his grip, "you will tell us, or you will tell the police. Which will it be?"

Mr. Ransom looked down at Mr. Heelis' hand, looked up at Beatrix, and yielded. "His name," he said in a sullen tone, "is Spry. I don't have an address for him. He merely stops in. On an irregular basis, that is."

A vivid flash of lightning lit the small room.

"Spry?" Mr. Heelis frowned. "I don't believe I know—"

The rest of the sentence was drowned out by a clap of thunder that seemed to shake the very floor. When its reverberating roll had died away, Beatrix spoke.

"I do," she said. "I know exactly who he is."

Fortunately, the thunder and lightning rolled away to the west as quickly as it had rolled in from the east, and Beatrix and Mr. Heelis—with the precious cargo wrapped in waterproof and stowed in the back of the gig—were soon on their way, with the idea of getting back to Sawrey in time for tea. The rain still came in hard, stinging volleys, however, and even though Mr. Heelis had put up the collapsible gig cover, they would have been quickly soaked if Beatrix had not unrolled her mackintosh (she had visited often enough in the Lake Country to know that a person should not go out for the day without her mackintosh) and draped it over both their heads as they huddled close together on the seat.

"Well, Miss Potter?" Mr. Heelis asked, as they drove smartly along the Hawkshead Road, the horse's hooves kicking up little bursts of spray. "Who is this Mr. Spry?"

"He is Mr. Henry Roberts' house agent," Beatrix said. She adjusted the mackintosh so that the rain did not fall on Mr. Heelis's shoulder. She felt uncomfortable sitting so close against him, and thought with a fleeting shiver of the scolding she would receive from her mother, should she ever be found out. But her companion's quiet matter-of-factness eased her, and she went on. "Mr. Roberts introduced him to Mrs. Lythecoe and me the day before yesterday."

"A house agent!" Mr. Heelis exclaimed, turning to look at her. "What a perfect arrangement for a thief!"

"A perfect arrangement?" Beatrix asked, puzzled, and then understood. "Of course! As a house agent, Mr. Spry is called in to make appraisals. When he's in the house, he notes valuable art objects that he thinks might find a ready market. Then he returns to steal them, with confidence that he will not be discovered, since he knows that the house is temporarily unoccupied."

"Exactly, Miss Potter," Mr. Heelis said in a congratulatory tone. "Exactly. I daresay this isn't the man's first theft. He's probably been at this for some time."

Beatrix frowned. "But how did you happen to approach Mr. Ransom about the painting? Was it just a lucky chance, or—?"

"Not quite," Mr. Heelis said, with a wry grin. "I had dealings with Ransom last year. A valuable Etruscan vase disappeared from the residence of a client of mine in Windermere. I had once admired it—very much as you admired the Constable, perhaps—and then happened, quite accidentally, to see it in Ransom's gallery. The vase was returned after some negotiation, and with an agreement that no questions would be asked. Ransom was the first person I thought of yesterday, when we determined that the painting had been taken out of Miss Tolliver's cottage."

"Excellent work, Mr. Heelis," Beatrix said approvingly.

He shook his head. "The work is yours, Miss Potter, and Miss Barwick has cause to be very grateful. If you had not pointed out to Mrs. Lythecoe that the painting was missing, its absence might very well have gone completely undetected.

And if you had not already identified the artist, its loss—
even if it had been known—would likely have been dis-
missed."

Beatrix felt herself coloring at the compliment, but she
only said, shyly, "You give me too much credit, Mr. Heelis.
I am only glad that I could be of help." She paused and inquired, "And what will happen next?"

"I suggest that we leave the painting with Captain
Woodcock," Mr. Heelis replied. "He can return it to Miss
Barwick the next time she comes to Anvil Cottage. And he
and Constable Braithwaite can discuss with the magistrate
how to deal with this man Spry. I should think that there's
enough evidence for his arrest."

"I'm glad of that," Beatrix said emphatically. "It will
be good to have that thief put out of business." She gave
Mr. Heelis a sidewise look. "And what about Mr. Ransom?
He's equally guilty, I should think."

"Indeed," Mr. Heelis said. "I intend to have a word with
the Ambleside police about the man, and ask them to keep
a close eye on him. I daresay they'll discover that he regularly receives stolen goods, and not just from this fellow
Spry." He smiled. "You may have put two thieves out of
business, Miss Potter. A ring of thieves, perhaps. Please accept my congratulations and profound gratitude."

And while it could not stop the rain, that last short, pleasant sentence had the remarkable effect of warming Beatrix,
inside and out, during the rest of the drive to Sawrey.

27

Many a Little Makes a Mickle

A great many interesting events were crowded into the next few days, so many and so interesting, in fact, that Beatrix was dazzled with the excitement. She was continually amazed by the difference between life in the little village of Sawrey, which was filled with such energetic and contradictory and *vivid* people, and life at Bolton Gardens, which seemed, in contrast, frigid and unchanging. It was the difference, she thought, between a scene viewed as a photograph, its black-and-gray subjects frozen forever in place and time, and the same scene in real life, with color and movement and smells and sounds all mixed together in a gloriously fluid muddle of changing images and blurred perceptions.

Of course, the Sawrey events were all small ones, but they certainly added up to a great deal of interesting activity—or, as Mrs. Crook liked to say, many a little certainly made a mickle. The Constable miniature had come home, a happy event that was marked by a celebratory tea party at Anvil Cottage. Miss Barwick herself baked a sampling of the tea cakes, scones, and biscuits she planned to produce in her new business, and insisted, quite firmly, that everyone should call her Sarah. In turn, she called everyone, even the men, by their first names, which seemed a shocking display of familiarity. To the disappointment of some, she did not wear trousers for the occasion, although her skirt was short enough to cause comment. Most of the villagers, however, had already seen her in trousers, astride her bicycle (which, it turned out, she had purchased in Hawkshead and expected to use to deliver her baked goods), and had already expressed their various opinions to their friends and neighbors.

As to the man who had stolen Miss Tolliver's painting, it was reported that a certain Oscar Spry had been apprehended by the Kendal constabulary, and that a police raid on the Ambleside shop of Lawrence Ransom had turned up several other stolen items and that Ransom himself had been arrested. A ring of clever art thieves had obviously been operating in the area, and their activities seemed to have been brought to an abrupt halt.

"So it was the other man you saw, climbing in the window," Tabitha Twitchit said in an accusing tone to Crumpet, when this news reached the animals—Tabitha, Crumpet, Rascal, and Max—sunning themselves in Anvil Cottage's back garden. *"The thief was Spry, the house agent, and not the draper from Kendal."*

Crumpet pretended to lick a grass burr from her paw. *"It was an easy mistake to make,"* she said defensively. *"They looked enough alike to be twins. Tweedledum and Tweedledee."*

"That's no excuse," Tabitha replied with a stern frown. *"If you're going to play at being Sherlock, you have an obligation to—"*

"Girls, girls," Rascal said, in a soothing tone. *"Let's not mar our achievements with a petty quarrel. After all, we were the ones who got the Roof Fund away from those greedy rats. It's thanks*

to us that Joseph Skead is mending the roof at this very moment."

Crumpet licked the other paw smugly. *"And I was the one who put Max up to sitting on the stairs so that Miss Crabbe could trip over him."*

"And I was the one who located the Parish Register," Max said, with a note of pride in his voice. Since the events at Castle Cottage, he had lost some of his shyness and had come down the hill to join the gang.

"But I am still the senior cat in this village," Tabitha said firmly, becoming bored with this self-congratulatory back-patting. *"I move that we all go round to Belle Green and see if Miss Potter's animals are interested in taking an excursion."*

There were no dissenting votes.

Where the Parish Register had been discovered was a mystery that only Vicar Sackett might have resolved—although he refused to reveal to anyone where and in what circumstance he had found it. He discussed the matter only with Miss Viola Crabbe, who confirmed that her sister had been working on the Crabbe family genealogy and had gone to the church to consult the Register. It was Viola's feeling that Myrtle had simply picked up the volume and taken it home with her; whether by design or by accident could not be determined, since her sisters were not anxious to ask her about it. As soon as her fracture was sufficiently mended, they were planning to take her for a few months to the south of England, away from the harsh Lake District winter.

Beatrix had an opportunity to see the elusive Register for herself one misty afternoon, when she, Sarah, and Dimity went to the churchyard to put chrysanthemums and Michaelmas daisies in front of the new headstone on Miss Tolliver's grave. After that simple ceremony, they went into the church, and Dimity showed them the Register, restored to its proper place beside the baptismal font.

Beatrix idly turned the pages, glancing at the names of people who had been born and baptized and married and died over the years. She recognized some of the village families—the Crooks, the Leeches, the Skeads, the Suttons. And then she saw another name she recognized: Abigail Tolliver.

"Look at this," she said to Dimity and Sarah. Bemused, she read the entry aloud: "Abigail Tolliver, bride, Wesley Barwick, groom, baker, of Hawkshead, first reading of banns, September 6, 1867."

Sarah pulled in her breath. "Wesley Barwick," she said wonderingly. "Why, that was my dad's name!"

Dimity's eyes widened. "Sarah!" she exclaimed. "Miss Tolliver must have been married to your father!" And then, realizing that this could not possibly be true, she corrected herself. "But she was always Miss Tolliver. So the wedding didn't take place." She ran her finger down the column below the lines where the banns had been posted. "There's no indication that the second and third readings of the banns ever occurred."

"Her father must have forbidden the marriage," Beatrix said, half under her breath, remembering what Grace Lythecoe had told her. She bit her lip, thinking of her own father and mother and how hateful they had been about her engagement to Norman. She felt a kind of melancholy kinship with Abigail Tolliver, and a deep sadness fell over her.

"Oh, dear," Sarah said. "Oh, how awful for her—to be bullied by her father in that way! Why did she put up with it? How could she stand it?"

"I think things were different back then," Dimity said, as if in explanation. "Girls were expected to stay home and take care of their parents. It's all different in these modern times, of course."

Beatrix was about to say that it wasn't, necessarily, but Sarah spoke first. "I know that Dad was happy with Mum, over the many years they were married," she said. She shook her head. "But poor Miss Tolliver never had anyone to love. It's very sad, don't you think?"

Dimity did not hesitate. "She must have loved *you*. She gave you her home, the place she cared for more than anything else in the world. Perhaps she began to think of you as the daughter she never had."

"Not good enough," Sarah said, in her hard, ringing voice. "I wasn't her daughter, and I couldn't have made up for all the years she missed with my dad. It's a tragedy, if you ask me."

"Yes," Beatrix agreed, very quietly, very sadly. "A tragedy."

But aside from these melancholy moments, the waning days of Beatrix's visit were, for the most part, quite happy.

For one thing, the cloud of suspicion that had settled over Jeremy Crosfield was lifted and he returned to Sawrey School. Miss Nash, who was now his teacher, saw to it that there was no more bullying, and that the boy's drawings (which really were quite good) were given pride of place in the school room. Beatrix had several spinning lessons from Jane Crosfield, and she and Jeremy went often to Cunsey Beck, to draw frogs. Each time, Beatrix thought, her sketches became more interesting and more full of life. She would have some good work to take back to London, and for the first time in a very long time, she almost began to look forward to being indoors all winter, in her studio in the old nursery at Bolton Gardens, completing the watercolors for *The Tale of Jeremy Fisher*.

For another thing, Beatrix received several letters from her publisher, a second parcel of books, and a very handsome check. "It will, I hope," she wrote in reply, with her tongue smartly in her cheek, "inspire the natives with rather more respect for me." The check would, of course, do more than that—it would pay for the alterations to the dairy, the pigsty, and, best of all, to the farmhouse itself.

For the thing that made Beatrix happier than anything else was the decision she had come to regarding the house at Hill Top Farm. She had been sitting in the garden at Hill Top one bright morning, dreamily sketching the old place, when she suddenly found that her pencil had drawn an addition onto the house, replacing the one-story kitchen on the farmyard end with a two-story wing, with a gable facing the garden. She had observed a great many Lake District buildings, some of which had been enlarged in just this way, and she must have known, unconsciously, that an addition could perfectly balance the old house without destroying its seventeenth-century lines.

She stared down at what she had drawn. *That's the answer!* she thought, with surprised delight. *I'll build a new wing onto the house for the Jenningses, and I will take the rest of the farmhouse for myself!*

The decision seemed to please Mrs. Jennings, who actually smiled when she boasted to Bertha Stubbs that she and Mr. J. were going to have a whole new house, all to themselves, as soon as Miss Potter could arrange to have it built—which might be quite a while, yet, with winter coming on. "It'll be ever' bit as good as a new house," she told Bertha. "And big, too. Oh, not as big as t' main part, but cert'nly newer."

And when Mrs. Jennings was contented, Mr. Jennings was contented, too, and he whistled as he went about the work of rebuilding the pigsty and carrying out the other changes upon which he and Beatrix had agreed.

Beatrix herself was delighted with the plan, and she persuaded Mrs. Jennings to allow her to go through the house with a tape measure, making notes of the dimensions of rooms so she could have some of her own pieces sent up from London, and planning the furniture and draperies and treasures she wanted. She couldn't actually live here—not, at least, for quite some time—but she could make Hill Top into her own domain, a house of her own, with everything in it just as she wanted it. The house would be the house of her dreams, the house where she *belonged*, where she could imagine herself leading the kind of life that would make her, at last, content. And all around her would lie her own land, fold and fallow, garden and green meadows and pretty patches of woods. And on it she would have her own animals: cows and pigs and chickens and sheep, yes, Herdwick sheep, those sheep who instinctively knew their own heaf.

The more Beatrix thought about the arrangements she was making, the happier she became, and she had a lively discussion with George Crook and Charlie Hotchkiss about the best contractor for the job. George (who seemed to be slowly reconciling himself to the fact that Beatrix had snatched Hill Top Farm out from under the nose of Silas Tadcastle) suggested the name of a man in Hawkshead, and Mr. Jennings and Beatrix drove to see him one afternoon in the pony cart. He seemed to be the right choice, and Beatrix celebrated their bargain by stopping at the cobbler's shop and ordering a pair of pattens for herself, those old-fashioned wooden-soled clogs that farm women wore to keep their feet out of the mud.

It was the proper footwear, she thought to herself as the cobbler drew carefully around her foot, for a proper farmer.

Historical Note

Beatrix Potter is best known to the world through her "little books"—the nearly two dozen children's books she wrote and illustrated between 1901 and 1913, beginning with the immortal *The Tale of Peter Rabbit*. But this intriguing Victorian woman lived many different lives, not only as a gifted artist and story-teller, but as an observant naturalist, a dedicated farmer, and an ardent conservationist who cared not only for the land but for the creatures who lived there. She was a late-bloomer who, at mid-life, began to insist on making her own place in the world.

Beatrix Potter was born in 1866 into a wealthy, upper-middle-class London family. Much of what we know about her early life comes from her journal, which she kept in a kind of miniature cipher that was not decoded until some fifteen years after her death, when a dedicated scholar managed to decode the exercise books and loose papers that had been found in at Castle Cottage, the house where Beatrix lived from 1913 until her death in 1943. (See *The Journal of Beatrix Potter, 1881–1897*, transcribed by Leslie Linder.) From her journal, we learn that she lived a secluded but

interesting life of books, art exhibitions, drawing and painting, and holiday travels with her family. She was educated at
home by governesses until she was nineteen, and had no formal education, except for art lessons. She and her brother
Bertram assembled their own miniature zoo in their third-
floor nursery, and even on holidays, the children brought
along their pet rabbits, mice, and birds. The Potters made
annual three-month visits to Scotland and the Lake District,
where Beatrix took great delight in learning all she could
about the natural world and making notes of her observa-
tions in her journal. She was especially interested in fossils
and fungi, and by the time she had reached her early twenties, she was well on the way to becoming a competent naturalist and botanical illustrator. The depth of her interest in
natural science and the power and authority of her botanical
work is clearly illustrated in *A Victorian Naturalist: Beatrix
Potter's Drawings from the Armitt Collection,* by Eileen Jay,
Mary Noble, and Anne Stevenson Hobbs.

But Beatrix sketched her pets, too, and it was her drawings of her favorite rabbit, Peter Piper, which led to *The Tale
of Peter Rabbit,* composed in 1893 as a letter to the son of her
favorite governess. (When Peter died in 1902, Beatrix wrote
in her journal: "Whatever the limitations of his intellect or
outward shortcomings of his fur, and his ears and toes, his
disposition was uniformly amiable and his temper unfail-
ingly sweet. An affectionate companion and a quiet friend.")
In 1901, after several attempts to interest a publisher in
her work, Beatrix paid to have *The Tale of Peter Rabbit* privately printed, and when the little book came to the notice
of Frederick Warne Publishers, they offered to publish it.
Her parents were opposed to the commercialization of their
daughter's art; they became even more opposed when the
books became best sellers and it began to seem that their
daughter's earnings might make her independent of them.

But Beatrix longed for the independence her mother and

father resisted. In her first act of defiance against her parents, she agreed that Warne should publish her first book and quickly began to make plans for more. The books—*Peter Rabbit* (October, 1902) was followed by *Squirrel Nutkin* (1903), *The Tailor of Gloucester* (1903), *Benjamin Bunny* (1904), *Two Bad Mice* (1904), *Mrs. Tiggy-Winkle* (September, 1905), and *The Pie and the Patty-Pan* (October, 1905)—turned out to be phenomenal best sellers. As the year 1905 began, there were a quarter of a million copies of Beatrix's books in print, and she was well on the way to financial independence. (The story of Beatrix's publications is told in *Beatrix Potter: Artist, Storyteller, and Countrywoman,* by Judy Taylor, who frames her early work and life in the context of her development as an artist and naturalist.)

Beatrix's success did not change her life in any outward way, for she was by nature reserved and shy and by training a dutiful daughter. She continued to attend her mother, by all accounts an exacting and not very pleasant old lady. With rare exceptions, her only excursions outside of London were with her parents; and in London, she was not even allowed to visit her publishers' office without a chaperone.

But in mid-1905, Beatrix's life took several unexpected and dramatic turns. In July, she received an offer of marriage from her editor, Norman Warne, on whose steady guidance she had come to rely. Like Beatrix, Norman was self-contained and modest, and their chaste love affair was restrained, even by Victorian standards. They were chaperoned at every meeting and were never once alone together. But their work brought them together regularly, and a real and deep affection began to grow between them. For three years they exchanged almost daily letters.

Beatrix's parents, however, were angrily opposed to their friendship, and when Beatrix told them of Norman's offer, they made it clear that marriage was out of the question. Despite the fact that both the Potter grandparents had been manufacturers, Mr. and Mrs. Potter looked down on the Warne family as being "in trade" and hence not of their class. Beatrix defied them to the extent that she agreed to marry Norman and accepted his ring, but no one except for Norman's family was to know and their marriage was to be delayed indefinitely. It must have been a time of mixed happiness and sadness, for while she could not marry the man she loved now, Beatrix could at least glimpse the future the two of them would share.

But tragedy struck with unexpected swiftness. Norman fell ill and by the end of August, 1905—just a month after their engagement—he was dead, the victim of lymphatic leucocythemia, a type of leukemia. Beatrix was bereft, devastated, alone. Now she knew that if she were to have any life of her own, separate from her parents, she would have to create it for herself.

It was at this point that Hill Top Farm came into Beatrix's already quite complicated life. About the time of her engagement to Norman, she had located a piece of property she wanted to purchase, a small farm in the Lakeland village of Sawrey, where she and her parents had gone on holiday in 1896, 1901, and 1902. She had visited Hill Top Farm during these periods, because her parents' coachman and his family (like other wealthy Victorians, Mr. and Mrs. Potter traveled with a full contingent of servants) were boarded there. Her parents were not happy about her purchase, but perhaps their objections were tempered by the fact that their daughter's marriage "into trade" was not to take place, and the farm, whatever it might represent to Beatrix, was a reasonably prudent investment of the income from her books and a small inheritance from an aunt.

Much of what we know of Beatrix's growing attachment to Hill Top Farm is recorded in her letters (*Beatrix Potter's Letters,* selected and edited by Judy Taylor). In October, six weeks after Norman's death, Beatrix traveled to Sawrey to inspect her new property. There, she threw herself into the Hill Top project with all the passion and dedication she gave to her books, planning what to do with her new acquisition, getting acquainted with the people in the village, and enjoying the release from her watchful parents. Perhaps the challenge of dealing with Hill Top Farm and making a place for herself in the village helped to divert her thoughts from her great loss: "My purchase seems to be regarded [by the villagers] as a huge joke; I have been going over my hill with a tape measure." In a postscript, she added, "It is most lovely autumn weather, I shall try to stop till the end of month if I am not sent for" (*Letters,* October 10, 1905).

While Beatrix was not to come to Sawrey to live for another eight years, she visited as often as she could and her heart was constantly there. Perhaps it is not an exaggeration to say that Hill Top saved her from despair. It gave her a sense of new possibilities for herself, exciting new hopes and new dreams and even—by 1913—a new and enduring love. It changed the course of her life.

And thereby hangs a tale . . .

Susan Wittig Albert

Resources

There are a great many excellent resources on Beatrix Potter's life and work, and on the Lake District of England. Here are a few of those that I have found most useful in the research for this series. Additional resource material is available on my website, www.mysterypartners.com.

Denyer, Susan. *At Home with Beatrix Potter,* Harry N. Abrams, Inc., New York, 2000.

Jay, Eileen, Mary Noble, and Anne Stevenson Hobbs. *A Victorian Naturalist: Beatrix Potter's Drawings from the Armitt Collection,* Frederick Warne, London, 1992.

Lane, Margaret. *The Tale of Beatrix Potter,* revised edition, Frederick Warne, London, 1968.

Paston-Williams, Sarah. *The Beatrix Potter Country Cooking Book.* Claremont Books, in association with Frederick Warne, London, 1995.

Potter, Beatrix. *The Journal of Beatrix Potter, 1881–1897,* transcribed by Leslie Linder, Frederick Warne, London, New Edition, 1966.

Potter, Beatrix. *Beatrix Potter's Letters,* selected and edited by Judy Taylor, Frederick Warne, London, 1989.

Potter, Beatrix. *Beatrix Potter: A Holiday Diary,* transcribed and edited, with a foreword and a history of the Warne family, by Judy Taylor. The Beatrix Potter Society, London, 1996.

Rollinson, William. *The Cumbrian Dictionary of Dialect, Tradition and Folklore.* Smith Settle, Otley, West Yorkshire, UK, 1997.

Taylor, Judy. *Beatrix Potter: Artist, Storyteller, and Countrywoman.* Frederick Warne, London, Revised Edition, 1996.

xx⟨⟨⟨⟩⟩⟩xx

Favorite Sawrey Village Recipes

Tatie Pot

This version of tatie pot comes from *Beatrix Potter's Country Cooking*, by Sarah Paston-Williams (Claremont/Warne) and is reprinted with permission.

Tatie pot is a familiar dish in the Lake District, and every cook had her own recipe. Black pudding (made from pig's blood and oatmeal) is a delicacy in northern England, and makes a dark, rich gravy; it can be omitted from the recipe if you can't find it, or you can substitute it with a dark sausage. Mathilda Crook would have used Herdwick mutton and vegetables and herbs from her garden, and served her tatie pot with mashed turnips, pickled onions, and pickled red cabbage.

1.6 kg (3½ lb) best end and middle neck of lamb, in chops
Seasoned flour
3 large onions, finely sliced

4 large carrots, thickly sliced
1 large turnip or swede, roughly chopped
Lamb stock or water, to cover
3 or 4 sprigs of fresh mint
1 bay leaf
Salt and freshly milled black pepper
450 g (1 lb) black pudding, thickly sliced
900 g (2 lb) potatoes, thinly sliced

Pre-heat the oven to 140 degrees C (275 degrees F, gas mark 1).

Trim the fat and skin from the meat and cut up the fat finely. Melt it in a large frying pan. Roll the trimmed chops in seasoned flour, then brown all over in the fat. Remove with a slotted spoon and arrange in a large, shallow oven-proof dish. Fry the onions, adding extra dripping if necessary, until soft. Add the carrots and turnip and fry for a few minutes more.

Transfer the vegetables to the ovenproof dish and pour over enough stock or water to cover. Add the mint and bay leaf and season well. Cover with a lid and cook in a very slow oven for 4–5 hours, or until the meat falls off the bone easily. Strain off the cooking liquor and leave until cold, preferably overnight.

The next day, pre-heat the oven to 190 degrees C (375 degrees F, gas mark 5).

Bone the meat and cut into bite-sized chunks. Discard the mint and bay leaf. Arrange back in the cleaned ovenproof dish with the vegetables and cover with slices of black pudding. Remove and reserve the fat from the cold stock, then boil the stock up in a pan. Taste and adjust the seasoning as necessary, and pour over the meat, to cover. Arrange overlapping slices of potato over the top and dot with the reserved lamb fat. Season the potato, then cover and cook in a fairly hot oven for about 1 hour, removing the cover after 30 minutes to crisp and brown the potatoes at the edges. (Brown under the grill for a few minutes if you wish.) *Serves 6.*

Elsa Grape's Gooseberry Sauce

1 cup gooseberries, tops and tails snipped off
2 tablespoons butter
1 tablespoon sugar
1 tablespoon lemon juice

Stew the gooseberries in as little water as possible until very soft. Drain and puree. Return to pan over low heat and add the butter, sugar, and lemon juice, stirring until blended. Serve hot with fish.

Sponge Cake

This recipe for sponge cake, a tea-time favorite, comes from Mrs. Beeton's *Book of Household Management.* Popularly called *Mrs. Beeton's,* the housekeeping manual, first published in 1861, was a Victorian publishing phenomenon, selling 60,000 copies in the first year and more than two million copies by 1868. It was an essential reference for every Victorian cook and housewife. In 1913, Beatrix wrote to a friend, "Now, if you want to get me a nice useful present that I shall always use and remember you by— get me Mrs. Beeton's Cookery, *please,* and write my name in it!"

INGREDIENTS: The weight of 5 eggs in flour, the weight of 8 in pounded loaf sugar; flavoring to taste. [Mrs. Beeton also intends you to use those 13 eggs!]

MODE: Let the flour be perfectly dry, and the sugar well pounded and sifted. Separate the whites from the yolks of the [13] eggs, and beat the latter up with the sugar; then whisk the whites until they become rather stiff, and mix them with the yolks, but do not stir them more than is just necessary to mingle the ingredients well together. Dredge in the flour by degrees, add the flavoring; butter the tins well, pour in the batter, sift a little sugar over the cakes, and bake them in a rather quick oven, but do not allow them to take too much color, as they should be rather pale. Remove them from the tins before they get cold, and turn them on their faces, where let them remain until quite cold, when store them away in a closed tin canister or wide-mouthed glass bottle.

TIME: 10 to 15 minutes in a quick oven. AVERAGE COST: 1 penny each.

Bertha Stubbs's Rhubarb and Strawberry Tart

Pastry for a 2-crust 9-inch pie
4 cups chopped rhubarb
2 cups sliced fresh strawberries
1⅓ cups sugar
¼ cup cornstarch
1 tablespoon lemon juice
¼ teaspoon cinnamon
1 egg, beaten
1 tablespoon sugar (for lattice top)

Preheat oven to 425 degrees F. Roll out half the pastry and line a 9-inch pie plate. Trim, leaving a ½-inch overhang over the edge of the pie plate. Combine rhubarb, sugar, cornstarch, lemon juice, and cinnamon. Mix well and pour into the pie shell. Roll out remaining pastry and cut into eight 1-inch strips. Place four strips at equal intervals across the filling. Crisscross these with remaining four strips, weaving them into a lattice. Trim the strips even with the edge of the pie plate. Fold the ½-inch of the bottom crust over the ends of the strips, and seal and flute the edges. Brush lattice top with egg, and sprinkle with sugar.

Place pie in the oven and bake for 15 minutes, until the crust starts to brown. Reduce heat to 375 degrees and continue to bake for 50 to 60 minutes, until crust is golden, rhubarb is tender, and filling is thickened. (For easy cleanup of spills, place a cookie sheet or sheet of foil on the bottom of the oven.) Serve with ice cream for a real treat.

Gingersnaps

Beatrix Potter recalled with pleasure her Grandmama Compton's "very hard gingersnap biscuits." These gingersnaps are chewy, rather than hard.

- ¾ cup shortening
- 1 cup sugar
- ¼ cup treacle (light or golden molasses)
- 1 egg
- 2 teaspoons soda
- 2 cups sifted flour
- ½ teaspoon cloves
- ½ teaspoon ginger
- 1 teaspoon cinnamon
- ½ teaspoon salt
- ¼ cup sugar mixed with ½ teaspoon cinnamon

Melt shortening in saucepan, over low heat. Cool. Beat in sugar, molasses, and egg. Sift flour, soda, cloves, ginger, cinnamon, and salt together, and add to first mixture in two batches, mixing well. Form into 1-inch balls, roll in granulated sugar, and place on cookie sheet about 2 inches apart. Bake in 350-degree oven for 8–10 minutes. Makes about 3 dozen.

Mrs. Stokes's Treacle Pudding

The traditional English treacle pudding is steamed on top of the range, but this oven-steamed adaptation is easier. Most English cooks prefer golden cane syrup (rather than corn syrup). This recipe includes a syrup sauce, but treacle pudding is often served with a thick vanilla custard. With regard to puddings, Mrs. Beeton observes wryly that, in Great Britain, flavor was less important than the size and number of portions, and that the most important feature of any pudding was its "substantiality." This rich pudding offers both flavor and substantiality.

> ½ cup softened butter
> ½ cup plus 2 tablespoons fine granulated sugar
> 2 eggs, beaten
> Grated zest of one lemon
> 1¼ cups flour
> 1 teaspoon baking powder
> 2 teaspoons milk
> 4 tablespooons syrup
>
> *SAUCE*
>
> Juice of one lemon
> 2 tablespoons water

4 tablespoons syrup (dark or light)
Light cream

Preheat oven to 400 degrees F. Cream butter and sugar until fluffy. Add eggs and lemon zest. Sift flour and baking powder together, and fold into creamed mixture. Gently stir in milk.

Grease a 3-cup ovenproof bowl and pour the syrup over the bottom. Pour pudding mixture over it. Grease a sheet of aluminum foil, place it *loosely* over the bowl, and place the bowl in a pan with 1 inch of water. (It's easier to put the bowl and pan in the oven, then pour in the water.) Bake 45 minutes, or until the pudding has set and the top has turned golden.

Turn the pudding onto a serving dish. With a spatula, scrape out any syrup left at the bottom of the bowl. To make sauce, slowly heat lemon juice, water, and syrup in a saucepan for 5 minutes. Pour it over the pudding. Serve warm, with a pitcher of cream. *Makes 6–8 servings*.

Glossary

Arval. Funeral refreshments made of the best ingredients and given to mourners at the graveside.

Babblement. Foolish chatter.

Barmy. Silly, weak-minded.

Beck. A small stream.

Black pudding. A traditional sausage made with pig's blood, beef suet, onions, and oatmeal.

Bodderment. Bother, trouble.

Bolter. A rabbit that jumps out of a burrow when it is chased by a ferret.

Chandler. Dealer in groceries, supplies, sundries.

Charabanc. A long, light horse-drawn vehicle with several seats, all facing forward.

Coppice. A small thicket of trees grown to be cut for fencing material and other farm purposes.

Daft ha'p'orth. Literally, daft halfpennyworth. A foolish little thing.

Dander. Walk slowly, dawdle.

Daytrippers. Tourists who come for only a day or two.

Draper. Originally, someone who made woollen cloth; later, a dealer in textiles.

Fash. Bother. As in *doan't fash thasel* (don't bother about it).

Fell. A mountain or a high hill.

Fortnight. Two weeks.

Girt. Great, large.

Heaf. An area of fellside where sheep graze. Herdwick sheep remember their native heaf and return instinctively to it; that is, they are *heafed* to the fell.

Joiner. A craftsman who constructs wooden furniture, cabinets, ship fittings, etc. by joining.

Ken. Know.

Mappen it may. Perhaps it will.

Nevvy. Nephew.

Nobbut: Nothing except, only. *He is nobbot a fool*.

Off-comers. Strangers, visitors, non-natives.

Pattens. Old-fashioned wooden shoes worn (mostly by women) for outdoor chores.

Reet. Right, proper.

Seed wigs (or whigs). Spiced buns, often dipped in ale or wine. Hawkshead was famous for its caraway seed wigs.

Sovereign. The gold coin that was equivalent to the British pound sterling, which at the time of this book was worth about 56 current pounds (approximately equal to 150 current U.S. dollars).

Tarn. A glacial lake. Moss Eccles Tarn is about a twenty-minute walk from Hill Top Farm. Beatrix Potter kept a rowboat and fished there.

Tupping time. Tupping (breeding of sheep) takes place in November, when the rams (*or tups*) are let in with the ewes, to ensure that the lambs will be born during the warm days of early spring.